JAMES, BY THE GRACE OF GOD

To be King of Scots was never the passport to peace or joy, and for young James the Fifth the throne made an uncomfortable seat indeed. As a boy he had been deliberately corrupted by his step-father, the Red Douglas, Earl of Angus, so that he might get both king and kingdom into his power. Even when James escaped from Angus's clutches, he still had that most rebellious and powerful house to cope with. Not to mention the Hamiltons, whose chief, the Earl of Arran, was next in line to the crown. So he did not have his troubles to seek.

Add to this, James himself was impetuous, hot-blooded, handsome, with no great interest in matters of state, but an enormous interest in women. While to the south, his uncle Henry the Eighth of England watched every move north of the border, poised to invade.

The royal advisers therefore faced a mighty task. Of these, the two Davids, Lindsay and Beaton, were among the most effective and loyal, without being uncritical of their liege-lord's weaknesses and escapades. David Beaton is now Lord Privy Seal, soon to be Cardinal, the poet David Lindsay is Lord Lyon King of Arms. Friends from their student days, they are very different characters and frequently find themselves at loggerheads as they try to keep the unruly, perplexed and endangered nation in some sort of order, and its king from disaster.

In this second of his trilogy of love and hatred, folly and statesmanship, poetry and martyrdom, Nigel Tranter paints a vivid picture of a turbulent period, a strange friendship, and of James Stewart, by God's grace King — but only just.

**Also by the same author,
and available from Coronet:**

THE BRUCE TRILOGY
THE MACGREGOR TRILOGY
THE STEWART TRILOGY
DAVID THE PRINCE
LORD OF THE ISLES
MACBETH THE KING
MARGARET THE QUEEN
MONTROSE: THE CAPTAIN GENERAL
AND THE YOUNG MONTROSE
RIVEN REALM
UNICORN RAMPANT
THE WALLACE

James, by the Grace of God

Nigel Tranter

CORONET BOOKS
Hodder and Stoughton

Copyright © 1985 by Nigel Tranter

First published in Great Britain in 1985 by Hodder and Stoughton Limited

Coronet Edition 1988

British Library C.I.P.

Tranter, Nigel
    James, by the grace of God.
    I. Title
823'.912[F]   PR6070.R34

ISBN 0 340 41900 8

Printed and bound in Great Britain for Hodder and Stoughton Paperbacks, a division of Hodder and Stoughton Ltd., Mill Road, Dunton Green, Sevenoaks, Kent TN13 2YA.
(Editorial Office: 47 Bedford Square, London WC1B 3DP) by Cox & Wyman Ltd., Reading

Principal Characters

IN ORDER OF APPEARANCE

DAVID BEATON: Rector of Campsie and secretary to the Primate.

DAVID LINDSAY OF THE MOUNT AND GARLETON: Usher to the King of Scots.

PATRICK, 4TH LORD LINDSAY OF THE BYRES: Father-in-law of David Lindsay.

ARCHIBALD, EARL OF ANGUS: Chief of the Red Douglases.

SIR ARCHIBALD DOUGLAS OF KILSPINDIE: Uncle of above, known as Graysteel.

MASTER WILLIAM DOUGLAS: Abbot of Holyrood. Another uncle of Angus.

JAMES BEATON, ARCHBISHOP OF ST. ANDREWS: Primate of the Church in Scotland.

JAMES HAMILTON, EARL OF ARRAN: Lord High Admiral.

JAMES THE FIFTH, KING OF SCOTS: Aged thirteen.

MARGARET TUDOR: Queen of the late James the Fourth and sister of Henry the Eighth.

SIR JAMES HAMILTON OF FINNART: Known as the Bastard of Arran. Illegitimate son of that Earl.

JOHN STEWART, EARL OF LENNOX: Chiefest of the non-royal Stewarts.

SIR WALTER SCOTT OF BUCCLEUCH: Warden of the Middle March and chief of the Borderland Scotts.

JOHN STEWART, EARL OF ATHOLL: Great Highland noble.

JANET DOUGLAS: Tirewoman and Wardrobe Mistress to the King, daughter of the Laird of Stonypath.

GAVIN DUNBAR, ARCHBISHOP OF GLASGOW: Chancellor.

ROBERT, 5TH LORD MAXWELL: Warden of the West March.

JOHNNIE ARMSTRONG OF GILNOCKIE: Known as King of the Border. Leader of that notorious clan.

MARGARET VON HAPSBURG, QUEEN OF HUNGARY: Aunt of the Emperor Charles and Governor of the Netherlands.

CHARLES VON HAPSBURG, EMPEROR.

MARION OGILVY: Former wife of Davie Beaton. Daughter of the 3RD LORD OGILVY OF AIRLIE.

BISHOP ANTONIO CAMPEGGIO: Papal Nuncio.

GEORGE, 4TH LORD HOME: Great Borders noble.

HENRY, 6TH EARL OF NORTHUMBERLAND: English Warden of the Marches.

MARIE DE BOURBON: Daughter of the Duc de Vendôme.

FRANCIS DE VALOIS, KING OF FRANCE.

MARIE DE GUISE, DUCHESS DE LONGUEVILLE: Sister of the Duc de Guise and Cardinal of Lorraine.

MADELEINE DE VALOIS, PRINCESS OF FRANCE: Daughter of King Francis.

PART ONE

1

Half-a-dozen men were working at the hay on the slantwise, south-facing field on the lower slopes of Lindifferon Hill that June afternoon, the horseman noted; but whilst five were toiling near to each other towards the bottom end, one was by himself towards the top. And while the group worked with a slow but steady rhythm of practice and custom, swinging their sickles in smooth, even sweeps, the lone individual seemed to be labouring much harder, stooping and rising more often with more frequent strokes, head down, even at that distance a picture of tense concentration, strange in a sunny hayfield. Without much hesitation, the visitor turned his mount's head in that direction and trotted across and up.

As he drew near, the toiling man seemed loth to stop cutting, even to glance up, although he could not have failed to hear the clip-clop of hooves and jingle of harness. The newcomer's handsome features took on a thoughtful, assessing look.

He reined in his splendid grey stallion only a few yards from the other, who at last looked up. "So, David—you are busy, I see. God bless the work! A fair hay crop, this year, all tell me. It is good to see you, friend."

The toiler straightened an obviously aching back, and nodded, stiff-faced. "Yes," he said, "and you." He did not sound over-joyed, voice level.

"They told me at your castle that you would be here," the horseman added. "Working, always working, they said. You are well enough, David? I have seen you looking better, and with more flesh to your bones."

"Well?" the man with the sickle repeated. "What is well? Or ill? I am not sick, if that is what you ask. Not sick of body."

"Mmm. I am sorry, David—sorry."

There was a pause as they eyed each other.

They made an extraordinary contrast in appearance, those two men, both in their early thirties, the one brilliantly good-looking

9

in a strangely delicate, fine-featured way which could have been almost effeminate save for the strong jawline, firm mouth and keen, lively eyes, the other more rugged both of face and build, muscular but gaunt-looking, clad in old breeches which had been well-cut once and were now stained and worn, with a sweat-darkened shirt of linen, open to the waist, while the horseman was dressed in the height of French fashion, all but dandified, crimson velvet slashed with gold, lace at throat and wrists, the curling feather of his flat jewelled cap held in place by a great ruby brooch.

When the standing man made no further comment, indeed turned to look away down over the lovely prospect of the part of the fertile Howe of Fife known as Stratheden—gentle green swelling hills enclosing the wide farm-dotted vale, with its winding river, scattered woodlands and red-roofed villages, over a thousand acres of which, closest at hand, were his own—then the horseman dismounted and came to stand beside his friend, for these two *were* friends, despite all appearances. He laid a hand on the other's arm.

"They say that time heals all, David," he murmured. "True or not, who knows? But activity makes time pass the faster—which may help. But hay-making, now? I doubt if that is the best time-passer for such as you! Too much time to think. Not so?"

"Perhaps," the other admitted. "But no time, however passed, will find me what I have lost."

"No. Agreed. But you have to go on living, man."

"Aye. All the years."

"To be sure, all the years. You have forty perhaps ahead of you. I say that you will need more than hay-making, or harvesting, or working the land, or yourself too weary to think, to remember. You will need more than that."

"Need? My needs are the least of it, Davie. And what I need I cannot have."

"But . . . there are other needs than just yours, friend. *My* needs. Others'. The realm's needs—this Scotland of ours. There are great and pressing needs thronging the land beyond all this." And he waved his gloved hand to encompass that fair vista. "Beyond the Mount of Lindifferon evil stalks through this kingdom. While you make hay, David Lindsay of the Mount!"

"No doubt. It usually does, God knows! If there is a God. But I cannot help that."

10

"You can, I think. You have done in the past and can do again."

"Davie Beaton—spare me your scheming and plots and ploys! I am in no state for such, I promise you. I know you. Moving men like chessmen—as you have moved me, in the past. That is over—like so much else."

"Is friendship over, then? Affection? Regard for others, man?"

Lindsay frowned down at his sickle. "No-o-o. Not that. You know that is not true. You know it."

"I know that I, your friend, need you. And, more important than I am, James Stewart needs you. Your liege-lord and mine."

That was shrewd thrusting, and Lindsay started to protest, but restrained himself with an effort. Twelve-year-old King James the Fifth was indeed his friend, as well as his monarch. "James is beyond any help of mine," he said.

"Perhaps not. Help he must have. If he is taken to England, to his Uncle Henry of accursed name, I doubt if we should ever see him again!"

"England? What do you mean, England? How could this be?"

"We have word at St. Andrews that his mother contemplates taking him there, secretly. To prevent him from falling into Angus's hands, she says. You have heard that Angus is back, and he and his Douglases have taken over Edinburgh town again?"

"No. No—I had not heard that. I hear but little here . . ."

"Perhaps you should hear more, listen more, David. For knowing nothing will not save any of us from trouble! Yes, the Earl of Angus and his Douglases descended upon the capital in strength some weeks ago, and took over the city. As he did once before. Arran and his son were at Hamilton, so they had an easy conquest. The Queen-Mother and young James contrived to get up to the castle from Holyrood, with the help of the English guard Henry has provided, and they are secure there, meantime at any rate. Without cannon, Angus cannot take the castle—but it is not beyond him to obtain artillery in time and bombard it. Although whether he would dare that, with the King therein, I doubt. But Margaret Tudor, it seems, thinks that he might—and she ought to know him, having wed him!—and so she is planning secretly to leave the fortress by night and flee with James to England. She has written to this effect to the Lord Dacre, the English Warden of the Marches, at Morpeth—our spies intercepted and read the letter. She asks him to be ready to

11

receive them, and to muster all available forces to invade Scotland thereafter, with King James at the head of his army so that the Scots will be loth to take arms against their own monarch. And so to drive the Douglases out of Edinburgh and restore Margaret to power."

Lindsay shook his head. "So—we are back to that! The same old folly and treachery. Will it never end?"

"Not so long as James is a child, I fear, and his mother holds him. And good men fail to act! It is all part of her brother, Henry Tudor's game to win Scotland for himself."

"Aye. Then I am well out of it all!"

"Spoken like a true friend of Jamie Stewart!" Beaton said, sourly for that honey-tongued individual.

The other drew a quick breath and the knuckles gripping the sickle gleamed white. "I was *put* out of it, I'd remind you!" he jerked. "Dismissed from being the King's procurator and usher—by the Queen-Mother, seven months ago. Besides, what could I do now? The boy himself may like me well enough but his mother hates me. She certainly would not listen to me, even admit me to her presence. I am but a simple Fife laird now. I have nothing to offer in this sorry situation—even if I would."

"I think that you mistake, David. It is not to Margaret Tudor I would have you go. But to someone who will listen to you. To Kate's father. Your own good-father at The Byres of Garleton—Patrick, Lord Lindsay."

His friend stiffened perceptibly at those names and turned to stare at Beaton, eyes narrowed.

Hurriedly the other went on. "The Lord Patrick is an honest man, one of the few on the present Privy Council. The Queen-Mother will have none of him, any more than of you. And that weak fool the Earl of Arran takes his line from her. So Lord Lindsay is squeezed out—like other honest men. And we have heard that Angus has twice been to The Byres to see him."

"What of it?"

"Angus, for that hot-tempered man, has been behaving with some care since he took Edinburgh. He is biding his time, keeping his Douglases under control. He has even moved out of the city himself, to lodge with the Black Douglas chief, the Earl of Morton, at Dalkeith, even though until now they were un-friends. We, my uncle and I, have hopes for the Earl of Angus. Faint perhaps, but hopes!"

12

"Then I misdoubt your judgement!"

"Ah, but the judgement is not of character but of circumstances! He remains a hot-head, ambitious, untrustworthy, but . . ."

"And in King Henry's pocket! Always he has been. If he has lately come back to Scotland, it is straight from Henry's court."

"Aye—but the conditions are changed, see you. Have you not heard this either? The divorce has been granted. Our friend the Duke of Albany in France has prevailed upon the new Pope to grant it. Paid all out of his own pocket, they say—Lord knows why, save that he hates Angus! So Margaret Tudor is no longer Countess of Angus, and he no longer Henry's good-brother. Thus, you see, he is no longer of the same use to England. Henry cannot command him as he did, or use him, the most powerful noble in Scotland. He has not the same hold over him."

Lindsay shrugged, waiting.

"So, as I say, we have hopes for Angus. In this coil. There are three great factions in this Scotland—the Queen-Mother's, the Earl of Arran's and Angus's. Four, if you count Holy Church! And the young King is the prize. Whoever hold James, rules in his name, now Albany is gone and there is no regent. Arran and his Hamiltons have taken sides with Margaret Tudor, and so presently rule—or *she* does, since he is a weakling. Thus, Holy Church must look elsewhere."

"You mean *you* must look elsewhere! Since you control your uncle, the Archbishop."

"Crudely put, David! As the Archbishop's and Primate's and Chancellor's secretary, I may have some small influence. But to control him, and through him Holy Church, is an . . . exaggeration! Incidentally, my friend, you should speak more respectfully to your old class-mate. For I am now not just Rector of Campsie and Cambuslang but Lord Abbot of Arbroath, no less!"

"You? You—Abbot? Arbroath! How can this be? You are not a priest. Not in holy orders . . ."

"Admittedly. But I am Abbot *in commendam*. A lay prelate, shall we say? A convenient arrangement, is it not? Since Arbroath is the second richest abbey in the land!"

"Convenient! It is shameful, rather. Disgraceful. That the Church should prostitute itself, to give such as you its high office, its wealth and power . . ."

"Sakes—you are in an ill mood this day, David, I must say! Why not me? I will use the revenues of Arbroath to better effect than any of its ordained and priestly abbots for long enough, I promise you—in *Scotland's* cause. Or half of them, for my uncle would only grant it if he retained half! If I am going to do what I seek to do for our realm, I need moneys. So I have prevailed on my good kinsman—unwilling as he was, mind you—to arrange this. And what is so shameful? If the late King, of beloved memory, could make his fifteen-year-old bastard son Archbishop of St. Andrews *in commendam*, why not your humble servant, who has a degree in theology from the Sorbonne? I warrant no other abbot in all Scotland has that! And I *was* Scots ambassador to France. But, you see, it is not only the moneys and status that is important to me, but the fact that the mitred abbacy carries a seat in parliament. *That* is what I require. Hitherto, at parliaments, I have had to sit dumb, like yourself, listen only, and nudge my august uncle, as Chancellor, when advisable! Now, friend, I can speak and urge and vote. Which is partly why I am here."

Lindsay nodded, almost wearily. "You will come to why, Davie, no doubt. In this flood of words. Always you could out-talk anyone I ever knew."

"Exactly! Hence the value of a seat in parliament! Well now, simple Fife laird—here is my mission, and, I hope, yours. If Margaret's wings are to be clipped and James saved, her own and Arran's factions have to be reduced, out-fought. And only by the other two factions working together can this be achieved— that is, Angus's and the Church. That is the simple fact of it. But less simple to achieve, for they have never had aught in common. My uncle and Angus have always been enemies. So— we need a mediator. Lord Lindsay should serve. Will you go to bespeak his good offices for us, David?"

"So that the Church can aid Angus to supreme power? Think you that any betterment for Scotland?"

"That is not the objective—although even Angus, suitably hobbled, might be better than Margaret Tudor, now that he is cut adrift from Henry of England."

"Have we not had enough of faction-fighting, feud and civil war, all these last years, since Flodden?"

"It is not fighting, war, we seek, but the rule of law, the rightful authority of the realm . . ."

"From Angus and his Douglases! Have you lost your famed wits, man?"

"It is a parliament we aim for—do you not understand? Votes in a parliament. My uncle, as Chancellor, can call a parliament in the King's name. The Church and the Douglases together could swing sufficient votes amongst the shire and burgh commissioners, I believe, to gain a majority. One reason why I wanted my abbacy—to speak in parliament. That way we could unite the nation, or enough of it to thwart Margaret and Arran. And to get the King out of her hands."

"And into Angus's?"

"Into the Privy Council's, with honest additions. Will you do it, friend? Go over to East Lothian, to The Byres of Garleton. Tell your good-father what is intended. Seek his good offices. Ask that he will go to Angus and tell him what is proposed. Ask the Earl to come to St. Andrews for a conference. We cannot go to him—my uncle is past skulking travel, so gross has he become. You come from East Lothian, know your way. We would put you across the firth by night, in a boat from Pittenweem, secretly. Go to The Byres. See your own father, whilst there. Back the next night. No difficulty for *you*. Will you do it, David?"

"I . . . I must consider . . ."

"Aye. Do that. And whilst you consider, man, will you not prove yourself more of a host towards an old friend and offer me some small refreshment better than the smell of cut hay? After all, I have ridden fifteen miles from St. Andrews to see you."

"Yes. To be sure. You will forgive me. I am remiss. Come—we will go back to The Mount . . ."

They walked side-by-side, leading the horse, across the field and down through open woodland where cuckoos were calling hauntingly, towards the dip between the twin hills, Beaton holding forth on the possibilities of his plans, the chances of Angus's co-operation and the methods which he would use to seek to ensure that Holy Church gained most from the association, rather than the Douglases—whose menace he by no means underestimated. A tinkling burn ran down the green cleft in the bosom of the hills, and as the well-defined track they were on neared this, to cross it by a plank-bridge, David Lindsay turned off the track right-handed to head through the trees to a lower crossing-place some way down. His companion, who had used the track and bridge on the way out, interrupted his talk to ask why the detour?

"That bridge is where Kate fell," he was told shortly.

Beaton asked no more. At the funeral two months earlier he had heard that Kate Lindsay, seven months pregnant, riding back from some visit, had been thrown from her shying horse at some hazard, to be eventually found dead and her part-born child with her, in some water. Her husband had been a stricken man since.

A narrower and new path leading lower indicated that David Lindsay could not bear to use that bridge any more.

In silence now they strode on round the base of the eastern hill, back on the track again.

Soon they came to the Castle of The Mount, rising before them on a sort of terrace of the hillside, a typical square stone keep of four storeys beneath a parapet and wall-walk, with a garret storey above, all surrounded by a barmekin or high defensive wall with a gatehouse, enclosing a courtyard containing lower lean-to domestic outbuildings. It had been David's inheritance from his mother, so that he had been nominal laird of the Mount of Lindifferon from childhood, although one day, when his father died, he would be Lindsay of Garleton, in East Lothian, a larger property where he had been born. He and Kate had only come to The Mount, hitherto stewarded for him by an older brother of his mother, in the previous November on being dismissed from the position of procurator and usher to King James, which he had held for all twelve years of the boy-monarch's life. Here he was to become the simple Fife laird he had spoken of so bitterly, and here their first child was to be born. Now he saw life bleak and grey, a changed man.

That was David Lindsay.

In the first-floor hall of his little castle, a housekeeping woman provided a cold meal, adequate but unambitious, to which Beaton did justice but at which his host merely picked. The conversation was almost all on one side, and fairly heavy going even for that most eloquent individual. It was not long before the visitor declared that he must be on his way back to St. Andrews Castle, a two-hour ride—and was not pressed to stay.

At the gatehouse farewell, Davie Beaton rode off sad and concerned for his friend. But at least he had his promise that he

16

would go on this mission to East Lothian for him, and with minimum delay, for time was of the essence.

* * *

Three nights later they made another farewell, this time some twenty-two miles to the south-east, at the fishing haven of Pittenweem below the walls of St. Ethernan's Priory. It was not dark—it is seldom really dark of a Scots June night—but after midnight, a strange time to be putting to sea in a small boat.

Both men had very much in mind the last time that they had been here, in similar if darker circumstances, in the previous November, but coming in the other direction—only that time there had been three of them, Kate agog at the adventure of thus clandestinely commencing a new life.

"It is a calm enough night," Beaton said. "You should be over in little more than two hours. Then a bare three-mile walk up to The Byres. There well before breakfast."

The other nodded.

"You have it all? What is proposed. What to tell the Lord Lindsay. What we wish him to put to the Earl of Angus. And the need for haste. A parliament takes time to mount. And Margaret Tudor might make her move any day."

Again Lindsay nodded. "It is all clear enough. Although whether it will come to anything is another matter."

"We must hope so, pray so. For the sake of young James and his realm, for all our sakes. Much will hang on this, I believe."

"*You* do the praying, my lord Abbot!" he was told, almost mockingly. "Which will be a change, I think!"

It was on the tip of Beaton's tongue to say that such words and attitude represented a still greater change in the David Lindsay he had known since they were youths at college, but instead he held out his hand.

"Good fortune and God speed," he said.

"Yes. I will come to you at St. Andrews two days hence. Or three—who knows?"

"Aye. The boat will wait for you at Luffness. And the Prior here will have your horse ready whenever you arrive, and an escort."

Lindsay stepped down into the broad-beamed coble, and the four fishermen, employed by the Priory, dipped in their long sweeps to manoeuvre the craft out from the cluster of other boats at the pier-side, to pull for the harbour-mouth. Their passenger sat hunched in the stern and did not look back.

Out in the open Firth of Forth the sea was less calm than it had seemed from the land, and the fourteen-mile crossing took longer than Beaton had estimated, largely because the oarsmen had to pull all the way, the square lug-sail being of no use to them, for the prevailing south-westerly breeze, although not strong, was in their faces going this way. The glimmer of the beacon on the Isle of May, to their left in the firth-mouth, was much paler in this half-light than it had been in the dark of November, and soon faded from sight altogether. It was chill out there on the water for the passenger who huddled in his riding-cloak. Occasionally a shower of spray came inboard. Only the creak of the rowlocks and the slap-slap and hiss of the seas broke the silence.

After a couple of hours of it, the loom of the land grew vaguely before them, but there was no certainty as to feature or distance, as the oarsmen pulled steadily, rhythmically on. It was sound rather than sight, in almost another hour, which offered any evidence of location, the continuous booming roar from half-right ahead, low but powerful, dominant. David knew what that was; strange if he did not, after all the flighting for wild-geese he had done to its accompaniment. It was the noise of breaking seas on the bar of Aberlady Bay, the three-mile-long, half-mile-wide sand-bar which all but closed the mouth of that great estuarine bight, something which was not to be mistaken in all the scores of miles of either side of the Firth of Forth.

Parallel with that daunting sound, but well back from its origin, the fishermen steered their craft for the bar's entire length, for the navigable entrance to the bay, at whatever state of the tide, was at the extreme west end of it, where the Water of Peffer found its way to the sea from behind the bar. Twin stone pinnacles marked the opening, only some two hundred yards apart, the gateway to the channel—for Aberlady was the port of Haddington—and these stood out clearly enough in the June half-light; but of a winter's night in a gale of wind and spume, it was not difficult to miss them, and many were the ships which had done so, to leave their timbers on that grievous submerged sand-bar.

Once within the calm waters of the bay itself, all was changed and it was like rowing over an inland loch. They turned the boat's blunt prow eastwards again now, well away from the long jetty at Kilspindie where the port shipping tied up, to head towards the very apex of the triangular-shaped bight, the water of which covered a full fifteen hundred acres. The tide was two-thirds in, fortunately, which meant that they would not be troubled by shallows in this fairly flat-bottomed coble.

Near the very tip of the bay, where the Peffer came in from its wide, level vale, they made their landfall at a boat-strand under quite a steep bank, above which reared the lofty curtain-walls and angle-towers of the great castle of Luffness, another Lindsay stronghold owned, but seldom visited, by the chief of all that renowned house, the Earl of Crawford. Below the castle, huddling between its frowning walls and the shore, was a row of cothouses, hovels, tarred shacks for smoking fish and drying nets hung on poles, the fishing hamlet of Luffness Haven. All was dark and asleep here still, although a dog barked at scent of the visitors.

David jumped out on to the shingle, leaving his boatmen there in their craft. They would do well enough with the local fisherfolk when these awakened. He hoped to be back the following night, for the return passage, but if not they should wait another day. If still he had not appeared, and no word sent, they were to go back to Pittenweem on their own—although he did not anticipate that.

Avoiding the castle, for he was uncertain as to its keeper's allegiances, he set off to the west of it, deliberately to pass a certain red-tiled cart-shed in a field belonging to the Carmelite monastery, sited that side of the castle, a place of bitter-sweet memories, where he and Kate had pledged their troth nine years before. Moving inland he came to the monastery chapel where they had been married. He did not go in but stood at the door amongst the ancient trees for a little, his mind a battle-ground for emotions, before sighing, and resuming his walking.

The light was growing now and he reckoned that the sun would be rising in another hour, by which time he ought to have reached his destination. Strangely enough, familiar as it all was to him, he could not remember ever having *walked* this way before, always having come on horseback, even as a boy.

Skirting the monastery grounds between it and its sister nunnery on the outskirts of Aberlady village, he crossed the water-logged Luffness Muir by a track which was almost a causeway, setting up quacking duck by the score and lazy-flapping herons and disturbing roe-deer and hares; a great place for hawking. Over a mile of this and he came to the hamlet of Ballencrieff, where the cocks were beginning to crow and more dogs remarked on his passage. Then the land began to rise, gently, towards the green ridge of the Garleton Hills, another mile or so. And up there, fairly close under the now abruptly soaring heights of the ridge itself, he came to the castle and castleton of The Byres of Garleton, just as the sun was rising in golden splendour above the rim of the Norse Sea, glimpsed from this altitude miles to the east, between North Berwick and Dunbar.

This place, the seat of the Lords Lindsay of The Byres, the second-most-senior line of that powerful family, and Kate's former home, was a fine establishment, not so large as Luffness but a noble house nevertheless, within its walled gardens and pleasances and orchards, a many-towered fortalice of reddish stone lording it over its slantwise fertile lands and cattle-dotted hummocks, with its own chapel, dovecotes, granaries, mill, ice-houses, even a brewery, its castleton greater than many a village. The first blue smokes of morning fires were lifting into the new slanting sunlight as David approached.

Crossing the moat by the drawbridge, which was not raised, as the portcullis was not lowered, he nevertheless had to beat on the massive timbers of the gatehouse double-doors with the hilt of his dirk, with some repetition, before a peep-hole at eye-level was opened and he was inspected.

"Lindsay of the Mount," he jerked, and there was an exclamation of recognition from within.

With a great creaking the gates were thrown open wide and the porter greeted him with warm respect, all incoherent half-sentences about him being a stranger, his sad loss, the earliness of the hour and where had he come from, to all of which he got little response save for a shake of the head and an enquiry as to whether his lordship was at home? He was, yes, he was told, but not likely to be out of his bed yet. No matter, David said, not to disturb him. He would go to the kitchen for some refreshment, and wait there. No need to escort him; he knew his way.

Presently, with a breakfast of porridge and cream, cold venison, oatcakes and honey washed down with ale, and not anxious to be put through an inquisition, however friendly, by the kitchen

20

staff, he allowed his head to droop at the great kitchen table, and promptly fell asleep.

He started awake with a hand on his shoulder and looked up to find a tall woman, still handsome although elderly, and with kind features, considering him.

"David—here's a surprise!" she said. "It is good, good to see you. But—how come you thus? Afoot, I am told. Why by night? Is it trouble, lad? More trouble?"

"Aunt Isabella!" He rose, to kiss and be kissed. Lady Lindsay was not his aunt but he had always called her that, although her husband he never named uncle. "No, no trouble. At least, not for us. Any more than for all. I come on a mission to my lord. From the Chancellor. And best that I be not seen. By unfriends."

"Ah—so that's the way of it! If it is the Chancellor, then it is young Beaton his nephew! And that one can mean trouble enough, I vow! But—at least it has brought you here, David. You are well enough? You look thin, lad."

"I am well enough, yes. I came in a boat, by night. Did not sleep . . ."

Patrick, fourth Lord Lindsay of The Byres appeared, a thin, high-coloured, grizzled man in his late fifties, with hawklike face and minus an arm lost at Flodden-field. An individual of few words, he greeted his son-in-law briefly. His wife informed him of the circumstances.

David, in no mood for small talk anyway, came straight to the point. "Chancellor Beaton has it that the Queen-Mother intends to take King James secretly to England, believing that her former husband, the Earl of Angus, seeks to lay hands on him and use him for his own ends. This would deliver the boy, and the kingdom, into King Henry's hands. It must be stopped. He believes that a parliament called could stop it. He can call a parliament, as Chancellor. But to win a vote against the Queen-Mother's and Arran's parties, he would require Angus's support. Also his assurance that he would not grab the King. So he seeks a conference with Angus, and quickly. You, my lord, he has word have been seeing Angus. The Archbishop asks that you go to Angus, as mediator. He has always been unfriends with the Earl, so he needs a go-between, in this."

The older man eyed him levelly. "I am no friend of Angus, either," he said.

"Yet Beaton says that he has been here to see you more than once, of late, my lord."

"Your churchman is devilishly well-informed! How that?"

"I know not. I think that it is not so much the Chancellor as his nephew. He seems to have spies everywhere . . ."

"Aye—your friend Davie Beaton! This is all *his* device, then, I warrant. Rather than the old man's. Is it not so?"

"It may be. But does that alter the need for this parliament? To save the King. Something must be done."

"Perhaps, but Angus is an ill man to deal with."

"Yet you have been dealing with him?"

"Not me with him, boy. *Him* seeking to use me! He wants my manpower, against Arran and the Hamiltons. He has Crawford on his side, so he wants the rest of the Lindsays."

"Then you have something with which to bargain."

"I am not giving my Lindsays to die for Angus! Or any of them. I have had enough of war and swordery!"

"So say I. And Davie Beaton! Better a parliament to decide matters, the vote not the sword. It's why I agreed to come here."

"Maybe so. But by the same token I have nothing to bargain with, with Angus. I told him that I am not lending him one man."

"Nevertheless, my lord, you still can reach him, have access to him. And Davie Beaton has not. Will you do this? For the young King's sake."

"Angus is one for the sword rather than talk, conferences, voting in parliament. He would laugh at me, belike. He is a devil, that one."

"It is not much to do, Pate," the Lady Isabella said. "Need Lindsay fear Douglas laughter?"

"My lord—at least ask him to come to St. Andrews, to confer with the Archbishop. Angus has an uncle, a churchman, Prior William Douglas. And many other Douglas clerics. *They* would not wish him to reject the Primate's call out-of-hand. He may prefer the sword, but would be a fool needlessly to antagonise the Church, I think."

"You are strong on this, David. Why? If you are so keen, go to Angus yourself."

"He would never see me, only a small laird now, of no consequence. He is proud, arrogant. Besides, I cannot travel the breadth of Scotland to seek him . . ."

"No need. He is not at Galloway or Douglasdale, mean-time. He is only at Tantallon—a dozen miles away. Has been these ten days. I will take you to him—but you can do the talking!"

The younger man bit his lip, uncertain now.

"Why not, David?" Lady Isabella asked. "Both go. Better two than one. He will not *eat* you!"

"I was to sail back tonight . . ."

"And still can, if you must. You could be at Tantallon before noon. Back in two hours . . ."

He shrugged.

So, presently, with a tail of a dozen well-mounted armed retainers, without which such as the Lord Lindsay never rode abroad, the two men trotted eastwards down into the Vale of Peffer, by Drem and Prora and Congalton, skirting to the north of the wide boglands where that most curious of rivers arose. For the Peffer was probably the only river in all Scotland to flow in two directions out of its swampy womb of waters, one branch westwards nine miles, eventually to enter Aberlady Bay; the other eastwards only four miles to reach the Norse Sea at Peffermouth; both called Peffer from the Celtic *pefr*, meaning fair, and forming one continuous waterway through one of the most fertile vales in the land.

By the village of Hamer, with its fine and ancient red-stone church, they came in sight of Tantallon, on its cliff-girt promon-tory, that seemed to shake a fist at sky and sea and the mighty mass of the Craig of Bass which reared out of the tide two miles offshore. It made a striking picture, a vast thrusting pile as red as Hamer Kirk, the Lothian seat of the Red Douglases—indeed some suggested that was how this branch of the family got its name, for its people were in truth no redder in hair or feature than the Black Douglases. No other fortalice in the land was quite like it, for it was really an enormous thirty-foot-high curtain-wall, topped by a wall-walk, cutting off its lofty trian-gular peninsula of cliff, with a massive gatehouse-keep in the centre and a tall tower at each end, the whole being defended from landward by water-filled moats and deep dry ditches, in series, which prevented even the most powerful cannon from being sited within range to do any damage. It required no defences on the seaward sides, so sheer were the precipices. From the end towers the great red-heart banners of Douglas flapped, while above the central keep flew the Earl's standard, quartering the arms of Angus and Douglas.

Impressed despite themselves, the Lindsays frowned at it all. They had been challenged by Douglas outposts long before they reached thus far, at Hamer and Scoughall and Auldhame, but Lord Lindsay's authoritative reaction had gained them passage without trouble. But at the final drawbridge before the arched pend through the basement of the massive central keep, they were held up for some time while, after demanding their business, the porter sent to discover whether they were to be admitted, scowling men-at-arms presenting a frieze of lances at them as though they were about to try to take the place by storm.

At length they were allowed in, although their escorts were curtly told to wait outside with the horses. They were led through the quite long vaulted passage beneath the great five-storeyed tower by a character dressed in the finery of a herald's tabard, with feathered bonnet, all emblazoned with the Douglas device, to an open space hardly to be described as a courtyard, for it was much larger than that. It was the flat cliff-top area enclosed by the tremendous barrier of masonry through which they had passed, part paved and part laid out in cropped grass as sports-ground for bowls, quoits and even archery, as well as a lady's pleasance with arbours, sundials, paths, shrubs and flowers, a strange place to find behind that frowning exterior. Most of it was surrounded by subsidiary outbuildings, chapel, domestic offices and accommodation, stabling and the like; but directly in front a gap had been left at the cliff's edge, providing an open view over the sea to the Bass and the distant Isle of May— although hoists and crane-like structures with ropes and pulleys and cranks indicated that it was not so much for the vista that the gap was there but for a raising and lowering device for men and goods, so that this all-but-impregnable establishment could be supplied and re-inforced by sea, a notable advantage. Their herald took them to a large well-shaft, with its own hoist, in the centre of the paved area, and there told them to wait.

The Lord Patrick snorted something about over-grown and blown puppies aping royal status, with their heralds and arrogant pretensions; but David was busy taking in his surroundings in detail and perceiving why Tantallon had never been successfully besieged, to date.

24

They were kept waiting for another considerable period, to the older man's wrath, before the herald returned to announce that the lord Earl would now see them. He conducted them up a straight stair in the thickness of the main curtain-walling—which provided some indication as to the width of the said masonry, since the stair itself was nearly four feet wide—and into an anteroom on the first floor of the central keep, to leave them once more and disappear beyond into a further chamber from which voices sounded. Again they had to wait, with two armed guards in the Douglas colours eyeing them at the connecting doorway. Lord Lindsay, something of an autocrat himself, inevitably stamped back and forth on the stone-flagged floor in unconcealed offence, spurs jingling.

At length the busy pursuivant reappeared, to usher them in, proclaiming in sonorous tones the Lord Lindsay of The Byres to see the most noble and puissant Earl of Angus, Lord of Douglas, Galloway, Nithsdale and Jed Forest, etcetera, whom God succour and assist. He did not mention David.

Lord Patrick stamped in, glaring. Four men lounged at ease around a table laden with flagons and beakers, drinking, and certainly giving no impression of being in council or doing serious business. Three were of later middle years, one much younger, in his late twenties.

"Ha—Lindsay!" the young man said. "So it is yourself. Have you come to see sense, then? Perceived that your refusal was unwise? Belatedly!"

"At Tantallon, so far, Angus, I have only perceived mummery and play-acting! If I had been looking for sense I would have gone elsewhere! To be kept waiting at your doors like packmen . . . !" Which was not how David would have wished to start the interview.

The Earl clenched his fists on that table-top. He was a handsome, fair-haired, hot-eyed man, well-built, richly if carelessly dressed. Undoubtedly he was a man to look twice at—but it was those eyes which made the greatest impression, of palest blue, staring, unblinking.

"Watch how you speak in Tantallon, sirrah!" he jerked. "You come un-announced. Like packmen! If you are not seeking sense, and you have not changed your mind over supporting me, what *do* you want of me, man?"

"Civility is all *I* seek—perhaps too much to expect from

25

Douglas! It is my friend here who has matters to put to you. Myself, I would have counselled him otherwise!"

"You would . . . ?" For the first time, as it seemed, Angus allowed himself to notice David, and then only briefly. He gave no sign of recognition, although he must have known him, having seen him often enough with the young King. "And what does *he* want?"

"My lord—I come from the Chancellor," David said. "The Archbishop. From St. Andrews. He sends greetings and seeks . . ."

"I addressed the Lord Lindsay—not you!" he was interrupted. "Speak only when you are spoken to, in this house. Well, Lindsay?"

The Lord Patrick stared. "Are you out of your mind, Angus?" he demanded. "Has association with Henry Tudor addled your wits to make-believe Tudor grandeur?"

The Earl half-rose from his seat, in a posture of menace. "If you wish to leave Tantallon a whole man, Lindsay, you will guard your ill tongue! While you still have *one* arm!"

"I lost the other, Angus, on Flodden-field, amongst better men than you! And where the previous Angus rode off the field before the battle started!" That was shrewd thrusting, but hardly fair, for although the fifth Earl, the notorious Bell-the-Cat, this man's grandfather, had indeed left the Scots army before the fighting began, out of disagreement over strategy with James the Fourth, not in fear, his eldest son, the Earl's father, had died there with his monarch.

David, exasperated beyond bearing by all this folly, turned to the other three who sat watching, listening. He knew them all, all Douglases, all uncles of Angus—Sir George Douglas of Pittendreich; Sir Archibald Douglas of Kilspindie, known as Graysteel, neighbour of The Byres and Garleton; and Master William Douglas, Prior of Coldinghame. It was to the last that he addressed himself.

"You, Master Prior—you are a churchman. I come from the Primate of Holy Church with a message. Is it not to be heard? Shall I return to the Archbishop and Chancellor and tell him . . ."

"Silence, fool! I told you—speak only when spoken to in my presence!" the Earl exclaimed. "Think you that coming from that fat slug Beaton commends you to me? If there is any worth

26

in what he has to say to me, then let your good-father reveal it. I do not deal with underlings."

David drew a deep breath. At least the man had revealed that he knew who he was.

The Lord Patrick snorted. "The message is his, not mine. I scarce know the matter. I but brought him here. Would God I had not!"

"Aye—the first fair word you have spoken here, Lindsay!"

There was a cough from the eldest uncle, Pittendreich, who glanced at the Prior. That plumply smooth individual, presumably taking this as a sign to intervene, spoke up.

"Do you not think, Archie, that we should hear at least what the Archbishop has to say?" he suggested. "And since my lord of Lindsay appears not to know the details, it looks as though we must have it from this Lindsay of the Mount. Briefly, to be sure."

His two brothers grunted agreement.

Angus eyed them all from under down-bent brows for a little, silent.

"Better from *this* Chancellor, perhaps, than from the other!" the Prior added, significantly.

That dart found its mark. For the Queen-Mother, Angus's late and hated wife, had recently declared the Archbishop, in the King's name, to be no longer Chancellor, and appointed to the office her present lover, Henry Stewart of Methven—although she had no true authority to do either, the chancellorship being an appointment of the King-in-Parliament. The Earl, who could not be expected to love his successor in Margaret Tudor's bed, shrugged.

"Very well," he acceded. "Out with it."

David felt himself to be at his least eloquent and persuasive, his most terse, in these circumstances. Which was perhaps unfair towards Davie Beaton's mission.

"My lord Archbishop proposes a conference at St. Andrews," he announced jerkily. "He would call a parliament thereafter and wishes to ensure a favourable vote. He has learned that the Queen-Mother intends to smuggle King James out of the country, into England. This must be stopped. He believes that only a parliament can do it, take the necessary steps. And the Douglases, my lord, could much aid the vote in parliament."

"So-o-o! That is the way of it. Henry is to get James into his hands—is that it?"

27

David nodded.

"When?"

"That is not known. But the Chancellor calls for haste. He believes that the Queen-Mother is but waiting for a message from the Lord Dacre, the English Warden, to whom she wrote."

Angus looked at his uncles. "She fears us, then!"

"Or else she fears that Arran may turn against her! Or that Bastard of his." That was Graysteel, Sir Archibald of Kilspindie.

"Aye, perhaps. You have heard naught of such talk?"

"No."

"It is said that Arran resents Margaret making so much of Henry Stewart," Sir George of Pittendreich said.

"Dacre has been in the south, at London," the Prior pointed out. Having Coldinghameshire property on the borders of Northumberland, and being in league with the Homes, he was in a position to know such things. "He may still be."

"So Margaret waits," Angus said. "And Beaton looks to Douglas to do his work for him!"

"Say, my lord, that he recognises that together Douglas and the Church can sway parliament, and so save the King. Whereas alone, neither could, possibly."

"You think so? Perhaps Douglas should take the King out of Margaret's hands without troubling a parliament! And save him the more surely, that way."

"Since she has His Grace safe in Edinburgh Castle, my lord, it is scarcely likely. It would require a siege, bombardment by cannon. Against the King's royal person . . ."

The Earl glared at David angrily.

"What does the Archbishop suggest . . . in return for this Douglas service?" the Prior asked suavely.

"I know not. But that, perhaps, is what the conference is for!"

"Ah."

There was a silence around that table. It had not been proposed that the Lindsays should sit down, or partake of the wines.

"When?" Angus demanded abruptly.

"So soon as is possible. Since the Queen-Mother may act at any time."

"Why can Beaton not come here? Why should we go to St. Andrews?"

"The Archbishop is not young, and less than well. Also there

28

is less danger for Douglas in travelling the country than for him, is there not?"

"By sea, Archie, we could be at St. Andrews in three hours," Pittendreich said.

David recognised that he had gained his objective.

"Tell Beaton that he had better have sufficient inducements for me, if I come!" Angus said grimly.

"Yes. When shall I tell him to look for you, my lord?"

"That remains to be seen. I do not discuss times and seasons with such as you, nor wait on the convenience of clerks in orders! Tell him so, likewise."

The Lord Patrick grinned. "When the clerk controls more riches than the rest of the realm put together, Angus, I think, will discover his convenience not so difficult!"

It was his turn to be ignored. "You have my permission to retire, Lindsay," the Earl said, but to David now.

"When do we start to name you Your Grace?" the older man mocked. "Come, David—we have had a sufficiency of play-acting for one day!" And without so much as an inclination of his grizzled head towards the Douglases, he turned for the door.

David hesitated, half-shrugged, bowed briefly, and followed him.

Surprisingly for so plump and comfortable a person, they found Prior William reaching the door before them. "I will see them out, Archie," he said, and waved them on.

The herald was waiting in the anteroom beyond, but the Prior gestured him aside. At the stair-foot, he paused.

"Give my lord Archbishop my duty and greetings," he said. "Tell him that I will do what I can, in my humble way. Give me three days, or four, and I think that I may promise that we will be at St. Andrews. A good day to you, Lindsay. And to you, my lord."

As the herald came to take them on to the porter's lodge and drawbridge, the Lord Patrick shook his head.

"An oily scoundrel that," he judged. "A snake, where Angus is but a boar! And greedy, I swear. Seeking a bishopric, no doubt!"

"Perhaps. But greed my be easier to deal with than arrogant pride, I think."

"Easier, man? That one will never be easy. Watch him! Remember how he won Coldinghame Priory—by having the

Homes slay the previous Prior and his monks in cold blood, he watching. The snake is more deadly than the boar—for one gives warning when he strikes and the other does not!"

They rode back westwards, thoughtful.

David called in at Garleton Castle to see his aging father and Mirren Livingstone his mistress, but did not stay long. He was back at Luffness Haven, to the waiting boat, by sundown.

2

David Lindsay certainly had not expected to be travelling back to the south shore of the Firth of Forth again so soon, even though in very different fashion. Again it was the persuasive Davie Beaton who had been responsible, convincing him that he ought to attend the session of parliament, purely as a spectator of course, partly because his advice might be useful, and partly as an opportunity to see his late charge and young friend, King James, impossible these days otherwise. Lindsay had once more been reluctant, but the other pressing—Beaton seemed to have taken it upon himself to try to rouse his namesake and former fellow-student out of his depths of depression.

So now, dressed in what passed for his best, he rode near the head of a glittering cavalcade westwards through the central Howe of Fife—for Archbishop Beaton hated the sea and refused to make the journey to Edinburgh by boat. In fact the Primate travelled very much at ease, lying in a handsome canopied litter, heraldically decorated, slung between two white horses, a gross, overweight, heavy-jowled man in his early sixties, almost purple of feature, with drooping eyelids above small, shrewd pig-like eyes, most splendidly garbed in ecclesiastical finery and decked with jewellery, even for the journey, Holy Church indicating temporal power to match the spiritual. Before and after rode at least one hundred of the archiepiscopal guard in mitred breastplates and liveries embroidered with the arms of the metropolitan see, and behind this personal escort, a colourful cavalcade of clerics, chaplains, confessors and officials; then a train of laden pack-horses burdened with gear, extra vestments, provisions, wines and candles, led by uniformed servitors, and finally another detachment of the guard. David, riding with his friend near the Primate's litter, considered it all a vulgar and unsuitable display, but the Lord Abbot of Arbroath—*in commendam*—declared otherwise, that it was a useful and salutary demonstration to all concerned of the fact that the Church was a potent and effective influence in the affairs of the realm, much needed in the present struggle for rule and government.

The conference at St. Andrews had duly taken place—if such it could be called, when it had been really only a bargaining session between Angus and the Archbishop, or more accurately between the latter's nephew and the former's uncle, Prior William Douglas, who between them had done most of the trading. Lindsay of course had not been present; but when young Beaton had come again to the Mount of Lindifferon, to persuade him to attend the parliament, he had given him some account of the proceedings, with typically humorous and scurrilous comments. Angus had hectored and threatened and insulted, but the fact that he was there at all indicated that he had judged the occasion worth while and therefore could be dealt with. There had been some hard bargaining nevertheless, and Prior William had proved himself an acute and wily opponent—whom Davie Beaton appeared to admire. He did not give details of the terms come to, but no doubt these would become evident in due course. Meantime, the parliament had been agreed to and, because of the necessity for haste, the normal forty days notice had been dispensed with. This would inevitably mean a low attendance, with lords and commissioners from the remoter areas of the country probably unable to make it in time; but it was calculated that the Douglas and Church representation would be apt to gain from that.

So, ten days later, here they were on the road.

With that horse-litter, and the clerical horsemen apt to be no pace-setters, progress was stately rather than speedy; but as Davie Beaton pointed out, the Queen-Mother was unlikely to try to smuggle her son off to England now, with a parliament arranged at which the young King was to be present, and hopefully a rallying-call for her supporters; and, moreover, with the Douglases alerted to the danger, keeping a night-and-day watch on any possible exits from Edinburgh's castle-rock. The Archbishop was prepared to face the mere mile-wide crossing of Forth at Queen Margaret's Ferry, where the great flat-bottomed barges could carry their many horses; but that demanded a journey, through Fife and Fothrif, of some thirty-five miles, and ten miles to Edinburgh on the other side. At their rate of progress, this would require an overnight halt, and the Primate was not the man to put up with scratch lodging in some small monkish hospice or ale-house. So it meant reaching his own princely Abbey of Dunfermline, the richest jewel in the metropolitan mitre—with Arbroath only in second place—even though it was those thirty-five miles from St. Andrews, a long journey for one day for the present travellers, even though the two Davids could have done twice that. If Davie Beaton, who could ride as hard as any, chafed at their unhurried pace, as did David Lindsay, he did not allow it to show.

Since the Archbishop slept for most of the way, his nephew was free to discuss with his friend—or more truly use him as a sounding-board in his calculations—how the parliament was likely to go. Even with Douglas support, they could by no means be sure of success. For the Douglases were hated as well as feared, and Arran's party was strong in the west. Much would depend on lesser factions, in especial the Stewarts. These were a somewhat divided lot, although all of them supported their Stewart monarch. But some, such as the Earl of Lennox, loathed Margaret Tudor, and others, like the Galloway branch, were apt to side with their Douglas neighbours. On the other hand, the main Lanarkshire and Renfrewshire stem, which included the Lords Avondale and Innermeath, were likely to support the Queen-Mother, since Henry Stewart of Methven, her present lover, was Avondale's son. All Davie Beaton's renowned artifice and eloquence was going to be required to win the day, Douglas or none.

It was evening before they reached Dunfermline and the comforts of its great abbey, in the splendid church of which so many of the King's ancestors were interred, including the hero-king Bruce himself. Because it had succeeded Iona as the place of royal sepulture, it had become so well-endowed with lands and riches over the centuries that it was now the wealthiest foundation in the land, and, coming as it did under the metropolitan see of St. Andrews, represented one of the Primate's greatest assets. It was understood that whoever was appointed its abbot passed on half of its vast revenues to the Archbishop; nevertheless there was never any difficulty in filling the position. If the present Abbot considered the invasion of nearly two hundred mouths to feed, with their beasts, an imposition, he was careful not to say so. He would come with them in the morning, for his was another mitred abbacy with a vote in parliament.

They made no early start next day, and, reinforced by the contingents of the Abbots of Lindores and Balmerino, both in Fife, made their way down to the narrows of the Firth of Forth at the Queen's Ferry. This was in fact one of the money-spinners of Dunfermline Abbey, run by that establishment ever since the days of St. Margaret, who had founded it over four centuries earlier. Now all other travellers were pushed aside—to the annoyance of certain lords, also heading for Edinburgh—while the major task of transporting the archiepiscopal following to the Lothian shore proceeded, a protracted business. Perceiving this, Davie Beaton urged his uncle to invite the Earl of Rothes and the Lord Glamis to accompany him across in the abbatical barge and to take wine with them in the hospice at the other side, as they waited—since it would be a pity to lose two votes out of mere injured pride.

It was a major company, therefore, which reached Edinburgh in the afternoon. The hilly city was already packed, seething with incomers, too large a proportion of whom appeared to be wearing the colours of Douglas, and behaving as though the capital belonged to them. Pushing slowly through the thronged narrow streets from the West Port, by the Grassmarket below the soaring castle-rock, to the Cowgate, they came to the Blackfriars Monastery, which was the Archbishop's Edinburgh headquarters—and which he had not dared to visit for long. Commodious as these quarters were, they were filled to overflowing by the new arrivals. The Prior thereof warned all that it would be unwise to venture out into the city streets after dusk, as the town was infested with roaming bands of Douglas and Hamilton supporters, based on Holyrood and the castle respectively, looking for trouble and not only with each other.

It made scarcely ideal conditions for a productive assembly to arrange the nation's affairs.

Of recent times parliaments had been apt to be held in the great church of the Holy Rood—largely because all too often the castle, with its Parliament Hall, was in the hands of one faction or another and barred against the rest. But on this occasion, with the Queen-Mother and her son therein, and she refusing to let King James be taken out, it had been agreed to hold the session there, however reluctantly, as giving advantage to Margaret's and Arran's parties, since it was essential for a true parliament, as distinct from a convention of the Estates, that the monarch should be present in person. It was not really anticipated that, at the last moment, the Queen-Mother would hold the citadel against them and refuse admittance, since that would be to proclaim to the nation that she feared that she had only minority support; but the possibility was always there, Davie Beaton admitted. What would happen if she did was hard to predict. Almost certainly outright civil war would follow.

*　　*　　*

Next noontide, David Lindsay sat in a corner, carefully chosen, of the great hammer-beam-roofed Parliament Hall of the capital's fortress, watching and waiting. So far, so good. There had been no attempt by the garrison to prevent ingress, although ranked men-at-arms, mainly wearing the Hamilton colours, lined the climbing route up from the gatehouse and drawbridge to this hall, glaring at all comers belligerently. But they had not done more than that—indeed the Douglases, thronging the tourney-ground approach to the castle, had been much more aggressive in challenging all who sought admittance, indicating that all who entered the citadel did so only with their permission, all unauthorised turned away out-of-hand. Lindsay undoubtedly would not have gained access had he not come with the Chancellor's party. Davie had found him this place to sit, on a stool in an alcove not far from the Chancellor's table and, in fact, directly across the dais from the throne. It was, Beaton said, where he would have sat himself, to be effectively near his uncle, had he not had to take his new place on the ecclesiastical benches, as Abbot of Arbroath.

The hall was by no means full, for it would hold hundreds—and there would be no hundreds attending this parliament. Indeed Davie calculated that there would be no more than sixty present entitled to vote—although of course

34

there were many others: burgh representatives who were permitted to come to ensure that their chosen commissioners voted as their burgh councils had instructed, the eldest sons or heirs of lords of parliament, senior churchmen not in the mitred class, and other privileged spectators. But even of these there were a deal fewer than usual.

With the city bells below the castle-rock striking the hour of noon, a fanfare of trumpets from outside the hall stilled the chatter. All stood, eyes turned to the double doors which opened on to this dais area and which were now thrown wide.

The Lord Lyon King-of-Arms and his heralds entered, all splendid in their colourful tabards, to announce the royal summons and authority for this parliament. Then, preceded by pikemen in the royal livery, he ushered in the procession of state, consisting of those high officers of the realm who were not otherwise involved, or indeed not banished, imprisoned or afraid to appear—the Clerk-Register, the Dempster, the Lord Privy Seal, the Lord High Treasurer—none other than Margaret's paramour and would-be Chancellor, Henry Stewart— the Earl Marischal and the High Constable, the last with the sword of state. These were followed by the justiciars, two-by-two.

There was a pause and then another trumpeting, and two men appeared side-by-side but walking as far apart as the access would permit, each managing to turn a shoulder away from the other in mutual disesteem, but each bearing a purple cushion. That was the only point of resemblance, for one, the Earl of Angus, was young, handsome, upstanding and, oddly for the occasion and a summer's day, clad in half-armour and thigh-length riding-boots, as though garbed for the fray; and the other, the Earl of Arran, chief of the Hamiltons, Lord High Admiral and second person to the King, his cousin, elderly, stooping and over-dressed in velvets and cloth-of-gold. On Arran's cushion lay the sceptre and on Angus's the crown. Clearly hating each other, they marched into the hall and up to the Chancellor's table, where the Clerk-Register had already taken up his position, to deposit their symbols of sovereignty beside the sword of state. They then moved down to the foremost benches of the assembly, there to sit together, but still contriving not to see each other.

Another pause and trumpet-blast and James Beaton came in,

the President of the High Court of Parliament, Chancellor of the Realm, a figure to catch and hold all eyes, his grossness hidden under the most magnificent and costly robes that even an archbishop might aspire to, alb, cope, pallium and stole, all so encrusted with jewels and gold as to make his every movement a blazing scintillation, Holy Church intent on preaching one of its more telling lessons. Archiepiscopal staff in one hand and Chancellor's gavel in the other, he paced his ponderous way to the table, there to remain, standing.

Sir Thomas Clephane, the Lord Lyon, bowing, retraced his steps to the door and out. All waited, on their feet.

The trumpeters this time excelled themselves in a flourish of brassy sound which seemed to shake the ancient stonework. There was a clanking of armour and grounding of pikes outside, but a distinct interval elapsed before Lyon reappeared, his baton upraised, pacing slowly now. Just within the hall he halted, and gazing about him, exclaimed with practised grandiloquence:

"James, fifth of his name, by God's grace, High King of Scots, Duke of Rothesay and Lord of the Isles, our most high and mighty prince and gracious sovereign-lord!"

It is to be feared that the sequel to this stirring announcement was something of an anticlimax, for neither the boy nor the woman who now appeared were such as to especially engage the attention in other circumstances. James, now thirteen, was good-looking enough, well-built for his years, and with a fine head of red hair; but he entered with that head down, and scowling, reluctance in every line of him; and he was dressed in nondescript, not to say outworn, clothing, probably the least fine in all that hall. And his mother, close behind, was neither beautiful nor elegant. Now aged thirty-four, Margaret Tudor looked older, heavily made, hair greying prematurely, her features puffy, pasty—although those close enough to perceive it would recognise spirit in her dull-glowing dark eyes, indicating that here was a woman who could have fierce emotions, who could hate with a smouldering intensity and whose rages were as notorious as her lasciviousness. David Lindsay, as she came near, from his alcove wondered anew that one so, to him, physically unsavoury, could be so concerned with her own body and its functions. Her brother, Henry the Eighth, was similarly gross—but at least he was said to have a certain animal attractiveness. Margaret, who had come to Scotland at the age

36

of thirteen as bride for the dashing and gallant James the Fourth, was undoubtedly one of the Auld Enemy England's most effective disservices to the northern kingdom.

Behind the pair, unlooked-for, unsuitable and causing gasps of offence from the deep-bowing assembly, clanked in a file of perhaps a score of armed men in red livery, their steel breast-plates painted with the five-lobed flower device of the Tudor Rose, part of the bodyguard of two hundred sent north by the King of England a month or two before, allegedly for his nephew's protection, a gesture much resented by the Scots.

James, reluctant as he obviously had been, once he was into the hall made for his place, the throne at the rear of the dais, at more speed than dignity, his mother's barked command to slow down ignored. As a consequence she also had to hurry, to keep up, and the men-at-arms behind likewise, making an unusual royal entry. At the handsome gold-painted chair of state, with its rampant lions as finials, set on its own plinth, the boy sat down without ceremony. Panting a little, and frowning as darkly as her son, the Queen-Mother came up, to pause before seating her-self on a chair placed beside and a little below the throne. The clanking escort shuffled to range themselves in a long line behind, facing the assembly.

After a moment or two of silence, all sat who had seats.

The Chancellor rose again, bowed to the throne and raising a beringed hand, uttered a prayer for the proceedings, remarkable in its brevity. He then declared the King-in-Parliament to be duly in session and called upon the Clerk-Register to read out the names of the Lords of the Articles appointed by the last parliament, a sort of executive committee charged with carrying out the broad decisions of each assembly, and whose responsibi-lities were now ended. It was noticeable that of the ten names given, five were not present today.

Hardly had the Clerk-Register finished before the Queen-Mother was on her feet. "My lord Chancellor, my lords and barons," she said in her clipped English voice which twenty-one years of residence in Scotland had not altered, ignoring the burgesses, "I declare that this parliament is untimely and unnecessary. I do regret, as does His Grace, the inconvenience and cost to which you have all been put, to attend it. The Lords Articular, with my guidance, were well able to conduct the affairs of His Grace's realm in the meantime, there having been no disaster or great event to warrant another parliament. I therefore move that the Lords Articular, those who have done their duty, be reappointed forthwith, and so save much unnecessary talk and labour here."

She sat down amidst a great outcry and stir of excitement. Never had the gauntlet been thrown down so swiftly and unexpectedly, in a trial of strength which could end the proceedings before they were begun.

The Chancellor banged his gavel on the table, jowls wobbling in indignation and outrage, but ignoring him, the Earl of Arran rose.

"I support the Queen's Grace," he exclaimed. "I call a vote."

Before he was finished, Angus, at his side, was on his feet. "My lord Chancellor," he cried, "with all respect for my late consort, I move the contrary. Douglas has not come here for such device. We have come to right the realm's business." No swords other than the sword of state were permitted within the Parliament Hall, but the Earl managed to beat his sheathed dagger metallically against his plate-armour as he sat down.

The Archbishop continued to bang his gavel, almost as though he did not know what else to do, his quandary most evident to all who knew the rules. As President of the session, procedure was difficult, to say the least. The fact was, Margaret Tudor had no authority to speak in that parliament at all. She was not the monarch, nor a lord of parliament, nor a commissioner of shire or burgh and certainly not a representative of the Church. So her speech and motion were *ultra vires*. But Arran, an earl, had seconded it and Angus, another, had made a contrary motion, both within their right. The situation was as complicated as it was embarrassing.

Strangely, relief came for the Chancellor from an unlikely source. It was at this difficult moment that King James, glowering around sulkily, suddenly caught sight of David Lindsay sitting in his corner. His expression transformed, he promptly leapt to his feet.

"Davie! Davie Lindsay!" he shouted gladly, and ignoring his mother's restraining hand, ran across the dais to the alcove and his former procurator and usher.

There was consternation in Parliament Hall.

David's mind became a battlefield of emotions, alarm, uncertainty and gladness that his one-time charge should so clearly delight in his presence. But—how to cope with the situation?

The boy hurled himself bodily upon his friend in a gabble of incoherent greetings and affection, and involuntarily the man's arms encircled his monarch's eager young person, however improper and unsuitable that might be. It was the best part of a year since they had been rudely parted, at Stirling Castle, and David sent packing by the Queen-Mother, James in tears. Nothing could have been more eloquent of the boy-king's misery and hatred for those months than his attitude shown hitherto this day compared with the joy displayed now before all.

But as the youngster clung and laughed and shook his friend in an excess of feeling, David sought desperately for ability to deal with the situation. And not only David; all present with any authority for the parliament were in a like quandary. Never had the like been seen, or any precedent established for dealing with it. James Stewart might be a newly-thirteen-year-old boy behaving in outrageous fashion on a great state occasion, but he was the sovereign-lord of all there, in theory the supreme authority in the parliament as in the realm. No-one was in a position to order him back to his place so that proceedings might be resumed, for although the Chancellor chaired the assembly, the monarch in effect presided over all.

There was an agitated interlude, with the hall loud in exclamation and talk. Margaret Tudor was on her feet, glaring. Archbishop Beaton was twisting his gavel round and round in his uncertainty. The Earl of Arran even turned to stare at his neighbour, who was grinning at it all. One man, however, did more than gaze. The Abbot of Arbroath left his place amongst the clerics to step up on to the dais-platform, to his uncle's side, there to whisper urgently.

The Queen-Mother it was who acted first. Striding out, she came for her son, hand out imperiously.

James, feeling his friend stiffen, turned. Seeing his mother there, he too held out a hand, but palm towards her, in the most eloquent thrusting-away gesture.

"No!" he shouted. "No! Go away. Davie—do not let her . . . !"

That made the situation worse than ever. The previous year Margaret and Arran had, on the Duke of Albany's return to France in resignation, managed to have the regency declared at

39

an end and the King old enough to rule personally as well as reign—they in fact ruling in his name. Nevertheless, James was nominally supreme ruler of his kingdom from that day, and his royal command unchallengeable—even if he would scarcely realise it. Whether the Queen-Mother accepted this momentarily, or was merely shaken by this public exhibition of her son's hatred for her, she faltered.

No-one else was in a position to intervene. Henry the Eighth's English guards looked on helplessly.

Margaret Tudor could not just stand there, in mid-dais. She had to either go forward or back to her seat. "James," she said loudly, "come back to your throne. I, I beg of you." For that woman, that last must have taken a deal of saying.

"No!" her son answered. "Go away."

In the ensuing silence, with all at a loss what to do now, Davie Beaton made a gesture of his hand towards Lindsay and the latter gave a single nod of the head. It had come to him that he alone in all that gathering might solve this problem, and must try to, for everyone's sake, not least that of the boy who still clutched his arm. He drew a deep breath.

"Sire," he said, low-voiced, "I think that you should go back to your place. I will come with you, if you wish. Until you do, this parliament cannot go on. And it should, for your kingdom's sake. The sooner it resumes, the sooner it will be over. Go back to your throne, Sire."

"*You* will come, Davie? You will stay with me?"

"Yes. I will stand behind you. As I have done before."

"Very well. But you must not leave me. Where have you been, Davie, all this time?"

"At my house in Fife, Highness. Come . . ."

Hand-in-hand they crossed the dais, James deliberately looking away from his mother as he passed her. He sat on the throne again, and David stood beside it, close but a little behind on the left, where the boy could, and did, pat his arm. So much for his discreet attendance as a spectator in a corner.

The Queen-Mother returned to her seat, set-faced. Sighs of relief prevailed around. Davie Beaton moved back to his own place, in his splendid prelatical robes for the first time.

Whatever else might result from this incident, it had had more than one effect on the Chancellor who, possibly with his nephew's advice, appeared to have gathered his wits about him in the interim. Bowing elaborately to the throne, he banged his gavel.

"With His Grace's royal permission, we will resume," he announced. "A motion was before the parliament regarding the Lords of the Articles. But I have to rule this out-of-order, as the proposal was not made by a commissioner. I also rule that the appointment of Lords Articular is always made at the *end* of a session, not the beginning, when the decisions which they have to implement are known. It is within my authority to decide. The order of business is the Chancellor's responsibility. Therefore I so rule. We shall now proceed with the agenda. The first matter I have down for consideration is the necessary extension of the panning of salt. The trade to Muscovy and other parts in salted fish demands not only an increase in salt-making but a spreading of manufacture over a wider area of the kingdom. Certain burghs, which have coals nearby, must be encouraged to build salt-pans and take up such manufacture. Holy Church has long taken the lead in this matter, but the realm's trade demands more general development. I understand that the royal burgh of Inverkeithing has proposals?"

If the Chancellor believed that Margaret Tudor had been quelled, and that the introduction of a safe and non-controversial subject such as this would get the session established in orderly and businesslike fashion after a deplorable start, he was to be disappointed. The Queen-Mother was not so easily put down. Before the Archbishop had finished speaking she was on her feet again.

"My lords," she said strongly, "it may suit churchmen and traders to discuss this matter of salt and fish before the vital affairs of the kingdom, but I swear that this is not why most of your lordships have come here today! First things first, I say! And since the conducting of the business of this parliament, since it *has* been called, however unnecessarily, is important, as is the managing of the realm's affairs thereafter, from day to day, I say that the assembly should appoint, as is its right, a new Chancellor, one in better health and fitness of mind, the present cleric being of sere age and having over-long borne the burden of office. He deserves relief! I propose for the chancellorship the present Lord High Treasurer."

At first that bombshell was greeted with an astonished hush. Then uproar broke out, exclamation and shouting. Nor was it all

41

indignation. There was debate, glee—for the Archbishop was not everyone's favourite—even admiration for the sheer effrontery of the Englishwoman in thus making such telling recovery from her humiliation at the hands of her son.

The Chancellor gobbled and blinked, as though scarcely able to believe his ears. He had indeed held the great office of chief minister of the realm for long years, since Flodden indeed, so that he had come to look on it as his own, almost as by divine right, as indeed did others. When he recovered his voice sufficiently to enunciate, however chokingly, he could only fall back on his previous contention.

"Madame," he got out, "I, I must remind you that you have no authority here to propose anything such. Nor indeed even to speak in this parliament, save by my permission. Only members of the Three Estates, lords of parliament, spiritual and temporal, and commissioners of shires and burghs may propose a motion. I must again rule you out-of-order, therefore."

"Then I, my lord Chancellor, move the same instead!" That was the Lord Avondale, Henry Stewart's father, from the lords' benches.

"And I second," came from the Lord Innermeath, his kinsman.

There was pandemonium in the hall, as everywhere men objected, disputed or acclaimed. This cut across all faction-siding and alignments, a totally unexpected issue, irrelevant to most there. Even Angus and Arran for once need not be on opposite sides, Angus because he was against anything his former wife might propose, Arran because he resented her infatuation with and promotion of the upstart Stewart, nine years her junior. Yet the Stewart faction could be strong, if it could be united, which it seldom was; and James Beaton had his enemies.

That man glowered around the assembly heavily. He could not reject the motion, duly moved and seconded by lords entitled to vote. "Any contrary motion?" he demanded.

"I move the contrary," Angus declared briefly.

Arran was half-way to his feet to second, and then just could not bring himself to seem to support his hated rival.

In the pause, Master William Douglas, no longer just Prior of Coldinghame but mitred Abbot of Holyrood with a vote in parliament, part of the price the Archbishop had had to pay at the St. Andrews conference, was first of half-a-dozen Douglases to second his nephew.

Shrugging massive shoulders, the Chancellor nodded to the Clerk-Register, whose duty it was to supervise the counting of votes.

It made an unlikely subject for the first vote of the day, one which would give no true indication as to the way major decisions would go thereafter. Admittedly no Douglases or their close supporters were likely to vote against Angus's counter-motion; but otherwise the result was unpredictable, all depending on how many found Henry Stewart intolerable and how many disliked the Archbishop sufficiently, who had never sought popularity.

On this first vote, the procedure was formal and lengthy, each voter being named and answering individually, a system normally helpful for the humbler and undecided, since the more important came first and so gave an indication as to relative strengths and wise alignments—which was why this first vote was important. The Estate of Holy Church came first, and since the Chancellor himself had to vote last of all, the question was put to the second most important prelate, Gavin Dunbar, Archbishop of Glasgow, the former tutor to the King, who had in fact succeeded Beaton on his promotion to St. Andrews.

"I abstain," that man said levelly, "since I conceive it unsuitable that one archbishop should seem to uphold another in secular office."

There were gasps at this, and immediate conjecture as to whether this lead would be followed by other clerics, the Chancellor and Primate shooting venomous glances at his colleague, with whom he had never got on.

Perhaps fortunately for his cause, the next name to be read out was the previous voter's uncle, of the same name, Gavin Dunbar, Bishop of Aberdeen. He was sound in his Primate's support, and voted accordingly.

Thereafter, although certain of the churchmen abstained, most voted for the amendment, only one against, the Abbot of Paisley, who was a brother of Arran. The lords temporal divided in no recognisable pattern on this curious issue, save that the Stewarts were solid in favour of the motion except, oddly, for their most senior representative, the Earl of Lennox, who abstained. The commissioners of shires and burghs, who unless themselves involved, usually tended to follow the lead of their local magnates, now did just that. The motion was defeated by twenty-three to fifteen, with almost a score abstaining.

The Chancellor looked relieved, but, glancing over to his nephew, David Lindsay saw that Davie seemed less so. This had been no true test of strengths. The real challenge was yet to come.

Clearly Angus also recognised this, and, hardly waiting for the Clerk-Register to finish, was on his feet.

"Before the Chancellor gets back to his salted fish," he announced grimly, "I too say first things first! We are here for one main purpose, on which all hangs—the weal and safety of the King's Grace and therefore the realm's also. Both have been much endangered. There has even been word of His Grace being taken to England." And he stared balefully at his late wife. "The present situation of the King is unsuitable and should be changed—forthwith. Douglas will take better care of the King!" Abruptly he sat down.

All around, men stared at each other, unsure, alarmed. There was no doubt as to what this meant—the Douglases were for taking over the rule of the land if they could, grabbing the monarch. But how? That had sounded like a naked threat. No motion had been proposed. What now?

The Chancellor looked as uncertain as most others as to how to proceed after this flinging down of the gauntlet.

Two people there were in no doubts, the Queen-Mother and Davie Beaton. As the former, white with fury, stabbed a finger towards the Earl of Arran in clearest command for him to rise and rend her late spouse, the Abbot of Arbroath was on his feet, to seek to repair and regularise the situation well before the not-very-effective Lord High Admiral could move into any sort of action.

"My lord Chancellor," he said in clear but modest, almost diffident tones, as though in awe of the company he kept, "I rise reluctantly to speak, well aware of my inexperience and lack of standing in this my first parliament in which I have had a vote. But I beg all to bear with me, for I yield to none in my love for our liege-lord James, whom God defend, and my concern for this my native land—I, who have sought to serve it, and His Grace, these last years, to my best if humble abilities, as the realm's ambassador to France."

The company stirred uncomfortably. It was not used to this sort of embarrassing talk about love and inexperience and humble abilities, from a whey-faced young man almost beautiful enough to be a woman. It might be how they did things in France, but in Scotland its legislators were apt to speak more through clenched teeth and with clenched fists.

As though aware of this reaction, Davie Beaton changed all, with a remark in the same mild and deferential voice, almost as an aside, as though it had just occurred to him.

"And speaking of France, Your Grace, my lords and friends all, I think that you may not have heard—since I only received the news this morning from France—that the King of France has been defeated at Pavia in Italy, and is now captured and in the Emperor's hands. Which, as you will perceive, may well alter much on the stage of our Christendom! I therefore . . ."

His voice was drowned in the clamour of less nicely modulated tongues, as everywhere men exclaimed, agog. For this news did change the entire international prospect, with Scotland bound to feel the effects in a major way, much more closely than the misfortunes of a foreign monarch might seem to imply. Because of the Auld Alliance, the mutual defence treaty, centuries old, between Scotland and France, whereby England could be threatened on its northern and southern flanks if she attacked one or the other, the French dimension was vital for the northern kingdom. Moreover, the balance of power in Europe was maintained largely through the relative positions of the Empire, Spain, the Vatican, France and England, with ever-changing affiliations, to keep any from becoming too powerful. So a weakened France, and her King a prisoner, was bound to change Henry of England's present stance. He had recently been pro-Empire and pro-Vatican, to help keep France in her place; but now, with an imperial victory, and Spain linked dynastically to the Emperor, France would be no danger—whereas the others would. And if Henry came to terms with France, however temporarily, he would have no fears for his southern flank and could turn his aggressive attentions against Scotland with impunity. It had all happened before and all knew the possible consequences.

Having thus exploded, however moderately, his own bomb-shell and thereby changed the atmosphere in the hall, not least towards himself and his position, Davie Beaton went on as the hubbub died down.

"So, my lord Chancellor, I say that it behoves this realm to take all necessary steps for the defence of its borders and the protection of its sovereign-lord King James. With all respect towards the King of England's royal sister," and he bowed towards that lady, "I submit that King James requires more strong hands for his safety than any woman's can be, however kindly and gentle." If the speaker's references to a gracious kindly, gentle woman were in profoundest mockery towards Margaret Tudor, neither by intonation nor expression did he give the slightest sign of it. "Accordingly, I say that parliament itself, the supreme authority of this realm, under the King himself, should take His Grace's royal person into its own good keeping, for his security. Since, to be sure, a parliament cannot, by its nature, remain permanently in session, nor itself cherish the King from day to day, I propose that it chooses four of its number, of high repute, to be the royal protectors, in turn. Perhaps for three months each, sharing the burden and privilege each year, in the name of the Three Estates of the Realm. My lord Chancellor, with your permission, I so move." He sat down.

There was no doubt as to the impression he had made now, how he had altered the entire temper of the meeting by his news, his skill and eloquence, and his pointing to a seemingly decent way out of the dilemma facing them all. The unctuous voice of William, Abbot of Holyrood, emphasised acceptability by Douglas at least.

"I have pleasure in seconding the motion of my young friend, *in commendam*, of Arbroath."

Arran rose, belatedly. "My lord Chancellor, I move rejection of this motion, this quite unnecessary motion," he declared. "His Grace is well cared for and protected as it is, here in this strong fortress. It is not only his royal mother who tends and cherishes him. *I* do, his Admiral and cousin, second person in this realm. And I have no lack of men to aid me in it! King James requires no change in his care. From Douglas, not long come from England, or other!"

There was something like a cheer for that—and it was not often that lack-lustre individual drew cheers.

"I second rejection," Sir James Hamilton of Finnart, known generally as the Bastard of Arran, the Earl's illegitimate son, called strongly. "When the King requires Douglas protection, things have reached a pretty pass in Scotland!"

As growls and hoots, cheers and counter-cheers filled the hall, Davie Beaton was on his feet again.

"My lord Chancellor, Your Grace, I crave your indulgence, and that of all here," he said earnestly. "Perhaps I did not make myself clear? In which case I tender my apologies. You must put the fault down to my lack of experience in parliamentary speaking. My motion was not that His Grace should be put into the keeping of any one house or party, but that parliament itself should accept the responsibility for his royal care, and appoint its own four guardians."

If that were an urgent attempt to avoid the house having to vote baldly for or against Douglas, it was not to be the last word, for Angus claimed that. Not bothering to rise, but clashing dirk-hilt against his gold-engraved steel breastplate, to draw adequate attention, he barked:

"Douglas has power to protect the King. Greater power, I'd mind all, than any other in this land! And how well does Hamilton presently cherish His Grace?" He jabbed out that dirk towards the rank of impassive English guards standing behind the throne. "Are *those* Hamiltons? Has Hamilton adopted the Tudor Rose as his emblem now? There are two hundred of these in this castle—Henry's men. *They* hold the King! Who votes for that? Vote, I say! And no more talk."

The Chancellor, glancing towards his nephew, shrugged. "Vote, then," he called, flat-voiced. "The amendment first." And he nodded to the Clerk-Register.

This time it was by show of hands. Angus promptly rose to his feet, and turning his back on monarch and Chancellor, stood staring at the company, clearly to note well who dared to vote against Douglas. After a moment or two, Arran did likewise, although he bowed to the throne before turning.

Most hands were slow to go up. The Bastard of Arran's was the first, Archbishop Dunbar's the second, the Abbot of Paisley's the third. Then the Stewart lords, again excepting Lennox. Encouraged by these, the hands of others rose, notably the Earls of Glencairn and Cassillis, west country neighbours of Hamilton, the Earl of Moray and the Lords Maxwell and Ruthven. Lesser men then began to risk a decision. Presently, David Lindsay, at the King's side, was able to count twenty-six hands upraised, three more than the winning total of the previous vote.

There was a tense silence now in that hall, as all perceived how close a thing this was going to be.

"All finished?" the Clerk-Register intoned. "I declare twenty-six against the motion."

"*For* the motion, vote," the Chancellor said.

There was little delay this time, as hands shot up. Assessing, Lindsay knew a thick sensation in his throat. One or two, he noted, had still not voted, the Earl of Lennox and his own father-in-law the Lord Lindsay amongst them. Counting and counting again, he made it exactly twenty-six again, the same as the counter-motion.

As everyone else reached the same conclusion there was uproar, men on their feet, voices raised, fists shaken.

When he could gain approximate silence, the Clerk-Register turned to the Chancellor. "My lord Archbishop of St. Andrews?" he asked, clearing his throat. "Do you vote?"

"I do. I vote for the motion."

If the noise had been vehement before, it was redoubled now.

David Lindsay let his own breath out as he perceived Beaton's brief expression of triumph, quickly replaced by one of more moderate satisfaction. He had won, thanks to his uncle.

"I declare the motion carried." The Clerk-Register had to shout, but probably few heard him. Not that it mattered. Scotland's course had been changed, for good or ill, by that one vote.

Half-a-dozen Douglases rose to speak, but when they saw Angus himself rise, they sat down. Their chief was brief, and definite as always.

"As well this parliament has chosen rightly," he said, nodding significantly. "As well, I say! If I mind aright, the motion said that four guardians should be appointed. These must be of the highest rank and fit for the task. Four earls, then. I nominate, besides myself, my lord of Erroll, the High Constable; my lord of Lennox, and . . ." he turned to his nearest neighbour and bowed, mockingly, "my lord of Arran, the Admiral!"

Swift seizing of the initiative as this was, none could deny that it was shrewd also, indicating that Angus was not all mailed fist and bluster. For these names, on the face of it, were suitable, fair, such as most present could vote for, covering the main factions, Stewart as well as Douglas and Hamilton. The hereditary High Constable, Erroll, chief of the Hays, was in a different category, but senior of the high officers of state, a young man who had recently married the daughter of Lennox. If four were to be the number chosen, it would be difficult to fault these, even though men wondered at Angus's unprejudiced choice.

There was a chorus of seconding.

The Chancellor, recognising the general acceptance, announced that, assuming these lords were willing to accept the duty and responsibility, he saw no reason to seek alternative names and to vote therefor. With parliament's agreement, then, he would nominate the Earls of Angus, Arran, Lennox and Erroll as responsible for His Grace's royal security. In sequence.

There was no contrary reaction, only Angus himself commenting.

"Since the motion was mine, I will accept the first such responsibility!" he observed, again significantly.

For moments there was a sort of general hush, as the assembly considered something about the way that was said.

King James turned to look up at David Lindsay. "I do not like that man!" he said—and in the quiet, most must have heard him.

The Chancellor coughed. "On the matter of the salt . . ." he began, and was interrupted.

"A plague on your salted fish!" Angus cried, now firmly in command. "The Council can deal with siclike merchandise! Douglas did not come here to bicker about salt!" Clearly the Earl's diplomatic interlude was over. "We have settled our day's business. Let us have done."

"My lord Chancellor—the Lords of the Articles . . ." someone called.

"None are required!" That was Angus again.

"My lord!" the Archbishop protested. "This parliament is presided over by His Grace and myself. I . . ."

But it was too late. The Douglas now had the bit between his teeth, and was already on his feet. Ignoring the Chancellor and all others, he strode forward, up on to the dais and straight to the throne. With the sketchiest of bows, he held out his hand.

"Come, Sire," he said, commanded.

The gathering watched, dumbfounded.

James rose from his gilded chair, but not to take that out-stretched hand. He shrank back, shaking his red head. He turned to clutch David Lindsay.

The Queen-Mother, too, was on her feet now. "How dare you!" she got out.

"I dare much, anything, in the service of . . . our liege-lord!" Angus answered, with a derisive bow so elaborate as to be almost a genuflection. He looked past her, to the row of Tudor guards. "Out!" he snapped, with a flick of his hand, still holding that dirk, to reinforce his scornful order.

"Fool!" his ex-wife exclaimed. "There are ten score more waiting outside this hall! Have you lost such few wits as you ever had?"

The Earl grinned. "Lady—while this parliament has been sitting, my Douglases have been entering the castle by ten times your ten score! For His Grace's better security! There is some value in talk, perhaps—it gives time for the more active to act!" He raised his voice. "All here will now do as I say—parliament having kindly granted me that authority! *You* may go. Go to your Linlithgow—or to your royal brother in England, if you wish. But send *these* back to him, forthwith, for King James has no further use for them." He turned. "You, boy—come with me. We go to Holyrood. Away from this ill prison on its cold rock, so bad for Your Grace's good health, with its foul airs rising from the Nor' Loch! You, Lindsay, had better come with him, since he seems to esteem you. You will see that he behaves suitably—as you value your skin! Come, both of you." And without so much as a glance at any other, he strode for the dais doorway, and out.

Lindsay looked from James to his mother, to the Chancellor, and got no help from them, or any other. Was there any point in refusing? Would anything such not merely cause more distress for the King? It was utterly deplorable, shameful—but Angus appeared to hold all the cards and everybody there saw it, even the English guards, who were now milling around looking unhappy. Then, with his young charge demanding of him, "What now?" he found the scarlet-robed figure of Davie Beaton at his side.

"Your Grace," that man said, hurriedly for him. "David—better go. No choice. Angus will have it this way, meantime. But—there may be advantage in it, too. If he keeps you with His Grace at Holyrood, you could learn much of use, be of great help hereafter, within Angus's household. I will find a way to reach you. Go now—before there is trouble. Your Grace." Bowing, he hastened over to his uncle.

Lindsay, expressionless, put an arm around the boy's shoulders. "Come, Sire," he said. "I will stay with you."

Without a glance at his mother, James Stewart went with his friend.

3

The man and boy climbed steadily, deep-breathing both, close together, picking their way with practised eyes up the steep grassy slope, avoiding the outcropping rocks, the slippery wet patches and the prickly gorse-bushes, while Holyrood and the burgh of the Canongate and all Edinburgh, hilly as itself was, dwindled and sank below them. But as well as watching where they put their feet their glances were apt to range somewhat further afield too, if not so far as the spread of the city, planning not only the line of their further ascent but picking out hollows, bluffs, dead ground, features of the hill which could hide them in their upwards progress and so confuse the half-dozen horse-men who dotted the slopes below and on their flanks. It was a sort of game that these two played most days, temporarily to lose and alarm the Douglas guards who so assiduously dogged their steps, ordered never to let them out of their sight. These, being mounted men and no hill-climbers, had to take different routes up Arthur's Seat, Edinburgh's main mountain which reared over eight hundred feet above the Abbey, and which, with its surroundings, constituted a royal hunting-park. It gave the climbing pair a certain satisfaction the more they could agitate and upset their inevitable escort, even though they could never elude them entirely. The ascent of a bare, conical-shaped hill precluded any ultimate escape from horsemen.

Most days that summer David and James climbed Arthur's

Seat, from the Abbey at its foot. It was something to do, a kind of challenge, both the mountain and the confounding of the guards, something they could pit their wits and energies against, confined prisoners in all but name as they were. Lindsay had always been a man for action, physical activity, fretting at the constrictions of fortress life when he had been the young monarch's procurator in Edinburgh and Stirling Castles; and latterly at the Mount of Lindifferon, seeking to hammer down the ever-rearing sense of loss of his Kate by sheer, unremitting toil. And James, a growing boy, strongly-built and burgeoning now into youth, as good as a captive all his days, ever sought bodily freedom, any kind of freedom. He was permitted to go riding, even hawking occasionally, and hunting in this his own great royal park, but always with that armed escort of Douglas guards—which ruined all. Only in climbing this mighty hill could he escape their close proximity for a little and gain a momentary illusion of freedom.

It was six weeks since the parliament, six weeks of constraint and surveillance and ordering for both of them. David was kept with the King all the time, slept in the same room and, with his master's degree from St. Andrews University, acted as tutor as well as attendant and companion. They were not ill-treated, so long as they did what they were told, but any resistance or display of independence was dealt with forcefully, the young monarch purely a hostage, an asset to be exploited for its nominal authority, Lindsay a useful servant whose duty was to ensure maximum co-operation. Angus himself was apt to hector them when he deigned to acknowledge their existence; but fortunately Angus was seldom at Holyrood, ever ranging the land he now ruled, putting down any signs of opposition, wielding that mailed fist. His uncle, the Abbot William, was their real captor, a much cleverer man than the Earl and a deal less abrasive to cope with—although by no means to be underestimated as a menace on that account, for he was quite as unscrupulous as his nephew, only more subtle and superficially amiable about it. He was a man unhesitatingly prepared to commit any act—indeed multiple murder, as he had already demonstrated at Coldinghame—to further his ambitions and gain his ends.

In these weeks the Douglases had ruthlessly transformed the governance of Scotland to their own liking—all in the name of James, High King of Scots. Practically every major office of state was now held by one of them, or their nominees. Henry Stewart was dismissed as Lord High Treasurer, and Graysteel, Douglas of Kilspindie appointed in his place, which gave Angus control of the Exchequer, depleted as it was by Margaret's extravagances. Abbot William himself was Lord Privy Seal. Their brother, Pittendreich, was Master of the Household. Douglas of Parkhead was Captain of the Guard, and Master of the Wine-Cellar, Douglas of Drumlanrig was Master of the Larder—positions of more power than their titles suggested. The judiciary, the sheriffdoms, the keeperships of the royal castles, the controllerships of customs and taxation, and naturally the armed forces, were all in the hands of their people. Angus appointed himself, amongst other things, Chief Warden of the Marches, which ensured him personal command of the vital Borders area. The Privy Council had been purged and reconstructed, so that men who could scarcely be got rid of without major armed challenge, such as Arran, the Earl of Argyll, the Campbell chief, Erroll the Constable and the Lord Lindsay, David's father-in-law, could always be voted down with ease. The Chancellor, or chief minister of the realm, was still James Beaton, but he was little heard of and Angus took all the decisions. Scotland was in fact governed from Tantallon Castle now.

The climbers had surmounted the major northern shoulder of the hill and had to circle the corrie at the head of the central probing valley, known as the Hunter's Bog, when James, keen-eyed, scanning the positions of the scattered horsemen now coming into view, noted something else, three riders coming cantering up the slantwise floor of the valley itself, from the lower ground of St. Margaret's Loch. These three looked different from the others, riding purposefully and close together, the central one even at half-a-mile's range seen to be clad in vivid red.

"See, Davie—strangers," the boy said.

Lindsay paused, staring. "Aye. So-o-o! And who do we know who wears scarlet? And only the one, James?" When they were alone, titles of Sire, Grace and Highness were dispensed with.

"Davie Beaton—who brought me my papingo." On a visit from France, years before, Beaton had given the child-king a present of a parrot, which the boy still cherished.

"The same. Now what, say you? We will wait, I think."

"He comes to us?"

"Who else? Up here?"

Their waiting there at the head of the corrie allowed their guards to reach them before the newcomers, suspicious at this change from their usual eluding tactics. The Douglas men sat their beasts a little way off, and were ignored.

The three others, superbly mounted, came pounding up, Davie Beaton sure enough, with two armed attendants wearing the mitred emblems of the archdiocese of St. Andrews on their chests. A splendid figure in his scarlet travelling-clothes, the Abbot of Arbroath jumped down from the saddle, to bow low before the King.

"Your Grace's most devoted subject!" he greeted. And to Lindsay, "Lord, David—you are a hard man to reach! To have to chase you to the top of Arthur's Seat!"

"It gets us out of that Holyrood Abbey, where we are little better than prisoners." The other gestured towards the watching Douglas guards.

"Aye—no doubt. At least you look well on it! A deal better than when last we forgathered."

That was true. Despite the frustrations and constrictions of his present existence, David Lindsay had lost much of the embittered and drawn attitude which had settled on him after his Kate's death.

"And *you* look . . . extraordinary? Less than suitably clad for hill-climbing, I fear!"

"Ha! You would not condemn the Lord Abbot of Arbroath to looking ordinary, man? Especially when he has to make his presence felt. But I daresay that I can climb your hill as well as the next. If I must, to have privy speech with you?"

Grimly Lindsay considered the other's magnificent scarlet-dyed thigh-length riding-boots of softest doe-leather, with their high and spurred heels. "Can you mount yonder steeps in those?" he demanded, and pointed to the roughest and rockiest route up towards the summit. "Where we may get away from those horses."

"Ah—is that the ploy! To be sure, I can." Beaton turned to his two escorts. "Lead my beast and keep us in sight," he directed. "These others will no doubt be doing the same. Now, Sire—lead on!"

Laughing—and it was not often that James Stewart laughed

these days—the King started off upwards, deliberately choosing the most difficult and abruptly-rising route, amongst the outcrops, scree, stunted gorse and wet green aprons of surface-water. The horsemen were left behind to find an alternative way up. But if this might have been a successful device for gaining them private speech, it proved less so in that Davie Beaton was so busy picking his way in those awkward boots, and panting for breath as he did so, that he had little ability to talk. Perceiving this, after letting James have his fun for a little, Lindsay pointed half-right to a sort of narrow terrace on the hill-face, where they could pause, and where no horses could get within three hundred yards at least. Thankfully Beaton made his way thither.

They stood for a minute or two on that eyrie-like ledge, surveying all the land spread like a variegated carpet beneath, down to the blue waters of the Firth of Forth and beyond to the gentle green hills of Fife, before Davie was in a state to talk. He sat down, on a sun-warmed outcrop.

"God save us—I prefer Lindifferon Hill to Arthur's Crag!" he got out. "Why can you not stay on level ground, like other folk, Master Pursuivant Lindsay of The Mount?" David had been appointed an Extra Pursuivant, or herald, to the King, by the Douglases, not out of any desire to accord him status but so that his board and keep could be charged to the crown revenues as part of the Lord Lyon King-of-Arms' establishment.

"Save your breath for more useful talk!" his friend advised. "What brings you here that could not have waited until we were returned to Holyrood?"

"I do not trust that sleek William Douglas. I trust none of them, to be sure, but him least of all. He would be unlikely to let us be alone together—and if he did, might well have listeners behind doors or arras! And what I have to say is for your ears alone. And yours, Sire, to be sure."

"I hope that you are going to contrive some way of getting us out of Douglas clutches?"

"That, too. But seven weeks more, and Arran takes over as guardian of His Grace. It may be better, easier then—if all goes as it should! Meantime we must be as patient as is in us."

"Patient . . . !" Lindsay snorted.

"Aye, just that, David. Patience, using our wits, gathering

support, seeking out Angus's weaknesses. Which is where you are well-placed to learn much. We need to know how united are the Douglases themselves. Angus is not a kindly man—they cannot all love him! How sure is he of his allies—the Homes, the Kers, the Hepburns and the rest? What does he plan for the future—if he has to yield His Grace to Arran? Are all the royal fortresses firm in his support? You, biding within Holyrood, with his Uncle William, who has the wits of the family—however great a scoundrel—must hear much. The other uncles are there frequently, we know. And the rest of Angus's kin. What have you learned?"

"Sakes—have you come only to pick my brains? I had hoped for better than that!"

"All in good time, friend. Do not tell me that you have learned nothing in these six weeks?"

"I have learned to hate the Douglases! And to grieve the more for King James, here." He shrugged. "For the rest—I agree that the Abbot William is the cleverest of them. That he is not to be trusted. That Kilspindie is probably the least ill of them, and disapproves of much that Angus does. He does not like his brother William. Nor does Pittendreich—but he is as big a rogue, only less clever. Angus himself is little here, ever riding about the land, sword in hand. But—all this you must know, and can be of little use to you. What do you want of me?"

"Better than that, yes. Although it is of use to know that Kilspindie, Graysteel, does not always agree with Angus and does not love his brother William, since he is now Treasurer. Perhaps we can use that. What of the Earl of Morton, chief of the *Black* Douglases? How close is he? Angus and he used to be unfriends."

"Nor are they friends now, I think. Morton is seldom at Holyrood. But William and his brothers speak little good of him."

"That is well, then. But Drumlanrig, now Master of the Larder, is one of that line."

"He *is* a friend of Angus, yes. The only one of the Black sort, I think. But—why do you concern yourself with all this? What good can such knowledge do? Angus controls Scotland. Who loves him signifies little—so long they all fear him!"

"Now, perhaps. Because Angus now holds His Grace, here.

But that situation is due to change in October. Then we may see."

"You believe that? From the way the Douglases talk, they see no sudden ending of their power, in October or other. They plan to remain in power."

"Have you heard any word of *what* they intend to do in October, man?"

"No. Nothing plainly, just their general attitude. That they will still be holding Scotland firmly in the future."

"Aye. David—do you think that Angus will refuse to deliver up His Grace to Arran, in October? Despite parliament's instructions—his own proposal?"

"I do not know. But I would not put it past him. That one will care nothing for parliaments, or even for his own given word. Power is what he wants—and he has that power now. I would expect him to try to hold on to it. Would not you?"

"If he believes that he can, that way, any way, yes. If he defies parliament and refuses to yield up His Grace, he unites many against him, since parliament, however muted, is still the voice of the nation. Not only Arran and his Hamiltons, their friends and the Stewarts, but Lennox and Erroll and their people, the other two guardians. And others who voted for that motion—including Holy Church! Argyll, the Campbell chief, resents not being included as a guardian—he was always one of the old Privy Council. Your good-father, Lord Lindsay. The Earl Marischal. Angus could weld most of the realm against him if he did that."

"So long as he holds King James, does that matter?"

"See you—he could avoid that uniting against him if he came to terms with Arran."

"Arran? The Douglases and the Hamiltons in harness! They have ever been foes."

"To be sure. I do not say that they would start to love each other. But if they were to *work* together . . . ! If *I* was in Angus's saddle, that is what I would do. Arran is weak and Angus would dominate, inevitably."

David shook his head, wordless, but obviously disbelieving.

James Stewart it was who spoke now. "The Earl of Arran would like to be King," he said. "He might kill me."

That silenced even Davie Beaton for a moment or two. Lindsay reached out to grip the boy's arm.

"Never that, James—do not fear. Arran is no killer. Never think that."

"But his son, the Bastard is!"

Beaton stared at his young monarch, clearly astonished at the boy's perception rather than his fear, for that was shrewd judging. Sir James Hamilton of Finnart, the Bastard of Arran, *would* kill, to advance himself. His father, second person in the kingdom, was the nearest heir to the throne, with the Duke of Albany gone, a French citizen and obviously no longer interested in Scotland. Arran's mother was the Princess Mary, a daughter of James the Second. The Bastard, being illegitimate, could never aspire to the throne himself, but could hope to rule the kingdom through his weak father.

"Sire—you must not fear anything such," Beaton said urgently. "There is no danger, I swear to you! Sir James Hamilton would never seek to lay hands on the Lord's Anointed. Nor would any . . ."

"Others *have*! Why not him? I would rather be held by my lord of Angus, who would not seek to be King!"

The two men eyed each other, in mutual agreement that the subject should be changed.

"Angus will undoubtedly protect Your Grace—since you are the source of his present authority," Beaton said. "As for Arran, he has become weaker, not stronger, of late. Since Your Grace's royal mother married Henry Stewart . . ."

"Married!" That was Lindsay. "They are *wed*?"

"Yes. Had you not heard? A week past, at Linlithgow."

"But—this is folly! Worse than folly! A man of no account, eight or nine years younger than she is. A young coxcomb! For the former Queen, the King's mother, to wed such . . . !" Glancing at James, David coughed. "I crave your pardon, Sire."

The boy shrugged that aside, clearly not interested in his mother or her antics. "You will always stay with me, Davie?" he demanded. "Even if my lord of Arran gets me?"

"To be sure—if I may, Sire. I shall not leave you willingly. Fear nothing . . ."

"This marriage has driven a wedge between Arran and the Queen-Mother," Beaton went on. "He was wroth when she made Stewart Lord Treasurer without consulting him, or any. For old Avondale, Stewart's father, is a long-time foe of Arran's. But this marriage is too much for him. He has left her side and

58

returned to his castle of Cadzow. So her cause also is the weaker. As is his. If Angus were to approach him now, who knows . . . ?"

"You are not *hoping* for this, man?"

"No. Far from it. But we must consider it, the possibility. So I ask that you listen well to the talk at Holyrood. If you hear any word that Angus is in touch with Arran and the Hamiltons, contrive to let me know. It is vital that we should learn of it at St. Andrews at the earliest."

"Why?"

"Because such alliance would be the worst that could happen for Scotland, and we would have to move heaven and earth to stop it! Douglas and Hamilton together would make a league almost impossible to beat. We would have to try to halt it before it was established."

"How could you? How could any?"

"It would not be easy. But there *are* forces in this land which have not been harnessed as yet in the King's cause, powerful forces seldom considered. In the north, the Highlands, the clans. They are part of the realm, are they not? Always over-busy fighting each other, and so overlooked. Yet they represent a mighty power—if they could be brought into it."

"Aye—but how? Since Harlaw, a hundred years ago, they have shown little interest in Lowland Scotland. Why should they now?"

"Two reasons. Or three. Two men have been ignored by Angus and Arran both—and resent it. Both from the north: Argyll, the Campbell chief, and Huntly, the Gordon; both on the old Regency Council, and now overlooked. Each could put three thousand broadswords in the field—more, if they brought in their friends and neighbours. And the third—Lennox. Also on the fringes of the Highlands. See you, if Arran joined Angus, it would leave the Stewarts stranded. They are not strong enough of themselves to stand alone. They would have either to join Angus likewise, or retire from all but local influence in the land. But there are Highland Stewarts too—Appin, Ardvoirlich, Garth, and of course, Atholl."

"These will not love the Campbells, I think!"

"No. But if it were that or nothing, bowing to Angus, I say that they might well be persuaded. And Lennox, the senior of the non-royal Stewarts, is the key. He is a sound man and of influence, one of the chosen guardians, and holder of one of the most ancient Celtic earldoms. He might bring in Erroll and the Hays."

"I like my lord of Lennox," James put in.

"Might! Could! May be! It is all so much supposition, hope, Davie. Hope, that is all. A Highland host, to beat Douglas! I do not see it."

"It would not be easy, no. But do not forget two other influences, both linked—the Church and siller! Money, friend—money! My uncle controls the deepest purse in this kingdom—and the Highlanders are ever hungry for siller."

"You would seek to buy them? Buy the clans? To fight against Lowlanders."

"If necessary. We must use whatever tools come to hand. Mind—it may never come to this. Angus may yield His Grace to Arran. And even if he does not, he may not think of coming to terms with the Hamiltons. And Arran might reject it. But—we have to be prepared. So you understand how important it is that we have prior knowledge of any movement, any link, between Douglas and Hamilton? *You* are the best situated to learn this, David."

"Mmm. I think you over-estimate the length of my ears! But, if I did hear aught, how would I get word to you? I am never permitted to be outside Holyrood Abbey without guards. As now."

"I know it. But the Sub-Chantor at the Abbey here is one of my people, from St. Andrews. He will convey your messages to me. John Balfour his name—of distant kin."

"I will do what I can . . ."

They moved on, but, taking pity on Beaton in those boots, did not climb all the way to the top of the hill. He was probably glad to reach his horse again.

Before parting company, he retailed one other item of news which might interest them. His minions, notably proficient at intercepting and suborning couriers crossing the border, by means unspecified, but almost certainly at the monkish hospices for travellers at the Tweed crossings, had read a letter from the Queen-Mother to her brother Henry, via Lord Dacre, request-ing the despatch of ten thousand English troops to Scotland under the Duke of Norfolk, to enable her to recover possession of her son and so to restore her rule. Later, word from a spy in

Cardinal Wolsey's London establishment informed that this request was refused on the grounds that the King of England believed that it was not necessary, as the Earl of Angus would do his work for him.

On that note they parted, Lindsay thoughtful indeed—not least as to the uses its Abbot made of the rich revenues of Arbroath in maintaining his information network, presumably something else he had learned in France.

As it happened, soon after their return to Holyrood, David learned something from the talk therein, namely that Angus, having heard about the marriage, had gone to Linlithgow and arrested Henry Stewart of Methven on a charge of treason for having wed the King's mother without the King's sanction or knowledge. He was now confined in nearby Blackness Castle, a prisoner. Margaret herself had been conveyed to Stirling Castle and placed in the strict keeping of the Lord Erskine.

Lindsay did not seek to forward this news to Beaton, assuming that he would learn of it speedily enough from his normal sources. It certainly made clear who was in command in Scotland.

4

It was All Hallows Eve, the last day of October—and no change so far had become evident in the dull routine at the Abbey, no arrangements for handing over the King to Arran, or anybody else, nor any suggestions of such a thing. So it seemed that the fears expressed on Arthur's Seat all those weeks before were well-founded; Angus did not intend to yield up his royal hostage to other guardians, parliament or none. There was, however, no air of tension at Holyrood; the reverse, in fact, for the Abbot William, in an excess of amiability, announced that a diet of study and lessons was not natural or proper for young folk, even the Lord's Anointed, and that His Grace deserved a little entertainment. So, it being All Hallows, the traditional time for mummery, guizards and such-like frivolities, he had arranged some small diversion for that evening. There would be a modest banquet in the refectory, with music, dancing, play-acting and the like. His Grace's spirits must be maintained.

David was a little suspicious at this sudden concern for the royal feelings, even whilst welcoming any lightening of the boy's distinctly trying circumstances.

That night the monks' eating-hall was transformed, ablaze with candles, lamps and lanterns (many contrived to look like grinning faces), yew, fir and holly branches decking the walls. The abbatical dais was provided with laden tables flanking a central one which was accorded five chairs instead of the benches elsewhere, leaving the main floor clear for the entertainment.

Led in by the abbey choir chanting a more spirited refrain than usual, James made a formal entry, flanked by the Abbot and his brother, Sir Archibald of Kilspindie—who, as Treasurer, was no doubt paying for all this. David Lindsay and the Prior came behind—and the former was interested to note that there were women present on this occasion amongst the brethren, and not nuns either, something he had not seen before. All bowed to the monarch, the first time anything of the sort had been staged. David wondered the more.

James was seated in the middle, between William and Archibald Douglas, while David sat on the left and the Prior on the right. The latter rose to say a brief grace-before-meat in Latin, and then the lay-brother servitors brought in the steaming dishes. Flagons of wine were already on the tables.

It proved to be quite the finest repast Lindsay for one had tasted for years—soups, salmon, wild duck, venison, pork, sweetmeats, fruits and a variety of liquors. He noted how assiduously the Douglases urged James to partake of all, particularly the wines, and he grew a little apprehensive. Presently he mentioned to his neighbour, Kilspindie, that the boy was not used to so much, especially the liquor—but was pooh-poohed as though a spoilsport.

Whilst the meal proceeded there was entertainment in the form of juggling, singing, fiddling and dancing, taking place on the main refectory floor, not perhaps of the highest standards—save for the last, which was performed by a gipsy group of four. The two men and two women were exceedingly

62

active and talented, the women in especial, who might have been sisters, both darkly striking in appearance, one, seemingly the younger, almost beautiful in a coarse-grained way. They were well-formed creatures and, disporting themselves to the fiddle-music with rhythmic abandon, their notably low-cut bodices and brief skirts hid little of their persons, their breasts bouncing about with eye-catching freedom, indeed those of the younger woman tending to escape their cover altogether on occasion—and not to be put back with any embarrassment or even haste. David noted how young James's eyes were concentrated in that direction, to the neglect of his viands.

When the performance ended, unusual perhaps for an abbey, the King was loudly enthusiastic in his applause, and Abbot William, patting his shoulder, assured him that they would have more of this, if he enjoyed it, when the dancers had recovered their breaths. Beckoning a servitor, he murmered something to him, accompanied by an odd gesture indicating the upper body.

Thereafter there was an interlude with a distinctly moth-eaten performing bear, and some more singing, before the gipsies reappeared, but this time only the two women. And now their offering was frankly and provocatively sexual where before it had appeared to be so only, as it were, by accident. Moreover, both bodices were now so low-slung that quickly the jouncing, twisting movement caused them to slip down to the waist, and after only a token pull or two upwards, so they remained throughout the dance. The older woman was rather less well-endowed but just as active, and the entire display challenging indeed.

When it too finished, to prolonged acclaim, Sir Archibald beckoned both females up to the dais, where he offered the elder his own beaker of wine to drink from, in congratulation, indicating to the King that he should do the same for the younger. James was nothing loth, although clearly suffering from acute embarrassment and fascination mixed—for the tucking-in process as the women advanced had been only partially successful and one of the younger woman's breasts was still fully exposed, and at close range, with the large dark aureola and thrusting nipple, having an almost mesmeric effect on the boy.

While still the dancers, panting effectively from their exertions and exuding a heavy female scent, were sipping the wine, bold-eyed, Abbot William rose to announce that the entertainment would now be general, and that all who cared to dance should do so—adding, with a smile, that for this evening he gave leave for such holy brethren as knew how to join in. He called on the fiddlers to strike up, and then moved round the top table to take the hand of the older gipsy woman and lead her down on to the main floor, beckoning to James to do the like with the younger. It now became apparent that the other women guests were there to provide dancing-partners for at least some of the monks and lay-brothers.

David Lindsay sat still. He had not danced since Kate died, and certainly did not feel like restarting now. He was unsure what to do, if anything. It seemed very clear that all this had been arranged at some expense and for some purpose—and for young James's benefit, if that was the word. Equally clear, that these tough Douglases were not suddenly smitten with concern over their hostage's dull existence and lack of amusement. So what was the object of this peculiar All Hallows celebration, particularly this deliberate exposure of the women to the boy?

Lindsay was no prude, but as well as being fond of James he felt himself to have a duty to guide and protect him in more than tutoring and personal attendance. But was there anything that ought to be done, or could be done, here? Was there any harm in it all, for the King? He was thirteen and although, having been as good as a prisoner all his life, he had inevitably been sheltered from fleshly matters—whatever he thought of his mother's behaviour—he was bound in the nature of things, to learn about women and sex in the near future. Was this way so objectionable? And even if it was, would *his* objections be paid any attention to by those who had gone to the trouble to stage the evening?

At first the general dancing was notably different from what had gone before, formal, graceful, in set patterns, lines and circlings with pacings and much bowing and curtsying. James had done little of this previously, but his present partner was assiduous in his instruction, and no doubt the wine imbibed helped to counter his inhibitions. He was scarcely graceful about it, coltish rather, but picked up the rhythm quickly enough. About a dozen couples took part, Abbot William leading.

Presently the fiddle-music changed tempo and style to a less dignified and more jigging pace, and the formal grouping split up into little clusters and pairs, steps growing lively, the two gipsy women emphasising the change. Abbot William, panting, soon had enough of this and retired, his partner being joined instead by one of the gipsy men, and these two now set a pace which grew ever more vehement. James, out of his depth, was nevertheless guided and led and put up with by the younger woman, in much laughter, suiting herself to his gangling cavortings—which of course soon shook her bosom quite free again. Her partner's concentration on the dancing-steps was no doubt thereby distracted. Presently, either by his own initiative or her guidance, one royal hand was holding at least one of those mobile breasts approximately steady, leaving the other to its jigging.

It was at this stage that David's frowning attention also became distracted. For the Abbot, back at the top table and puffing noticeably, his plump features pink and beaded with sweat, addressed himself to the younger man.

"You do not dance, Lindsay? Because you cannot, or will not?"

"To dance worthily, my lord Abbot, one must feel so disposed. I do not."

"Ah. Do I detect some . . . criticism?"

"Wonder, rather. I wonder what you are at?"

"What but to celebrate All Hallows Eve in a fashion to amuse our young liege-lord. You would not grudge him? He, at least, appears to find it all to his taste."

"As you have gone to some trouble to ensure!"

"We do what we can, although little enough." The other glanced along the table, and gestured. "My brother is no dancer, either! And seems to have had a sufficiency of entertainment for one night! He will be the better of his bed. Will you conduct him to his chamber, Lindsay?"

Surprised, David looked at his neighbour, Sir Archibald, who now lay slumped over the table, head on arms amongst the flagons and beakers, apparently asleep or drunken or both.

"He seems well content!"

"Nevertheless, he would do better elsewhere. He sleeps in the chamber in the foot of the bell-tower."

Shrugging, David rose. He could scarcely refuse this strange request, or command, although one of the monks or lay-brothers would have seemed a more suitable escort if such was indeed required.

The Abbot shook his brother's shoulder. "Rouse yourself, Archie," he exclaimed. "Lindsay here, who appears to think as little of our entertainment as do you, will aid you to your couch. You could do with it. Come, man—on your feet."

Graysteel looked up, blinked, and obediently rose, if unsteadily. But he was sufficiently rational to grab David's arm rather than his brother's. He said nothing, but leaning heavily on the younger man, promptly began to weave his way across the dais towards the door.

Leaving the refectory building, which was separate from the main residential conventual range, they crossed the wide courtyard to the cloisters which skirted the chapter-house and church itself, the bell-tower being at the far south end of the range. The chill night air appeared to do Sir Archibald good, for he began to walk fairly normally, although he clung to the younger man's arm nevertheless—otherwise David would have sought to excuse himself and return to the refectory. They exchanged no conversation.

Even within the main building's candle-lit corridors he was not released. The place seemed to be deserted, all the inmates being at the entertainment, no doubt. Reaching the Treasurer's bedchamber, David's services were still required whilst more candles were to be found and lit, Graysteel suddenly becoming talkative and detaining his escort further with enquiries about the King's progress in his studies, his general abilities and the like, all notably unlike the Douglases.

Wondering the more, David made his escape and headed back for the refectory.

There the dancing was still in progress, amidst much noise. It did not take him long to discern that James was no longer present, nor indeed was the Abbot William. It took only a little longer to recognise that the King's dancing-partner was missing also, although her gipsy colleagues were still there. The Prior was likewise gone from the dais-table.

David sat for a little, sipping his wine, not exactly perturbed, since it all might be explained perfectly naturally no doubt, but just slightly uneasy. That unease grew as time passed and James made no reappearance. At length, he beckoned to a lay-brother servitor and asked him where His Grace had gone. The man expressed ignorance. He moved down amongst the dancers, seeking out the older gipsy woman. Panting, at his enquiry, she too appeared to have no knowledge—but smilingly offered to dance with him. He approached another servitor, and when he gained the same response, asked where the Abbot had gone, frowning now. He was little more successful in that, save for the suggestion that he might well have retired to his own quarters, as indeed might His Grace.

David had to admit that this was a sensible enough supposition, especially if James had noticed that he himself had disappeared from the dais. Perhaps William Douglas had escorted the boy back to his bedchamber, if he had had enough dancing.

So, leaving the refectory again, he returned to the main building and up to the room he shared with his charge. James was not there.

He waited, growing ever more uneasy, as the minutes went by. At length, never a notably patient man, he could stand it no longer. He knew where the Abbot William's rooms were. He would go and enquire there, however unlikely to be well received.

But downstairs, in the most handsome suite of apartments in the great establishment, although candles blazed, and a fine fire crackled on the hearth, there was no sign of the incumbent.

At a loss, David considered. The certainty grew on him that this entire night's proceedings were altogether too out-of-character to be explained away naturally.

It had all been thought out. Why? The Douglases did not usually do things by stealth and subterfuge; they were far too sure of themselves for that. If they had intended to remove James from his own charge and care, they could have done it openly, without all this elaborate play-acting. He could not have prevented it. So, what?

He decided that he at least knew where one of the play-actors was; and Archibald Douglas was easier to deal with and less subtle than his brother. He would go to the bell-tower and try to get to the bottom of this business, even if the Treasurer was now asleep in his bed.

He went out into the chill night air again.

At the door of Graysteel's room he paused, hearing voices

within. After only a moment's hesitation he knocked, and without waiting for permission opened and entered.

The two Douglas brothers sat therein at a table, wine-beakers in hand. They stared at him.

"What's to do? What do you want, Lindsay?" the Abbot jerked, less smoothly than usual.

"I am looking for His Grace," David said flatly.

"Indeed? And why look for him here, sirrah?"

"I left him in your care, my lord Abbot. When you required me to escort Sir Archibald hither." David made a brief mock bow. "I rejoice to see your brother so well recovered!"

The Treasurer cleared his throat. "Is the King not still dancing?" he asked.

"No, sir. Nor is he in the refectory, nor in his own chamber. The hour is late. Where is he?"

"Sakes, Lindsay—what's this? What a pother!" William Douglas had changed his tone. "It is All Hallows Eve, a time for merry-making—not for auld hens' cluckings! His Grace is but a lad—let him have his bit fling."

"As you have most carefully devised!"

"Tut, man—we but contrived a little entertainment for the lad. He has had little enough of such, I jalouse. Let him be, for once."

"He is in my care, my lord. I could let him be more readily if I knew where he was and what was being done with him."

"*Done* with him? Nothing is being done with him, man! Or . . . how could it be? Here in this my Abbey? What he is at, wherever he is, he cannot come to any harm. It is none so large a place, and he'll no' get out. Probably, like Sir Archibald here, he found the wine, the provender and the noise and dancing overcame him somewhat. He will be sleeping it off, belike, somewhere."

"But not where he should be—in his own bed. I must find him."

"You speak like any auld wife, Lindsay! Spare us more of it. Go seek His young Grace, if you must, but leave us in peace, of a mercy!"

"That I will, sir," David said, and turned on his heel. He slammed that door behind him.

Out in the cloisters, he tried to clear his mind of anger and to think constructively. It did not look as though the Douglases were for spiriting James out of the Abbey or planning any major change—not this night, at least. It *could* be all as the Abbot pretended. Yet all this *had* been planned, of that he was convinced, for some purpose. That purpose he must discover. First he must find James in this rambling establishment. Where to look? He could not go prying into every room, dormitory, corner. Between eighty and one hundred souls lived in the Abbey of the Holy Rood. He would have to return to the refectory, to start there, question folk again, try to gain some hint.

On the way, he looked in once more at their own quarters— which were still empty. Back at the eating-hall, he found conditions changed, the dancing superseded by general revelry, drunken singing, horse-play and the like, shameful in such a place consecrated to worship, nobody apparently in charge any more. But James had not returned nor could David see the younger gipsy woman either, although her companions were still present.

So—the chances were that the pair of them were still together, with all that implied. Was that it, then? An assault on the boy's pudency, modesty, virtue? And if so, why? What would that gain the Douglases? These people did nothing without a reason . . .

Putting the whys and wherefores to the back of his mind meantime, David concentrated on the task of finding James. Where to look? If the woman was indeed involved and had taken the lead, then the probability was that, a gipsy and an outsider, she would not know the abbey-precincts throughly and would therefore tend to take the King somewhere near-at-hand and available, easily reached—unless some more elaborate place had been specially prepared for them. So, try this same refectory building, for a start. He had never been through it before. None of the company looking sober, unoccupied or helpful, he went exploring.

Behind the main eating-hall he found the kitchens, larders, storerooms and wine-cellars, in vaulted basements. He unearthed two couples in the warm kitchens, one copulating, the other sprawled in each other's arms asleep—but neither known to him. There was another pair comfortable in an adjoining room full of blankets. Half-way along the connecting vaulted corridor there was a circular stair-tower containing a turnpike.

Two more revellers had reached thus far, one a monk, but presumably had been either in too great a hurry for their satisfaction or found themselves unable to climb the stair, for there on the lowermost treads they lay, clothing markedly disarranged, dead to the world. Deciding to try the upper floor, David stepped carefully over them and mounted the winding stair.

There was a dormitory above, presumably for the domestic and kitchen staff, and from it snores emanated. The door open, David looked in, but although some of the beds were occupied none appeared to contain women or King James. At the far end of this, however, was a shut door with light gleaming above and below. To this the searcher proceeded, and in no mood now for polite knocking, opened and entered without pause.

His quest was over. It was a much smaller apartment, probably the bedchamber of the chief cook, and on the bed two naked figures lay, one on top of the other, the woman uppermost. She at least was not asleep, for she raised her dark head to look towards the doorway. Clothing lay in a pile on the floor. As she lifted her well-made upper half, languorously, James Stewart's red head came into view beneath.

David moved into the room and closed the door behind him, to stand tight-lipped, contemplating the scene.

"Davie!" the King got out, chokingly. He heaved convulsively beneath his partner, managed to wriggle free and rolled over the far edge of the bed and down, out of sight.

The woman, quite unabashed, turned lithely, lowered her feet to the floor and stood up, facing the intruder. She was certainly magnificently formed, a sight to stir any man—or boy.

She smiled invitingly. "You now, sir? Your turn?" she wondered, with an eloquent flourish of the hand.

"Thank you, no!" David said shortly. "This, this is . . . shameful! How dare you! The King's Grace!"

"Och, I dared very well, sir. Nae trouble! And so did this one! For a first time, he did well enough. A quick learner! But, och—you, now, will be mair practised?"

"Be quiet, woman!" he commanded. "Have you no shame? No decency? Our sovereign-lord . . ." As she laughed, he moved round the foot of the bed to where James crouched on his knees, hands over his private parts, peering up, flushed, in an agony of guilt and apprehension.

"Dress yourself," he was told, in no humble tones. "Quickly. We shall talk later." David turned back to the woman. "You were brought here to do this? Paid?"

She shrugged shapely shoulders, her breasts quivering effectively.

"Who by?"

She said nothing, but went to sit on the bed, making no move to pick up and don her clothing.

"Was it Sir Archibald Douglas? The Abbot?" he demanded. "Tell me. Who contrived this, this wickedness?"

"Nothing wicked in it, sir," she assured, easily. "The laddie enjoyed it fine—I saw to that! So did I. So might your ain sel', if you'd tak the glower off your face!"

David realised that he was going to get nothing out of this gipsy. James was struggling into his clothes, not entirely effectively. He turned to give the boy a hand, less than gently. The woman sat watching, amused evidently, and unconcerned with her nakedness.

When he was approximately dressed, the man took the King's shoulder and pushed him towards the door.

"Guid night to you, laddie," came from behind them amiably. "You'll no' forget Jeannie!" That was a statement, and no plea nor question.

James did not look round.

On the way to their quarters across the courtyard, man and boy exchanged scarcely a word. James kept his head down, and David decided that this was not the time for serious talking. Even up in their own bedchamber little was said, the youngster obviously anxious only to get his head down under the blankets in oblivion. The man knew a certain sympathy with him, for it was scarcely James's fault. When he said good night before getting into his own bed, he tried to make his voice sound as normal as possible, not unfriendly. He got only a muffled grunt in reply.

Lying awake thereafter, David went over it all in his mind time and again, trying to discern what was behind the night's events, the reasons for this deliberate seduction of the young monarch. It must have been important, for the Douglases to have gone to so much trouble. It could scarcely be sheer depraved evil-mindedness, in the corruption of a youth. Nor hatred, for they had no reason to hate James. Policy, then? But

71

to what end? To gain some power over the boy? To strike at his now-hated mother through him? To loosen his own, David Lindsay's, hold over the King's affections, for their own purposes? None of these seemed adequate—but he could not think of anything more significant before he slept.

In the morning he saw things more clearly. James was silent, reserved, eyes never meeting his own, so unlike his normal affectionate reliance. Was that it, then—a means of driving a wedge between them? But could that have any importance for the Douglases?

Their silent breakfast over, the inevitable inquest on the affair, which the boy so clearly dreaded, had to be got out of the way before the day's studies began. David sought to be fair, moderate, reasonable, recognising all too well his own difficulties in the matter. After all, this was the King of Scots he was to talk to, his liege-lord; and he had no moral authority over him either now, no longer even his official procurator and usher, but only the ties of friendship and loyalty.

"James," he said, at last, "what happened last night was wrong, very wrong—as I think that you know very well. Wrong in more ways than one. We have to speak of it."

The boy did not answer, looking away.

"What that woman did with you was . . . unsuitable, shameful. Not the act itself only, see you—but how it was done, and with *you*. Men and women do have this, this congress, can fit their bodies together, to enjoy each other, to much satisfaction. But it should be done in love and affection, not coupling in haste like farmyard animals! And you are not a man, not yet fourteen years. Much too young for such."

"I, I was not too young to, to . . ." His voice faded away.

"No, perhaps not. Your body might be able for it—but not *you*, yourself, your inner self. And forby, you are the King. And that woman was a, a gipsy whore, a paid trull, hired to ensnare you."

No response.

"James—we have to speak of this. Why the Douglases did this, I do not know. But they did it out of no love for you, that is sure. They are your enemies, holding you captive for their own purposes. Last night's doings were for their own advantage likewise—no question of that. They hired this woman and her friends to attract you with their dancing, their bodies. They made you to drink more wine than was good for you. Then they got you dancing with her and she making you very free of her person. They pretended that Sir Archibald was drunk, and had me to convey him to his chamber—and while I was away the woman took you off. And you know what followed. Why, think you?"

James shook his head but found words at last. "She was . . . kind," he said.

David sighed. "Kind is not how I would name it. She would be well paid to do what she did. That was no kindness, James."

"How do you know? You were not there!" That was almost defiance.

"For a woman to seduce a half-drunken boy of thirteen years, and her liege-lord, for money, is scarcely kindness. But—she is not the greatest sinner, I admit. Those who paid her to do it are worse. Would that I knew why they did it. But they went to much expense to achieve it. I suspect, to gain some power over you. So—apart from all else, we must not play the Douglases' game for them. Enough that we have to suffer this captivity. Do you understand? Can you not see it?"

The boy certainly gave little indication of understanding, staring down at his hands, set-faced.

"We shall speak no more of this, meantime, lad. I just ask that you consider who are your friends—the Douglases, who devised it all? Or myself, Davie Lindsay, who loves you well? So—enough of that. Now for the Latin . . ."

Throughout that day David debated with himself whether to go and challenge William and Archibald Douglas with his accusations and condemnation, but came to the conclusion that it would achieve nothing. He would leave them in no doubt as to his reaction, but recognised that this was unlikely to distress them unduly.

So his relationship with their captors deteriorated markedly, although the All Hallows Eve incident was not actually discussed. This in itself did not distress David; but what did was that his relationship with James had also suffered some change. They were still close, but the affair with the woman had introduced a shadow between them, something which was not spoken of but which was there, and on which the boy held a view very different from the man's. This was sad, but what made it worse was the fact that the Douglases began to adopt a different

73

attitude towards the King, seeking not exactly to ingratiate themselves with the boy but to show him more respect, to talk to him, even to defer to him on occasion. Especially Sir Archibald who, with sons of his own, was more used to dealing with youngsters than was the Abbot. He presented James with a handsome dirk, which much pleased the recipient, and took him hawking in the adjacent royal park, the first time accompanied by David, the second time not. As Treasurer, he had to be much in the capital, and so was more or less in residence at the Abbey.

Then, one day in late November, Angus himself made one of his infrequent visits, and that night James was invited to dine with the Earl and his uncles—and David was not. When he was brought back, late, the King was distinctly the worse for liquor, and inclined to boast of his success with these Douglases, who were none so ill when one got to know them. His friend was the more anxious. Clearly a new policy was being established—and it was clear that Angus had no intention of yielding up his hostage to Arran or any other. And his own, Lindsay's, influence with the monarch was to be reduced. Presumably, then, the Douglases considered him to be in their way. He guessed that it might be only a matter of time before he was dismissed. Which implied for James—what?

When, just before Yule, another caller at Holyrood was the Bastard of Arran, and his call all but secret, David decided that Beaton should be informed, both of this last and of the new treatment for James. Going in search of the monk Balfour, the sub-chantor whom Davie had named as go-between, he found himself in a part of the establishment hitherto unvisited, and passing the laundry was surprised to see a woman working there—the gipsy Jeannie. She hastily turned her back on him, and disappeared further within, but there was no doubt as to who it was. Considerably concerned, he judged this to be an added threat.

His message to Beaton was the more emphatic.

David's fears were soon substantiated. With the wintry weather limiting his ranging the country, Angus spent most of the Christmas and Yuletide period at Holyrood—and although he was not the man to go in for festivities in any large way, he and his uncles did celebrate to some extent, with feastings and gatherings. In some of these James was included, but David never. On two such occasions the boy was again brought back to his quarters very late and drink-taken, guilt and defiance writ large in his attitude, to be followed in the mornings by sulks and heaviness. When, on a third such night, Hogmanay, he did not return to their room at all, nor reappearing until the forenoon of New Year's Day of 1526, David's anxiety and distress was not to be damped down any longer.

"James—you have been with that woman again!" he charged. "I know it. Every line of you proclaims it. After all I said, all my warnings. Do not seek to deny it. The Douglases have set you to drinking and whoring—and you are playing their game. She is still about this abbey—I have seen her."

The King nibbled his lip, wagging his red head. He looked slack and dull-eyed.

"They are working your ruin, boy—can you not see it? To get you into their pockets, dependent upon them. And you their willing dupe!"

"There is no harm in it," James burst out, thickly. "We hurt none. I . . . I like it. I am old enough, not a child any more. Others do it. Jeannie is kind. She likes me well, says that I am good at it! You, you are hard, would deny me all pleasure."

"Och, James, laddie—I am your friend. Your only friend in this place. That woman is no friend, however warm she seems towards you. She does what she does not out of love for a thirteen-year-old boy but because the Douglases pay her. Like it you may, but it is evil . . ."

"You say that. Others do not. Bedding is natural for any lusty person . . ."

"Who said that to you? Was it Angus? The Abbot? The Treasurer? I swear that you did not make that up for yourself!"

The other looked away. "My mother—she beds whom she will! And my father, they tell me, had many mistresses. When he was young, too . . ."

David looked grim. "Aye—they teach you skilfully! Can you not see what they do? You are not a fool. They make you to *need* them. And they separate *us*, drive a wedge between you and me. Is that what *you* want?"

"No-o-o. But I am no longer to be treated like a child. I am the King!"

"Ha—so that is it, *Sire*! Yes, you are King of Scots, and I am but your humble subject, no more than that. But we have been

75

friends all your days. Your royal father put you in my care. But, if that time is past and Your Grace wishes to be free of me and my guidance and caring, then so be it. You have but to say the word."

Doubtfully now James eyed him.

"See you, Sire—I mislike it here, held as good as prisoner. The Douglases hate me and would be quit of me. I need not be a captive in this abbey. I have my lands in Fife to tend, my own life to live. Only *your* service, and my love of Your Grace keeps me here. If you have no longer need of me, and find my lord of Angus more to your taste, the Douglases' care kinder—then, Highness, say so. I vow none here now would seek to keep me!"

"Davie—no! Oh, Davie!" Abruptly the boy's entire attitude changed. Wide-eyed now he flung himself forward into David's arms. "Do not say it. You must not leave me, Davie. Never! You *must* not. I need you, need you. I will not see her again—Jeannie. I promise! Do not go away."

Much moved, the man nodded. "Very well. I will stay, lad—if they will let me. They may not, mind. Since they wish to separate us, clearly, surely the easiest way to do it would be to send me away . . ."

"I will not let them! If you go, I go. I am the King—my royal command! You stay with me."

"If it was as simple as that, James, neither of us would be here! But—I will stay whilst they allow me . . ."

In the aftermath of that scene there was a marked improvement in their relations and no further talk about women and bodily needs. And when, a few days later, another invitation to dine with Angus came, James curtly refused. This presently brought the Abbot William to the royal quarters, ostensibly to enquire after the King's health, the assumption being that he must be feeling unwell. The boy's jerked assertion that he was not sick but had no wish to dine again with the Earl and his friends, caused the Douglas to look very thoughtful, eyeing David equally with James. He did not cross-question nor seek further details, however, and left them ominously silent.

"I fear that we shall not be long in hearing more of this!" David commented.

They did. The next day it was the man's turn to be

summoned to Angus's presence—and not for dinner. As ever, the Earl did not beat about the bush.

"Lindsay," he said, "we have supported you here sufficiently long. The King, I judge, no longer requires your attendance. We shall provide other and more suitable companionship for him. You will make your arrangements to leave, forthwith."

David took his time to answer that. "I am in the King's employ, my lord—not yours. If His Grace asks that I leave him, I shall leave."

The other's hot eyes flared. "You will leave whether he asks you or no! From all I hear, your influence with him is not good. You are stubborn and unhelpful, and would make him so. He deserves and requires better company."

"Female, I take it? A gipsy laundry-wench. For the King's Grace!"

"Fool! You will address me civilly, or suffer for it. I speak of a tutor and more worthy attendant. Now—be off."

"Gladly. Only, I tell you—if the King stays, I stay. That is his royal wish . . ."

"We shall see . . ."

David waited for three days. But when the summons came it was for James. Angus had gone to Tantallon in the interim but had now returned. At the order, brought by a servitor, the King was for refusing to attend—it was not for a monarch to be summoned by one of his carls. David agreed but, since they were in the Douglas's power, it would serve for James to announce that he would see Angus somewhere of his own choosing, not the Earl's. Say in the abbey-church—a suitable venue to emphasise dignity; for it would be a hard and brow-beating interview concerned with his, David's dismissal. He did not see that James could win.

The boy went, with a mixture of apprehension and determination.

When he returned, it was still with mixed feelings, but now the mixture was different—there was triumph in it. They had won, he declared excitedly. Davie was not to be sent away—he could stay. He had told Angus so, and forced him to agree. They were not to be parted.

That David was surprised went without saying, so improbable did this outcome seem. But behind the boy's satisfaction the man sensed something else, some hint of reservation.

"You won, then. I am glad," he said. "But—at a price, I think? What did you have to pay, James? Angus is not the man to yield to mere pleading, even from his sovereign-lord."

The King looked down. "I have to write a letter—that is all."

"A letter? To whom?"

"To my mother. To tell her that all is well with me. Just a letter."

"James—what is this? Why such a letter? Now? There is something strange here. This was Angus's demand?"

"Yes. That was why he sent for me—that, and to say that you must go. I was to write to my mother, to say that I was well content here, that I was treated kindly. And that I was well pleased to continue to bide with the Earl of Angus."

"So-o-o! That is it! And—you agreed?"

"I said that I would only do it if you were allowed to stay with me, Davie."

"Och, laddie, laddie . . . !"

"It is none so much to do. They *are* being kinder to me now. And my mother cares nothing for me—only to use me, as King, for her own purposes. It is not much to do to keep you, Davie. Is it?"

"More than you think, James. Do you not see? That letter is not really for your mother, at all. Oh, she will get it, no doubt. But others will read it, or learn of it, as well—all the realm will. Scotland will learn that its King is well content with the Earl of Angus and the Douglases, happy in his keeping. This is not for *her* comfort! No—it is for others. In especial, I think, for Arran, Lennox and Erroll, the lords to whom Angus should have delivered you after his three months—and has not. Which means, to be sure, that he is going to keep you still. And more than that, I think. For most will have come to that belief already. He must have some further plan for you, which requires that he seems to have your agreement. What, who knows? But—there is a deal more in this than just a son's letter to his mother. Some subtle scheme—more like the Abbot William's work than Angus's, I'd say. Was *he* there?"

"Yes, he came to the church with the Earl, but said little."

"Aye—that one is a devil . . . !"

"But, Davie—what of it? The Douglases will do what they

will, anyway. We cannot stop them. But *you* stay with me. That is what is important. I'd do more than write any letter, to hold you. You stay!"

"At what cost, I wonder . . . ?"

5

Although superficially the months that followed at the Abbey of the Holy Rood were little different from those which had gone before, there was in fact a notable change. The roles of David and James had altered. The man was there now only on sufferance, dependent wholly on the boy's continuing demand and active bargaining. Their captors demonstrated that all too clearly, showing with scorn and insult that they had no further use for him. And, perhaps inevitably, something of the shift in emphasis began to show in the relationship between the two. James was more and more the King and David the subject, even if the boy did not consciously so intend. It was partly, no doubt, that he was growing up fast now, spurred on almost certainly by his sexual awakening; also the fact that the Douglases were treating him ever more respectfully, on the face of it at least. The pair remained good friends but the balance was changing, especially in authority.

The dinners with Angus or his uncles resumed, David excluded; and after one such, when the boy returned very late, David suspected that he had been with that woman again. A stroll round to the laundry next day revealed that she was still working there. Then, a week later, he was sure of it—James actually smelt of woman when he came back.

In bed thereafter, David debated long with himself what he should do. Was there any point in challenging the boy with breaking his promise and yielding to what was undoubtedly strong temptation deliberately put in his way? Would it do any good? On the contrary, would it not merely worsen the situation between them? Better probably to make no comment, whilst

79

letting James realise that he *knew* what was happening. If they were going to continue to live thus close, for both their sakes he must strive to keep relations as harmonious as possible.

So nothing was said about drinking and womanising, although the King could have little doubt as to his friend's attitude and knowledge.

Then, on the 10th of April, the boy's fourteenth birthday, they learned what was partly behind that letter written to the Queen-Mother. Angus was at Holyrood again, and invited James to attend a ceremony in the abbey-church in celebration, at noon. Wondering, the boy could hardly refuse to attend—but he took David along with him. They were escorted into the chapter-house, to discover Lyon King-of-Arms there, with his heralds and trumpeters. Presently Angus himself came in, bowed low to the monarch, glared at David, and announced that proceedings would commence and the royal birthday be suitably honoured. The trumpets would sound, Lyon would lead the way, and they would enter the church by the chancel doorway. He himself would guide His Grace as to what to do.

James looked doubtfully at David, but the Earl forestalled any questions by signing to the trumpeters to sound. In the confined space of the chapter-house the noise of their fanfare was deafening. The inner doorway was thrown open by a herald, and Lyon formed up his colourful court of pursuivants—at the last moment beckoning for David to join them, since he was, officially at least, one of them—and in great dignity marched in, Angus and the King coming behind together, followed by the instrumentalists, still blowing lustily.

They found the church full, surprisingly, Arran and his son the Bastard with a clutch of Douglas lairds, waiting there in the chancel, with Abbot William and the robed clergy. The abbot's chair had been brought forward to a central position, and to this Angus led the King and, with a flourish, indicated that he should sit. The heraldic group formed up nearby. Angus remained standing beside James.

When the fanfare ended at last, the Earl stepped forward and held up his hand for silence.

"My lords and fellow subjects," he said loudly, "we are here for a purpose. To celebrate the birthday of our gracious sovereign-lord King James. He has now reached the age of fourteen years and enters into manhood. I say that we all wish him well." That was jerked out with more force than eloquence, for Angus was no speech-maker. He turned and bowed towards the throne-like chair.

"His Grace has been well prepared for his high calling," he resumed. "And having now reached years of discretion and judgement, his Council have decided that he is fit and able to govern as well as to reign. Accordingly, as from this birthday, King James the Fifth assumes the rule of his realm. God save the King!"

How much surprise there might be in the crowded church at this announcement, David had no means of knowing—for it might have been bruited abroad beforehand. But for himself, he was astonished. Angus did nothing without hope of advantage for himself and his house—and what advantage was there for Douglas in this? If it meant little or nothing, a mere empty ceremony, as had been the case when the Queen-Mother had made a similar statement almost a couple of years before, then why go to all this trouble? And if it was indeed a significant act—why? Fourteen was still far too young an age for any true rule. And nothing was more improbable than that Angus was voluntarily yielding up effective power and influence.

David's wonderings were interrupted by a further development. Abbot William moved from behind the altar to the King's side, carrying now a handsome cloak of purple velvet trimmed with fur. He placed this ceremoniously about the wary boy's shoulders, and then bowed deeply before him.

"God save the King's Grace! Long may he reign and his rule be glorious!" he intoned, with a practised eloquence in marked contrast to his nephew. "We all acclaim the King's Highness."

Led by the ranked Douglas lairds, the congregation took up the traditional refrain. "God save the King! God save the King! God save the King!" all chanted loudly.

At a sign from Lyon, the trumpeters raised their instruments and blew another stirring flourish.

When this died away, Angus spoke again. "A new beginning. All, I say, wish His Grace well in it. At this fresh start in the realm's governance, all appointments of the crown fall back into the monarch's hands, to be renewed . . . or otherwise." There was a significant pause there. "I myself yield up my position of Chief Warden of the Marches. Others likewise. The King now rules. God save him!"

81

A little less fervently now the congregation repeated the phrase, but only once.

So that was it! The reason behind all this play-acting—for David was sure that it was little more than that. All offices of state were forfeit at a new rule—to be reallocated to men of Angus's choosing without a doubt. All direction of the realm put lawfully into the hands of a boy who was controlled by Douglas. This was the rest of the plan foreshadowed by that letter to the Queen-Mother—Angus the effective master of Scotland, and for years to come.

As though to emphasise the accuracy of that assessment, Angus now turned and strode back to James's chair, held out a hand to raise the King from it, and taking his arm through that fine cloak, led him off across the chancel to the door by which they had entered, and out, without pause or further ceremony.

Reality had returned, play-acting over.

Apparently taken by surprise, Lyon looked around him uncertainly, decided on a final fanfare, and gestured to his trumpeters. As, somewhat raggedly, this rang out, he looked over at Abbot William, evidently wondering who should go first, and then more or less shooed his heralds out rather like barn-door fowls. The entire proceedings had lasted only a few minutes.

In the chapter-house, David found Angus already gone and James waiting alone, uncertain as to what would happen next, in a notable atmosphere of anticlimax. David nodded to the boy, took his velvet cloak and handed it to the Lord Lyon, for it was fairly evident that in fact nothing happened next, and together man and boy went out into the cloisters and across the courtyard to their own quarters.

The new dispensation and fresh start seemed markedly similar to the old.

And so it remained, in the summer weeks that followed, all as it had been, except for one development—signings. Now, almost daily, large numbers of papers, documents and charters were brought to the King for signature. No explanations and elucidations came with them, just the requirement to sign. This, it seemed, was the monarch ruling in person. It was no part of David Lindsay's remit or duty to advise James not to sign, since refusal would result only in pressure and unpleasantness. But he did suggest a policy of reading first, where possible, so that at least they might be made aware of what the Douglases were up to. Most which they read were appointments to office under the crown and transfers of lands, mainly to Douglases and their friends—although, significantly, some to Arran and his Hamiltons, clearly in token of a bargain struck. But most significant of all was a document addressed to the Archbishop of St. Andrews informing him that his position of Chancellor of the realm and chief minister now, like others, reverted to the crown; and that he, James, had appointed the Earl of Angus thereto, and ordered the return of the Great Seal of Scotland to the said Earl, forthwith.

What the Beatons would do about that remained to be seen.

In early July there were two developments. James was informed that Angus intended to hold justice-ayres in the Borderland—one of the first papers he had had to sign had been the reappointment of Angus as Chief Warden of the Marches—and the Earl deemed it right that the monarch should accompany him on this occasion and learn at first-hand of the administration of justice in his realm; this in a week's time. The second, a day later, was the arrival at Holyrood of the Earl of Lennox, to see Angus—who had gone off to Tantallon only that morning. Before following on thither, Lennox came to pay his respects to the King—and was sufficiently senior to be able to dismiss the functionary who brought him there, so as to have some private converse with the monarch. He was a personable, youngish man, fine-featured but slightly-built, descendant of the ancient Celtic mormaors through the female line, although himself a Stewart.

Alone with James, who kept David by him, he knelt down on one knee to take the royal hand within both of his own, in the traditional gesture of fealty, declaring urgently that he was His Grace's man until his life's end. Rising, he spoke low-voiced and hurriedly. He said that they might well not be left long alone, and so he must say what he had to tell him quickly. First, he had brought a letter from the Archbishop of St. Andrews and the Abbot of Arbroath. This he handed over, recommending that it be hidden meantime—James passing it to David, who pocketed it within his doublet. Secondly, Lennox told them that the King's predicament and shameful captivity was not forgotten or accepted by many of his loyal subjects. Angus seemed to have all his own way for the time being, but forces were being mustered against him and it would not be long before a move would be made to right the wrong. He himself was actively gathering support, especially in the Highlands. Once the harvest was in up there they would march south. The clans would never rise before harvest, since the cattle, their life's-blood, depended on the winter-feed the hay and oats represented. In September then, God willing, they should be in a position to challenge Angus. Not only the Highlanders, of course; many others would rise. From his own Lennox, from the Stewart lands of Renfrew and Bute, from Gowrie, Menteith, Fife and Galloway, even in the Borders many hated Angus who bore hardly on them, using the Homes to do his ill work for him . . .

At mention of the Borders, James interrupted to declare that he was going there, with Angus, in a week's time, on justice-ayres. He had never been to the Borderland, never really been anywhere in the realm save Stirling, Linlithgow and Edinburgh. Could they do anything, speak to any who would help, while they were there?

It was at this stage that Lennox's fears about interruption were proved valid, for the door was thrown open and Abbot William and Sir Archibald Douglas came in, with no pretence at by-your-leave even though they bowed briefly to the King. Graysteel announced that they had some papers urgently requiring the royal signature, and his brother produced some documents.

Lennox took the hint and bowed himself out.

The documents proved to be far from pressing, merely an excuse.

The Douglas brothers gone, David produced the letter Lennox had brought.

It was from Davie Beaton. He too announced that the Holyrood captives were not forgotten and that Angus's power was less complete than it probably seemed to them. Moves were afoot to unite the forces against Douglas. No details in this letter, which could fall into wrong hands; but it was to be hoped that their ordeal would soon be over. Needless to say, the Archbishop would not resign the Chancellorship nor return the Great Seal, recognising that King James would have signed the order only under duress. The Earl of Lennox was to be trusted and had large influence, especially in the Highlands; and Argyll was helping, with his Campbells. Once read, this letter should be burned.

Much heartened, the recipients complied with that last. James was cock-a-hoop, and fell to be warned by his friend not to be over-optimistic, for the Douglases were very strong and in a position to bring much pressure to bear on the fearful and the hesitant. Admittedly their power did not extend into the Highlands, where lay James's best hopes—if those strange warrior-clans could be coaxed southwards. James must seek not to reveal by any evident good spirits that they had received encouraging news, which could alert their captors.

That wise advice was more easily given than acted upon. However, the King's obvious satisfaction at the whole idea of the Borderland assize trip and the comparative freedom it represented, was not dangerous and probably the Douglases put his high spirits down to that. David was to go too, the boy declaring that he himself would refuse otherwise.

*   *   *

The Borderland episode of 1526 had an extraordinary effect on James Stewart—more so than even David anticipated. Just how enclosed a life the fourteen-year-old had led, shut up in fortresses all his days, was apt to be forgotten. He had been allowed to hunt and hawk and ride short distances from his places of captivity, of course, but always under strict guard, never permitted to roam the land, see new scenes and faces, mix with his subjects, meet the common people. All beyond his keepers and their courts was a new world for him—the more intriguing in that he was nominally the lord of it all. The sheer feeling of space, release from confinement, the illusion of liberty, with the changing scenery, towns, villages, houses, rivers and lochs and moors, gripped him with the excitement of what could be round the next bend in the track. He was still under close watch, to be sure, and still not allowed to mix with others than their hosts at abbeys, castles and towers where they rested and put up; but he was seeing new faces all the time, undergoing new experiences, listening to litigants in the various court-sittings of the justice-ayres, witnessing justice being done, even men being hanged or having their hands chopped off or their genitals emasculated—although blessedly these cases were in a minority, for each holder of a barony had his own powers of pit and gallows and did not require the royal justiciar's authority to imprison or hang in other than pleas of the crown. These summary jurisdictions applied to Holy Church also. Treason, rebellion, theft of royal revenues, assault or robbery on the King's highways, high-seas piracy and such-like did not occur every day. So most of the cases before the justiciar, sitting in the King's name, were disputes about lands and boundaries, rights, privileges and servitudes infringed, inheritances withheld, slanderous accusations circulated, mainly concerning the land-owning classes. All of which was of much educative value for the young monarch, as well as providing interest.

And, strangely enough, it all showed up Angus himself in another light. Where his own personal interests and advantage were not involved, nor those of his friends, he made a generally fair and honest judge, never gentle, admittedly, but equitable, listening attentively to both sides and coming to reasonable and often shrewd decisions. And he was no respecter of persons. James did indeed learn much, sitting by his side in judgement seats.

They went down Lauderdale, to the burgh of Lauder itself, where they hanged certain thieves who had been terrorising and robbing the lieges who had to use the desolate road over the Lammermuirs by Soutra and Fala; and settled a dispute between the barons of Thirlestane and Whitslaid. Then on to the Earlstoun of Ersildoune, where James was more interested in the tower which had belonged to the famous poet and seer, Thomas the Rhymer, than in the rather dull litigation over a boundary demarkation between the common lands and the barony of Cowdenknowes—which being a Home property, the case was decided in their favour. Then on to Melrose, where they passed the night in the great Abbey. No justice was dispensed there, for the Cistercians' foundation had it own regality jurisdiction. Here was the burial-place of many of the Douglases, including the second Earl of Douglas, the hero of Otterburn, and Sir William, the Knight of Liddesdale, alleged Flower of Chivalry. Also, of course, of the heart of Robert the Bruce.

Making their way up Tweed thereafter, they entered the great Forest of Ettrick, for what proved to be a major hanging session at Selkirk, for the Forest, royal lands and covering an enormous area of the Middle March, was the notorious haunt of robbers and broken men; and every now and again batches of these, caught in the interim, fell to be tried and executed by the score, more or less a routine exercise for the justiciar. David Lindsay had expected young James to recoil in horror from all these hangings, but the boy seemed fascinated, observing and commenting on the different attitudes of the victims and how long each took to die.

At Selkirk, Angus's party was joined by a quite large contingent of armed men from the Douglas lands of Yarrow and Megget and around St. Mary's Loch. With these they moved southwards over the hills, by Ashkirk and Synton to the Teviot valley where, at Hawick, a further assize was held and their strength further added to by considerable numbers of the retainers of the Douglases of Drumlanrig and Cavers, the latter hereditary Sheriff of Teviotdale. When they moved on, south-westwards now, climbing towards the high central spine of Lowland Scotland, they had almost a small army with them—which seemed a strange development. Soon it transpired that this was in fact one of the main objectives of the entire expedition—a drive against the Armstrongs.

The Armstrongs were a large and warlike clan of mosstroopers and freebooters inhabiting what was known as the Debateable Lands, of the Middle and West Marches, on both sides of the Borderline—indeed, the term border hardly applied in their area, as the word debateable implied, for the Armstrongs just did not recognise it, and held sway on each side, a law unto themselves. They were a fierce and powerful lot, able to muster thousands on occasion, and normally the Scots and English Wardens left them very much to themselves, as too hot to handle conveniently. But every now and again they tended to overstep the mark and raid properties lying around the perimeter of their area—which, on the Scots side, were apt to be Douglas lands. And when this became serious, punitive measures were called for, and had to be prosecuted in major force, as now.

When James learned of all this, he was much excited, seeing it all as a great adventure, the sort of thing that he had often dreamed of, shut up within fortress walls, stirring battle between knightly hosts and outlaws and rebels. Sadly, however, the King was disappointed, for it seemed that the Armstrongs possessed an excellent information system and were well warned of this Douglas approach. Whether it was the fact that the King was present with Angus inhibiting them, or merely that this July was not a convenient time for them to muster in strength, was not to be known; but they proved entirely elusive, not only not to be brought to battle but not even to be seen. As the Douglas force moved up past Teviothead and over the great watershed at Mosspaul and so down into Ewesdale, heading for the Esk at Langholm, they had scouts well ahead, but these encountered no opposition. Langholm-town itself huddled fearful as they rode through; and beyond was Armstrong country. But it was a deserted land they entered—although only recently deserted. These green hills and dales were never densely populated, but there were not a few farms and upland properties surrounding small stone peel-towers, and all those readily reached from the passes and roads were empty, cattle and even poultry gone with their owners, even though in some peat-fires still smouldered on hearths. That Angus's men left more than peat smouldering at most of these was scant consolation for lack of either slaughter or booty—and anyway, bare stone towers do not burn readily. Where the Armstrongs and their beasts had gone was not clear, but the hills and the hidden valleys stretched away to infinity on every hand, and could swallow up hundreds.

Angus was making specifically for Gilnockie Tower, the seat of the most prominent and notorious of the Armstrong leaders, not the chief himself but his brother, Johnnie Armstrong of Gilnockie, who was renowned far beyond the Borderland for his daring, his disrespect for all authority other than his own, the style he kept—he was reputed seldom to ride abroad without a tail of up to thirty Armstrong lairds—and the fact that he boasted he could raise one thousand mounted men in three days and two thousand in a week. Angus had every intention of hanging this insolent individual out-of-hand if he could catch him; but when they reached Gilnockie, on Eskside some five miles south of Langholm, it was to find the place deserted like the rest. Not only this, but the tower itself was a disappointment for it was no more than a square stone keep within a courtyard, four storeys and a garret in height, with a parapet and wall-walk, sturdy and strong but little larger or more impressive than the other Armstrong fortalices they had already so unsuccessfully tried to burn. It certainly gave no aspect of being able to house and support so puissant a character as the famous Johnnie, much less his reputed entourage, almost the only distinction of Gilnockie Tower being the stone beacon surmounting its topmost gable—this presumably the means by which he summoned his supporting hordes from near and far, with a blazing signal which would touch off other beacons in prominent positions on the surrounding hills, a sort of static fiery-cross.

Angus went to great exertions to ravage if not demolish this small empty stronghold; but with walls six feet thick and precious little woodwork, and no cannon nor gunpowder available, little could be done save to burn the notably simple furnishings left behind, the hay and straw in the stables and byres, and such other perishables as could be found. Presumably more gear was hidden not too far away, but search-parties failed to locate any.

The justiciar's force reluctantly turned northwards again, recognising the hopelessness of probing further into this Debateable Land, and leaving a great column of smoke rising above Gilnockie—mainly burning hay and the thatches of the surrounding shacks and cot-houses—which Angus hopefully described as an alternative beacon to let the Armstrongs know who ruled in Scotland. But it all made a very hollow triumph, and the Earl made irritable company for the next day or two.

A surprise greeted them back at Hawick, where they found the Earl of Lennox and a small company awaiting them. He said that he had come to pay a visit to his kinsman, Sir Walter Scott of Buccleuch, at nearby Branxholm, but had found him from home; and hearing that His Grace and Angus were in the area, he thought it only civil to wait and pay his respects. Angus demonstrated no joy at this encounter, but could hardly banish his fellow-earl from the King's company when he indicated that he would ride on with them.

That evening at Jedburgh, Lennox contrived a brief private word with David Lindsay, having been unable to find James alone. He said that when they had told him at Holyrood of this borders expedition, he had decided to try to make some attempt to rescue the King. He had in fact seen Scott of Buccleuch, who was the Warden of the Middle March, and put the attempt into his hands—for the Borderers were always loth to fight under any but their own leaders. Buccleuch was away now drumming up support amongst his own Scotts, the Elliots and Turnbulls and Pringles of these parts. But they had not expected Angus back from the Armstrong country so soon, and any attack would have to be hastened on or it would be too late to effect it in the Borderland. So he himself was remaining with the royal party, to try to send messengers secretly to Buccleuch as to details of positions and numbers. It was unfortunate that Angus had so

89

large a force with him on a justice-ayres. They had not reckoned on so many.

David, whilst grateful that efforts should be made to free them, was distinctly doubtful over this situation. He understood that Angus was making for Roxburgh, where Teviot and Tweed met, then to move north up Tweed again to Melrose on their way back to Edinburgh. So there would not be much time for Scott to gather an adequate force. It was probable that the Douglases of Cavers and Drumlanrig would leave Angus when he moved out of Teviotdale, so his numbers might be considerably lessened; but even so, there might not be time to assemble . . .

In fact, next day, although the Teviotdale Douglases did turn back, reducing Angus's company by some four hundred, this sadly was more than made up for by the appearance in the afternoon, in the St. Boswells area, of a mixed band of Homes and Kerrs to the number of almost six hundred. And worse, these came because there was a rumour circulating in the East March that Scott of Buccleuch was planning some sort of attack on the King and his guardians.

So Angus was not only reinforced but warned. He ordered more support from the nearby Kerr and Home lands and put his people on the alert, riding in tight formation now. And he turned on Lennox with some suspicion, since he had recently been in touch with Buccleuch. For his part Lennox denied all knowledge of where Scott was or what he was about, and suggested that the tale was a nonsense, for he would swear that none was a more loyal subject than Sir Walter.

Thus, wary and keyed up, they came to Melrose again. Angus decided to remain at the Abbey there for another full day, to give opportunity for further Homes and Kerrs to arrive. These did appear, over the next thirty-six hours, in batches small and quite large, so that the Douglas was able to count a force of little less than two thousand—with Melrose groaning under the impact. No signs of Buccleuch's muster was reported. Whether Lennox had been able to reach them with messengers was not to be known.

They left Melrose on the morning of the 25th of July, to head northwards by a different route, up the Allen Water valley, parallel with the Leader, as being less likely to be watched by potential enemies, and so headed westwards at first, to cross

Tweed by the Darnlee ford. They had gone, in fact, not much more than a mile from the Abbey and were nearing Darnick Tower and hamlet, before the approach to the ford, when all at the head of the long and necessarily strung-out column were surprised by the sounding of horns blown from ahead and to the flank. There was a low wooded hill, scarcely high enough to be so-called in the Borderland, between the road and the river, and rounding the shoulder of this, Angus and his leadership group were astonished to find the track ahead of them barred by a solid phalanx of mounted men, armoured and with banners, more and more riders emerging from the cover of the woodland, more horns blowing. The Douglases drew rein abruptly, with consequent considerable bunching and confusion behind. Angus had no scouts out thus early after leaving the Abbey, and scarcely out of the town.

The barrier of men and horses was perhaps two hundred yards ahead, and at its centre was a group of knightly figures in fine armour and plumed helmets under the blue-and-gold standard of Scott. One of these reined forward a little way and held up a steel-gauntleted hand.

"Hail the King's Highness!" he shouted. "I, Buccleuch, Warden of the Middle March, greet the King's Grace, and request the honour of his escort whilst he is in this March—as is my undoubted right. Will you so honour me, Sire, and receive my homage?"

For moments all around the King were struck dumb by this unexpected development, so different from any assault or ambush such as had been anticipated. Then Angus found his voice.

"Buccleuch—what are you at?" he demanded, having necessarily to shout also, at that range. "This is Angus. King James is in *my* keeping. His Grace requires no further escort."

"In the Middle March he should be in *mine*, my lord. You know it."

"Not so. I am Chief Warden of all the Marches, His Grace remains with me."

It was a highly dramatic and extraordinary situation, the two Wardens facing each other some one hundred and fifty yards apart, each backed by a cohort of armed men—and not only Wardens but cousins, for Buccleuch's grandfather had married the sister of Bell-the-Cat, fourth Earl of Angus, the present

91

Earl's grandfather. David Lindsay sat tense beside James's horse. Lennox watched, still-faced, nearby.

"Angus—my words are for the King's Grace, not for you," Scott cried. "In the presence of his royal person you have no authority over me or any. Sire—will you come to my good care . . . ?"

Angus precluded any answer from James. "Buccleuch—if you wish to pay your humble duty to His Grace, come you here and do so," he called. "But come alone."

"Is the King of Scots not to be allowed to speak his own mind in the presence of Douglas!"

"Fool! In your insolence you deny His Grace passage. Clear your ruffians from this road. Before I clear it for him! And a new Warden for the Middle March will be required, I swear!"

Lennox raised his voice. "My lords," he began reasonably. "This is folly! King James should surely go forward to receive the homage of these his illustrious subjects. *I* will escort him, Angus, if you fear aught . . ."

"No!" the Douglas barked. "Enough! Begone, Scott—while you still have a head on your shoulders!"

"Not so, Angus. You have held His Grace captive sufficiently long, to your shame and his royal hurt. Now he will go free. Sire—come forward, I pray you . . ."

Angus reined his mount round, almost unsaddling his Uncle Archibald in the process, to lean over and grab James's bridle—eloquent enough answer.

It was sufficiently so for Buccleuch, at any rate. Turning, he raised a curling bull's-horn to his lips and blew a long quivering blast, then lifted his steel-clad arm again and thrust it forward, pointing. And with a roar the ranked horsemen blocking the way lowered lances and whipped out swords and spurred into action. "A Bellendaine! A Bellendaine!" they yelled, the Scott slogan.

There was inevitable confusion in the royal cavalcade at this sudden charge. Most of the column was still out-of-sight around the shoulder of the hill. The leaders wheeled their beasts to get out of the way of the Scott onslaught, some spurring off into the flanking trees, some heading directly back, some seeking to prepare those behind to stand their ground. Angus himself, rearing his mount on its hind legs, yelled to Graysteel to bring the King, and then dashed headlong through the press behind him, cannoning men and horses aside, clearly not in any panic to escape but to gain control of his host further back and to dispose it to face this challenge.

James, David and Lennox found themselves surrounded by a group of Douglas lairds under Sir Archibald, and rudely forced round and driven towards the rear. It crossed David's mind to try to resist, but unarmed and alone he reckoned it would be pointless and might result in danger to the King; besides, the mass of shouting men hurtling towards them in a thunder of hooves was sufficiently daunting to vanquish every other urge than to get out of their way. Back they went amongst the jostling throng.

That bend in the road round the shoulder of hill was the key to the entire encounter. It meant that neither side, at the start, had any clear idea of the other's strength. Also no broad front was possible for the attacking charge, which inevitably had the effect of slowing it down and diluting its force, whilst at the same time preventing those behind the leadership from perceiving what went on, or even being able to receive signals and commands. A better place for a hidden and waiting ambush, and a worse for an onrushing assault, would have been difficult to envisage.

After the first undignified scurry rearwards, the reverse applied to Angus's force. Once back round the bend, there was plenty of space for his people to form up and manoeuvre; likewise to see and follow their lord's orders. The Earl was quick to recognise all this, and acted decisively. Spurring furiously towards his own bewildered and milling main body, he waved his arm urgently right and left, right and left, yelling to divide, divide, divide. How many perceived the implications of his tactics was doubtful; but the way he drove down on his own column, with the waving and shouting, was unmistakable. Men reined aside hurriedly to get out of his way and to give him passage. But once in their midst, he wheeled his spirited but long-suffering charger right round again, it pawing the air, and went on yelling and gesturing to divide into two, that command at least now entirely clear. Jostling and sidling, in something not far from chaos, his following, or the front half of it, did somehow split into two uneven sections, with himself and some of his lieutenants, including David, the King and Lennox, left in the centre.

This was the situation which confronted Buccleuch as he and

his foremost ranks came pounding round the bend. And Angus had guessed aright—not very difficult to do perhaps, for the attackers' obvious strategy on so narrow a front was to constitute themselves into the traditional wedge or spearhead formation and to drive headlong at the enemy front and leadership, bore through it and break it up in confusion, then to wheel round on its rear, a well-proved cavalry device. Buccleuch attempted just that—but found the enemy already divided into two and awaiting him, and only the little group left in the centre as target, leaders though they were. And so close were they that there was no time to change tactics in a thundering charge. Buccleuch, at the head of the wedge, could try to switch his attack somewhat to one side or the other, but that would leave the unassailed section free to assault his wedge in flank, where it was most vulnerable.

Decision had to be taken almost instantly, and Scott, probably advisedly in the circumstances, elected to continue for the centre, where at least he might bring down Angus himself and his leaders and just possibly capture the prize of the King. But this too the Earl had foreseen, using himself as bait. As Buccleuch bore down on him, sword swinging, he yelled to Graysteel, pointing, to take James into the press of his people on the left or south side, while he flung himself, with some others, into the temporary anonymity of the throng on the right—and with only brief seconds to spare. The attackers, quite unable to change course at that range, came crashing down into the now empty gap, still shouting, "A Bellendaine! A Bellendaine!"

What happened thereafter was all but indescribable. Horses at full charge cannot be pulled up in short space, so Buccleuch's formation went plunging down the corridor between the two sections of Angus's force, and these promptly turned in on them on both sides in smiting fury. In moments the scene was utter turmoil, a wild mêlée of flailing, hacking, shouting men and rearing, stumbling, neighing horses. Adding to the pandemonium was the pressure from behind, as more and more of Buccleuch's people came piling in at the gallop, and the rearmost hundreds of Angus's column did the same. It became complete, savage tumult and disorder, with no sort of planning nor direction possible on either side, the leaders themselves lost in the general shambles. Angus was a born fighter and Buccleuch a veteran Border warrior, but as the encounter had so swiftly developed, they were both all but helpless to control their followings. What ensued was not so much a battle as a medley of countless individual combats, in closest proximity and constriction, hopelessly entangled in bloody riot.

In these circumstances, inevitably numbers told, and when everything became evident it was that there was a lot more with Angus than with Buccleuch.

Whenever the clash commenced, David Lindsay saw the safety of the King as his one duty. So, whilst all around him were pressing inwards to the attack, grabbing James's bridle, he sought to push in the other direction, outwards away from the battling. It was anything but easy, forcing their alarmed mounts against the tide of struggling, plunging horseflesh and bawling, sword-wielding men, and more then once they were all but unseated, their knees were bruised, their bodies buffeted. But at length, more perhaps by the tide leaving them than themselves gaining on it, they found themselves free of the press and on a slight grassy rise, from which they could turn and view all.

James was trembling, not with fear but with excitement, gasping incoherent exclamations, questions. Scanning the terrible scene of passion and hatred and bloodshed, David pointed and pointed again.

"Outnumbered!" he cried, above the din. "Aye, outnumbered. Two to one, I'd say. Hard to see . . . who is who. But, see you—Buccleuch can have no more than a thousand there, if that. And Angus twice as many. I fear, I greatly fear . . ."

"Perhaps they will . . . I cannot tell . . . where is Buccleuch? All the banners are down. Davie—what can we do? Surely we can aid them . . ."

"No—we cannot. Nothing that we can do, unarmed. You, the King, must stand safe. That is our only part. *Your* part. You are the King . . ."

For how long that dire struggle lasted there was no knowing, for time was irrelevant, went unnoticed. But gradually some pattern in the disarray did begin to evolve, some recognisable drift—and that drift was westward almost imperceptible at first, then becoming more evident, westwards and north-westwards, the direction from which the attack had come, round that bend in the road and into the woodland. More and more of Buccleuch's people were breaking away, perceiving their fight as hopeless and making their escape whilst they could.

Whether Angus was content with this gradual exodus of his enemies, or was in no position to halt it anyway, the watchers, joined now by Lennox, could not tell. They could not even pick out Angus's person in the mêlée. But presently the trickle became a flow, a flood, and the battle, if such it could be called, more or less ground to a halt.

The Douglases and their allies were left in possession of the field. And that field was a grievous sight, littered with the dead and wounded, riderless horses everywhere, the dark-red stains of blood seemingly splashed over all.

Angus, himself bleeding from a grazed forehead and cheek—for, like most of his lieutenants, he had been caught helmetless by the attack—materialised from the milling throng and came spurring up to the King, hot eyes hotter than ever.

"So much for your friends!" he jerked. "How Buccleuch pays his homage! You are going to require a new Warden of the Middle March!" He swung on Lennox. "And you, my lord—what part did *you* play in that onset? Little that was honest, I swear!"

His fellow earl shrugged. "What part should I have played, Angus?" he asked. "Save to take concern for His Grace's safety. Do you require me to aid you put down but half your numbers of Buccleuch's people?"

"So you stood by and lifted no hand! God's wounds—if I thought that you had helped to bring down those dastards upon us, Lennox, I would, would . . . !" The mailed fist rose, quivering.

Lennox reined back, involuntarily.

"Is, is Buccleuch . . . ? Is he . . . fallen?" That was James, thick-voiced.

"I know not—nor care!" Angus reined his mount round, to ride back to the scene of carnage, where wounded were being picked out from dead, friend from foe. Over his shoulder, he threw back the command. "Lindsay—take His Grace back to the Abbey. Kilspindie will accompany you. We shall wait until the morrow to ride north."

Lennox, when the other was gone, shook his head. "A bungled business!" he said. "A sorry outcome, ill-managed. Myself, I will be off. Nothing for me here. But, Sire—do not lose heart. We shall do better than this, for Your Grace. At the least, it has shown that the Lowlands are not waiting for the Highlands to save the King. The clans will now heed me, I think. This is only the first blow struck in Your Grace's cause." He reached out to take the King's hand, and kissed it, before riding off.

Doubtfully the other two looked after him, as Archibald Douglas came up to escort them back to Melrose Abbey.

They learned, later, that Buccleuch was not amongst the eighty dead and many more left wounded on the field of what Angus called the Scott Skirmish of Darnick.

Next day, still heavily escorted by Homes and Kerrs, they rode by the shortest route, up Lauderdale, for Edinburgh. The Earl was in a black mood, not triumphant over his victory but angry that such a revolt against his authority should have taken place, especially in his own Borderland. Also that he had been caught in a position where he had been unable properly to control and direct his forces, so that they had fought like any rabble. He exemplified his ill-humour, on arrival at Holyrood, by swinging on David Lindsay and telling him, without warning, that he was dismissed from the King's service, and to be gone. He declared that he had seen his head close to Lennox's on more than one occasion—and he believed Lennox to be behind the affair at Darnick. He must leave forthwith.

In vain James pleaded, threatened that he would do nothing that he was told, would sign no more papers, wept even. Angus was scornfully adamant.

David was not allowed even to see the King alone thereafter. With a strained and almost tearful farewell, he rode away from the Abbey of the Holy Rood that same evening.

6

It was almost a repetition of the previous occasion fifteen months before, when Davie Beaton came riding back to The Mount of Lindifferon—save that this time it was the oat harvest, not the hay, which was being gathered, in early September, and a different field in which Lindsay was wielding his sickle, in line with his men. Beaton perceived another difference too, as he came up—his friend no longer bore the former dour, grim expression and bearing but, without being especially lively or demonstrative on this warm afternoon of hard labour, was much more his normal self.

"Is it the scourging of your body for the weal of your soul? Or do you *like* to labour and toil with your hands?" Beaton greeted him, dismounting. "I never knew the like."

"Some honest toil would do *you* no harm!" he was told. "Sweat some of the intrigue and plotting out of you."

"I think not, friend. The talents the good Lord has given my unworthy self to use reside in my head rather than my muscles, I judge! For every man of wits there are a thousand with mere thews. You, it seems, have both, in some degree."

"I thank you! After the months shut up in Holyrood, I find this labour in the fields to my taste. But—what brings you here, Davie? When you come visiting, I fear the worst!"

"Ingrate! You must agree that I bring diversity and interest into your life? Yes, I have word for you of something more lively than reaping oats." Beaton took his friend's arm, to lead him out of earshot of the other workers. "Affairs are on the move, David—at last. Lennox has achieved it—with some help from St. Andrews! He has mustered an army and is ready to march, from beyond the Highland Line. To sweep Angus from power and win James his freedom."

The other made no comment.

"Come, man—this is what we have been waiting for, what I have been working for. In God's name, show some heed!"

"I heed you, yes. But—I was at Darnick!"

"Darnick! That was but a gesture, a shaken fist—and a palsied one! This is otherwise—a stabbing sword! Not a few mosstroopers, ill led, but a great army on the march, the clans moving south. And more than the clans—Gowrie, The Stormounth, Strathearn, Menteith, The Lennox, and others south of the Line. This is the challenge to Angus. Argyll, Atholl, Erroll, Huntly, the Marischal—all these earls are in it, lords and chiefs by the score. And Holy Church paying the siller! This time Angus has war on his hands, not gestures! Do not tell me that you, of all men do not rejoice?"

The other shrugged. "As to rejoicing, I reserve mine, mean-time. If James can be won out of Angus's grip, then none will be more glad than I. So long as he is not to fall into other hands little less harsh. But—major war? Scots slaying Scots by the hundred, the thousand—is that the price? Aye—and is that not what Henry Tudor seeks? To weaken the realm so that he can take it over?"

"Angus put down, and the realm united round the young King, would set Henry back, man. That is sure. This is the only way to get rid of Angus. I have been scheming and planning—aye, and paying—for this these many months. While you were shut up in Holyrood, I have been sowing the seed—now, pray God, is the harvest! And a deal more vital for Scotland than your wretched oats, David Lindsay! I lead a party of my uncle's retainers, and some of my own from Arbroath, to join the host at Stirling in four days time. I want you with me. You have had experience of warfare, under the late de la Bastie. I have had none. Nor have most of the Lowland lords who will be there—the legacy of Flodden where all our warriors fell. Do not say that you will not come? You, the King's friend."

Lindsay kicked almost savagely at a sheaf of oats lying there. "Damn you, man—you never let me be!" he cried. "Always you are at me to do this, to do that!"

"You can always refuse, can you not?"

"That is the curse of it! I *cannot* refuse. I never can, the way you charge me with it. Well you know it . . ."

Beaton smiled, and gripped his friend's shoulder. "That is well, then—you cannot refuse! Curse me as you will, so long as you come!"

"You are a devil, abbot as you may be . . . !"

So, three days later, Lindsay rode westwards again, en route for Stirling, with his so-demanding friend, at the head of some four score armed retainers in the fine livery of the archdiocese of St. Andrews, with more to be picked up at the great Abbey of Dunfermline and at the lesser one of Culross. Beaton was in high spirits, eager to see the consummation of all his planning.

By the time they left Culross they had almost two hundred—and had also collected Abbot John Inglis thereof, Lindsay's old former colleague and assistant tutor to James, now back less than enthusiastically to the life religious.

Fife and Fothrif left behind, fifteen miles further west, at Cambuskenneth Abbey under the soaring castle-rock of Stirling, despite almost doubling their strength again, from this place as well as the Abbeys of Lindores and Balmerino, they received news to perturb them. Lennox and Atholl with their army were no longer at Stirling, having left at first light that morning for the east, without waiting not only for the Church contingent but for the Earl of Argyll and his Campbells and the Earl of Moray and a further large company from the far north-east. It seemed that Lennox had learned that Angus had recently taken King James to Linlithgow, because Edinburgh was undergoing one of its periodic visitations of the plague—Linlithgow only eighteen miles east of Stirling. And only last night word had come from there that Angus himself had had to return to the capital temporarily for some reason, so that for the moment James was left in the care of George Douglas of Pittendreich, another of the Earl's uncles. Lennox saw it as a God-sent opportunity to strike swiftly, grab the King whilst Angus was still absent—and do the main fighting later, with James safely in their hands as figurehead. Linlithgow was a palace, no great castle or fortress, and should not be difficult to take.

If Davie Beaton was concerned over this sudden change of plan, he was not nearly so much so as David Lindsay. Lennox was no seasoned warrior, and even though his force, allegedly about five thousand, might well greatly outnumber the Douglases at Linlithgow, Angus would not be such a fool as to leave James less than adequately guarded. It was almost certain that he had heard that a host was gathering against him behind the Highland Line—indeed it was quite likely that he had gone to Edinburgh again to drum up and co-ordinate reinforcements. Besides, Linlithgow area was Hamilton territory and now that Arran was in league with Angus, the country round about would be against them. Not to have waited for Argyll and Moray, in especial, was folly.

That night the two Davids debated as to what they should do—whether to hurry on after Lennox, with their near four hundred, or to wait for the Campbells and Moray men. Lindsay was in favour of the latter, for the Campbells were seasoned fighters and Argyll could put a couple of thousand men in the field, at least; thus they would have a strong and well-led force to go to Lennox's aid, if he needed it. Beaton argued that immediacy was more important. Lennox would take only a few hours to reach Linlithgow. If he needed help, he needed it now rather than vaguely in the future. If Argyll or Moray were not reported nearby first thing in the morning, they should hurry on eastwards after Lennox, with all speed.

Beaton won, of course; the men were his, even though Lindsay was there as the experienced campaigner. And at sun-up, with no word of new arrivals from north or west, Holy Church's contingent set off along the south side of Forth for Linlithgow, with some trepidation.

They went by St. Ninians and the mustering-place for the Bruce's mighty victory at Bannockburn, passing the mill thereof where James's grandfather had died ingloriously, and on through the great Tor Wood which stretched for many miles to above Falkirk, where Wallace had suffered defeat—for this was the cockpit area of Scotland. Thereafter, keeping to the high ground of Muiravonside, they crossed the Redding and Polmont moors until presently they could see the green low hills around Linlithgow some miles ahead, and began to drop down to the lower levels. From here all looked entirely peaceful.

It was as they neared the valley of the Lothian Avon that they caught up with Lennox, relieved to find that so far there had been no hostilities. But that situation appeared to be about to end. Lennox, Atholl and the other lords and chiefs were clustered on the summit of a wooded knoll overlooking the quite deep river-valley, their troops resting all around, part Highland, part Lowland, each category keeping well apart from the other.

The two Davids rode up to the knoll—and Lindsay was surprised to find his father-in-law there, along with the Kennedy chief, the Earl of Cassillis, and a batch of Stewarts, the Lords Avondale and Innermeath, the Bishop of Caithness, and the Highland Stewarts of Appin, Ardvoirlich, Garth, Fasnacloich and Invernahyle. They were loud in argument, amidst much pointing and gesticulation.

The bridge over the Avon could not actually be seen from here—the only one upstream or down for many miles, and carrying the main Edinburgh-Stirling road. It seemed that their scouts reported that the bridge was held against them, by Hamiltons under Arran himself, with some Douglas support. The main enemy force was massed on the up-sloping far side of the river, but a strong party had been thrown forward to this side to hold a bridgehead. The dispute on the knoll was as to tactics. Atholl was a huge, golden man, shoulder-long hair and silky

101

beard gleaming, black armour so chased and engraved with gold that little of the steel was noticeable, known as The Magnificent, on account of his princely extravagance. He was advocating, demanding indeed, direct assault on the bridge, asserting that they could easily over-run the defenders there with a Highland charge and their superior numbers. Cassillis and most of the Highland Stewarts agreed with this. Lords Lindsay, Avondale and Innermeath however, declared that it would be too costly, that even though they won the bridge itself, they could be bottled up at the other side unable to get sufficient men across its narrow passage to break out. They must seek a crossing elsewhere. Lennox himself appeared undecided.

The arrival of the two newcomers went all but unnoticed, save by Lennox—who possibly saw in them the means to help him make up his mind.

"Beaton—Lindsay!" he greeted. "How say you? Linlithgow Bridge is held against us, and Arran masses his Hamiltons beyond. But less than our numbers. Shall we attack?"

Beaton gestured to his friend to speak first.

David shook his head. "It would be folly to assail a held bridge, with a large force waiting behind it. You might capture the bridge itself, but you could get only a few men across at a time. They would be wiped out as they reached the other side."

"What, then?"

"You have little choice. Either you wait here for the enemy—let *them* make the crossing. Or you cross the river elsewhere."

"Another craven!" Atholl exclaimed. "What are we? Bairns, to be given lessons? We have here a Highland host, man—they will take that bridge and swarm beyond it, like bees out of a bike!"

"Ringed in beyond by steel-clad men on horses, my lord, your bees will never win out of their bike to swarm!"

"Where else could we cross?" Lennox asked. "It is a steep valley, although the river itself is not very deep. We cannot just sit here, waiting. *They* will not cross to us, I swear!"

Beaton spoke. "There is a small nunnery something over a mile upstream, the Priory of Emmanuel. Under the protection of the Order of St. John of Jerusalem, whose Preceptory of Torphichen is but two miles further—but at the other side of this Avon. I know it well. There is much coming and going between the two houses. There is no bridge—but there is a ford—the Nuns' Ford. It is narrow for such a host as this, but . . ."

"A ford! Only a mile up . . . ?"

"Here's better talking," Lord Lindsay said.

"Narrow you say?" Lennox asked. "How narrow?"

"I cannot say. I did not measure it. Scarcely made for an army to cross. But . . ."

"Three abreast? Four . . . ?"

"Oh, yes—that, surely."

"Then let us be on our way. We had wasted overlong here . . ."

"Wait, my lord—wait a little," David Lindsay broke in. "This is Hamilton country. The Hamiltons may well know this Nuns' Ford. If Arran is waiting, and watching the bridge, he may be watching the ford also. And if it is narrow, it could be almost as easily defended as the bridge . . ."

"God save us from the fearful!" Atholl cried. "Are we men or, or nuns! I say, let us down to this bridge and see what steel can do, Highland steel! Enough of this talk."

"Wait, John," Lennox said. "Much depends on this." These two, chiefs of independent Stewart septs, were married to sisters. "Lindsay of the Mount learned war with de la Bastie, the First Knight of Christendom."

"Let my lord of Atholl lead his Highlandmen down to the bridge," David nodded. "This I was about to suggest, but to wait, in full view, not to attack. The rest, the horsed host, to make for the ford, unseen. See you, Arran and the Hamiltons will know that we are here—but they cannot see us yet. Nor we them. They cannot know our full numbers. If part of your force shows itself this side of the bridge and seems to prepare to attack, Arran will assume belike that this is the *entire* host. Especially if it displays all the banners, and not a few armoured knights as well as the clansmen. The rest of us, horsed, hasten up to the ford, to cross, out of sight, to win *behind* the Hamiltons. Then we have them front and rear. Even if the ford is watched and word sent to Arran, he will not dare to leave the bridge. He will have to split his force . . ."

"Good! There speaks good sense," Lennox cried. "John—you hear? Take you the clansmen and go show yourselves at the bridge. Make as though to assail it. I will take the horsed people and try to get behind Arran. Give me a little time . . ."

Atholl snorted, but swung his mount round.

With much blowing of horns thereafter the two distinct portions of the army divided, not difficult since they kept well apart anyway, the Lowland cavalry to mount their beasts and the Highlanders to cluster in their clans and sept groupings. There were far more of the latter than the former; nevertheless, the mounted force, including the new Church contingent, which presently set off at speed southwards, numbered above one thousand. Some lords and knights remained with Atholl, to make a show, with all the colourful flags and banners. Whether Atholl, on his own, would wait and be content merely to demonstrate rather than promptly hurl into the attack, was an open question.

Davie Beaton led the way up through the rolling grassy braes and open woodland which flanked this west bank of the Avon, safely hidden from the east or Linlithgow side. It proved to be somewhat more than a mile to the Priory of Emmanuel, but they were soon there. Leaving the cohorts of cavalry to be eyed askance by the alarmed nuns, with Abbot John Inglis to reassure them, the leaders rode down to the riverside, to inspect the ford.

It was as David had feared. A little group of Hamilton horsemen were hanging about on the far side of the river, watching. At sight of the newcomers, these bunched together and came down to the head of the ford, obviously prepared to contest passage.

"No more than a score," Lord Lindsay commented. "These cannot hold us up for long."

"But they can send to warn Arran," his son-in-law pointed out. "Only a mile away, if Arran is but behind the bridge. A mile back—and he could have a force here in only a short time. We will have to get our people across fast, these guards or none."

Davie Beaton was forward, peering into the river. "Twelve feet wide, the causeway, not much more," he reported. "Four abreast at the most. And slippery."

"No delay, then," Lennox decided. "Bring the men, with all haste." His sword drawn, he was the first to urge his horse down into the water.

"Wait, my lord," David advised. "Why fight against odds? Let *them* do that. Now they see only a few men here. But when our host appears, these Hamiltons will perceive that they have no chance of holding us up, and will bolt." He did not add that a field commander's task was to guide and control his force, not to act as outrider, however gallant.

Quickly the first files of the cavalry appeared, and were directed down into the water. Great blocks of stone had been set there, some two feet below the present surface, much shallowing the river. In this early September, after the summer, the water was running low; but this advantage was to some extent offset by the quantities of green slime on the stones, which would be swept clean by winter's floods. Davie Beaton was urgent in advising the horsemen to go slowly, carefully across, as their mounts could so easily slip and fall, to create havoc behind.

Fortunately, as more and more men appeared from the direction of the Priory, the waiting Hamiltons recognised that they could not possibly do more than hold up the first files for a brief interval, and evidently decided that this effort would be pointless. They wheeled around, then, and spurred away up the opposite bank and disappeared.

Lennox was not to be deterred from being one of the first to cross. And once over he still would not wait for all this force to make the passage, but himself pressed on, up the bank and then downstream again, with a mere hundred or so at his back. David Lindsay cursed, shouted to Beaton at the other side that he was going to try to restrain the Earl, and raced off in pursuit.

Up on the higher ground there was still no extended view, owing to the rolling nature of the land hereabouts, certainly no sign of the enemy. David pounded after Lennox, with others coming piecemeal behind him.

He came up with the Earl and his group at the lip of a steep ravine, where a tributary stream came in from the east, Lennox prospecting the best way across. David urged a general halt here meantime, to assemble their host in some sort of battle order before moving on. And if a detachment of Arran's force appeared in the interim, this was a good defensive position to withstand it.

But Lennox would not hear of it. He was not looking for any defensive position, he cried. He was here to rescue the King, at Linlithgow; and that was not to be done by sitting inactive and waiting to be attacked.

He set off zigzagging down into the ravine and up the other side, David following on unhappily.

After a little more riding, this advance-guard began to hear the din of strife ahead of them. Atholl was evidently making no mere demonstration at the bridge but was in action. Lennox grew the more eager.

Breasting one of the gentle green ridges of that terrain, suddenly they obtained something of the looked-for vista. Ahead of them the land sank to a wide area of grassy pastureland, still undulating but open now, dotted with wheeling agitated groups of cattle. Beyond, they could see a confused mass of men and banners, but owing to a further drop in the land-level towards the road and bridge, they could not distinguish details of what went on.

Although more of their mounted men had now caught up with them, including some of the lords and knights, Lennox still would not wait for any marshalling of his force. No point in that, he claimed, until they could see the whole field before them, how the enemy was placed, and decide how they were to attack. Clearly Atholl's people were engaged and would require assistance swiftly. He plunged on.

David found Beaton cantering alongside, and panted out his opinions of Lennox's odd generalship. But there seemed to be nothing that they could do meantime, save to keep up and try to control the situation somewhat once it was clarified.

It was as the Stewart host was thundering in great style but no order at all across the grassland, spread out over a great area, both in length and depth, that David became aware that some, many, of those milling cattle-beasts were behaving oddly, not just charging about in confusion as before but heading in a solid mass—and heading towards them, in a stampede, heads down and tails high, and covering quite a wide front. It took only a little longer to perceive the reason—the banners and pennons and lance-tips showing behind the steaming mass of bullocks. The Hamiltons had seen the Stewart advance and were using the old device of driving a herd of frightened cattle before them, to confuse and break up an enemy formation. The fact that there was no formation ahead of them would not lessen the confusion.

In fact what happened thereafter was even worse than that, absolute chaos, a wild clash of charging bullocks and rearing, toppling horses, riders flung from saddles and trampled on by bellowing cattle-beasts, weapons useless. Lennox, in the forefront, was one of the first to go down, disappearing in the steaming, stinking, neighing press, other leaders likewise. David Lindsay, a little behind, recognising what the impact would produce, had just time to take some avoiding action, pulling his mount cruelly back on its haunches and dragging it right round in the same movement, to spur it in the other direction, backwards, however craven-seeming, and yelling to Beaton to do the same. They did not escape all contact with the hurtling cattle, being cannoned into and jostled. But at least they were now proceeding approximately in the same direction as the crazed animals, and they kept their seats. It was a mad situation altogether, to find themselves actually smashing back amongst their own Church followers.

But, however unheroic in appearance, it served some purpose. For seeing their leaders thus in headlong retreat, the Churchmen sought to slow their onwards rush and slew round after them. This also resulted in dire disorder, but at least most of their people escaped the cattle stampede.

Probably the general wide scattered nature of the Stewart advance had its advantages in some degree, for it meant that quite a large proportion did not become involved in the shambles at the front, even though they were still unco-ordinated and more or less leaderless.

Lindsay and Beaton, once out of danger of being over-run, sought to produce at least some order out of the turmoil. Reining round again, David shouted:

"A wedge! A wedge! Here—to us. A Lindsay! A Beaton! Form a wedge. Quickly! A wedge . . ."

Probably few of those who heard him had any real understanding of what he meant, being only the personal guards of prelates and the like, not trained battle-fighters; but at least they rallied round, thankful for some leadership and command. Urgently David sought to marshal them into something of the traditional arrowhead formation, whilst Beaton, for his part, waved in latecomers of their own or of other groups. How many they mustered thus, they had no opportunity to assess, but there would be well over one hundred.

There was no time to wait for more or to try to form these up in better shape. The priorities were vital and immediate—to present some sort of organised opposition to the Hamiltons, for the rest to rally to; and if possible to rescue Lennox—for any force which discovers its commander fallen is in danger of losing its morale as well as its focal point.

Placing himself and Beaton together at the apex of the distinctly ragged wedge, David shouted for their men to keep tight formation, to protect each other, and if the outer riders tired or were wounded, the inner ones to replace them. That was as much as he could do in the circumstances. He flung his swordpoint forward in the advance gesture, and dug in his spurs, Davie at his side.

Ahead, the situation was still in disarray but less densely so, for a fair proportion of the cattle-beasts had made off, singly and in groups, the surviving horsemen were recovering and some of those unhorsed regaining their mounts. But as a fighting force it was a travesty and many bullocks remained in milling frenzy. A tight group of Stewart lairds, dismounted, stood around the fallen Lennox, swords and dirks at the ready. And beyond, a couple of hundred yards or so perhaps, the horsed Hamilton force had drawn up in line, on a minor grassy crest, clearly waiting for the right moment, with the cattle out of the way, to charge down and finish off their utterly disorganised enemy. A number of banners flew above them, but in the centre was one larger than the others, the undifferenced arms, red-on-white, of the Hamilton chief, Arran himself.

As David Lindsay took all this in, he had only moments to make up his mind. If he and his merely went to join the Stewart lairds round Lennox, they would lose all the advantage and impetus of their driving wedge, and just be there to be ridden down also when the Hamiltons charged. On the other hand, a direct assault on the waiting enemy line, whilst risky indeed, possibly disastrous, could have great impact, even change the entire situation by, in turn, disorganising Arran's front and giving more time for the scattered Stewarts elsewhere to rally. Arran was notoriously no warrior and might well not react swiftly. If it had been his son the Bastard's banner there in the middle, it would have been very different.

These thoughts flashing through his mind, another was no less evident. To assail Arran with any element of surprise, it would be necessary to plough his wedge first right through that entanglement of their own fellows, horses and bullocks, a grievous thought. But to seek to ride round it all would lose them impetus and also give the Hamiltons all the warning and time they would require to prepare to meet an attack. Lindsay made his decision and drove on the harder.

Yelling their slogans, mainly "A Beaton! A Beaton!" the wedge-formation crashed headlong into the mêlée of men and animals, hurling aside and knocking over right and left with the speed and weight of their impact. At the tip of it all, the two Davids were all but jerked out of their saddles, but were held approximately in position more by the impetus from behind and the pressure at the sides than by their own efforts. It was grievous to see the Stewarts going down around them, some trampled under hooves.

They drove on relentlessly, to thunder past within a score of yards of the ring around Lennox. Lindsay waved in that direction, but that was all, his attention concentrated on maintaining his position and cutting a way through the crush as nearly directly as possible towards that great banner of Arran's.

Pounding and shouting, at last they were through, leaving a trail of ruin behind, with only that couple of hundred yards between them and the long, stationary Hamilton line. Presumably it only then dawned upon Arran and his people that precipitate assault upon them was intended by this comparatively small company, and that something would have to be done immediately. But these were no more trained cavalry than were their opponents, and the instinctive reaction was to get out of the way of that menacing arrowhead—and Arran himself, although hereditary Lord High Admiral of Scotland, was no veteran general, despite his years. He was indeed almost the first to rein round and urgently seek a less exposed position, cannoning into his banner-bearer and those behind in the process. Others took prompt example from their chief, and the centre of the line broke in disorder.

It does not take many moments for even cantering horses to cover two hundred yards, and in the press and confusion little of escape, and certainly no defensive strategy, was achieved before the wedge struck. Although this clash was against sword- and lance-bearing riders, not cattle-beasts and unhorsed men, the difference was not so noticeable as might have been expected, for the Hamiltons were more concerned with getting out of the path of the attackers than the bullocks had been, jostling and impeding each other in their haste, and so close-packed in consequence that their lances were useless and even swords were difficult to wield. The long line, which had been formed thus mainly to act as a barrier to prevent the mounted Stewarts from reaching and rescuing Atholl's Highlanders at the bridge, although perhaps three hundred yards long was only three or four men deep, and this presented no great obstacle to the charging spearhead, which ploughed through in less time than it takes to tell. Admittedly its members had little opportunity to use their swords either, although they knocked over a few of the Hamiltons mainly by collision; but the principal objective was to break up the lines and to upset the leadership. This certainly was achieved.

Lindsay now was faced with his most difficult task, to swing round his wedge to drive in the reverse direction without losing all formation, a large enough problem even with trained cavalry and almost hopeless with these churchmen's retainers. Nevertheless, yelling repeated instructions and waving his sword in pointing gestures, he attempted just that manoeuvre, pulling round left-about, the direction in which he had seen Arran go, and seeking to make as tight an arc of it as was possible.

It was not very successful, in fact, and the resultant wedge was scarcely recognisable as such. Also speed and impetus inevitably dropped. But, determined to retain as much of their advantage as possible, he shouted his orders to reform, and without waiting for any real improvement, led the way back, still with Beaton at his side, spurring to regain speed.

At least his target was not difficult to identify, for Arran's banner-bearer was faithful and kept close to the Earl, round whom numbers of the Hamiltons were rallying. Directly for the great flag Lindsay headed his now oddly-shaped company.

It was scarcely an acceptable military manoeuvre, but at least it had purpose and drive, which elsewhere was notably lacking on that field. Arran's group were in the main leaders, not the led, but that did not make a unified force of them, especially as they got little lead from their chief. Some were for dispersing, some for forming a wedge of their own, some indeterminate. In these circumstances, the dispersers inevitably won, and the group disintegrated in various directions. David headed, as far as he was able, after Arran and his bannerman and a few others foremost in dispersing.

The situation developed almost farcically, with over one hundred churchmen chasing the Lord High Admiral and about a dozen others—the dozen darting hither and thither making for nowhere in particular. But in the nature of things, one hundred are less easy to twist and turn than are a dozen, also slower, and little was achieved. David was deciding to abandon this profitless exercise when Beaton reached over to grasp his arm, and point. Up on the ridge, almost half-a-mile to the east, a new situation was developing. A long line of horsemen were silhouetted, and being added to, many hundreds with banners innumerable, two in the centre large and unmistakable—the red-on-gold Lion Rampant of Scotland and the Red Heart of Douglas.

"See—Angus! With the King!" Beaton shouted. "Worse trouble, now!"

That Lindsay recognised all too well. The farce was in dire danger of becoming a disaster. He yelled and gesticulated to his following to break off and swing round. He would head for Lennox and his dismounted group, rescue them at least, and then race back to the ford before the Douglases came up with them.

Abandoning pursuit of Arran, this they attempted, and achieved in some measure, quickly driving off the comparatively small numbers attacking the Stewart lairds. Lennox they found to be wounded, but able to stand. Hastily recapturing a few of the riderless horses, they mounted some of the Stewarts and took up the rest behind their own saddles, all the time eyeing that ominous advancing array beneath the flapping standards. It was going to take them all their time to reach the Nuns' Ford unassailed.

They did not quite manage it. A company of the Douglas host detached itself from the left flank of that lengthy front and came driving hard, at a tangent, to cut them off. Spur as they would, David's party could not outride these, who were racing downhill and had not the intervening ravine to contend with. It became obvious that these Douglases knew of the ford and were determined to prevent their crossing.

"We must stand. And fight!" David jerked.

"To what end?" Beaton demanded. "They outnumber us already. The longer we stand the more will come. We will not reach that ford. We are held."

"What, then? Yield?"

"What else? No service to die! For nothing. Yield. Young

111

James—perhaps he will be the saving of us? If they have him under yonder standard. They will not execute the King's friend out-of-hand! Nor the Abbot of Arbroath, I think!"

It was a hard decision to take, tamely to surrender. But there seemed to be nothing else, in reason, for it. This battle was already lost—if it could be called a battle. Lindsay nodded, and reined over towards a little mound in the levellish area just beyond the ravine, to pull up, waving and shouting to his following fairly eloquently. None of his churchmen looked outraged at this development, whatever the Stewarts' attitude. Some of these spurred off on their own.

They had only moments to wait before the Douglases arrived, pounding up, shouting their slogan, swords drawn, lances lowered. Swiftly, expertly enough—trained mosstroopers these—they surrounded their stationary quarry.

From behind the two Davids one voice was upraised—Lennox's, weak, weary. "All is lost, then? Lost!"

"Only the day is lost, my lord," Beaton answered him. "There will be other days. You are something recovered?"

A burly, stocky, red-bearded man of middle years rode forward out of the milling circle of newcomers, well-armoured. He waved his sword at them, on their mound.

"You—like conies on a warren! Do you yield to me?" That was harshly demanded. "I am Mains. Douglas of Mains."

"We have heard of your name, Aye, we yield—to avoid unnecessary bloodshed," Beaton declared, now taking charge. "I am David, Abbot of Arbroath. And this is David Lindsay of the Mount, King's Procurator and Extra Pursuivant."

The other seemed unimpressed—looking past them, indeed. "Is that not Lennox, I see? The Earl?" Mains demanded, pointing. "Hiding there!"

"Yes. He is wounded, not hiding."

"You say so? My lord—your sword!" The Douglas was undoubtedly concerned for the ransom-value of his prisoners, and assessed one of the most ancient Earls of Scotland a notable prize—although a shrewder captor might have considered the Abbot of Arbroath, the second richest Abbacy in the land, and nephew of the Primate and Chancellor, as still more profitable.

Lennox, in evident pain and half-dazed, had lost his sword in the affray earlier and did not appear to understand what the Douglas wanted. Some of his Stewart lairds were protesting

112

angrily and there was much shouting and altercation, Mains clearly considered to be of insufficient status to yield to for such as themselves. It would have been almost amusing had it not been, in fact, grimly serious.

The real gravity of the situation, however, was demonstrated all too speedily. One of Mains' lieutenants reined close to Beaton, knocking the proffered sword out of his hand but reaching out to wrench the gold chain with the small crucifix from about his neck—the only symbol of his office other than the abbot's ring which he wore—when another company of horsemen came cantering up. This was still more numerous than the Douglas's and under a much larger banner—the white-on-red of Hamilton but differenced by a black diagonal band across from top-left to bottom-right, the bend-sinister or heraldic symbol for illegitimacy. More than one individual was entitled to blazon that device undoubtedly—but one only was likely to flaunt it thus in action—Sir James Hamilton of Finnart, the notorious Bastard of Arran, eldest of the Lord High Admiral's illegitimate brood. The two Davids knew him well, as an unscrupulous but able and ambitious man of about their own age. He was tall and darkly handsome, with fine features and a noble brow but notably thin cruel lips. He carried one shoulder slightly higher than the other. He ignored both Beaton and Lindsay meantime.

"Ho, Douglas," he called authoritatively. "Who commands here? You, Mains? I see that you have netted a pretty parcel of fish! But you have taken one of mine, man." He pointed. "Lennox. The traitor himself!"

"Lennox is mine—*my* prisoner," the Douglas growled. "What do you want with him?"

"Not yours—mine. My people unhorsed him, in fair fight. Before you saw fit to take the field! I want him."

"And shall not have him!" Mains roared. "To me he, and they all, surrendered. You are too late, Hamilton."

"Fool! Do you not know who I am? I am Finnart. Son to Arran, the Admiral, I demand . . ."

"Son o' a sort! I care na whether you were Arran himsel'! Or young Jamie Stewart on his bit throne! Yon's my prisoner—they all are. And bide mine." The older man grinned mockingly and waved a hand. "You can have one o' his esquires, if it suits you . . ."

113

But the Bastard, paying no least heed, kicked his magnificent mount through the press, to Lennox's side. Cold-eyed, he stared at the Earl.

"So, traitor—it comes to this, does it!" he jeered. "You thought to outmatch Hamilton and grasp the King. We shall teach you better, I swear, than to assail honester men."

Lennox clearly had to exert much effort to speak at all, even to remain upright in the saddle. "It ill . . . becomes you . . . such as you . . . to talk of honester men!" he declared thickly. "Seek you . . . honest parentage first! And to say traitor—you who aid Angus . . . to hold the King's Grace . . .!"

Hamilton's hand shot out, furiously to slap the Earl across the face.

Both Lindsay and Beaton started their beasts forward to intervene, in protest, but it was Mains who got there first.

"Hands off my prisoner, Finnart!" he cried. "Hear you? They all are mine. Douglas's."

"God's curse on you, scum! I told you . . ." The dark man gestured with the hand that had struck the Earl. "A pox—you may have some of these. And this milkmaster of a false priest!" And he flung a scornful glance at Beaton. "But Lennox is my property. Do not meddle with matters too high for you, man. I take him. After all, he is my cousin!"

That was true, at least. Lennox was son to Arran's sister.

"For the last time—no!" Mains raised his mailed arm towards the ranks of waiting Douglases. "Take him—if you dare! There are more Douglases nearby than these, I warn you!"

"Fiends of hell—dare? Finnart!" Handsome features contorted, the Bastard reined the yard or two closer to Lennox. His hand fell to his waist, to his dirk's hilt—he had not deigned to draw his sword. Like lightning he whipped out the gleaming dagger. "By the Christ—if *I* may not have him, none other shall!" he exclaimed.

Ferociously he lunged over, to plunge the steel into the Earl's throat, just above the armour's gorget. Twice, thrice, he stabbed expertly, then wrenched the reddened weapon clear and contemptuously wiped it clean on his victim's sagging person, as with a bubbling groan Lennox sank, slewed and toppled from the saddle to crash to the ground, spouting blood.

A short bark of a laugh and the Bastard of Arran spat, reined his horse round and spurred away, without a glance at anyone else, his men falling in behind him. Stupified, appalled, all others stared, at first too shocked to move.

David Lindsay was the first to jump down, to run and sink to his knees beside the prostrate Earl, whilst Douglas of Mains lifted his great voice in furious profanity.

John Stewart of Lennox's last breath choked in a bloody froth.

In the confusion, indignation and recriminations which followed, the other captives, at least, all but forgot their own dangers and problems.

Developments followed fast, however. Arran himself, no longer being chased, rode up, now in the company of none other than Angus. Presumably they had already been told of Lennox's death, for the former, a thin, lantern-jawed ageing man of fine but weak features, went straight to where the body lay, dismounted and bent down, gazing at his nephew, head ashake, slack lips moving.

All around men paused, to turn and watch.

It was Davie Beaton who broke the sudden silence. "Your son did this, my lord," he said evenly, levelly. "Finnart. Slew an unarmed and wounded man. Unprovoked, in wanton spleen. Your son . . ."

The other did not answer, did not so much as look up, but sank on his knees beside the corpse. His hand, trembling a little, went out to touch Lennox's face. Then rising, he took off the handsome cloak he wore over his armour, scarlet with the ermine cinquefoils of Hamilton, and spread it over his nephew. Perplexed, embarrassed, men looked on at the extraordinary scene.

Douglas of Mains found his rough voice. "My lord—Lennox was *my* prisoner. To me he yielded. Then that, that skellum, your Bastard, came up. I told him. But he slew him. *Mine* . . .!" It was to his chief, Angus that he now turned.

"Aye, that is Finnart! Never heed, Sandy—you will not suffer. But these others. *I* want Beaton, nephew to the former Chancellor. Do as you will with Lindsay and the rest. But keep Beaton for me—or, by God's eyes I'll have your head for him! Now—where is the King? Where is young James? I said that he was to be here, to Pittendreich. By the Rood—where is he?"

"Yonder, lord," one of his people said, pointing. "There he comes. Leastways, the royal standard . . ."

Coming now from the general direction of the bridge, the

party with the Lion Rampant flag approached. James was riding beside Douglas of Pittendreich, and Parkhead, the Captain of his Guard, and with a dark scowl on his attractive young face. At sight of Lindsay, however, this vanished, replaced by a wide grin, as he spurred his mount forward.

"Davie! Davie Lindsay!" he cried. "You, here! Good, good— here's joy! It has been long . . ." His voice tailed away as he caught sight of the body part-covered by the rich Hamilton cloak, but not sufficiently to hide the gold-and-blue Stewart surcoat Lennox had worn over his half-armour, and Arran still standing there. The boy stared. "That . . . that is . . . ?"

"Lennox, Your Grace. The Earl—foully slain." That was Beaton.

"Lennox! My lord, fallen? Dead?" It was at Lindsay that he looked, biting his lip. He reined closer to where Lindsay stood, and reached down to touch, to grasp his shoulder, gulping. "Is all lost, then? You—*you* are not hurt? You are well? And, and Abbot Beaton?"

"Unhurt, Sire—but prisoners, it seems. Meantime."

"All not lost, Your Grace—only this joust!" Beaton added, with an assumption of cheerfulness.

Angus, watching and listening with a sort of grim interest, snorted a laugh. "This joust—and the last! And the next, clerk!" he jerked. "Fear not, James—Your Grace is safe from all such feckless plotters and traitors."

"They are not traitors! They are not. They are my friends, my good friends, my lord," the King asserted. "You it is who, who . . ." He restrained himself, changing the direction of his accusation. "If there be any traitor here, I say that it is this man." And he pointed to Pittendreich. "He, he mistreated me. He threatened me, coming here. Is it not treason to threaten the person of the King? He said, he said that rather than his enemies should take me from him, he would lay hold on my body. And, and if it be rent in pieces, he would be sure to take one part of it! Pittendreich said that, in front of these others. Is that not treason?"

As men gasped, Angus glanced at his uncle, and shrugged. "I am sure that Sir George but jested, Sire. He meant no ill."

"He did! He did! All heard him, and laughed. At me, the King! He said he would lay hold on me, rend me in pieces! Davie—is that not treason most foul?"

116

"I would say that it was, Sire, assuredly."

Angus reined round, indifferent, to watch Arran remount and ride away, alone, seemingly stricken. "Enough of this," he said. "We have more to do here than bicker over words. I want Atholl now. Have these prisoners secured . . ."

"They are mine, lord," Mains repeated. "All mine. Lennox was, forby . . ."

"Yes, yes. Have done, man. You will get your ransoms. But—guard them well. This Beaton in especial. He is a fox! I'll require him at your hands. Your Grace—come."

"Davie—you come with me," James exclaimed.

Lindsay looked from the King to Angus and over to Mains. "Gladly, Sire. But—I am captive. Of Douglas, here . . ."

"No. I want you with me. You *must* come."

"Your Grace—Lindsay must bide with Mains. He has yielded to him. He has the disposal of him," Angus declared, frowning.

But James, having found his friend again, was not going to be parted from him without a fight. "I want Davie Lindsay. He is mine. And I am the King. It is, it is my royal command!" That was defiant.

Angus was put in an awkward position now. However much he might ignore and over-rule the boy in private and behind closed doors, in front of many others, as here, he could scarcely disobey an express royal command. Angrily he waved a mailed hand.

"Very well. Let him come along with us. But only Lindsay. Mains—you will not lose by this. Now—come."

So David made for his horse, receiving a surprisingly mirthful grin from Beaton in the by-going, mounted, and spurred over to the King's side. James patted his friend's arm, and they rode on together after Angus and the royal standard, smiling to each other.

Angus led them back to the bridge area, where, although there seemed to be much confused fighting still going on, it was obvious that the tide of warfare was now in reverse, with Atholl's people retreated but holding the narrow bridge itself against all attacks. This in itself could probably be kept up more or less indefinitely; but the Nuns' Ford was just as much of a back-door for one side as the other, and it would not be long before Angus's men used it to get behind the Stewart defence. No

doubt even the brash Atholl perceived this, and had retired from
the forefront of his fighters to organise the rear, probably with a
view to withdrawal from the scene. Or so Lindsay assessed it.
The day was now clearly lost. He wondered what had happened
to his father-in-law. He could not see the red-and-blue banners
of Lindsay anywhere. The Lord Patrick was an old campaigner
and no doubt had seen the way things were being mismanaged
and had reacted prudently.

Angus halted well above the bridge conflict to consult with
some of his lieutenants. James was chattering incoherently,
excitedly to David when the latter suddenly pointed. Coming
fast along the far, western side of the river-bank was a large
mounted company and at its head, distinguishable even at that
distance, was the diagonal black bend across the large banner in
the Hamilton colours.

"Finnart—the Bastard!" David exclaimed. "He who slew
Lennox. He who slew Lennox. He has crossed the ford. This
will finish Atholl, I fear."

The Highland Stewarts saw and recognised the threat, and
however martially aggressive, accepted that they had now no
chance, no choice. Everywhere the breaking-off process commenced.

Angus, shrugging, turned his horse's head round once more,
shouted commands to sundry of his lairds and beckoned for
Pittendreich to bring on James, back towards Linlithgow town
and palace. This day was done.

David Lindsay rode with them. From here he could not see
what had happened to his friend Beaton. He felt somehow guilty
of desertion.

7

David Lindsay found himself to be in a most peculiar position,
part prisoner yet the King's favourite, treated with hostility by
most yet the closest of all to the monarch's person. James, in his

118

determination to hold on to him, threw tantrums if there was any move towards separating them. The boy, if he had not actually matured in the interim, appeared to have become considerably more assertive, not to say hot-tempered. Indeed however warm he was towards David personally, that man grew a little troubled at James's general behaviour and attitude to life. His natural sunny disposition seemed to be somewhat clouded over, his converse abrupt, his manner suspicious. He drank too much wine, he played cards with some of the young Douglas blades, well supplied with money apparently, and his—and their—talk was much of women, in detail unsuitable for a youth of fifteen. It looked as though Angus's campaign to corrupt the lad was being all too successful, like his military efforts.

In his influence with the King, David did find that he had one ally, and a female one at that. James, it transpired, had acquired a tirewoman and seamstress, odd as this might seem. Angus, it appeared, was pursuing a new policy with the boy, whether as part of the corruption efforts or in an attempt to gain his co-operation, giving him splendid clothing, even some jewellery, keeping him supplied with money—most of which he lost at cards back to the Douglases—and similar pamperings. To attend to this new wardrobe, Janet Douglas, daughter of the Laird of Stonypath, had been appointed, a still-faced, quiet young woman, comely without being beautiful. At first, David assumed her to be another like the gipsy wench at Holyrood, but he soon realised that this was not so, that here was a modest, rather shy, not to say reserved creature, no whore nor bought woman. And that she was concerned for more than the King's clothes was soon equally apparent. She was watchful, protective without being assertive, occasionally gently chiding. James had obviously told her much about Davie Lindsay, and her interest in him, although veiled, was evident.

Angus was meantime occupying the Queen-Mother's palace of Linlithgow, a handsome and commodious establishment above its own broad loch, no stern fortress. The King had been given much better quarters than at Holyrood, so conditions were comfortable enough, physically at least.

Part of Lindsay's mental discomfort stemmed from the fact that Davie Beaton was here at Linlithgow too, removed from Mains' keeping and locked in a bare, semi-underground cell three floors below. James had asked that he be accorded better treatment, but Pittendreich, who was in charge while Angus himself was much away, ignored the plea. He was a hard man, the most sour and morose of that family.

However, on the fourth day at Linlithgow, Beaton achieved his own release from durance vile. He actually turned up in the royal quarters to say goodbye, much to Lindsay's surprise.

"How of a mercy did you effect this?" the latter demanded. "Lord—I'd have thought this beyond even *your* clever tongue!"

"I but struck a bargain with Angus," the other assured easily, "when he returned last night from Hamilton—where I gather he is now having trouble with Arran. I had to get out of here somehow."

"A bargain? With Angus? What could you give that man which he would value more than holding your person?"

"One thing only—the Great Seal of Scotland!"

Lindsay stared. "The Great Seal! You mean—man, you have not bartered the Seal for your freedom? Your uncle's office . . . ?"

"I have indeed. It is the one thing that Angus wants, needs. The Chancellor's symbol of office. He has been calling himself Chancellor, and seeking to act it, these many months. But he needs to hold the Great Seal to *make* him Chancellor. And that I can give him. It is at St. Andrews. What use is it to my uncle, in present circumstances? *He* cannot act the part, as matters are. As good as in hiding, cooped up there in his hold on the edge of the Norse Sea. And after that sorry battle at the bridge of Avon, possibly fled to France, when he heard that I was taken. The Seal is but a bauble to him, now . . ."

"Even so, next to the crown, it is the nation's symbol . . ."

"What advantage to the nation that is in chains to Angus? I must be free—to aid the nation. Do you not see? I am of no use to Scotland locked in a vaulted cell. Free, I can act, use my wits—and the power of Holy Church! Work for Angus's fall. Can you not see it, man?"

Lindsay shook his head. By this time, he ought to have been no longer surprised by the other's self-confidence, his utter faith in his own abilities and destiny—which, it had to be admitted, seldom was proved to be seriously misplaced.

"The Archbishop?" Lindsay asked. "Will he agree to yield up the Seal, entrusted to him by the realm?"

"I have no fears as to that. My one fear is that he may have already departed in our waiting ship, for France. And taken the Great Seal with him. But I did not tell Angus that!"

"And what will you do if he has? What will you do, anyway?"

"I go now to St. Andrews. And if Uncle James has gone, I will go after him and bring the Seal back. I have given my word—and even Angus accepts that. But—I think that he will probably be at St. Andrews still, and the Seal with him. I will bring it to Angus. That I have promised. And then—then I will work day and night to bring him down! Angus. I may no longer be secretary to the Chancellor—but I am still Abbot of Arbroath and secretary to the Primate of Scotland's Church. And the Church is rich, see you, rich beyond all telling! Gold, Davie. Gold and wits together may move mountains. With a little faith!"

"So-o-o! And once you start that, will St. Andrews remain a secure haven? Will not Angus come to prise you out of it? Then what of your uncle? And what of your wife and the child?"

"It may well come to that. I will move them to Arbroath Abbey. Then somewhere even more remote, secure, if need be. All Scotland lies before us, the Church everywhere. Angus will learn that!"

"And is this what Christ's Church is for? Fighting your battles?"

"Fighting the nation's battles. It is the nation's Church. It must fight to free the Lord's Anointed—James. If his anointing and kingship mean anything. Somebody must continue the fight—and fight more effectively than did Lennox and Buccleuch and the others."

"That I do agree. And shall do what little *I* can. But I too am as good as a captive here. And with nothing to exchange . . . !"

"You can do much—more than most. For you have the King's ear, and his love. You can influence James more than any, to resist and confound Angus in all ways possible. He needs the royal authority and signature to make his deeds lawful. He will take James with him where he can. If you can go also, you can do much, see you."

"I can try . . ."

They parted, then, Beaton to ride off a free man.

*　　*　　*

It was not so easy to deny the King's authority to Angus, however willing James was to co-operate. The Douglases made

121

harsh and determined taskmasters and the boy was entirely in their power. They could make conditions very unpleasant for him, and David saw it as no part of his duty to involve his liege-lord in more trouble and discomfort than was absolutely necessary. James did make himself more difficult to his captors, and suffered for it; but it only really came to delaying tactics. Indeed, one of their most galling failures related to none other than David's own father-in-law. Lord Lindsay, amongst others who had escaped from the disaster of Linlithgow Bridge, was declared to be in rebellion against the King, outwith the King's peace, and required to submit himself to the King's justice forthwith—and when he failed to do so, his lands and property were declared forfeit to the crown and handed over, in theory, to Graysteel of Kilspindie—if the latter could effectively take them. A royal warrant to this effect was amongst the many put before young James to sign—and one that he sought longest to delay, David naturally encouraging him. But the latter came to recognise that the Douglases might well be watching this warrant carefully, making a test-case of it, and could possibly make use of any opposition to give them grounds for parting him from the King's side. In the end, he actually urged James to sign the forfeiture, and in the presence of Abbot William Douglas, esteeming this the lesser evil. He imagined that the Lord Patrick was capable of fighting his own battles.

So that winter of 1527 passed uneasily, with Angus everywhere in command in Lowland Scotland, if not in the Highlands. Or, in command more in name that in fact, perhaps, for a fair proportion of the lords and chiefs were hostile, if meantime quiescent, merely biding their time. The situation could be exemplified by the fact that Graysteel did not indeed take over the Lindsay lands of The Byres of Garleton and elsewhere, contenting himself with a mere token occupation of some small properties in the Ballencrieff and Coates area adjoining his own lairdship of Kilspindie, which the Lord Patrick apparently was prepared to concede for the sake of a precarious peace; no doubt the Earl of Crawford, the Lindsay chief, a lukewarm ally of Angus, was not uninvolved in this, resenting any Douglas encroachment closer to his own superiority of Luffness. Such represented the checks and balances of the feudal realm.

At least Angus gained his official chancellorship, when Davie Beaton, in a couple of weeks, arrived again at Linlithgow with the Great Seal of Scotland. Under the excuse of paying his due homage to the King, he contrived a brief meeting with Lindsay—in which he revealed, in strictest confidence, an astonishing situation. When he had reached St. Andrews, it was to find his uncle fled. On word of the disaster at Linlithgow Bridge and the capture of Davie, the Primate had promptly lifted his archiepiscopal skirts and betaken himself off, anticipating attack by Angus. But he had not departed for France, as feared, but for pastures, sheep pastures, much nearer home. Instead of making for Arbroath Abbey or any other of the Church's major havens to hide in, he had surprisingly elected to go to one of the granges of Cambuskenneth Abbey, a sheep-run in the Ochil Hills called Bogrian Knowe, where he was ostensibly acting as an extra shepherd—although what sort of a hill shepherd the gross and over-weight prelate might make beggared the imagination. Presumably the ex-Chancellor felt safer thus, where he would be unlikely to be traced by the Douglases, the Church's chief shepherd of men become a pastor of sheep. His nephew seemed to find all this amusing in the extreme, but was quite prepared to leave his relative where he was meantime, out of the way, whilst he himself, in the Primate's name, got on with his efforts to deal with Angus.

To Lindsay's questions as to how the other proposed to set about this, Beaton was less specific than usual. In very general terms he indicated that Fife, being notably under Church influence, with its abbeys of Dunfermline, Culross, Inchcolm, Lindores and Balmerino, and its priories of Inverkeithing, Dysart, Cupar, Crail, Pittenweem, Aberdour and others, as well as the great metropolitan complex of St. Andrews itself, might suitably initiate a kind of non-military revolt against the Douglas regime which Angus would find difficulty in countering and which, he hoped, might encourage lords and great ones elsewhere, with Church urging and gold, to do likewise, nationwide, until the Douglases were so stretched and preoccupied, over the country, that a successful military venture could be mounted. If all this seemed distinctly vague, not to say improbable, to his friend, Lindsay did not say so in so many words, acknowledging that the other had a remarkable ability to effect the most un-expected developments.

Before leaving, Beaton divulged that he had removed his wife Marion and their son from St. Andrews to the remote castle of

Ethie, on the Angus coast south of Montrose, which he had purchased and put in Marion's own name, as her property, to give her security and a safe base in the possible event of disaster befalling himself. It was the first time that Lindsay could recollect his so-confident friend ever conceding that such failure was even remotely possible. It took Marion Ogilvy to get beneath his armour.

That difficult and unhappy winter the Lindsay family received three blows in quick succession. First, David's father died, at Garleton. Sir David, in his sixties, had been ailing for some time, nursed by Mirren Livingstone, so this was no great shock, however sad. It made David laird of Garleton as well as of the Mount of Lindifferon; but he was well content to leave the management of the estate in the hands of his brother. What did shock was the news, when he was barely back at Linlithgow from attending the funeral under Douglas guard in Athelstaneford kirkyard, that the Master of Lindsay, Kate's brother, had been killed in a hunting accident in Fife. And this was followed, only a few weeks later, by the sudden death of the Lord Patrick himself, at The Byres, seemingly from natural causes, however unexpected, leaving the Master's young son John to become fifth Lord Lindsay.

David grieved for the old lord, with whom he had always got on well in an undemonstrative way; and more so for the Lady Isabella, his surrogate aunt, who had now lost husband, eldest son and daughter. And of course it left the Lindsay strength in the land direly reduced, with only a child as lord, and the chief of the name, the Earl of Crawford, a feeble and bumbling character.

It was in a belated spring of chill east winds and rain-storms that word of troubles in Fife began to reach Linlithgow. At first it took pinprick form, prayers and preaching against Angus in churches, refusals by parish priests to baptise, marry and give Christian burials to Douglases; threats of excommunication. This might not greatly have worried Angus, but soon what had obviously become a campaign grew, with access to monastic mills being denied to Douglases and their tenants and friends—and two-thirds of all Fife grain was ground at Church mills. Fairs and trysts were barred to them also, grazings of the vast Church lands cancelled, increased tithes and payments demanded, and so on. All this tended to make a laughing-stock of the name of Douglas, and quickly the Fife and Fothrif Douglases and their allies were up in arms, demanding redress and vengeance on the insolent churchmen. Eventually Angus could not ignore this. And when the news was whispered that the Queen-Mother and her new husband, Henry Stewart, now living in Methven Castle in Strathearn, were in some measure behind it all, with Atholl and the Beatons, he had to make a move, despite other pressing problems connected with King Henry, Lord Dacre, the Homes and the Border Armstrongs again. But for policy reasons he was not going to make too much of it, with no desire to give the impression that this was any serious threat. So, in May, he announced that he would escort the King for a visit to the royal hunting palace of Falkland in Fife.

They set off in mid-month, a notably large company for a hunting-party, sending the main body round Forth by Stirling and Kinross whilst Angus himself, with James and his close entourage, proceeded down to the Forth shore nearby to take Queen Margaret's Ferry across by the short cut. Thereafter, carefully avoiding Dunfermline meantime, they rode by Inverkeithing's royal burgh, noting particularly its Dominican priory, and on by Lochgelly and Kinglassie and Leslie, making for the shapely breasts of the twin Lomond Hills, so prominent a sight from the East Lothian coast. They reached Falkland, nestling under the East Lomond, by early evening, although it would take their main company all of another day to get there by the Stirling bridge-crossing.

James had never seen his palace of Falkland, and David had only on occasion passed through its surrounding castleton. It was a pleasant, sleepy sort of place, comparatively small, the palace not in the best state of repair—for the late King had never used it much and it had been neglected since his death. It was famous, of course, the seat of the Stewartry of Fife, having been founded by the MacDuffs, ancient Mormaors of Fife, and taken over by the line of the Celtic kings. Here David, Duke of Rothesay, heir to the throne of Robert the Third, had been starved to death by his uncle, a previous Regent Albany. The palace itself was restricted as to accommodation, having grown out of a simple stone keep, so the township adjoining, raised to the status of a royal burgh despite its modest size, was always used for housing courtiers, and thus possessed some better houses. The royal forest, which included the Lomond Hills, came almost up to the doors.

It became obvious, even the very next day and before the rest of the Douglas contingent arrived, that Angus had not come here to hunt. He and his lieutenants did not even stay in the little palace but lodged outside. Douglas of Parkhead, the Captain of the King's Guard, was in charge of the monarch and remained in close attendance, with his minions; but the others disappeared in the morning and were not seen again for two days.

The Earl was, in fact, showing the Douglas flag in no uncertain fashion and making clear how he felt about Holy Church's campaign against him. He had few doubts, of course, as to who was principally behind it all; but he did not assail St. Andrews at first, electing to take his reprisals against Dunfermline, the richest abbey in the land and not protected by any strong castle, as was St. Andrews, so no siege would be involved. He did not destroy the abbey itself, but much of the town went up in flames, the granaries, mills, brewhouses and warehouses pillaged and destroyed and sundry folk hanged—not clergy, which might have caused repercussions elsewhere. Thereafter, he turned his attention to the Inverkeithing Dominican priory. Presumably he intended to work his way eastwards, ever nearer to St. Andrews itself.

In the meantime, James was taken hunting by Parkhead and Balfour of Fernie, Keeper of Falkland Forest, David Lindsay in attendance. For three days they hunted stags and roe on the Lomonds, revelling in the comparative freedom of the chase even though their guards were ever with them. On the third evening, with Angus said to have gone over to Edinburgh on some urgent business, but with Kilspindie and Pittendreich and others returned to Falkland, there was a diversion. Beaton of Creich, a far-out kinsman of Davie's, who was hereditary Keeper of Falkland Palace but had not so far been in evidence, arrived from St. Andrews bringing a message from the Abbot of Arbroath in the name of the Primate. This was to invite Graysteel and Pittendreich to St. Andrews next day or the day after, to discuss a solution of the present differences between Holy Church and the house of Douglas, which all must agree were to be deplored. Safe conduct for the Douglases was assured and every courtesy proffered. The distressing events at

126

Dunfermline and Inverkeithing must not be repeated, it was emphasised. It was understood that the Earl of Angus was not presently available, but no doubt his uncles would be able to negotiate in his stead. The said uncles were grimly amused, but apparently prepared to go to see Davie Beaton—and no doubt spy out the land in case of any later assault on St. Andrews.

Beaton of Creich himself did not approach King James. But, for all that, he had a communication, and a significant one, for the monarch and David Lindsay. This was surreptitiously delivered to Lindsay by one of the Falkland grooms, Jockie Hart by name, one of Creich's men, who attended to the horses of the royal party and who had acted as something of a guide and extra huntsman in the chases. Hart, contriving to get David alone, informed him that the proposed St. Andrews meeting was a ruse, in order to get the senior Douglases away from Falkland with most of their following, while Angus was absent. This for the purpose of facilitating the King's escape.

The plan was for James to request and devise a special hunt at some distance from Falkland itself, say in the Balharvie Loch and Moss area, where boars and wolves were reputed still to lurk, and which would require an early start two mornings hence, assuming that the Douglas lords would be away. Parkhead could scarcely refuse this. They would make much preparation for the expedition, and claim to require early bedding the night before. But once the palace was bedded down, Lindsay and the King should slip out quietly, disguised in servants' clothing, and make for the North Park, where the horses were grazed. There he, Jockie Hart, would be waiting for them, with three beasts saddled, and they would make their secret departure and ride for Stirling. The Abbot of Arbroath would have a party waiting to meet them at Strathmiglo, and they would then ride on westwards through the night. Lord Erskine and the Earl of Atholl would be ready to welcome them into Stirling Castle.

Needless to say, David was much exercised by this plot, perceiving more than one point where it could go hopelessly wrong. On the other hand it would be a pity not to try it, an opportunity, carefully contrived, which might not occur again for long enough. When he told James, the boy was agog, eager and in no doubts. They would do it—of course they would do it.

So, all the next day, with Graysteel and his brother departed for St. Andrews, the King made almost too much fuss about his desire to go hunt boar at Balharvie Moss and the preparations which would be necessary, special long spears to be collected for the occasion, extra local men to be engaged as beaters who knew the area and the ways of boar, and so on. James Douglas of Parkhead could scarcely refuse co-operation, and agreed that an early start would be necessary, for Balharvie was on the other side of the Lomonds, on the hillskirts between the two peaks, and a roundabout approach would be advisable to ensure that the hunt took place on ground firm enough for the horses, for much of the Moss was impassable swamp. Sunrise would be around five o'clock, when they would make a start. So the insistence was on early bedding for all concerned.

Jockie Hart managed to smuggle in some rough outer wear, suitable for concealing identity, into the royal apartments that evening, and James and David made the pretence of retiring almost immediately after the evening meal. From then until midnight, the King was in a state of excitement and impatience to be gone, restrained by David. They had to be as certain as possible that no late-bedders remained up and about, to observe the departure.

In the event, there were no problems as the pair tip-toed down the turnpike stair along the vaulted basement corridor to a rear door. This was barred, but the massive draw-bar was well-greased with goose-fat and slid into its wall-socket noiselessly. The door open, they carefully pulled the bar back into place behind them, before closing the door again, so that no early riser would be alerted in the morning to anything unusual. Then they slipped across the courtyard, making for the posterngate in the surrounding curtain-walling.

This also had a draw-bar but again it was kept greased and presented no difficulty. However, the door itself gave them their only breath-catching moments, for it creaked loudly as they opened it and this set off a dog barking somewhere in the adjoining stables. In their haste to be away from there, they omitted to pull back this draw-bar into the closed position.

Outside the walling they all but ran. It was not really dark—it seldom is in late May in Scotland. They knew the North Park well enough, only some three hundred yards from the palace, where the horses, too many for the available stabling, were enclosed to graze overnight. Here they found Hart anxiously awaiting them, worried at having heard the dog barking. He had the three mounts saddled and ready, and explained that he had deliberately not taken the King's and David's fine beasts, just in case their absence would be noted and cause an alarm any earlier than need be. James suggested leaving the park gate open, so that the other horses might stray out and cause delay in any pursuit; but both David and Hart advised against this, as again capable of drawing early attention to an abnormal situation.

Mounting, they circled the park at a quiet walk and headed northwards into the woodland, before spurring into a trot.

There was a fair road through the forest the three miles to the little burgh of Strathmiglo in the upper Eden vale, but they did not risk a canter, for the trees increased the darkness and they must go carefully however impatient the sixteen-year-old monarch.

At Strathmiglo there was a hitch, for there was no sign of Beaton's promised party as they rode through the sleeping town. There developed, however, a great barking of dogs here also, alarming David and Hart and causing them to decide that they dared not hang about in the town waiting for the missing escort. But as they hastened on, swinging westwards now up the Eden, just beyond the outskirts they were met by a single horseman who greeted them relievedly and explained that his party was hiding in some birch-scrub just a little further on, by the river-side, they also having been scared out of the burgh by the barking dogs.

Their guide led them to a group of about a score waiting in the cover of the young trees, under Beaton of Balfour, Davie's eldest brother, whom Lindsay had not come across hitherto. He had the family's good looks but was much more heavily-built. It was a surprise to find in the company Balfour of Fernie, the keeper of this royal forest, who was to have been one of the leaders of the boar-hunt—and who now proved to have been in the plot from the start; indeed had been supplying St. Andrews with up-to-the-minute information throughout. He would return to Falkland now, and turn up for the hunt at sunrise, his implication unsuspected, he hoped. There were only the briefest and almost casual respects paid to the monarch.

There was no delay thereafter, none anxious to linger in the vicinity. They bade farewell to Fernie and set off up the river-side road, west by south.

129

It was calculated that they had some thirty miles to go to reach Stirling, following the River Eden almost to Milnathort, then avoiding that town and nearby Kinross by keeping to the higher ground of the Ochil foothills, to join the hillfoots drove-road again in the Carnbo area, with thereafter a straight ride by Yetts of Muckhart, Dollar, Tillicoultry, Alva and Menstrie to the causewayhead of Stirling. They would not be able to ride really fast until Carnbo and daylight, but from then on it should be a clear run of some seventeen or eighteen miles.

At first David and James at least tended to keep glancing behind them, fearing pursuit; but as the light strengthened and they left the riverside flats for the foothill slopes, beginning to be able to see for considerable distances, with no sign of trouble, they were able to relax. Jockie Hart, the only local man, acted as guide.

A pale pink-and-gold sunrise behind them began to fill the Ochil valleys and hollows with purple shadow when they were midway between Carnbo and Yetts of Muckhart. Save for the cattle and sheep which they disturbed, they still seemed to have the morning to themselves. They settled down to steady hard riding. James was an excellent horseman and no hold-up.

They were following down the ever-widening vale of the River Devon now, as breakfast fires began to send up their blue plumes of wood-smoke into the still air; and even David Lindsay, anxious for his charge, was able to accept that they had almost succeeded in their efforts, and the King's long spell of captivity in Douglas hands was over, meantime at least. When, in the distance, the thrusting skyline of Stirling Castle could be distinguished above the morning mists of the vale, to the west, the thing was assured. A new chapter was beginning for Scotland.

Tired and mud-spattered but elated, they clattered through the climbing streets of Stirling town, drawing but little attention from the populace intent on some cattle-fair, and up to the tourney-ground fronting the castle gatehouse. The portcullis was up and the drawbridge down, although the gates were shut. But the newcomers' shouts that here was the King of Scots requiring entry to his royal fortress had scarcely begun when they were thrown wide and the Earl Marischal and the Lord Erskine came, almost at the run, out on to the bridge-timbers, to sink to their knees thereon, before their sovereign-lord, too moved even to speak.

James dismounted and went to raise them up, himself suddenly overcome with emotion. For moments they gazed at each other, words an incoherent jumble when they came. Then urgently the King pushed past them, under the portcullis and into the gatehouse pend, to turn and wave his party in after him.

"Come!" he cried. "In with you, all of you. Down with the portcullis. Up with that bridge. Bar the gates. I am free—free! Back in my own Stirling—the King! Let Archibald Douglas come for me now, and see, and see . . . !" His young voice broke. "Oh, Davie, Davie Lindsay—we're free!"

"Yes, Sire," that man said, riding in. "God save the King!"

8

James Stewart had been a king for fifteen years, but only in name. Suddenly all that was changed. Always he had had some-one controlling him, usually more or less sternly, if not harshly; now, that no longer applied. There was no regent; his mother was utterly discredited and living privately in Strathearn; Angus had lost him; Arran held no authority meantime save his nominal position of Lord Admiral. James was in his seventeenth year, a youth rather than a boy, and in many ways, precocious for his age. It dawned on him, as on those around him in Stirling Castle, that he was now the King indeed, nobody in a position to do more than advise him, ruler as well as reigner—so long as Angus could be thwarted.

And, to be sure, now the very means by which Angus had sustained his usurped authority, in the possession of the monarch's person, the royal signature and seal, the final sanctions in the kingdom, were abruptly James's own, to use against Douglas. It took only a little while for this to sink in, although David Lindsay had been thinking along these lines since their escape. James now, as it were, reached out to grasp his sceptre.

But all depended on Angus's effective suppression, and with it, the breaking up of the Douglas power. Nothing was more sure than that Angus would not be long in asserting himself. He probably would not be able to winkle James out of Scotland's strongest fortress, although he might well try; but what use was a monarch permanently shut up in a fortress? To escape was not enough—James had to act.

That very first evening, after he and David had had a sleep, on the latter's advice he called a Privy Council meeting. Nominally this was possible, Atholl, the Marischal and Erskine all being privy councillors, as was the Lord Maxwell who happened to be visiting the castle; and in theory James could swear in anyone else he chose. He wanted to make Lindsay a council member there and then, but David dissuaded him, asserting that this would be unsuitable and could cause resentment amongst the others. If he could attend, as acting-secretary say, that would serve.

So the four lords sat down with the monarch in a corner of the parliament hall, almost like conspirators in that great apartment, with Lindsay sitting in, a little back from the table to emphasise his lower status. But James was not long in demonstrating that council member or none, David was expected to take full part in the proceedings, by addressing direct remarks and questions to him—which, of course, he could by no means fail to answer. James was perhaps slightly over-assertive on this his first council meeting with himself in charge, and of course no Lord Privy Seal present to act chairman. Without preamble he plunged straight into the main urgent business—what were they to do about Angus? He would be wroth and would certainly seek to recapture the King. And he was still as powerful as ever. How was he to be countered?

Atholl, ever brash, declared that *he* would raise the Highlands, the clans again, and come to the aid of their High King. This time there would be no folly of splitting forces, as at Linlithgow Bridge. He would send for Argyll to bring his Campbell hordes, and together they would stamp the Douglas and his Lowland ruffians into their Lowland earth!

This, needless to say, raised Lowland eyebrows round that table, the Earl Marischal snorting, Erskine starting to speak and then thinking better of it, although Maxwell agreed that they should certainly send for the Earl of Argyll, who for too long had been so busy making himself a little king in the Highland west that he had quite neglected his duties to his sovereign-lord and the realm. He was after all, Lord Justice General and hereditary Master of the Household . . .

Erskine frowned. He was married to Argyll's sister.

James interrupted impatiently. "That is as may be, my lords. But anything such will take long, mustering the clans. Angus will be here any day. He will come for me. He will besiege us here, in this castle."

"He will not have cannon, Sire," the Marischal said. "It would take him time to fetch cannon from Edinburgh or Dumbarton. And he cannot take this fortress without cannon. That will give time to muster forces against him."

"And even Angus would scarce bombard a castle, I think, containing his own liege-lord," Erskine asserted.

"But he would shut us up, in siege," James exclaimed. "I would be as good as a prisoner again—only in Stirling instead of Linlithgow or Holyrood. Davie—how say you?"

"We need time, Sire, yes. To summon the leal lords and chiefs and their people, Lowland as well as Highland. But I think that Your Grace has powers which you could use, mean-time—against Angus. You can declare him outwith your royal peace. Announce that he must submit himself for trial before either parliament or this Privy Council, on charge of having constrained Your Grace's royal person. Then, if he refused so to submit himself, you can order his apprehension. And meantime, he must not approach your person save to submit, and alone. He must keep a distance of so many miles. If he does bring armed men within such distance, he is openly guilty of highest treason, and when taken must be executed."

They all stared at him.

"Angus would laugh at anything such," Atholl scorned.

"With respect, my lord—will he? Even he will not wish to have a sentence for high treason hanging over his head. Anyone who aids a man under that sentence is himself guilty of treason, I'd mind you. Which means that all his people, his friends and allies, would have this hanging over them also, if they lifted a hand in his service. All such cannot go about guarded all the time. It would become the duty of all leal men to apprehend them in the King's name. Angus would become outlaw, and all who supported him actively likewise. How many would choose to put themselves in that position? All this is in the King's power to proclaim. I have thought much on it, as to what could be done when the King was free."

"My God—he is right!" Maxwell cried. "It could give Angus pause, trouble his people, leave them reluctant."

"I could *do* this?" James asked. "Make such pronouncement?"

"You are the King. It is within your royal prerogative, Sire, to condemn for high treason to yourself."

"How could it be proclaimed?" Erskine demanded. "To be effective, all must know it, hear it."

"This Council can announce it, my lord, in the first instance. Then a parliament should be called, to endorse it. A parliament is now needed, anyway . . ."

"That would take more time. Angus could be here tomorrow," James said.

"If he comes so quickly, then he must be told in person. An envoy from Your Grace must warn him as he approaches."

"He might but spurn it as an empty threat and mistreat the envoy."

"Send someone with authority . . ."

"Send Lyon," Maxwell suggested. "The King-of-Arms. It is in itself treason to mistreat the Lord Lyon on the King's business."

"Yes . . ."

"If there is to be a parliament, you will require a Chancellor," the Marischal put in. "Angus himself is at present Chancellor. Or claims to be . . ."

"Then he must be replaced at once. Who?"

They eyed each other. The chancellorship held great power and authority; but not everyone would want the position or could sustain it. It demanded eloquence, secretarial and clerkly skills, nimble wits, the ability to compromise and deal. Many of the greatest lords could not do much more than pen their own names. Traditionally, too, the office went to a senior churchman.

"Beaton grows old and slow. He held the Seal perhaps over long," Atholl asserted. "He has enough to do as Primate. Forby, none knows where he is! I say appoint my brother Andrew,

Bishop of Caithness. He is to be trusted, leal, and has sound wits."

The Earl Marischal demurred. "He is not so long a bishop. Others are a deal more senior. Holy Church might not like it, when there is the Archbishop of Glasgow, Dunbar, who was Your Grace's preceptor, here."

James made a face. He had scarcely loved Dunbar.

"Aye—if not Beaton, Dunbar. He is sound enough—even if he does write poetry!" Erskine cast a glance at Lindsay.

James also looked at that man, doubtfully. "How say you, Davie?"

The other hesitated. He felt that he owed it to Davie Beaton to support his uncle. Yet he was well aware that the Primate had been neglecting his duties as Chancellor for some time—Davie himself admitted it. But being the Chancellor's secretary gave the nephew much influence.

"The Abbot of Arbroath, Sire—would he not make an excellent Chancellor himself? Few more able in your kingdom. Your true friend. And he did contrive your escape here."

But there were murmurs from the others, mutterings that Beaton was too young, too clever by half, sufficiently up-jumped already, and the like. James darted uncertain glances around.

Lindsay realised that he had probably done his friend no service. "If not Chancellor, Sire, then perhaps some other office, close to your royal self. He has great influence with the Church, the Primate's right hand."

"Yes. Some other place. I would not be here but for him. Archbishop Dunbar, then, for Chancellor meantime? Tell him to call a parliament. Here?"

"I think not, Sire." That was Maxwell again. "It must not look as though you were beleaguered in this fortress. Edinburgh is your capital. It should be there for your first parliament as ruling monarch . . ."

So it was agreed. In Edinburgh, as soon as it could be made effective—for this parliament must be well-attended and successful, a demonstration of the nation's support and regard for the young sovereign. Always, of course, assuming that Angus could be contained, if not disposed of.

They did not have long to wait for some indication as to the answer to that question. The very next day, around noon, John Inglis, the Abbot of Culross, sent a mounted messenger

135

hot-foot to Stirling to inform the King that a large company of Douglases under Kilspindie and Pittendreich had halted briefly at his Forth-side abbey on their way to Stirling, declaring openly that they were going to collect the King there, and that the Earl of Angus himself, coming from Edinburgh, would join them at Stirling Bridge. This dire news sent James and many of his people up to the topmost towers of the castle to gaze eastwards by north. And, sure enough, just above the windings of the Forth, spread like a map before them from this lofty vantage-point, some three miles away and plain enough to be seen in the levels of the Powis area, was the dark mass of a sizeable body of mounted men.

The King gripped David Lindsay's arm. "They come! They come!" he exclaimed, thick-voiced. "Davie—what can we do? So soon! Angus coming . . . !"

"Fear nothing—you are safe here, Sire. At the worst, they cannot reach you in this hold. But we must do as we decided. At once. Send to inform Angus, warn him about his being outwith your peace and liable to a charge of high treason. An envoy . . ."

"But it is too late to send Lyon. He is not here. Who else could we send? The Marischal? He is the one of the great officers of state."

"Yes. But . . . better a herald. Not the Marischal himself. Or one of the others. Angus could lay hands on any such without it being treason, claim that he, or other, was but one of the lords against him. But a herald is different, protected. A royal herald . . ."

"But none are here! Save, save *yourself*, Davie. You are a pursuivant, now. They made you a pursuivant . . . You could go."

Lindsay frowned. "Willingly, Your Grace. But I would scarce carry sufficient authority. They know me too well and do not love me! Besides, I was only made Extra Pursuivant by Angus himself at Holyrood to have me paid for by your Treasury. He did it in your name, of course—but he is not going to be impressed by *my* position!"

"But—you say in my name? The King makes the heralds, then? So—I can make you greater than an Extra Pursuivant. Could I not make you Lord Lyon? Now, instead of the man—Clephane, is it?"

"Not Lyon, Sire, that would not do. The Lord Lyon

King-of-Arms cannot be replaced like some servitor. Sir Thomas Clephane is one of the most important officers of your realm. You cannot start by supplanting him out-of-hand."

"Then another, a new important herald, next to Lyon. What are they? Albany? Rothesay? Carrick—no, that is but a pursuivant." James swung on Erskine who had come up. "My lord, what herald could I make Davie Lindsay here so that he can go to Angus in my name and tell him, tell him what we decided last night about high treason? Rothesay and Albany and . . . is there not Marchmont? Marchmont Herald?"

"Marchmont is held, Your Grace. All these are held, already filled. You cannot use them. Likewise Unicorn and Carrick Pursuivants. Aye, and Kintyre also . . ."

"I must! It must be a herald who goes to Angus. So that if he seeks to misuse him it is high treason. There must be something . . ."

"Wait, Sire—there *is* something. There used to be a Snowdoun Herald. Here. This castle of Stirling used to be called Snowdoun, in early days, and there was a Snowdoun Herald. I have heard of it, many times. It has not been used for long, I think, but, yes, it was a senior herald, called after the strongest royal fortress."

"Snowdoun! Aye—Snowdoun! That is it. The old name for Stirling. Davie, I name you Snowdoun Herald, next to Lyon. You go to Angus, to Stirling Bridge, if that is where they meet. Tell him my royal command, he is not to come nearer. Indeed, he is to go away. Not nearer than, than . . ."

"Six miles, Sire, was the old limit," Erskine prompted. "Within six miles of the monarch, when he was in residence, was the royal bourne, precinct . . ."

"Yes. Then six miles. Not to come nearer me than six miles. Indeed, further . . ." In his excitement James all but pushed his friend. "Go, Davie, go quickly, or Angus will be here."

"I will go, Sire, yes. But I have no herald's clothing, no tabard. Nothing to show that I am what I say. They may well disbelieve me."

"A royal standard? Surely there is a royal standard flag in this royal castle? Ride under that. Jockie Hart will carry it for you . . ."

Although it was all the result of his own suggestions, David Lindsay thereafter found himself in a very doubtful frame of

137

mind as he and Hart rode down through the town under an enormous Lion Rampant standard meant for flying from a flag-pole—which seemed quite ridiculous for only two men—heading the half-mile for Stirling Bridge. Just what he had let himself in for he did not know, save that it would almost certainly be unpleasant. Nevertheless he still reckoned it to be their best move in present circumstances, however disagreeable the process.

As they neared the north end of the town they became aware of two aspects of the situation; first, an almost complete lack of citizenry in the narrow streets, an ominous sign; and second, nearing the bridge-head across the now narrowed Forth and the start of the mile-long causeway over the marshland beyond, where Wallace had won his famous victory, the sight of a great concourse of men and horses gathered at this end of the arched bridge, blocking all—the Douglases arrived. The fact that this crowd appeared to be stationary however, waiting, appeared to indicate that Angus himself had not come yet from Edinburgh.

David would have been inclined to hang back and wait, for it was Angus himself to whom his message applied and who would make the decisions, and a preliminary encounter with his uncles was of no benefit. But if he could see the Douglases, they could also see him, especially under this huge and colourful banner; and for the royal standard to hang about in the close-mouth of a Stirling street just would not do.

They rode on.

Their reception at the bridge end was all that David had feared, in laughter, jeers, catcalls. When Lindsay's identity was evident, the mockery became tinged with anger, at least on the part of the leadership, and there were distinctly threatening gestures.

Setting his jaw, David moved forward to well within hailing distance before reining up. "I come in the name of the King," he called. "To speak with the Earl of Angus. Is he there?"

An incoherent volley of shouts answered him. But out of it presently one voice prevailed, authoritative, harsh, Pittendreich's.

"You, Lindsay, you treacherous dog! You dare to show your insolent face before Douglas!"

"I am sent only to speak with the Earl of Angus, Sir George. Where is he?" David tried to keep his voice level.

"Fool! Think you that Angus, or any of us, will pay *you* any heed?"

"I do—since I speak in the name of our sovereign-lord and of his Privy Council. But not to you, sir. Only to Angus."

"We await the Earl of Angus, Lindsay." That was Graysteel, less aggressively. "I cannot think that he will greet you kindly!"

"I do not come for kindly greetings, Sir Archibald. I come only to state the King's and the Council's decisions."

"Such so-called Council can make no decision to effect—since Douglas was not at the making!" Pittendreich threw back. "Angus is Chancellor. Kilspindie is Treasurer. Abbot William is Privy Seal. I am Master of the Household . . ."

"Were, Sir George—*were*! Are no longer. You are replaced, all."

"Dizzard! Have you lost any wits the good God allowed you? Douglas places or displaces—none other!"

"You err. The King makes and unmakes. Have you forgot, sir? The King only, whoever may advise him. Only because you held the King and gained his seal and signature could Douglas hold any places, or bestow them. You no longer hold the King— and he makes other arrangements."

"We shall see about that, numbskull . . . !"

David drew a deep breath. This would not do, it was what he had determined to avoid, a profitless exchange with the uncles. Yet what could he do, until Angus arrived? He could not just sit his horse there, silent. He made up his mind, half-turning in the saddle, and pointing. There was a small mound a couple of hundred yards to the east.

"I shall await Angus there," he called, and reined around, Hart with the standard following.

To the accompaniment of more shouting and jeers they took up their stance on the mound, feeling somewhat foolish and embarrassed but thankful that the Douglases at least did not seem to be going to attack them.

For how long they could maintain this odd situation David dared not assess. But, to his relief, at least for the meantime, after only a minute or two a different quality of shouting rose from the Douglas ranks, with pointing and cheers. Looking behind him, he saw a hard-riding party emerging from St. Mary's Wynd and the North Port, under the great undifferenced banner of the Red Heart. Now for the real test.

Angus and his escort clattered up to the bridge-end company, and if he noted the pair under the royal standard in passing, the Earl gave no sign of it. There followed an interval of evident consultation and discussion amongst the leaders, with occasional glances towards the mound. Then, David staying where he was, Angus and his kinsmen appeared to reach a decision and came spurring over to him.

"Lindsay—what is this?" the Earl demanded hotly. "You have shamefully abused our trust, treacherously removed the King from our good keeping, and now come seeking my presence like some nuncio, some ambassador! It is scarcely to be credited!"

"I come thus because that is what I am, my lord. Not ambassador, since that would imply too high a status for you! But envoy, yes, representing King James. I come as Snowdoun Herald, duly appointed to the Lyon Court, in the name of the King and his Privy Council, to inform you of decisions taken concerning yourself."

"You . . . you do? *You*, an impudent upstart, come to me, Angus, with your empty talk of things too high for you!"

"I do. Since I am come in the King's name and by his express commission. And if anyone knows the worth and power of the King's expressed authority, it is you, my lord of Angus, since you have been using it, or misusing it, for long. But for no longer. I am here to inform you that you are now proclaimed to be outwith the King's peace; that you are now deprived of all office and position under the crown, no longer Chancellor, and will yield up the Great Seal to Archbishop Dunbar of Glasgow who is appointed in your place. All your kin and friends' appointments likewise are revoked, as from last night. Moreover, as outwith the King's peace you will not approach within six miles of the royal person, under pain of treason, save alone, unarmed, to make submission. Finally, you and your kind are required to appear before a session of parliament, day to be decided upon, to answer for your offences against the King's person and freedom. Failure so to appear, unarmed, will be adjudged as highest treason and be visited with the most extreme penalty provided by the law—public execution." If all that tended to come out in somewhat breathless fashion, it was scarcely to be wondered at.

For moments the Douglases seemed to be bereft of speech,

staring, unbelieving. Then a gabble broke out, in furious protest and hot challenge, all talking at once, Pittendreich actually urging his horse forward in menace.

But Angus's voice prevailed. "Have you gone crazed, Lindsay? Forgotten to whom you speak—*Angus*? You threaten Douglas thus? The Douglas power?"

"Not I, my lord—the King! And Council. Nor threaten—proclaim, condemn. Here is not threat. The thing is done. You are proscribed, *now*. Outwith the King's peace. Already you are guilty of treason. Since you are here within the bourne, the six miles distance of the royal presence. That may be overlooked this once if you withdraw immediately, now that you are informed. I have so informed you. I have fulfilled my duty, as Snowdoun Herald. I return to His Grace."

"Think you that I will accept this, this insane folly, man?" Angus was visibly quivering with ill-suppressed rage and resentment. "Douglas will soon show who holds the power in this land."

"I care not, my lord, whether you accept it or no. You are informed, that is all my duty. Indeed, for myself, I would prefer it that you did not accept it, I think—since then you are openly guilty of treason most assuredly, disobeying the King's express command, and so liable to the penalty, you and yours, outlawry, apprehension in due course, and execution when apprehended without need for trial. You, my lord, know well enough this process and what it means. You have used it, in the King's name and recollect the late Lord Home and his kin! I advise you to think well. Now I return to His Grace whom in your prideful disloyalty you can by no means reach in Stirling Castle! You are warned." And with only a curt bow from the saddle, David Lindsay wheeled his horse round and set off for the North Port. He felt like cantering, galloping even, his back as naked as a babe's. But somehow he managed to keep his mount to only a steady walk, under the flapping standard, and did not look back.

Ears stretched for beat of hooves behind them, he all but held his breath—and doubtless Jockie Hart did the same. But, half-way to the town-gate, with no evident developments at their backs, David risked a quick glance over his shoulder. Angus and his lieutenants remained where he had left them, heads together in seemingly earnest debate. With an enormous sigh of relief, he kicked heels to his beast's flanks and headed, at a quick trot now, for the town's streets.

A little later, from the heights of the tourney-ground before the castle, he drew rein, to gaze back and down and his heart lifted. The Douglas host was on the move—but northwards. Banners at the front, it was streaming in a long snaking column back over the narrow causeway, away from Stirling. Whether out of decided policy, prudence, a recognition of facts, frustration, or something of all these, Angus was distancing himself from the King's presence, six miles or otherwise. The first hurdle seemed to be surmounted.

* * *

The days that followed were busy ones at Stirling Castle, with messengers being sent out near and far and, as the news spread, visitors arrived in numbers, important visitors. The leal lords found their courage at last—and others who were perhaps less leal but adept at reading the signs. Soon the Earls of Moray, Eglinton, Cassillis, Glencairn, Rothes, Huntly, and even Arran himself, and Morton of the Black Douglases had come. It was fairly clear that the tide had indeed turned, at least for the time being. The lords of parliament were too numerous to list, but significantly included the new Lord Home, and Glamis, who was married to Angus's sister. And the prelates, headed by Archbishop Dunbar, came in force; also the nearer Highland chiefs, the Stewarts notable despite the memory of Linlithgow Bridge. Even the Queen-Mother's third husband, Henry Stewart of Methven, turned up, to offer his duty and congratulations to the monarch—and James's obvious embarrassment was somewhat dissipated by his councillors' wise advice to make a gesture towards his mother, if possible to prevent more intrigues and complications from that quarter, by creating Stewart Lord Methven there and then.

But in all this influx of well-wishers and place-seekers, it was not until Davie Beaton arrived, with a handsome train, from St. Andrews, that they learned any detailed news as to what Angus was doing. Beaton, always well-informed, announced that the Douglas had retired to his all-but-impregnable stronghold of Tantallon, on the East Lothian coast, presumably to sit out the storm there and await possibly more favourable conditions for regaining power. Although there was no hint of submission or coming to terms, at least there was no present indication of major mustering or armed attack, and it looked as though the treason proclamation was having its effect. Davie Beaton also explained that he would have been to Stirling earlier, but once he learned of Angus's retiral he felt it his personal duty to rescue his uncle from his shepherd's hut in the Ochils and restore him to his archiepiscopal castle of St. Andrews.

James, who seemed to have added years to his stature and carriage in a few days, if at the expense of his temper and patience, welcomed Beaton warmly, suitably grateful for arranging the escape from Falkland, as for all else. He somewhat apologetically explained the appointment of Archbishop Dunbar as Chancellor, pleading the Primate's age and state of health; but sought to compensate by offering Davie a seat on the Privy Council and the grant of any office he chose to ask. Beaton, never backward, there and then suggested the Lord Privy Seal's position so recently held by Abbot William Douglas—which, of course, involved the keeping of the monarch's own personal seal, provided the closest links with the crown, constant access to the royal ear and consequent major influence. James agreed without hesitation, although some of his advisers were less sure. The Abbot of Arbroath quickly showed that he had in fact come there with such appointment very much in mind, and prepared to stay.

When David Lindsay later asked whether his friend was now relinquishing his position as secretary to the Primate, he was informed that it was not so. He believed that he could fulfil both functions. After all, previously he had been secretary not only to the Primate but to the Chancellor. He looked upon this Lord Privy Seal's task as more or less similar to the latter, as senior secretary to the monarch—and he, having some knowledge as to the man Dunbar, rather anticipated that the new Chancellor would have considerably less impact on the realm than had his predecessors. Davie Beaton, in fact, was moving in, with unerring instinct, to assume administrative authority in the new dispensation.

At a second and much enlarged Privy Council meeting, with Lindsay merely sitting back as an observer this time, the Lord Privy Seal, however tactful about it, made it abundantly clear that he, rather than the Chancellor, was going to make most of the running in the developing situation. Dunbar, a quiet and studious man, unlike not a few poets, was watchful and adequate but neither forceful nor initiatory, and Beaton was careful not to seem to be in the ascendant, to him nor indeed to other senior councillors. Nevertheless, most of the decisions taken either started with him or were steered into final form by him, and none which he found occasion to oppose were in the end adopted. James most evidently paid more heed to him than to any other.

Measures against Angus were still the prime consideration, and it was agreed that considerable forces should be mustered for an assault on Tantallon Castle, and before King Henry might seek to take advantage of the situation. Tantallon, as well as being so strongly sited, could be supplied by sea, which would offer Henry opportunity; so the project would have to be very carefully planned. The Earl of Argyll had by now arrived from his West Highland fastnesses, and with so much campaigning experience—as well as his huge numbers of Campbell clansmen—was the obvious choice as military leader; although Arran, as Lord Admiral had to have nominal authority and Atholl be kept sweet by being given a secondary command. To achieve this difficult leadership acceptance, without major clashes of interests, the Lord Privy Seal blandly suggested that His Grace should personally accompany the military expedition, as commander-in-chief—which should ensure Argyll's supremacy. James agreed enthusiastically. The other measures against the Red Douglases, bannings, forfeitures, treason-sanctions, were all approved and added to.

It was decided that a parliament should be held in Edinburgh at the beginning of September when the harvest should be in and this bar to a good attendance removed. In preparation for this, and also better to arrange the assault on Tantallon, the court should remove to the capital city just as soon as sufficient troops were assembled to ensure the monarch's safety from any surprise Douglas attempt.

Many new appointments fell to be made to offices of state. And at Beaton's suggestion, certain prominent lords and barons, not present, who had hitherto supported Angus, were specifically absolved from any punishment and offered acceptance of the King's peace, as a gesture towards unity. Arran and his son, the Bastard, who of course came into that category themselves,

144

made no comment, the father eyeing his fingernails, the son grinning cynically.

Although David Lindsay now reverted to a comparatively modest station, as merely Snowdoun Herald and chief usher to the King, he nevertheless occupied a position of considerable influence, for he remained James's closest companion, as well as being in the confidence of the Lord Privy Seal, and in that of the Chancellor, who had associated with David for years as tutor to the young monarch. Another figure from James's childhood, Abbot John Inglis, was brought back from Culross to be royal chaplain.

In all these appointments there was one in which James himself had a particular interest and which seemed to concern no-one else. That was the Mistress of the Wardrobe. Before being taken to Falkland, the King had been growing ever more interested in fine clothing, a taste which Angus had seen fit to encourage, to strengthen his hold over the youth. James had grown fond of the quiet Janet Douglas, whom Angus had installed as wardrobe mistress and seamstress, and now was worried, both that she could have been whisked away from Linlithgow with the other Douglases, and that his clothes might have gone with her. He ordered David Lindsay, therefore, to go to Linlithgow to discover the situation, and if Janet was still there to bring her back to Stirling, and all his splendid apparel with her. He had been dressed in nothing but his hunting clothes since his release.

David, never loth to escape from fortress walls, found himself quite looking forward to seeing Janet again—if indeed she was still at the palace. He had not realised that he had missed her gentle, unassuming but far from negligible presence; now he had recognised that in fact he had done so, that she had been good and satisfactory company, undemanding but sympathetic, as well as his ally in the task of influencing James for the better.

So it was with a small surge of pleasure that, on arriving at the handsome brown-stone establishment above the loch, he learned from the gatehouse-porter that Mistress Douglas was indeed still there, in fact the only Douglas remaining in the place.

He found her down in the high pleasance near the lochside, amongst the fruit-trees, picking gooseberries.

"David!" she exclaimed. "How good!" That was all, but she

smiled warmly. She was a slightly-built creature but sufficiently womanly, with sensitive features and fine darkly expressive eyes. She was simply dressed, as a country-woman rather than any court lady.

Almost involuntarily he moved forward, hands out—then thought better of it. "Yes," he agreed, making his voice sober, factual. "It is. You . . . look well, Janet. A flower amongst other flowers!" He blinked at himself; he had certainly not intended to say anything like that.

"Thank you, sir." She dipped the hint of a curtsy. "Here is a most pleasant surprise. Is His Grace come back to Linlithgow?"

"No. He is at Stirling. He sent me for you."

"He did? I would have thought that he would have had enough of Douglases to last him for a lifetime! Unless, to be sure, I am to be . . . punished?"

"No, no—far from it, Janet. You are his friend. Mistress of the Wardrobe. He wishes you to be at court. He is his own master now, and chooses his own folk to be about him." He coughed, and being an honest man, added, "And wants his fine gear, the said wardrobe, to be sure!"

She smiled again. "That is more like it. I have been concerned about all the clothing, the jewels and the like, that he would be requiring them. When I heard, I thought to send all to Stirling, but had scarcely the authority. No-one instructed me. So I waited here, caring for it. And, and—oh, I am glad to see you, David!"

That was not her usual, either. They gazed at each other for a little, strangely moved.

"It will be difficult for you, here. Since, since Angus's fall," he said. He had hardly thought of that before, but recognised it now. "Alone, I mean, as a Douglas. All the rest gone and you left. Without word, wondering. We should have thought of you, before." That sounded lame, he realised. "There has been so much to see to."

"To be sure. I rejoiced when I heard of your escape from Falkland. Although it meant, meant problems for me. Is King James happier now, free? And can he remain free?"

"I believe so, yes. We must see that he does. The signs now are good. Angus is isolated. I think that we have his measure. The threat of treason, held over the Douglases." He paused. "I am sorry. You, a Douglas . . ."

146

"I have not been proud to bear that name, of late," she said. She stooped, to resume her berry-picking. "Even though I have to thank them for bringing me here, to serve His Grace, in however lowly degree as seamstress . . ."

"Mistress of his royal Wardrobe, he calls you now. See—give me your basket . . ."

They moved along the bushes together, the man picking also, and their talking drifted into more casual and companionable vein. Until presently she looked up.

"This is unnecessary now—this of the gooseberries," she said. "If I am to go with you to Stirling, no need for grossarts."

David hesitated, but not for long. "We can eat them when we dine, can we not? Stewed in honey they are very good." It was only early afternoon and, it being but eighteen miles to Stirling, they could be there within three hours. But the man knew an inclination to linger. "No doubt it will take you some time to gather together the King's gear and pack it for the taking. Tomorrow will serve very well."

"It is all but ready. I have kept it so. But—yes, I will cook you grossarts in honey, gladly."

They left it at that, and resumed their picking.

Later, in the royal quarters of the now largely empty palace, after their meal, they sat before a small fire of birch-logs, for the July evening had grown chilly. David told her the details of the Falkland escape and what had transpired since, emphasising Davie Beaton's prominence in all. Janet was a good listener, saying little herself. But she did comment that, grateful as they all must be to the Abbot of Arbroath, she judged him to be a man worth watching.

"You mean that by way of warning?" he asked, interested.

"Partly, yes. He is very able, to be sure, and of great spirit. Charm, also. But he could be quite ruthless, I think. And so, dangerous."

"Possibly. Fortunately, he is the King's friend, and my own. Perhaps James has need of some ruthless friends—since he has ruthless enemies!"

"Perhaps. But if he turned against you . . ." She stopped. "Forgive me speaking so, David, if he is your friend. It is presumptuous of me. I bide here alone, and think too much!"

"So long as you think of such as myself!" he told her, and surprised himself again.

147

She did not answer that, but changed the subject to James's behaviour. Now that he was his own master, as it were, was he still as concerned with the cards, wine, wagery and, and women?

The way that she said that last gave the man pause. "Did he, did he ever trouble you, Janet, in that fashion?"

"No, no. To me he was always . . . correct. But I knew of his failings, his weakness. I have heard him talking lewdly. So ill to hear in one of his years. And he so pleasing and kind, otherwise."

"Yes. That was Angus's doing. Of set purpose to get James further into his power. And finding women for him—an evil thing. At first, when you came, I, I . . ." He coughed. "I soon perceived that it was not so, that you were . . . different, very different."

She bit her lip. "You thought that? You thought . . . ? And others, perhaps? James himself?"

"Not when we saw you and recognised your, your worth." Hurriedly he changed to another aspect of the subject. "He has been better since Falkland and Stirling. Has been too busy, first with hunting then with taking over the reins of kingship. But I fear that he will always be so inclined. His mother, after all, is a woman of appetites, considerable appetites, as we all know! And his father was ever a lady's man. No doubt Angus reckoned on that when he ordered these temptations to corrupt the boy."

"You believe the Earl so wicked?"

"I do. I was there, saw it all. But James has strengths as well as weaknesses. These must be cherished, nurtured. That is one of the reasons why I am so glad that he wants you at court again. You can have so much effect on him, for good, as a woman whom he likes and admires. But is, is . . ."

She smiled slightly at his hesitation. "But is not attracting him towards her bed?" she finished for him.

"No, no. I mean, yes. Or not in that way. I did not mean . . ." Confused he started again. "Forgive me—you are indeed attractive as a woman to men. But you do not flaunt it, as do some. You will be good for James."

"I thank you. The other reasons you spoke of? You are glad I will be looking after his wardrobe, his clothing, yes?"

"That, of course. But I meant otherwise. I meant that *I* would be glad to have you there. Near to me also. I find your company to my taste, Janet."

"You are kind." She sounded as formal as he did. "I thank you again. I do not find it hard to seek to please such as yourself." As though she were thankful to get that little speech off her mind, she leant slightly forward. "I know how distressed you have been over your wife's sad death. My heart has gone out in sympathy to you. I know something of what you have suffered. For I too lost a dear one. We were not wed—but were going to be. He was slain at the Melrose battle."

"I am sorry. I did not know. I saw that battle. You must have felt very badly towards Douglas's enemies. Of which you must count me one."

"No. Only towards war and the folly of men's ambitions which result in war and battle."

They sat silent for a little after that, thinking their own thoughts. Presently the young woman rose.

"I will go now and prepare all for the morrow, pack the King's clothing for the road," she said.

"And I will aid you."

So together they gathered and parcelled up the contents of the royal wardrobe, the scanty jewels and other personal belongings, no great endowment for a monarch but quite a lot for a sixteen-year-old youth, stowing all in bags and baskets for carriage by pack-horse. It made a companionable task and they became the more at ease with each other. When they had finished, she filled a warming-pan with glowing ashes from the fire, to air his bed in the chamber he had used before, adjoining James's. Then she said that she would seek her couch.

He escorted her to her chamber-door, and reached out to take her arm. "Janet—I have been happier tonight, more, more complete, than I have been for long. Thanks to you," he told her.

"Then I am glad," she said simply.

"You are good for me, I think." The hand which held her slid round to encircle her waist. "I fear that I have been only half a man for too long."

She let him hold her close for a moment or two, and then gently pushed him away.

"Never that, David. Always a full man. Tonight has been good, yes. We both were perhaps . . . lonely. Perhaps *only* that. Perhaps more. We shall see. There is time ahead of us to discover. Good night, my dear." Turning, she left him there, and closed her door firmly behind her.

He went back to his own room, his feelings in something of a turmoil. He could admit to himself that, with the least encouragement, he would have gone in with her and taken her to her bed. Undoubtedly he was attracted, as he had not been since Kate died. Was it just because he needed a woman? A man's need? Or was it more than that? He admired her, as well as being attracted, and admired more than just her person. Was that being disloyal to Kate's memory? Or was he just lonely, as she had said? He did not know—he just did not know. All he knew for certain was that some part of him, the bodily part undoubtedly, felt disappointed, balked. But somewhere, he was relieved also. If she had let him in, so soon, would he have continued to admire her?

He went to bed without the answers to all that, but with the underlying conviction that it had been a good and somehow important evening.

In the morning, enjoying each other's company, with the laden pack-horses, they rode the eighteen miles to Stirling.

9

On the Privy Council's almost unanimous advice, the court moved to Edinburgh in later July; and with the lords and chiefs already mustering their forces in strength around the capital, it was deemed safe enough for James to take up residence in Holyrood Abbey rather than in the forbidding confines of the rock-top castle. And there, although the arrangements for the important parliament went ahead, the preparations for the expedition against Tantallon were the more urgent and enthusiastic, for most. This time, the Douglases were to be taught who ruled as well as reigned in Scotland.

The Abbey was full to overflowing, with nobles, lairds and prelates, and the city teeming with their retainers and clansmen, with consequent disharmony, riot and confusion. James entered into it all with energy and eagerness, the military side of it in especial. But not all his energies were so chanelled, for whether it was the ambience of Holyrood again or the mere availability of the city population, he began to renew his association with young women—and some not so young—despite David's and Janet's influence.

In this matter he found a new purveyor. Arran was amongst the residents at the Abbey, his large Hamilton manpower now judiciously at the disposal of the monarch; and the Bastard came with him. And from the first that determined character perceived priorities and set about making himself useful to the King. No doubt he had similar tastes himself and sensed James's needs. At first James was cold, prejudiced against the man who had murdered his friend Lennox. But Hamilton could be attractive and excellent company when he chose, and quite quickly the King came to accept his company. He played cards, and sometimes let James win. He raced horses, he sang and danced and told hair-curling stories, especially about French women and France—where he had lived for some years. And he appeared to have an inexhaustible supply of girls to make available for the young monarch, outdoing Angus himself in this respect, also a train of young gallants to cater to James's gaming, wagering and other weaknesses.

This situation had the effect of drawing David and Janet still closer together in a sort of frustrated partnership. They plotted and planned to circumvent the Bastard's efforts, not with much success. At the young woman's suggestion David actually composed a poem in aid of their cause, since James was interested in his friend's poetic efforts, indeed tried his own hand at the business on occasion. David left this effusion lying around so that the King was bound to see it. Its lines went thus:

> Each man after his quality
> 　They did solicit His Majesty,
> Some gart him revel at the racket,
> 　Some haled him to the hurly-hackit,
> And some to show their courtly courses
> 　Would ride to Leith and race their horses
> And wightily wallop o'er the sands
> 　They neither sparing spur nor wands,
> Casting gambols with bends and becks
> 　So wantonly might break their necks;

151

> There was no play but cards and dice
>> Aye aye Sir Flattery bore the price;
> Methinks it was a piteous thing
>> To see that fair young tender King
> To whom these gallants stood none awe,
>> To play with him, pluckt at the craw;
> They became rich, I you assure,
>> But aye the Prince remainit poor;
> There was few of that garrison
>> That learned him any good lesson.

It was not one of Lindsay's most profound efforts but they hoped that it might have some effect. The Sir Flattery was, of course, the Bastard.

But it was not left to poetry to insert a spoke in Finnart's wheel. One night, at Holyrood, when he was returning to his own quarters after a roystering evening with the King, he was set upon by a hidden assailant armed with a dagger, in one of the abbey corridors, stabbed in several places and left lying for dead. When he was discovered there was a great hue and cry, the entire establishment aroused. They found the culprit, who had failed to clean his blood-stained dirk, and he proved to be a servant of the late Earl of Lennox, come in the tail of one of the other Stewart lords. The Bastard recovered slowly, and his imprisoned attacker was made to pay the penalty with a vengeance, Hamilton vengeance, for he was tortured to death, paraded through the streets of the city while every part of his body was being nipped with red-hot pincers, a brazier accompanying his cart. His right hand was chopped off before he expired. The man's last words were that it deserved worse than that in having failed to slay his late master's murderer, a remarkable demonstration of Highland loyalty to a chief.

This incident set off a great alarm about the security of the Abbey; if a Stewart clansman could do this, what might not the Douglases attempt? So a twenty-four-hour guard was instituted, and even James insisted on taking his turn as guard-commander of a night—although David Lindsay at least suspected that this was very largely an excuse for secret chambering, the guard being on the lax side about women intruders.

Meantime Davie Beaton was working hard to ensure that

the parliament was a major success, to consolidate the King's new-found power. He coaxed, lobbied, bought with Church money, bribed with promises of position, threatened subtly. He was in a strong position and used it to the full.

The military preparations were more straightforward, assembling troops, arms, horses, stores and searching for suitable artillery. Short-range cannon would be of no use, for the Tantallon approaches were defended by a series of deep ditches to landward, keeping artillery at a distance. Mons Meg was the only really powerful piece available and unfortunately it was said to be not functioning at its best. Argyll was in charge of all this, and although an able and practised campaigner, David wondered how his experiences in West Highland warfare amongst the island clans would fit him to lead an assault on such as Angus and a major fortress like Tantallon.

By the beginning of September, with no sign of any of the Douglases yielding themselves up into ward in response to the Privy Council command—not that anyone expected them to do so—the parliament assembled at the castle, to promulgate the necessary measures and establish to all, not least to Henry of England, King James's new and due mastery. As these affairs went, it was a major success, thanks to Davie Beaton's efforts; but also thanks to James's own contribution, for he played his part well, showing authority tempered with modesty, no cipher now, but courteous with it. He was tall, well-built for his age, and good-looking in his red-haired way, indeed seeming older than his sixteen years, appearing quite the man. The two Davids had schooled him well for this occasion. If the Chancellor, in the chair, was somewhat hesitant, the monarch on the throne was not—any more than was the Lord Privy Seal. David Lindsay for the first time had an official role to play; for Clephane, the Lyon King-of-Arms, had been ill and was now unfit to carry out his duties. James had wanted to replace him and make Lindsay Lyon there and then, but was advised that such quick promotion for a new herald would offend others longer established—and Clephane might recover; so he had put the office into commission, in the names of the five senior heralds, Albany, Ross, Islay, Marchmont and Snowdoun. He had insisted, however, that David took this first important parliamentary duty. So, dressed in Lyon's gorgeous emblazoned tabard and regalia, Lindsay did the ushering, proclaiming and stage-managing for the occasion and thereafter stood close behind the throne—as indeed he had been wont to do in the past in unofficial capacity.

The principal business, the declaring of Angus and the other senior Douglases as guilty of treason, of holding of the sovereign's person against his will by the space of two years, of exposing of his person to battle, and the refusal to yield themselves up to his justice as at present commanded, resulting in their forfeiture and sentence of death, was passed almost without opposition, the nominal disposal of their lives, titles, lands and properties following automatically. Then there was the authorisation for all means necessary to enforce parliament's will, including of course armed assault on Douglas strongholds. This out of the way, the remainder of the programme, the appointment to offices of state, the keeperships of royal palaces, provisions for taxation and revenue-raising to rehabilitate the plundered Treasury, the purging of the judiciary and sheriffdoms, appointment of new ambassadors, and so on, took considerably longer and involved a deal of horse-trading and special-pleading. But it was done at last, and most there were reasonably well satisfied, even Davie Beaton.

Now for Angus.

It was quite a major host which set out four days later for Tantallon, no fewer than twelve thousand men, although David Lindsay, for one, saw little point in taking so many, with all the provisioning and tentage necessary; he knew Tantallon and recognised that it was artillery alone which could encompass its downfall, numbers of men being all but immaterial, and mere siege unlikely to be effective since the place could be supplied by sea. But Argyll was in charge, and he and Atholl—and indeed James also—seemed to have great faith in numbers. At least this host would serve to impress the countryside and commonality with the King's new power.

The artillery-train looked impressive but in fact, apart from Mons Meg itself, there was nothing there which, in Lindsay's estimation, Tantallon would take seriously, falcons, half-falcons, quarter-falcons, sakers, culverins and the like, mainly from Edinburgh Castle, with an effective range of little more than two or three hundred yards. The cannon, drawn by teams of slow-plodding oxen, creaked along behind the infantry, while the cavalry, moss-troopers and mounted lairds and lords rode far ahead.

They went by Musselburgh and Cockenzie, and at Longniddry and Kilspindie gestures were made at 'spoiling' these two Douglas houses. But at neither was there any resistance, and it was tame work, their owners being absent; indeed at Kilspindie it was merely a token harrying, burning a few barns and cowsheds—for James looked at Graysteel with less animosity than on the rest of the Douglases and sought to be lenient, although, to be sure, parliament had passed sentence of death on him also. The King also sent a party to assail Whittinghame Tower, but expressly forbade any attack on nearby Stonypath, this being Janet's home.

Although the advance guard had reached there earlier, the King and his leadership group came to Tantallon that same evening, to set up camp near the Castleton, about half-a-mile inland from the fortress. The place looked serene from a distance, assured, invincible, its towers and battlements rose-red in the glow of the setting sun. But it was not at the soaring walls and pinnacles that the knowledgeable gazed there and then but at those parallel lines, five of them, now filling with the purple shadows of evening, which barred off the entire headland, deep, water-filled ditches, perhaps one hundred yards apart and each with its own earthen rampart in front, to keep cannon out of range. These might be bridged, of course, but only at a price, for all most certainly would be defended, and under the muzzles of the castle's own artillery. Angus had often boasted that he could sit behind his defences from any force in Christendom.

Just before darkening, James sent David and the other heralds, with trumpeters, forward under the royal standard to the first rampart and ditch where, after a brassy flourish, they shouted formal announcement that the King's Grace in person hereby called upon Archibald, Earl of Angus to yield himself, his company and this stronghold, into the King's hands forthwith, or suffer from direst consequences.

There was no least reply from fortress or ramparts; the place might have been empty, abandoned. But later, beacon-fires began to blaze at strategic points along the walling and ditches, revealing that these were manned and that darkness was not to be allowed to provide cover for attack.

In the morning a council of war was held, after scouts had been sent out to investigate all possible aspects and approaches and had come back to report. They said that there was no other access to the castle than the ditched area before them. Right and left were only sheer cliffs and precipices dropping to the sea, and these ditches went right to the cliff-edges. They were well-manned behind their system of ramparts, trenches and saps; and some of the scouts had been shot at by archers hidden there.

The conference thereafter was noisy, incoherent and less than decisive. The up-and-at-them school, led by Atholl of course advocated a headlong assault and capture of the ditches, overcoming by sheer weight of numbers; but wiser counsels prevailed against this as much too costly in men and far from assured of success at that. Some believed that a night attack, despite the fires, would be the best hope, but most agreed that they should wait for the artillery. David Falconer, a noted sea-captain and expert on naval gunnery, whom Arran as Lord Admiral had brought along, advocated an attack by sea, from fishing-craft, using scaling-ladders to mount the cliffs; but that was received with scant enthusiasm.

The ox-drawn cannon still did not arrive, and David Lindsay, who had experience of using fishing-boats and their crews along this coast, volunteered to make an investigatory reconnoitre, taking the man Falconer with him. They rode eastwards by south, to Beilhaven, the nearest fishing village, where they hired a boat and crew to row them up the coast again, the five miles or so.

Two items they learned on that brief reconnaissance. Firstly, that three large vessels were in sight, lying well out to sea, almost hull-down and seemingly stationary, near the Isle of May—and Falconer had little hesitation in declaring them English, even at that range, warships of which the Scots had none on this coast, so it looked as though Angus had not been sitting idle in Tantallon all these weeks but had been in touch with Henry Tudor, soliciting aid, so that no assault on the castle by sea would be practicable. And secondly, close under the Tantallon cliffs themselves, they perceived that any attempted attack by scaling the said cliffs by ladder or otherwise was out of the question. So tall, beetling and over-hung were they, the only access from sea-level was a single, narrow stairway cut in the living rock, a dizzy ascent which could be guarded easily by only two or three men, from fortified ledges, a hoist alongside for the drawing up of supplies from boats. Recognising defeat on this front, they turned and rowed back to Beilhaven, to mocking waving from the soaring battlements above.

There was one less option open to the royal forces.

Next day, with the cannon arrived, hopes rose—but were quickly dashed. The artillery made a heartening banging, when ranged in an impressive row, sending up the seabirds from the cliff-edges in screaming thousands—but making no least impact on the castle, none of the cannon-balls, even from Mons Meg, reaching anywhere near the masonry. Try as he would, by raising muzzle-elevations and using dangerously enlarged charges of powder, the Lord Borthwick, Master of the Ordnance, could not bring those walls within range. Admittedly the shots fell amongst the ditches and ramparts, and may possibly have worked some havoc amongst unseen Douglas men-at-arms, but this was not very likely, for the cannon could not really fire dropping-shots and the earthen banks protected the men behind. So, however satisfying the noise and seeming dramatic activity, it was all fairly profitless.

Argyll accepted that there was nothing for it but to attempt a bridging operation. So parties were sent off to find and fell suitable trees with which to construct the bridges and ramps. There were none near at hand on this open coastline, and all had to be trimmed and dragged for substantial distances. This took much time, and those not so menially engaged perforce had to employ and amuse themselves as best they might. So races were run, knightly joustings held, deeds of physical prowess performed, with wrestling, javelin-throwing and other sports, and altogether an atmosphere of holiday and relaxation began to prevail—less than suitable in a serious military endeavour. Aggressive hostility and daring were hard to maintain.

It took another day to assemble and fabricate the bridges, which had to be light enough to drag and position but strong enough to bear the weight of the cannon. There was some suggestion of making the attempt by night, but with such un-wieldy material to transport and position in darkness over uneven ground, this would be more likely to work against them-selves than the defenders, even if they manhandled it instead of using oxen.

In the morning, then, in thin rain and a chill wind off the sea, a start was made, a screen of infantry in half-armour behind shields pushing forward to the first of the ramparts, surprisingly without being fired on. More surprising still, when brave men, cautiously clambering up, peered over the earthworks, it was to find the ditch beyond unmanned. Much relieved, they signalled back for the bridging parties to come on.

Dragging the heavy timbers behind long files of men was slow work, and to save time some of the cannon were also manhandled forward immediately behind. Still there was no reaction from the enemy.

The bridging process was fairly straightforward, the only problem being that the ditch was both deeper and wider than they had calculated, so that the timbering had to be laid lower than bargained for, with a consequent longer and steeper descent for the cannon. But the work went reasonably well and presently they had three bridges spanning this first hazard. The builders beckoned on the cannon-teams.

Getting those pieces, heavy in themselves even though light artillery, so-called, up over the rampart and then down the steep slope behind to the bridges, was hard work indeed—and one of the sakers actually rolled off out-of-control, to plunge down into the slimy water of the ditch, whence no amount of heaving would pull it out. But so encouraged were the handlers by being left in peace to do it that there was little grumbling. The pieces had to be pushed across the three bridges and then hauled up the bank on the other side, for further advance almost to the next line of ditch, where it was hoped that the castle walls might be within range. It was just as the first cannon were being positioned there, amidst much shouting and directing, that there came a series of popping noises from the castle, scarcely loud enough to do more than draw a few glances and comments. But swiftly all that was changed, as without further warning, stone and iron balls began to descend upon the would-be attackers, the very dropping shots which they themselves were unable to fire. Bombards. Tantallon must be equipped with bombards, a mortar-type of cannon which fired its missiles high into the air, for the balls to drop on the targets instead of being aimed directly at them. Such fire was less accurate, to be sure, but had the great advantage of being able to hit behind defensive barriers. With carefully calculated charges of powder, and elevations of the short barrels, it was possible to gauge the fall of shot in any given area with a fair exactitude, given practice—and clearly Angus's gunners had had ample practice and knew the precise procedure for dropping their shots on this particular area between the fourth and fifth ditches.

Somehow, missiles falling from the sky seemed direly more alarming than those fired in normal fashion, no cover being possible, no point in crouching or hiding, no way of taking avoiding action. As the balls, the size of a man's head, plummeted down, there was panic amongst the royalist advance parties, those with the cannon, those working at the bridging and those bringing up ammunition. When, added to this, archery opened up from behind the next line of rampart, at short range and with deadly accuracy, the position was seen to be all but untenable. Men went streaming back to the safety of the encampment, abandoning all.

The bombardment continued, however. Clearly the intent was to destroy those cannon and bridges.

It was some considerable time after the cannonade eventually ceased, that a couple of scouts crept cautiously forward to inspect damage. They found two of the three bridges shattered, the third shaky and two of five cannon damaged. These scouts were permitted to return, with their report, unassailed.

Gloom prevailed in the King's entourage.

The demand now was for bombards of their own, so that at least they could hit back behind the nearer ramparts, even if they might achieve little against the castle itself. These pieces were of French origin, called bocards and moyons, founded in brass, mainly used on ships-of-war, where they were useful for reaching behind the defensive bulwarks which protected the vessels' decking. They had been little used in Scotland, where naval warfare had been neglected until James the Fourth had sought to remedy this; and although Falconer had had them on ships of his, none were nearer than the Clyde ports. But David Lindsay seemed to recollect that Antoine de la Bastie had installed one or two at Dunbar Castle, when he was using that place as Warden of the Marches. He offered to go and see whether they were still there, to borrow them, if so.

Dunbar was only a mile or two beyond Beilhaven, its strange castle, so very different from but as unique as Tantallon, projecting into the sea at the mouth of the town's harbour, built on rock-stacks above the waves, these individual towers linked by covered and vaulted bridge-corridors, an odd-looking but very strong establishment. It had been a royal fortress for almost exactly one hundred years, since the downfall of the Earls of Dunbar and March; but parliament had ceded it to the late Regent, the present Duke of Albany, now back in France, who had left his deputy, de Gonzolles, in charge. This Frenchman was notoriously jealous for his master's interests, and on David's enquiry, whilst admitting that there were two bocards and sundry other brass cannon at the castle, refused to yield them up without the firmest surety as to their safe return. When Lindsay, at a loss, asked what sureties de Gonzolles would consider adequate, the Frenchman came up with the extraordinary requirement that three Scots lords or their heirs should be delivered to him as hostages for the return of the undamaged bocards, a demand from which he would not budge. So David had to go back to Tantallon with this odd proposal; and so concerned was the royal leadership over the stalemate in their siege that the terms were agreed. As it transpired, too, they had little difficulty in finding volunteers for the part, some of the less warlike and enthusiastic campaigners being quite content to exchange the discomforts and dangers of this so-far unsuccessful operation against the Douglases for the shelter and ease of a stay in Dunbar Castle. David therefore returned with his three willing hostages, plus an escort, and duly brought back the two bocards and some other pieces, with a supply of ammunition.

However, despite all this trouble gone to, no major breakthrough was achieved with the bombards. Clearly much practice was necessary to obtain accuracy with these weapons, and the royal gunners did not have the ammunition for such practice. Shooting beyond the ditches, they were unable to recover the spent cannon-balls—as the Douglases were able to do of a night. They blazed off their supply of powder and shot, but with only disappointing results as far as their observation could establish. Certainly the effect on the castle was minimal.

There appeared to be nothing for it but to settle down to a prolonged siege, or else pack up and depart in humiliation. Nor was there any real conviction that a siege, however long, would be any more successful, especially with those English ships-of-war standing off to supply the beleaguered garrison and even take off the senior Douglases, if required. And with harvesttime already upon them and most lords wanting their people back on their lands for that most essential activity.

All this much depressed the royal party, with James himself

crestfallen that his first major military venture should be proving so fruitless. He would not hear of giving up, however. Frustration prevailed.

There was a kind of relief from an unexpected source. Home of Aytoun, although nominally an ally of the Douglases, like the other Homes, had a bone to pick with that house. For it had been a kinsman of his who was the Prior of Coldinghame whom Abbot William Douglas had had murdered in order to gain the extensive Priory lands and wealth, Aytoun adjoining Coldinghame. Now he arrived at the King's camp with the surprising information that Angus himself had slipped out of Tantallon, presumably by boat and by night, and was now in fact at Coldinghame conferring secretly with his Uncle William—it was thought with a view to organising a Home and other Border clans uprising in the King's rear. This news coincided with reports coming in that bands of Douglases elsewhere had raided and sacked the two Midlothian villages and estates of Cousland and Cranstoun, likewise two further places near to Stirling, crown properties, clearly as distraction and counter-threat. The King, much excited, insisted there and then on personally leading a hard-riding detachment down into the Merse to catch and apprehend Angus at Coldinghame.

Leading a company of some five hundred of the best-mounted lairds, their retainers and mosstroopers, Lindsay in attendance, James headed southwards that same day, at speed, all glad enough for the activity, something positive to attempt after all the heel-kicking idleness and discomfiture of the past days. They had some thirty miles to go, by Beilhaven again, Dunbar, the Home castle of Dunglass, Colbrandspath Tower—where David had vivid recollections of de la Bastie—and on over the high wilderness of Coldinghame Muir where he sighed for Kate and their honeymoon at Fast Castle there. It was dusk when they arrived in the vicinity of the Priory, set in a deep, hidden valley, on a defensive site at the confluence of two steep-sided burns, not far from St. Abb's Head. The monastic buildings were more like another castle than any sacred edifice, even the church four-square, tough-looking and battlemented—no doubt with reason, in that blood-stained Merse area. Whether warned of the royal approach or not, the place was all shut up for the night behind its high walls, and no amount of trumpeted summonsing produced any acknowledgement or other reaction.

161

James ordered his force to encircle the establishment, to prevent any escape by Angus, assuming that he was still there, and settled down for a chilly night in the open.

In the morning, although the occasional bell sounded from within the Priory, there was still no response to royal demands for the appearance of the Earl of Angus, Abbot William, the Sub-Prior or anyone else in authority, an infuriating situation which again left James and his people at something of a loss. They had no artillery and no means of storming the high walling. They might contrive scaling-ladders but defenders could fairly easily cast such down and overcome the climbers. In the end it was decided to cut down some trees and try to use the trimmed trunks as battering-rams against the massive wooden gates in the walling. If that failed, they might attempt to burn the gates down by heaping blazing brushwood against them; but that would require the construction of some sort of strong canopy to act as shield over the fire-tenders to protect them from possible missiles, javelins or arrows from above, and such would take time to fashion.

The tree-felling was proceeding, with some local help enforced when, around noon, an alarm was sounded. A large mounted force was approaching down the valley of one of the streams, from the west. They bore no banners to indicate identity.

This disturbed David Lindsay more than it did the King or his other officers, who saw no reason to assume that any hostility was intended to the monarch of them all, that indeed it might well represent support and reinforcement from loyal Border clans, Turnbulls, Elliots, Pringles, Scotts, perhaps Buccleuch himself. David, who had had all too much experience of Border attitudes, under de la Bastie, feared otherwise. This was Home country, after all, and that warlike and unruly house were seldom loyal to any save their friends, usually pro-English, and traditional allies of Douglas, Aytoun being something of an exception. Indeed, at that moment, it suddenly occurred to Lindsay that there might be typical Home double-dealing here. Aytoun, after bringing the tidings of Angus's Coldinghame visit to the King, had not himself come back with them here, although his castle was only a few miles away, pleading weariness of men and horses after his dash north to Tantallon—on consideration a strange admission from a mosstrooping Border laird. Suppose in fact that this was all a plot to get the King detached from his army and into Home and Douglas hands? Suppose, after their departure from Tantallon yesterday, Aytoun had quickly recovered his energies and hurried southwards again on a different route, to inform his Home and other allies that James was now at Coldinghame with a comparatively small company and could be readily captured? Angus indeed might not be here at all! Voicing something of this to the King, he made little impression, the general reaction being that Lindsay was letting his poetic imagination run away with him. But when another scout posted on high ground came down to report that a second sizable cavalry contingent was heading hitherwards down the other burn's valley, from the north this time, there was no more mockery and some serious faces.

David, considerably perturbed now, urged James to order an immediate concentration of their people around his person. They were, at present, hopelessly dispersed, still forming a wide circle around the Priory, to prevent any possible break-out by Angus. If this was indeed an attack developing, then they could hardly be worse placed to withstand it.

James hesitated. If these were friendly folk approaching, as surely was most likely, he would look a fool to summon back all his own men, and offer Angus just the chance he might well be looking for to make a dash for it, and all their effort wasted. Others agreed.

So they waited, David fretting. But when, presently, the first-reported force came into general view topping a gentle rise to the west, a mere quarter-mile away, and there drew up and massed, without signal nor friendly indication, even the most optimistic of the King's companions fell silent. At David's agitated plea, James at last ordered his trumpeters to sound the recall for his scattered company.

And as though those trumpets had been their own command, the serried ranks of the newcomers raised a shout, drew swords, couched lances and surged forward. "A Douglas! A Douglas!" they cried, and "A Home! A Home!"

David took charge, since someone must. He reached out to grasp the King's arm, and pointed due eastwards. There was little choice of direction, with enemy approaching from west and north and the river to the south, but that way also would best enable most of their dispersed people to rejoin them; and the valley narrowing again after the open space around the Priory and its homestead, would help to limit any large-scale fighting.

The royal party that rode behind James and his companion were added to all the time by others from the encirclement obeying the trumpet-call. David, having taken the lead, felt responsible for their further moves and always he felt responsible for the King. He racked his brains. He had been here before more than once and could remember something of the layout of the valley, but little detail. Should they seek a place to stand and fight? Or, with the monarch's safety paramount, was that precluded? What were their chances if they did? Numbers were vital. He had no means of knowing the enemy strength but, at a glance, he would have put the company they had seen on the rise as at least as large as their own. And there was another, of unknown size, bearing down on their left. So they could be outnumbered two to one, or more. And these Homes and Douglases were tough Border reivers, fighting on their own ground, while their own party, hastily culled from the royal army, were untried as fighters. Dare they risk the King's safety, then, possibly his life, in such circumstances? It did not take him long to decide that they dared not.

But flight, however humiliating and feeble-seeming was not likely to be easy or straightforward. Their pursuers were probably just as well mounted and would know the country better. In a long chase, they might well win—and it was thirty miles back to Tantallon. So some sort of diversion, some hold-up of the enemy was called for. An ambush? That would take time to set up and would require suitable ground conditions, unlikely to be readily available. A split-up of their people, to confuse the chase? A rearguard action by the majority, to allow the King to win clear? But would James agree to such a move?

It was while all this was racing through his mind as they galloped, that David suddenly perceived something ahead which he had not recollected, if ever he had noticed it. The St. Abb's road they were pounding along crossed still another stream from the north, by a narrow bridge. It was in no deep or steep valley, this one, to serve as a difficult barrier for horsemen, but a broad and shallow and open declivity. However, by that very token, this burn here had spread itself in marshy meadowland and wet grazing, where cattle stood knee-deep amongst reeds and rushes. Through this the water meandered, the recent rains adding to the boglike aspect, with small pools showing. In consequence, the bridge had to be no high-arched stone structure but long and low and timber-built. Even as they began to thud across this, its planking shaking to the beat of hooves, David decided that here was a chance, possibly their only chance. Taking James's agreement for granted, turning in his saddle, he yelled and gestured right and left.

"Hold the bridge! Hold this bridge!" he shouted back. "Line the bog. Both sides. Hold them here. Here, I say!"

Chaos ensued. It was not possible to halt some hundreds of fleeing horsemen abruptly, especially crossing a long and narrow bridge, to deploy them in a defensive posture at the bridge-end and along an uneven marshy front on both sides, without considerable confusion, misunderstanding and dispute. But the King's presence helped, and he excitedly supported Lindsay.

They were fortunate in that the pursuers had evidently decided on a tactic which allowed their quarry a breathing-space. For although they had sent a group racing on behind the stragglers of the royal party, to keep them in view, the bulk of them had halted near the Priory, no doubt to link up with the second contingent. Which probably indicated confidence that their prey could not escape them. So now this detachment of the enemy, no more than fifty, drew rein near the southern end of the bridge, after the last of the stragglers were over, prudently to await the main body. How many of the royal force had failed to rejoin the King there was no means of telling meantime.

David had a little time, therefore, to seek to organise a defensive stance. There was perhaps four hundred yards of the marshland on the west side of the bridge and a bare two hundred on the east, which offered fair scope for a stand—this being emphasised when the hooves of the flanking parties' horses began to sink into the moss and mire, some up to the hocks. No enemy assault across the stream itself, and then through this, would be easy. But of course a mere six-hundred-yard front could be turned fairly quickly, and David had little idea as to what lay beyond, out of sight, right and left.

So, having made as effective a disposal of their manpower as was possible in these conditions, with about one hundred still congregated at the bridge-end itself, he turned to the King.

"Sire—we can hold them up here, I think, for a little. Not for long, for almost certainly they can outflank us, one side or both.

165

You must go now. Head back over Coldinghame Muir, with a small escort, for Tantallon. Once there, you can send ample troops to our aid."

"Leave you here, Davie? Whilst I flee? No—never!"

"But, Sire—the only point in making a stand, here or elsewhere, is to effect your escape. It is *you* they want, the King. You escape, and they are defeated."

"I will not go. Like some craven!"

"James, heed me, of a mercy! You are the *King*, the whole realm's sovereign-lord. All the kingdom needs you—not just a few men here. You can do nothing here to advantage the issue, one sword in five hundred. If you are captured, or struck down, or slain, you have failed your realm! Throw away all that we have been struggling for since Flodden-field. Think, James—think! Think what your own father cost the realm there, by fighting like a man-at-arms instead of a monarch, and dying, to leave his kingdom in ruin. Do you not the same!"

"He is right, Your Grace," Lord Maxwell, the most lofty member of this party agreed. "If you were captured here, Scotland would be struck a dire blow. In Douglas hands again, all could be lost."

"Can we not outfight them?"

"Not if they are double our numbers," David said. "And there could be more coming. This is a carefully-laid plot." He tried another tack. "We are near the border here. If you are taken, Sire, the Douglases and Homes could well convey you over into England and hand you to Dacre and King Henry, then Henry could make Angus his governor of Scotland, in your name and his!"

That served. James looked shaken. "No—not that!" he exclaimed. "Not Henry!"

"Then, Sire, go! My lord, will you escort His Grace with a small party? A mile this side of St. Abb's there is a farmery and hamlet, I mind. From it a road of sorts strikes northwards across the muir to Fast. Take that. We will follow—when we can!" David paused. "But wait. Not yet. If those yonder see you go now, leaving most here, they may guess what is done and send a company to cut you off. They will know this country better than we do. Wait, then, until there is the stir of attack—then go. Not openly, two or three at a time . . ."

They did not have long to wait. For even as Lindsay spoke the main mass of the enemy appeared around a bend in the valley, and it was very quickly obvious that they far outnumbered the King's force—perhaps twelve hundred of them, at a guess. They came on at speed to the bridge-end and there halted with the others, a bare two hundred yards away. It was something of an alarming experience just to sit inactive, watching them come so near.

Whoever was leading them was a man of decision for, after only a brief pause, he deployed his people left and right, while keeping about one-third of the total clustered at the bridge-head. Clearly there was to be a concerted attack without delay.

David asked himself what his late friend de la Bastie would have done, the most experienced and able commander he had known. Surprise. Surprise had always been Antoine's tactic—but what surprise was open to them here? The smaller force, and very much on the defensive, the only real surprise would be to attack. But how could that possibly be contrived?

The bridge itself was the only feature to offer the least scope. Its width was no more than eight feet, only just sufficient to allow a cart to cross. So it would take no more than two horses abreast at a time. But it could accommodate four to five dismounted men, shoulder to shoulder. If he were to put forward a screen of say fifty of the best-armoured of his people on foot, they could hold the bridge for some time in hand-to-hand fighting, lancemen in front. The enemy, then, would also have to attack on foot. And while this was going on, others of his folk behind them could be working on the bridge-planking, tearing and prising it up, so that thereafter it would be impassable for horses. So any mounted attack must then be pushed through the river itself and the soft marshy gound on either side, much better for defence than attack.

There was no time for trying to think up alternative strategies. Hurriedly explaining this to the bridge-end grouping, he called for volunteers to dismount and go forward at once. There was no great rush to respond; these were cavalrymen and like all such despised foot-fighters. That is until horns blowing from the opposite end of the bridge indicated that the enemy attack was about to develop, and battle would be joined anyway at one side of the stream or the other, and some choice was still theirs. Not fifty but perhaps thirty stout characters thereupon flung themselves down from their mounts, retaining their lances, and hurried out on to the bridge timbers before the enemy could advance.

So far the device worked. David's men were able to get most of the way across the lengthy bridge before the surprised opposition reacted by spurring forward in a mounted mass. But at the beginning of the timbering they pulled up in very evident doubt as to how to tackle this situation. A few daredevils were either ordered, or elected themselves, to ride on, as though to charge the men on the bridge; and not only the men but the frieze of lances, the front rank kneeling. No doubt the intention was to ride the defenders down by sheer weight of charging horseflesh; but two men side-by-side hardly make a successful charge, even though backed up by other pairs. Also horses have their own perceptions, and that tight wall of men and lances was a daunting barrier for any animal, with the sun glinting on spear-heads and armour. The first two beasts began to rear and shy.

Their riders drove them on, their own lances lowered—indeed, they were pushed on from behind willy-nilly. But it was ten lances against two, for the second rank of dismounted men, standing close behind their kneeling comrades, could thrust their weapons out over the others' shoulders, almost as far. Admittedly the horsemen had the height, but that very elevation took almost three feet off the length of the nine-foot pikes; and they had armoured breastplates and helmets to strike at while the others had unprotected horses' legs—for it was on the horses that the defenders concentrated.

The result was all but inevitable. In whinnying, screaming panic and hurt the front beasts reared up on hind-quarters and sidled. One, tottering, fell over the edge of the railless bridge, throwing its rider before it into the water; the other, hooves lashing, swung back and was cannoned into by the animal behind, and both went down in kicking ruin, totally blocking the bridge. On top of this the following horsemen piled, unable to draw up in time, in indescribable chaos, their long lances adding to the havoc. Two more beasts fell off into the stream, and men were thrown right and left. That assault was over.

David had not waited, however enthralling it might be to watch, but had forthwith sent forward his demolition people to break up the bridge-planking. This was not so easy, lacking tools, on solid, massive timbering; and sundry swords were snapped when used as levers. But enough of the planking came up to make the bridge useless for horses, which was what mattered.

David also had to observe the mounted attacks on the flanks, with hundreds of horsemen seeking to pick their way across wet ground, the muddy-bedded stream and more marshy ground beyond, and the defenders ready to stop any routes which seemed relatively easy. Clearly, whatever the eventual outcome, this was going to be a slow process and no major break-through was likely for some time.

He turned, to find Maxwell urging James to be off, the latter still reluctant. "Now!" David cried. "All are engaged. Slip away now, of a mercy! Go, James—go!" That was as near a command as any subject could give to his monarch.

Maxwell took the King's arm.

David returned to the management of his peculiar battle, the first that he had ever sought to command on his own. He sent a runner forward to tell the people holding the bridge to move back behind the gap made by the demolishers, but to do it in stages behind a protective screen, in case the enemy rushed them again. It would be an awkward process for there was only the supporting framework of the bridge to edge over for about a dozen yards. Belatedly he thought of sending mounted scouts up and down stream to spy out and report back on what lay beyond present vision, and whether their flanks could be easily turned. Then he sent a party to reinforce a point where it seemed as though the enemy might achieve a minor break-through.

Looking behind, he was thankful to see now no sign of the King or of Maxwell.

The enemy leadership appeared to be at something of a loss. It looked as though they were waiting to see how their flanking attacks went before making any new initiative, which suited David.

It was only a question of time before sheer numbers told. Timing, therefore, for himself also. If he could grant James a sufficient start, and then begin to withdraw his force gradually, leaving only a hard-riding rearguard . . . ? So much would depend on what the ground was like, left and right, out of sight.

He ordered more men off to plug another gap in the marsh-line to the west.

His scouts returned. Downstream, it seemed, there was more wet ground, even wider than here, indeed a mere of sorts. But the other's report was less encouraging. Round the upstream bend this side-valley narrowed in, with firm ground, and although the banks were quite steep and the burn itself deeper, there was nothing to seriously hold up determined cavalry for long. Sooner or later the enemy was going to turn that flank.

It was difficult for David to calculate timing in all this stress. How long had James had now? Sufficient to let him get clear away? Probably. So it would be wise to try to begin extricating his force almost at once. Where could he pull out first?

His consideration was interrupted by a new move, an enemy assault on foot on the bridge. This had to be unimpeded until the gap was reached, after which it would pose a problem indeed. Men creeping across the supporting framework could easily be picked off one by one. The enemy answer was to hurl missiles, javelins, stones, even pikes and dirks, across the dozen-yard break, to keep the defenders hiding behind their shields, and at the same time to send a proportion of their dismounted men to jump down and wade the river, which was not sufficiently deep to drown in.

David had anticipated something of the sort from the first, and relied on the muddy bottom of the stream to bog waders down, and the fact that there was at least thirty yards of very soft margin thereafter to cross before firm ground was reached. He sent reinforcements to contest this.

In fact, these were not required. The attackers, being cavalrymen, were almost all wearing spurred leather thigh-boots, and few thought to discard these before jumping. They were the last thing in which to wade a waist-deep stream, for they promptly filled with water, becoming little better than anchors, and the spurs apt to catch on weeds and other obstacles in the mud. So the river-front was no success. Nor was the bridge assault. The missiles, at that range, did little damage, and the few hardy souls who ventured over the bridge-skeleton were quickly disposed of. The entire attack petered out, with minimal effect.

David decided to try to disguise the first withdrawals by seeming to send a mounted group of about seventy dashing upstream and out of sight, as though they had just thought of the outflanking danger, but with the instruction to swing off northwards thereafter, for Coldinghame Muir. When there was no evident reaction to this departure by the enemy, he risked sending a still larger party in the other direction, downstream. This left his defensive force very much depleted, of course, reduced now to about three hundred, but he could not have it both ways.

And now he saw what he had been expecting all along, the opposition deciding on the outflanking attempt and despatching almost half their number upstream—whether in belated reaction to the defenders' recent move or not, who could tell?

Now, then, there could be no more delay nor diversionary tactics. In mere minutes they could be cut off by overwhelming numbers. David ordered their remaining trumpeter to sound the recall, and hoped that the foe would not immediately recognise it for what it was.

His people, needless to say, had been waiting for this and lost no time in obeying the summons. They came streaming back to their horses from marsh and riverside and bridge, and as they came, not waiting for any assembling or formation, David sent them off at speed along the St. Abb's road. Their opponents certainly could perceive what was happening, but there was little that they could do to interfere at this stage, with the barriers still between. All depended on the speed of the flanking-force.

David, fretting with impatience as he was, felt bound to be almost the last to leave. There was still no view of the upstream enemy.

A mere rearguard, they pounded along the road eastwards, David wondering how much of a start they had. At least he had ensured that most of the King's force would escape. That was a satisfaction. Also it was good that his first battle as leader, self-appointed as he might be, had been fairly successful and comparatively bloodless. Moreover, he had a sneaking idea that the enemy pursuit might be less energetically pressed now. After all, this entire plot almost certainly had been arranged to capture the King; and it must be fairly obvious to all now that there was little chance of that happening.

At the farmery a mile short of St. Abb's they swung off due northwards, by the track he had first explored with Kate on their honeymoon, passing behind the mighty headland. They began to climb almost at once, and now, on bare, treeless upland, could see many of their own folk streaming ahead of them. David kept glancing back and presently indeed spied pursuit, almost

171

a mile behind, strung-out and no very large numbers as yet. Encouraged, he spurred on.

They were well up on the moor, half-way to Fast Castle, when they recognised that the chase was being given up. Their pursuers could be seen on a grassy ridge far behind, and it took only moments to perceive that they were stationary there. Even as they looked, they saw these horsemen rein round and turn back.

Some of his people cheered, but David was content to sigh his relief.

About two hours later, near Dunglass, they were met by a large company sent by the King to their aid.

* * *

David Lindsay might have been reasonably satisfied with the outcome of that day's doings but James Stewart certainly was not. Indeed Lindsay had never seen him so dejected and ill-tempered. The youth appeared to see himself as a failure, both in his first military venture, the siege of Tantallon, and in the Coldinghame expedition—and in the latter, moreover, he had been compelled to seem the craven, to flee, leaving his people to their fate. No amount of contrary representation by David had any effect—indeed, David rather bore the brunt of the King's ill-humour, as the one who had insisted on his flight and there-after won praise where he had failed.

James's disappointment and resentment took practical form. The siege was to be abandoned and a return made to Edinburgh the very next day. Actually this decision was more or less inevitable, for there had been considerable desertion even in the short time he had been away, the entire situation at Tantallon being most evidently unprofitable and the harvest calling men away urgently—for in the long run most Scots lairds depended on cattle for their basic sustenance, and if the harvest was not successfully gathered in, the cattle would not survive the long winter; the economics were as simple as that.

So next morning the packing-up began, a gloomy business but few protesting. They did not know whether Angus was back in Tantallon—whether in fact he had ever left it—but if he was, he would be chuckling, and the thought was galling in the extreme. In his present mood, desirous of putting the entire wretched business behind him as quickly as possible, James

172

was certainly not inclined to wait for the cumbersome artillery, ammunition, tentage and waggon-train; and after sending back the Dunbar cannon to the man de Gonzolles for the relief of his hostages, he rode off westwards with his main force, with scarcely a backward glance, leaving Lord Borthwick, Master of the Ordnance, and the seaman David Falconer, to command the rearguard and bring on the artillery and baggage.

The King rode ahead, silent, desiring no company.

They were at Athelstaneford and David Lindsay was about to seek permission to pay calls at Garleton and The Byres, since his presence did not appear to be particularly welcome to the monarch meantime, when couriers caught up with them from the east. These brought dire tidings. Scarcely had the royal army departed than Angus himself had sallied out of his castle in force to attack the rearguard busy packing up the baggage. He had made an easy conquest, capturing the cannon and burning all the gear and supplies. The man Falconer and many others were slain and the Lord Borthwick a prisoner.

This news was not calculated to raise the royal spirits, but there was nothing that could usefully be done about it all now. James, in a passion, raised clenched fists high and swore on oath that so long as he lived Angus and his Douglases should never have their banishment revoked, nor find resting-place in Scotland.

Lindsay thought it an injudicious moment to seek leave of absence.

10

At Holyrood, in the weeks that followed, James was hard indeed to live with. His pride humbled, his self-esteem shattered, the worst side of his character came to the fore. He was bad-tempered, cross-grained, drank too much, demanded a succession of women, gambled recklessly and generally misbehaved. This was distressing for those fond of him and for those who were concerned with the quality of his rule; but it did have the effect of drawing David Lindsay and Janet Douglas ever closer together, in their joint efforts to save their young monarch from his weaknesses. The less successful they were the more they tried, and the better they came to know each other and appreciate the efforts made. David came to the conclusion that his earlier assessment of Janet's worth and virtues had been well founded, indeed an under-estimate, and that something should be done about it. He did not pretend to himself, or to her, that here was any headlong romance, nothing such as he had had with Kate; but he much liked, admired and even desired this young woman. He had no real urge to remarry, but respecting her, he concluded that it had to be a proposal of marriage.

A suitable occasion arose in mid-November after a distinctly shamefaced Lord Borthwick had presented himself at the Abbey, new-come from Tantallon. He reported that he had had a message for the King from Angus, who had casually released him without ransom, saying that James was welcome to have back him and the royal cannon, which were poor things, he having much better himself. He advised that if His Grace thought of a further call at Tantallon or other Douglas house, he should provide himself with more effective pieces than these, capable at least of knocking holes in a dovecote. So furious was James at this sarcastic and insulting gesture that he there and then commanded Arran, Argyll, Bothwell, Maxwell and everyone else about him out his presence, berating them for failing to rid him and his realm of this vile and arrogant traitor, and declaring on his royal word that they were none of them to dare to return to his court until they had disposed of Angus once and for all. On Argyll, as commander of his land forces, he laid the charge in especial, telling him that he should go forthwith and use any and every means and device known to God or man to cleanse the kingdom of this plague. Thereafter, dismissing them all, he deliberately drank himself into a stupor, and in that state David, with Janet's help, more or less carried him to bed.

Together they stood, side by side at the royal couch, looking from the handsome features of their young lord, flushed and open-lipped in drink, to each other; and suddenly, on impulse, David reached out to grasp the young woman's hand.

"This is . . . this is . . ." he began. "This is our lot, lass—our strange lot. Yours and mine. To cherish and defend and try

174

to succour this, this foolish yet lovable lad. Janet—will you wed me?"

She eyed him, searching his face. She did not seek to release her hand. "Wed, David?" she wondered. "Wed, you say? You would marry me?" She might have been playing for time.

"Aye, wed. You and me. Become man and wife."

"Why?" That was not curt but probing, questioning.

"Why? Need you ask, lass?" He sounded almost impatient. "Is it not clear that we should? Here we stand. Just you and I. Close, together, a man and a woman. Sharing so much. Needed, aye, and needing! Just ourselves—and him. James—in name he has a whole kingdom, multitudes, but in fact he has only us two."

"And does that mean that we should wed, David?"

"Why not? We know each other, now. Trust each other, rely on each other. As he relies on us."

"Yes. But is that sufficient reason?"

"Janet, I greatly admire you. I have come to, to require you, I think."

"You do? How do you require me, David?"

"Why, in all ways, woman!"

"All ways? My company you have, and can have, any time. My friendship and trust and regard is yours already. Fortune I have none. Is it my body, then?"

He wagged his head. "No. Or, yes—that also. But—see you, lass, must we put words to it? Can we not *know* what is best, right, good for us?" He all but shook the hand which he still clutched.

"I think that if we know, we shall find words," she said slowly. "You, a man of words, a poet, should perceive that, surely?"

He stared, biting his lip. "*I* know, if you do not," he asserted. "I know that I want you for my wife."

"And will you think hardly of me, David, if I say that that is not enough? For . . . marriage. *My* marriage."

"What am I to say?"

"If you do not know, my dear, then who am I to tell you!"

"So—you will not wed me, Janet Douglas?"

"I think not. Not . . . at this present. But, I thank you for the asking. And hope that this will not spoil our good friendship, David? Do not let it do that."

He looked down at the slightly snoring youth and shook his head dumbly.

She gently released her hand and left them both there.

Profoundly disturbed, dissatisfied, perplexed, David sought his own chamber. It was his turn for failure. Yet he could not see why, where he had gone wrong. She seemed fond enough of him. All this talk of words, of his being a poet, seemed pointless, lacking in significance—and it was a significant-enough occasion surely, a proposal of marriage? It all appeared contrary to his estimation of Janet's character, as though she were insufficiently serious. And yet . . . ?

In the morning the young woman seemed no different from usual, although the man realised that he himself might well be sounding stiff and abrupt. But there was in fact little scope for any private association anyway, for James awoke in a foul mood, contrary and demanding; and Davie Beaton arrived from St. Andrews, on a matter of urgency, seeking the King's co-operation and not getting it. With all Edinburgh in a stir—for Argyll appeared to be taking his new commission against Angus seriously and was commandeering money and materials as well as men in the city—personal preoccupations were precluded.

After a difficult interview with the monarch, Beaton came seeking Lindsay's help. "What is wrong with James?" he demanded. "He is as cross-grained as a Muscovy bear! I can get nowhere with him."

"He is not at his best, no. He has a sore head, from drinking too much, and otherwise working off his disappointments. You have heard of this latest affair of Angus?"

"The sending of Borthwick back with the cannon? Yes, the city buzzes with it. And Argyll's intentions with the Homes . . ."

"The Homes? What is this?"

"It seems that he intends to detach the Homes from Angus somehow. The word is that the King has given him a free hand, all the royal power, to get rid of Angus; and he sees the Homes as the Douglas's weak spot. Many of them are under sentence of banishment and forfeiture for their crimes on the border, as well as for supporting Angus. They say that Argyll will offer to remit these, and even give them moneys, in exchange for Angus's betrayal. Who knows—it might serve some purpose."

"It will not prise Angus out of Tantallon Castle."

Beaton shrugged. "The Campbells are cunning cairds. Argyll will have some scheme. But that is not my concern. I require the

King's assent to a matter of some importance to the Church—and he will scarce listen to me."

"The Church? Do *you* require the royal authority in Church matters?"

"It is not quite that. It is the matter of Patrick Hamilton, Abbot of Fearn. You will have heard of him?"

"I have heard the name, that is all. Is he not some kin of Arran's?"

"That is the trouble, or part of it—the lesser part. The greater is that he is therefore also some kin to James. His father is Sir Patrick Hamilton of Kincavil, Arran's brother. Which puts him in cousinship to the King."

"And that is . . . awkward?"

"Very. For the Abbot is a thorn in the flesh of Holy Church, which requires to be plucked out!"

"I see. So James's permission is advisable? What has this Hamilton done? Fearn is far away, is it not? In Ross?"

"Aye. But our Patrick unfortunately does not confine his activities to Ross. Indeed, I would say that he has not visited Fearn for years. He was given the abbacy as a mere youth, to provide him with funds and a seat in parliament. No—he elects to make a nuisance of himself much nearer home. In St. Andrews itself, in fact!"

"Ah—too close to the bone! What is his offence?"

"He is one of the so-called reformers, and determined with it. And voluble. At St. Andrews he studied under John Major, the historian—not noted for his orthodoxy! There he appears to have imbibed even more dangerous doctrines than we did! Then he went to the Continent, to Wittenberg, where he sat under the man Martin Luther, the schismatic, and then went to this new dissenting university of Marburg. Now he has come home, full of these heresies, and insists in trumpeting them abroad. Even in my uncle's own city. He must be stopped."

"Why? The Church stands in great need of reform, surely? You have said so yourself. The very fact that you are Abbot of Arbroath, yet not in holy orders, and he is Abbot of Fearn from youth, speaks for itself."

"To be sure. But such reform must be orderly, come from the Church itself, from the top, not from beneath. Hamilton preaches otherwise, to the masses, fomenting strife. It is revolt that he advocates rather than reform. He objects to churchmen having any power in the state—as did Major—a dangerous doctrine."

Lindsay grinned.

"You may smile, my friend—but if the Church did not play her part in the state, it would be in a sorrier case than it is! Lord—half of the lords secular can scarcely sign their names! But this Patrick Hamilton preaches other follies—that man has no free will, that children, after baptism, are sinners, that no man is justified by works, only faith, that faith, hope and charity are so knit together that lacking one, a man lacks all. And so on. Many are heeding him and he must be silenced."

"You admit the need for reform, man. But say that it must come from the top. But all know that Rome is the last place to look for betterment. The very worst shameful abuses come from the Vatican itself, the corrupt papacy, the sale of bishoprics and other benefices, even cardinalates, child prelates, the trade in indulgences and the like. Who can look to Rome?"

"Watch your words, Snowdoun Herald, when speaking to the Primate's secretary!" The other smiled as he said that. "You could find yourself excommunicated! But, no—I do not mean that the papacy itself will initiate reform. Not as present minded. By the top, I meant the Church hierarchy in other lands, where is vision and vigour. As here in Scotland! And in those Germanic states and the Netherlands. Even in England, where Wolsey seeks the papal throne for himself. There are stirrings. But the movement must come from above, from the appointed leadership, or Rome will never accept it."

"But *will* it? Can it? It is the very hierarchies which are most at fault. Here not least, man."

"Oh, it can, yes. Many times Holy Church has reformed itself, from within. Nearly all the great orders represent a reformation of sorts—the most recent, the Cistercians. But others, the Benedictines, the Dominicans, the Franciscans, the Observantines and the like, they all started as reformist movements. That is the way it must be done, not by fanatics and mobs."

"And *you*? You who now all but control the Primate and so much of the Scots Church—do you intend reform?"

"I do. Reform in many ways. But not Patrick Hamilton's way. Challenging all established authority, advocating *dis*order and violent change. He must be silenced, or he will do untold harm."

"And you need James's agreement?"

"Not need it perhaps, but prefer it. James himself has little interest in the Church, I think, in religion itself. Nor, probably, have Arran and his Hamiltons, in the main. But they are interested in power, wealth and kinship. Another of Arran's brothers is Abbot of Paisley, and a difficult man. Then there is the Bastard, who could well be awkward. This Patrick is his cousin. They could all bear on the King. So I must needs act, and quickly."

"You? Or your uncle?"

"Let us say both!"

"And what do you want of me?"

"Only your good offices with James. I cannot wait long. Hamilton is apprehended and in a cell at St. Andrews Castle, to appear before a court of the Church in a matter of days."

"I see. I fear that I cannot help you, Davie—even if I would. At present James scarcely loves me. He blames me for making him seem to act the craven at Coldinghame when I persuaded him to flee to avoid capture by the Douglases and Homes. No advocacy of mine would help your cause."

"And, do I take it, you would be loth to give that advocacy anyway?"

"Yes. I am sorry. But I would not be a party to persecution of reformers however . . . inconvenient! I believe that the Church *needs* reform, and is unlikely to get it from your hierarchies."

Beaton eyed him thoughtfully. They had disagreed on minor points and procedures before on many an occasion, but this was the first time that Lindsay had taken an opposing stance on a matter of principle.

"Then I too am sorry," he said simply.

The Lord Privy Seal remained only two days at Holyrood, and on the second came to take his leave of Lindsay in the royal ante-room. On this occasion Janet Douglas was present.

"I have made a little progress with James," he reported. "But only a little. He accepts that authority must be maintained, in Church as in state. But does not commit himself as to Patrick Hamilton. So—now I go to see the Bastard of Arran, who so largely sways his father, and who is all but recovered of his wounds, they say."

"And what do you hope for, from that one? He will have little love for Holy Church, I think."

179

"No—but he will have much love for James Hamilton of Finnart, unless I much mistake! So I must seek to provide for that."

"Provide? Then you will be wagering with the Devil!"

"No doubt. But I have had some practice at that!"

"My lord Abbot—that man is wicked, a murderer," Janet said. "Surely the Church can have no truck with such."

"It is a wicked world, my dear. If the Church has no truck with wicked men, how shall it make any headway?"

"Headway towards what?" Lindsay demanded. "Can it deliberately use evil to bring forth good?"

"If there is no other road open, and we have a fair destination, we must take the one there is, friend."

"Are you so sure? That way could lead to damnation!"

"Not if one watches where one treads! Use the wits God has given. Though I walk through the valley of the shadow of death, I will fear no evil!"

That silenced Lindsay, but not Janet Douglas.

"I think that David is right," she said. "Is there not a road to hell, to destruction, broad and fair? How is it paved?"

"Ha—wisdom crieth without, she uttereth her voice! Even Solomon had to accept it. I swear I have no chance with the pair of you!"

"But you *will* go to chaffer and deal with James Hamilton of Finnart?"

"I will, yes. And seek to prove you both wrong."

"We shall see. If I cannot wish you well, I can at least wish the Church well."

"Then with that I must rest content. Mistress Janet—of your charity, do not think too hardly of me. I have much on my shoulders, and must carry the burden as best I may."

"Did you not *choose* your burden, my lord? Elect to carry it your own way? David is right, surely. For myself, a mere woman, my notions matter little. But you should heed David Lindsay. Now I will leave you . . ."

"A notable and attractive young woman, with a mind of her own," Beaton observed, when she had gone. "Interesting. And not uninterested in yourself, I would say?"

"That *I* have not noticed."

"No? But perhaps you are hardly a noticing man, where women are concerned?"

"On the contrary. I . . . I much appreciate women."

"But not this one?"

"Why, yes—since you ask. I find her to my taste. But . . ."

"But not sufficiently to seek her favours?"

The other frowned. "If by favours you mean seeking to bed her—no! She is not that sort of woman."

"Ah, do I detect more interest than I had thought? A more serious concern? You could do with a wife, you know, my friend."

"Whether I could or no is of little matter. Since she will not have me."

"You say that? Sakes—that I can scarce credit! The way she looks at you. Have you asked her?"

"I have. And she refused me."

"Then I must indeed be losing my judgement! I would have said . . ." He paused. "You really asked her to wed? Not merely hinted, gave her to understand?"

"I asked her to be my wife, and she said no. As you say, she has a mind of her own."

"I esteemed that I knew women better than this! You must have trodden wrongly, somewhere."

"I asked her plainly, honestly. I could do no more."

"So! Plainly? Honestly? Perhaps now we have it? How plainly, Davie? Women may not always esteem mere plainness in a proposal of marriage."

"You are become very knowledgeable, of a sudden about women! I do not remember you being so sure of yourself when you were courting Marion Ogilvy! I told Janet that I admired her, trusted her, even needed her—at least, I think that I did. That we could rely on each other . . ."

"Admire? Trust? Rely? Aye, but did you tell her that you loved her? Love—that is what women want to hear. Did you tell her that?"

"Why, perhaps not. Love is, is a word which can mean much or little, anything or all but nothing . . ."

"Nevertheless, it is the word that women want. If you denied it her, it may be that she likewise denied you her hand. Until you should . . . learn!"

"But that would be madness! To refuse marriage for lack of one foolish word!"

"Madness or none, it could be your trouble. Try her again,

181

man. And tell her that you love her. Tell her again and again. I think that it might serve."

"That would be folly . . ."

"Folly? You do love the woman, do you not? After your fashion?"

"What mean you—after my fashion? Of course I love her. Would I ask her to wed me if I did not?"

Beaton threw up his hands in defeat. "I go. I go. Have it as you will. But I have given you good advice—better than you have given me! Now for the Bastard of Arran!"

David Lindsay, of course, was not going to take seriously his peculiar friend's theories on the approaches to matrimony—who was Davie Beaton, after all, to pontificate, a man who had taken years to put his own case to the test and who, once wed, could leave wife and bairns for months at a time? This talk of love was ridiculous as a kind of key to open the gate to marriage, surely. Marriage, the sharing of a man's whole life and future and fortune with another person, was much too important a step to contemplate to depend on any mere form of words, this one or other. Yet, to be sure, Janet had said that about words, claimed that as a poet he should be something of a master of words. So he might be; he seldom had any difficulty in finding apt words for his verses. But matrimony was not poetry, it was reality if anything was. He had *been* married, after all, even if Janet had not, and he knew. This of love—he did love her, to be sure, not as he had loved Kate, of course, but sufficiently to want her to share his life as well as his bed. He supposed that there might be no harm in saying so . . .

He did not see Janet alone again that day; but next evening, with James entertaining a wild party—with, it was interesting to note, the Bastard of Arran attending, and providing some of the women—David sought alternative accommodation and, it being cold outside, after a brief walk, thought of the warmth of the abbey kitchens. And there he found Janet, likewise escaping the riot in the royal quarters, and being entertained by the monkish cooks. He was glad to join that quietly cheerful company and to participate in their provision.

When, presently, the young woman declared that she would seek her bed, David pointed out that, with the noise generated by the King's group, sleep would be impossible for hours yet, and suggested that they might go walking for a little while, a couple of monkish cloaks borrowed against the cold . . .

If she thought this an odd suggestion for a winter's night, she did not say so, and they sallied out of the warmth into the starlit dark, making for the slopes of Arthur's Seat.

When Janet stumbled over an unseen stone, David took her arm and, this being awkward through the heavy cloth of the cloak, she drew aside that flap of it so that he might hold her more comfortably. It was pleasant, companionable, walking together thus, and leaving the lights of the Abbey behind them. They did not talk much. But at length the man spoke up.

"Davie Beaton thinks that I should marry again," he declared, rather abruptly, "that I need a wife."

"Oh," she said. And, after a pause, "Perhaps, in that, he is right."

"Yes. It may be so. But, it is not so simple. Since, since I cannot marry anyone whom I do not love." He had got it out.

He felt rather than heard the intake of her breathing, the lift of her bosom against his arm. But she made no other comment.

"So, my choice is much restricted," he went on—and felt very self-conscious, something of a fool even, as he did so. "Since *you* will not have me."

Still she was silent.

"Perhaps I seek too much?" If that sounded ponderous, she certainly was not making it easy for him. "Love, as well as trust? And, and admiration, was it?"

She halted now. "David!" she got out, distinctly breathless. "What are you saying? Is it . . . ? Are you . . . ? Oh, Davie!" She was clutching him now, hard.

"Why, lass, I am but trying to say what I said before. Only . . . better! I am not good at this, I fear. Saying that I love you and need you and want you. Want you for always, to be my wife. And if you will not wed me, I must needs go wifeless all my days. For I can love no other. It is as simple as that . . ."

And astonishingly, she burst into tears and threw herself against him, small fists beating at his chest—which was difficult in all the monkish cloaking.

Somehow he got his arms around her and rocked her to and fro, his lips in her hair. His sudden spate of eloquence was gone now, so that it was only incoherencies which he mumbled against her head.

But Janet found her tongue instead, however muffled it was. "Oh, Davie, Davie! You fool! You fool! Why could you not say so before? My dear, my very foolish dear! Or is it myself the fool? To have been so lack-witted, childish? So difficult? But I, I needed to know, to be sure. Forgive me, a wilful, silly woman!"

Through all that he picked his way. "Are you saying that . . . perhaps you will? That you might wed me, after all? Or, or . . . no?"

She raised her head, to peer up at him in the darkness. "Davie, my beloved—can you not understand? I love you, have loved you for long. But dared not hope that you might love *me*. I feared . . . and because I feared, I had to be sure. Do you not see? To be sure that you *loved* me also. Not only liked, wanted. You did not say so. Although I tried, I tried, to make you say it! Nothing else would do. Oh, I have been so wilful, stupid."

"Then it is true, Janet? You will wed me? Dear God—you *will*!"

"Of course I will! It is my heart's desire. I tell you, I . . ."

But she had told him enough, at last, words no longer necessary. He picked her up, bodily, seeking her mouth with his. "A plague on these cloaks!" he gasped.

Her peal of laughter was breathless still, but joyous. He stopped all that with his lips.

It was hours before they won back to Holyrood Abbey, by which time even the royal cantrips had died down and peace of a sort reigned, however drunken. They had been quite unaware of the cold, as of the passage of time.

* * *

Neither of them desired a large or spectacular wedding, nor did either want delay. So they decided just to ask the Sub-Prior at the Abbey to marry them, there in its church, or in one of its side-chapels, in ten days' time.

Those were an eventful ten days, as it happened. For they saw, after so long, the removal of the Angus threat, meantime at any rate. Considering all that had gone before, it all seemed somehow ridiculously simple and undramatic. Argyll's strategy worked where that of more straightforward, chivalrous or merely warlike characters did not. The Home bribery move was successful, the Earl decoyed back to Coldinghame—if he had ever been there in the first place—and there he was cornered in a

184

secret raid by Argyll. Cornered, but not captured, for Angus was holed up in his uncle's well-defended priory, and, it being traditional Home property, those curious folk would not hear of it being bombarded by artillery or otherwise damaged, even threatening to use their full force against Argyll if he attempted it. However, Angus himself presumably did not know of this and, unable to break out against the Campbells' vastly superior force, agreed, in exchange for his personal liberty, to yield, go under escort to St. Abb's and there take boat to exile in England, his uncle and other Douglases with him. So now he was gone, and Scotland could heave a sigh of relief. Admittedly he could come back—although he had promised not to until the King recalled him and cancelled the sentence of treason—for Tantallon was still unsubdued and he could reach it from the sea at any time. But it was all a notably improved situation, and Argyll came back to general plaudits and royal favour.

This success had the effect of much restoring James's good humour, so much so that he expressed himself delighted with David's and Janet's betrothal and indeed assumed that he would attend their wedding celebration.

So, the King present, others of the court came too, and the affair became much more ambitious than the principals had planned, being held in the great church itself, not in any side-chapel, even the Bastard of Arran being there. Davie Beaton came specially from St. Andrews—of all attending probably the best entitled. But none of all this, if undesired, in any way invalidated the essential joining together of the pair in one and at least they were spared the embarrassment of any attempt at a bedding ceremony, thanks to James who, strangely, considering his own behaviour and tastes, was much offended at any suggestion of it for these two. Probably he esteemed them in something like a parental role.

They made their own bedding ceremony later, and bliss it was—with promise of still better thereafter. And next day they left, on leave-of-absence, for The Mount of Lindifferon in Fife, Beaton and his archiepiscopal bodyguard as escort for most of the way. James would summon them back when he so desired.

PART TWO

At Janet's urging, David sought to develop further his un-doubted poetic gifts. In the first happy carefree weeks of their marriage he did turn out two or three small things, mainly on the themes of feminine beauty and wedded bliss, even love, suitable for the occasion. But for some time he had been contemplating a much more ambitious project, something which indeed he had started in a modest way long before but had laid aside—a major poem dealing with the manners and conceits, the moral and political follies of the day and the state of the realm, which he had tentatively entitled *The Dream*. Kate had encouraged him in this, but after her death he had not had the heart to continue with it. Now he returned to it, or rather, largely rewrote what he had previously penned, in the light of his own greater experience and maturity—and the impact of ongoing events. He was now thirty-eight and recognised some of his earlier views and judge-ments as all but juvenile, however finely poetic. So, as the weeks passed into months, and still the King did not send for them, did not even communicate in any way, and he grew just a little hurt, not to say resentful, the role of the monarchy and James himself tended to be alluded to more frequently in the composition, something not contemplated before. Janet backed him in this aspect, indeed they discussed the matter and its relevance and suitability. They assured each other that it was not just injured pride and pique, but for James's own good and guidance—for undoubtedly the poem would eventually go to the King when completed. After all, David had been James's closest companion and trusted friend all his life, his keeper as an infant, his boyhood guide and guard, his youthful instructor, his fellow-captive and now his personal herald. To be seemingly forgotten after all that was galling, for affection was involved as well as service and duty; but it was not so much that as with the King's own moral well-being that they were concerned—or so they told each other—for the monarch, of all people, must learn who to trust, who to turn to in need, how to reward faithful service, and so on. Presumably this present neglect or disfavour still stemmed from the business at Coldinghame, although Janet thought that it was more likely to be because of their united and undoubted disapproval of the King's present excesses in the matter of women, drink and gaming. At any rate, this poetry was a good way of working off disgruntlement and feelings, as well as making comment on, as it were from afar, the way they thought that Church and state were being mismanaged.

All this did not imply that these weeks and months were less than happy ones, or that they were much concerned with matters other than personal. On the contrary, they were prolonged satisfaction in living together, working together, learning to know each other to the full. And there was always plenty to be done at The Mount of Lindifferon, which had been neglected of late. But that was a long winter and late spring, and evenings by the fire lent themselves to such talk and composition.

If there was no news from James at Stirling (whence he had apparently removed again) there was plenty from nearer at hand, enough to resound throughout the kingdom and further afield—to Rome, undoubtedly. For the reformist Abbot of Fearn, Patrick Hamilton, was haled before a consistory court, found guilty of major, prolonged and unrepentant heresy and condemned to be burnt at the stake. At his trial, Sir James Hamilton of Finnart, the Bastard, had been one of the principal witnesses against his cousin.

These unpleasant tidings much concerned David, mainly in the new light it threw on his friend's character. For undoubtedly much of the responsibility for the entire affair must lie with Davie Beaton, even though the fate of the unfortunate Abbot was promulgated by a court of Holy Church. Without Beaton almost certainly little of it would have taken place, the final burning in especial, with the details of that horrific in the extreme, the gunpowder charges which were intended to expedite the burning of the wood twice failing to do so but each time blowing pieces off the wretched victim before he succumbed to the flames. That Davie could have approved of anything such, as well as contriving the situation whereby the Bastard (and therefore his father Arran) far from being a danger became an accomplice, revealed a side of him profoundly disturbing to Lindsay. And that the Church in Scotland could descend to such methods, whatever went on elsewhere, was a dire thought, and indicative both of the malaise which afflicted it and the threat it considered these reformist clergy posed, reforms which Lindsay for one largely agreed with.

As if that were not enough, a further and almost unbelievable aspect of Beaton's attitude towards the Church, and indeed towards life in general, was revealed shortly afterwards. He appeared to have been keeping his distance from the Mount— understandably enough, in Lindsay's opinion—but one day in May he turned up there, unannounced and without his usual impressive escort. He was greeted rather less warmly than usual. Nevertheless he seemed his normal, cheerful if slightly cynical self, behaving as though nothing had transpired to in any way alter their long-standing friendly association. But even he could not ignore indefinitely his host's stiff reaction and Janet's cool correctness.

"Do I detect some hint of reserve, possibly even some soupçon of criticism?" he wondered presently, smiling unabashed. "Or do you deem me a carrier of the plague, perhaps?"

"Can you expect us, or any decent folk, to approve of what you did to that Patrick Hamilton?" Lindsay demanded. "You sickened not only ourselves but most of the land, I would say."

"Then you, and most of the land, lack judgement and a due responsibility, my friends. Your responsibility, as well as others', see you. For you are all members of Holy Church, baptised into its fellowship, are you not? Bound by solemn vows to its support and maintenance. Yet when the Church is under dire threat and attack from those who would destroy its very foundations, you turn the other way, do nothing and condemn those who do act!"

"Is the burning of a man, a priest, any way to serve God's cause, the God of love?"

"If that priest is destroying the faith of others, the faith of thousands, he must be stopped, punished . . ."

"But burned to death! How could you authorise that?"

"Burning is the Church's long-standing penalty for persistent and unrepented heresy, not mine. Cleansing by fire. Hamilton knew the price he would have to pay, was warned, pleaded with, time and again, but was obdurate. He had to be silenced, and others given warning."

"Surely you could have banished him, spared him, a young man, so cruel a death?" Janet said.

"And sent him back to Luther and Melancthon and the rest,

to learn worse heresies? The Church is world-wide, Janet. Despatching a heretic merely to another part of it is no answer."

"Was the answer to make a martyr of this Hamilton?" Lindsay asked. "You talk of warning others. A martyr could do the reverse, *encourage* others."

"Perhaps. But scarcely so many. There will be a deal fewer candidates for martyrdom than for mere attack on the Church! We must choose the lesser evil."

"God's Church surely should not choose *any* evil? We said that you were playing with evil when you chose to trade with the Bastard of Arran. We were right, it seems. Anything that man touches is tainted. For immunity from the other Hamiltons you bought him in. Now *you* are stained with his evil."

"I doubt your judgement, friend. But if I am, and it is to the benefit of Holy Church, then I must just thole it. As I and my Marion are tholing a more personal burden."

"Marion . . . ? What has Marion to do with your Church's burdens?"

"A deal, to my sorrow. I fear that I must take holy orders."

"What . . . ? You! How can that be? It is impossible."

"Not so. It is . . . inconvenient, but not impossible."

"But—you are married, with a family. How can such be a priest?"

"It is difficult. But steps can be taken to alter that situation, in cases of great need. And such need is now. Seldom greater."

"What do you mean? Steps—and great need?"

Even Davie Beaton took a breath before answering that. "It is necessary," he said slowly. "My uncle, as you know, has long been failing, less than himself. Now not only his body but his wits are going. He is becoming senile, and it will grow worse. Yet, he is the head of Holy Church in this land, and seldom has that Church more needed a strong, able and vigorous leader."

"I am sorry for your uncle. But, there is always Dunbar. Archbishop Dunbar of Glasgow, the Chancellor."

"He will not serve, in this pass. He is essentially a weak man, talented but weak. You have seen how he acts at a parliament. He holds back, hesitates, thinks perhaps, but does not act. *He* will not save the Church."

"*Save* the Church?"

"Aye, save. It is as serious as that. See you—why do you think I was so strong against Patrick Hamilton? I, who believe that the

Church needs reform. Because he represented a much greater threat, he only the froth on the top of the ale. There are much more powerful figures behind him, who required to be warned. Henry is behind this . . ."

"Henry? King Henry Tudor?"

"The same. You heard that he has, they say, four hundred Scots in his pocket, pensioners? I do not know about four hundred—but I do know he has many. And some of these are bishops, as well as abbots and priors. All accepting Henry's accursed gold."

"Bishops? Save us—for what?"

"The old story. Henry wants Scotland, at any cost. All the English kings have done so, but he in especial. He sees Scotland as a threat in his rear to his continental ambitions. And Wolsey, his Chancellor, aims for the papal throne and would have the Scots Church behind his claim as well as the English. Moreover, he is Archbishop of York, and York has always sought ecclesiastical hegemony over the Scots Church. These two see us with a failing Primate and a weak Chancellor-Archbishop, and the reformist agitation growing. Likewise a young, inexperienced and headstrong king. And the Douglas power still, in fact, unbroken. So, the Church, instead of being the nation's strength and stay, as in the past, could be its weakness. And the bishops—many are ignorant, unlettered and corrupt anyway, the bastards of lords and other bishops! That is Holy Church today! Now do you see what I am fighting against?"

"Save us, is it so bad as that?"

"Worse. I do not know one prelate strong enough to be trusted to succeed my uncle as Primate, to keep the Church together and hold off Henry and Wolsey. Not one. So, I must take holy orders, it seems."

"*You* must? I do not understand?"

"Yet it is simple enough. As Abbot of Arbroath, *lay* Abbot, I am well enough, fit to be the Primate's secretary and aide, but not to be the Primate himself. That requires priesthood, holy orders. Although, mind you, our late liege-lord's bastard son Alexander was made Archbishop of St. Andrews and Primate at fifteen years, lacking holy orders. But that was, shall we say, a special case. I am no king's son . . ."

"But, but . . . ? You mean that *you* . . . ?"

"To be sure. I plan to take over from my uncle. When finally

193

he becomes too addle-pated and feeble to provide even a figure-head, as now. Or dies first. None other can I be sure of."

They stared at him, wide-eyed, trying to take in all that was implied in this extraordinary announcement.

"You, you think to be Archbishop of St. Andrews, Davie? You?" Lindsay demanded. "Head of the Church and all the bishops. You cannot mean it? How? Who would ever allow that? Who agree to it?"

"Why, the Pope in Rome would—which is what signifies, is it not? If I have put down heresy in Scotland, and maintained the Church, where others have not."

"Ha—so that is it! Hence Patrick Hamilton! This is scarcely to be credited!"

"And what of your wife?" Janet wondered. "What of Marion? And the children?"

"Marion understands. She has . . . agreed."

"Agreed to what?" Lindsay demanded. "How can this be? A married man may not be a priest. Whatever steps you claim to take, you are still a married man. In the old Celtic Church it would have been different, but Rome is stern on this."

The other was less than his usual assured self. "It will be necessary to alter Marion's status," he said carefully. "Unfortunate, but necessary. She, she will no longer be called my wife. We shall, to be sure, remain together as before. It will be but a matter of name."

"Name! You are saying that you will actually put Marion away, as wife? Your Marion!"

"No, no—not put away. All will be the same, I tell you. Save that in Church matters I will not call her wife."

"But this is . . . damnable! She *is* your wife, mother of your bairns. To shame her thus, before all. What of *your* vows? To keep, honour and cherish her all your days, till death do you part?"

"And so I shall, man. I tell you, nothing will be changed. Save that so far as Church affairs go, she will no longer be called wife . . ."

"What, then? Concubine? Marion!"

Even Davie Beaton flushed, the first time Lindsay had ever seen such a thing. "That is an ill name. Can you not see it? To all save the officials at the Vatican she will still be my wife. There I will have dispensation, setting the marriage aside, so

194

that I may take holy orders. It is a device, no more. But a device which could save Scotland!"

"You say so! I say that you rate yourself altogether too high—and Marion Ogilvy altogether too low!"

"Then you are wholly wrong. I love and respect Marion more than I can say. This grieves me more than anything that I have ever had to do, believe me, but I see no other way. Somehow I have got to take over my uncle's position, to save Holy Church. Then to displace Dunbar as Chancellor, to save the realm, and your James's throne. Otherwise, this time, Henry Tudor will win. And Scotland will become but a poor and despised province of England, with Angus Henry's viceroy."

There was silence for a while.

"So your mind is made up?" Lindsay said at length. "When does this . . . demotion take place?"

"I have already made the first moves. Letters to Rome." Beaton hesitated. "David—I wish with all my heart that you could see this as I do, or more nearly. If Marion can, why not you? So much hangs on it. Your fate, as well as mine, and so many others. Try to understand. You are my friend . . ."

"I cannot believe it to be right, whatever the cause. I am sorry, but I cannot."

They perforce left it at that. Beaton took his departure shortly afterwards, the atmosphere at the Mount of Lindifferon less than happy.

Afterwards, for long, David and Janet discussed it all, trying to see light in the darkness. Since they had to respect Beaton's wits and abilities and believed him when he said that he loved and respected Marion, there had to be something to be said for his extraordinary point of view, however hard for them to perceive. That he was personally ambitious went without saying; but surely not to the extent of deliberately wrecking the lives of his wife and children? Could he really be so devoted to the Church that he would sacrifice all else? David had known him since college days, and did not believe that; indeed he had never thought him as even a very religiously-minded man. It was merely that he used the Church to advance himself and his causes. What, then? It could only be Scotland itself, the realm and nation. Was Davie Beaton a patriot before all else? Did his love for his native land so consume him that he was prepared to give up all for it? Others without number had given their lives for their country, admittedly, down the ages. Was Beaton's patriotism of a still more determined kind? Whereby he planned and schemed and sacrificed all for the sake of his country? He was no modest man, and had infinite faith in his own abilities—and had proved that assessment right, time and again. He appeared to believe that he could save Scotland from disaster and that only he could do so. Could he be right? Was the danger indeed so great? It seemed less so, on the face of it, than for some years. But clearly he believed otherwise.

That he apparently planned to replace Dunbar as Chancellor, however arrogant the sound of it, could all be part of the same assessment and conviction, the belief that he would make a more effective chief minister than the Archbishop, or anyone else. Whether, of course, all the necessary personal advancement could be achieved, was another matter; but obviously he conceived it as possible.

David, debating all this, wondered whether there was something here, more than merely dramatic, for him to put into his poem, *The Dream*? Or was that unsuitable, as well as unkind?

12

Curiously enough, despite the disagreements and lack of harmony on that last meeting, it was Davie Beaton who, having as Lord Privy Seal frequent audiences with the King, arranged Lindsay's eventual return to court. Or, more properly, to James's service, for it was for military duties that he was recalled, fairly early in 1529.

A parliament had been called the previous December, to deal with developments on the English and Border fronts. King Henry had sent a peremptory demand for the reinstatement of his friend Angus, with sundry other requirements, to James's fury and that of most of the parliament. But Davie Beaton had managed to convince them that, in view of their own military unpreparedness and the disaffection of the Douglases and their allies, most of the Border clans, any outright challenge to the English might at this stage would be major folly. So, a diplomatic and comparatively soft answer had been sent to Henry, rejecting any outright pardon for Angus but remitting the sentence of death, so long as he remained in England, and on condition that Tantallon and the other Douglas strongholds were yielded up. James also added, at Beaton's suggestion, that he was grateful to Henry for all the many favours shown to him during his long minority; but now that he had attained man's estate, he would endeavour to stand on his own feet and hoped no longer to be any concern to his uncle or to require further guidance. This piece of semi-hypocrisy took a deal of swallowing by James, but was acceded to in the end as a wise precaution against the difficult, vain and unpredictable Tudor. It was also an indication of Beaton's influence with the King, and to the possibilities of obtaining his desired advancement.

In addition to this measure it was decided that something must be done to demonstrate both to Henry and to the rest of Scotland that James was no weakling nor puppet any more and that the Douglases and their Border allies must be warned as to the consequences of rebellion or any moves in favour of Angus. That individual, as chief Warden of the Marches, had set up an elaborate system of bonds of manrent, as they were termed, whereby each chief and leader of a borderland clan was bound to him and to each other in mutual armed support against all others, even the monarchy. This had to be countered and shown to be worthless. So an expedition through the Borderland was organised and David Lindsay, considered rightly or wrongly to be experienced in Border warfare, was sent for.

As a preliminary gesture of warning, again on Beaton's advice, a number of the most prominent Border lords, many of them more or less attendant on the King, were placed under token arrest at Stirling, with varying degrees of willingness. These even included the Hepburn Earl of Bothwell who had succeeded Angus as Warden of the Marches. Also the new Lord Home, the Lord Maxwell, Scott of Buccleuch himself, Home of Polwarth, the Kers of Ferniehurst and Cessford and the chief of the Johnstones of Annandale. These, allegedly as prisoners and hostages for their clans' good behaviour, were to accompany the royal army of some eight thousand.

James greeted David Lindsay in casual friendliness, as though there had been no rift and no prolonged parting. He was now entering his eighteenth year and had grown and filled-out considerably, looking older than his years, quite the man in his handsome, red-headed way. He had gained much in bearing and confidence of manner in the interim, but there were clear signs of his addiction to liquor and other excesses and his eye was apt to have a cynical glint. This expedition was accompanied by three ladies for his entertainment.

Argyll, under the monarch, was in overall command, with Lindsay somewhat unsure as to his own role. Beaton did not go along; he did not see military affairs as his responsibility.

They marched southwards by Falkirk and across the bleak moorlands of Central Scotland, making for Clydesdale, where they were to pick up Hamilton of Finnart at his castle of Craignethan—for the Bastard was now a firm favourite of James—and an accession of strength. David, for one, did not greet Hamilton with any enthusiasm, although admittedly he was an able soldier and useful man in any battle. Increased in numbers, they proceeded on into Douglasdale, to show the royal standard in that birthplace of the troublesome house. They found the area all but deserted—that is, by the lairdly occupants, the common folk being less able to up and depart when it seemed wise to do so. They did some token burning and despoiling, the Bastard foremost in this, and pressed on. More and more it was Armstrong which was the name on the men's lips now.

With vivid memories of the last time that they had sought to settle differences with that unruly and far-flung clan, under Angus himself three years before, David was very doubtful as to success whatever their armed strength and military expertise. But James was determined to show who ruled here—for Armstrong of Gilnockie was known as the uncrowned King of the Border, capable of raising all the Debateable Land in arms in a day or two, threatening both the Scots and English Wardens of the Marches with dire reprisals should they interfere with him, and acknowledging no man as his master. James also was anxious to prove that he could succeed where Angus had failed. Moreover, the Bastard appeared to have some private quarrel with Johnnie of Gilnockie and was vociferous for his fall.

However, they did not proceed directly to Annandale and Eskdale, electing to march by upper Tweed and down Ettrick and Yarrow, through the great Forest of Ettrick, haunt of thieves and outlaws from time immemorial. Apparently they had lesser fish to fry before seeking to arrive at conclusions with the formidable Johnnie Armstrong.

The Ettrick Forest, generally known merely as The Forest in Scotland, was vast, indeterminate of boundary but covering an area of perhaps some one-hundred-and-fifty square miles, from mid-Tweeddale and mid-Teviotdale westwards and southwards and including much of the high watershed of Southern Scotland where rose the great rivers of Clyde, Tweed, Annan, Nith, Esk and Teviot and a host of lesser streams, refuge for broken men, outcasts and patriots too on occasion, where Wallace and Bruce had been able to elude and defy their hugely-outnumbering foes. In this inaccessible sanctuary certain robbers and reivers were inevitably more successful and powerful than others, especially those with the deepest roots in the Forest, and Adam Scott of Tushielaw actually rejoiced in the self-styled title of King of Thieves—not quite bold enough to risk offending the much more powerful Armstrong of Gilnockie further south by calling himself monarch of more than reivers. James Stewart proposed to show them both what the royal style and title really meant.

Leaving Tweed near Selkirk they went up Ettrick past its junction with Yarrow, where they entered the more constricted dale. Now the great cavalcade grew elongated indeed, winding through the narrow valley mile after mile, with David urgent on sending out scouting parties in front, rear and flanks, recollecting all too clearly how de la Bastie had ambushed even the experienced Lord Home in such country, dividing up a large strung-out company into gobbets to be devoured piecemeal, starting with the main leadership group. Little attention was paid to his representations however, the King, Argyll, the Bastard and the other nobles being quite satisfied that their daunting strength in armoured knights, horsed men-at-arms and running, bare-shanked Highland swordsmen would inhibit even the most aggressive Border thieves and mosstroopers from provoking attack.

Whether or not this was an accurate assessment, they were not challenged as they proceeded up Ettrick Water. In the upper reaches of the twisting valley, with the trees thinning to scrub birch and hawthorn, James was persuaded to send out fairly strong flanking parties to seal off the various side-glens of Hindhope and Gilmanscleuch, Deloraine and Rankle, by which Scott of Tushielaw might seek to make his escape from any direct approach to his peel-tower.

It was as well that this was done for, a bare three miles short of Tushielaw, one of the said parties came back in triumph with Adam Scott himself, captured when departing discreetly over the high pass of Rankle, southwards towards Buccleuch, with a score of his mosstroopers. These had put up a spirited resistance but had been overcome, with heavy loss, and those remaining alive brought back, all wounded.

Their leader and laird proved to be a brash character in his late thirties, with a ruddy countenance, a fleering eye and a distinctly twisted neck—which the Bastard promptly declared to be in need of straightening with a rope. James agreed, but ordained that all must be done lawfully and in due order. So the wounded captives, tied to their own shaggy horses, were carried on to that hub of waters where four major streams joined Ettrick and Tushielaw Tower sat on its hillside high above all.

There was no resistance. The tower, a typical plain Border keep, square, gaunt and tall within a high-walled courtyard, appeared to have been hastily abandoned, although smoke still rose from one of its chimneys, poultry clucked around and women's clothing lay drying over a garden-wall.

James wasted no time. Calling on Argyll, who amongst other offices held that of Lord Justice General, to try the prisoners there and then, the Earl, without so much as getting off his horse, asked the near-swooning Scott if he could deny giving himself the style of King of Thieves. The other found strength to correct that to King of Reivers. Argyll pointed out that that was the same thing, even though it implied that it was cattle only which were stolen. Therefore they had an admission of stealing cattle, siller on the hoof, which was all that was required in law for judgement and sentence. The said judgement therefore was guilty and the said sentence was hanging. Turning in the saddle, the Earl pointed grimly to a nearby isolated tree, ancient and gnarled, from a limb of which three desiccated, shrivelled corpses already dangled, the laird's gallows-tree—for, as holder of the old barony of Tushielaw, he had the power of pit and gallows. Hamilton of Finnart, laughing, volunteered to carry out the sentence, and, finding halter-rope in the tower stabling, went to work with zest. Scott and the seven of his following who had survived thus far—and who could be assumed not to require any separate trial—were strung up, as it were at his own door and with his own facilities, all in the most businesslike fashion. Thereafter the King ordered Tushielaw's head to be cut off, to be sent back to Edinburgh for due and proper exposure on a spike above the Tolbooth.

Most of the royal army, far from being able to enjoy this spectacle, did not even glimpse it, for they were still winding their way up the long, narrow Ettrick valley.

James did not wait for them. The afternoon was well advanced and he had further justice to dispense before they camped for the night. With Scott of Buccleuch as guide—not mourning his fellow-clansman, who had been a thorn in his flesh for long—they turned due northwards, up the Tushielaw Burn, to commence a long climb through bare wild hills, by a well-trodden drove-road, all but paved with the dried droppings of cattle innumerable, no doubt the highway by which the late freebooter had brought home his reived beasts from near and far, over the years. Near the lofty pass at the head of this, they turned off left-handed, westwards again, downhill now by a much less well-defined track, from which presently they could gaze down over a wide-opening vista of upper Yarrow, where two lochs gleamed in the sinking sunlight, one large and one small, separated only by a tiny neck of land, St. Mary's Loch and the Loch of the Lowes, where the Meggat Water joined Yarrow. Down to this narrow isthmus their track led them, to cross it to the far side at Oxcleuch. Buccleuch explained. This way, their approach would remain hidden by intervening ridges from Henderland Tower, their next target, up its side-glen at Cappercleuch, whereas had they continued on the main drove-road over the pass, they could have been visible for miles, and Piers Cockburn warned.

As it was, turning right again along St. Mary's Loch, after less than two miles they reached and forded the inflowing Meggat Water, proceeding up it for another half-mile, and there, sitting in the mouth of its steep little glen, not much more than a corrie, was Henderland Tower, almost a replica of Tushielaw but slightly smaller.

Here, with no warning and no chance of escape for the Cockburns, all went rather differently. Piers Cockburn, younger than might have been expected from his freebooterly reputation, came out from his gatehouse in his shirt-sleeves to greet the newcomers, surprised but not apparently alarmed; and was promptly informed that he was in the presence of the monarch and that his sins had caught up with him, that he would be tried forthwith and the penalty paid. He made no least protest at this abrupt intimation of doom, no comment even, but requested that he might be permitted to take leave of his wife and bairns. This was granted by James, but Argyll advised that any farewells should take place in their sight, lest Cockburn tried any tricks. Many castles and towers had secret underground passages, after all, and escape into the hills might be attempted. So the wife, Marjory, and two children, a boy and a girl aged six or seven, were brought out from the tower, fearful and bewildered, the woman attractive, dark where her husband was fair. They ran to the man's side where he stood, held by half-naked Highlanders, and presently a wail went up as the woman learned his fate—to Cockburn's very obvious embarrassment. As the distressful noise went on, fearing hysteria and an unsuitable scene the Bastard hustled mother and children away, pointing her guards down into a deep ravine nearby, with its rushing stream where, as he thoughtfully pointed out, they would not hear her caterwauling any more than she would hear what went on up here.

All this satisfactorily arranged, James decided that the most telling place to hang Piers Cockburn, since he did not appear to possess a gallows-tree, Henderland not being a barony, was from his own gatehouse. So, that individual's quiet acceptance of his doom, plus his farewell to his wife, being taken as acknowledgement of guilt and no trial necessary, without more ado the miscreant was conducted up to the little gatehouse above the pend into his courtyard, and there dropped out of its only window on the end of a length of harness-chain, to be brought up sharp, to dangle and twitch over the archway. It was all over in seconds, for almost certainly the sudden jerk on the chain broke the young man's neck, despite the subsequent convulsive movements of the body.

James had thought to pass the night at Henderland but its situation within the jaws of this little side-glen was quite inadequate for a large encampment—not to mention the disturbance which might well be caused by a hysterical female. Buccleuch however, whose clan territory this was in the main, pointed out that there was an intrusive Douglas property nearby, down Yarrow, only some four miles away, where they had insolently actually given their name to a glen and burn. Almost certainly these Douglases would be aware by now of this force's presence, and would probably have abandoned their Blackhouse Tower there. But it would be salutary to spoil their glen and farmeries, and there would be plenty of room for the army to camp around their hamlet of Craig Douglas at the mouth of the glen.

This was agreed and a move made down the main dale to Glen Douglas, where that township perforce provided cattle and poultry and meal to feed the host; and while the slaughtering and cooking went on, a sizeable company was sent up the valley, under the ever-enthusiastic Bastard of Arran to deal with Blackhouse Tower and its associated homesteads and crofts, some two miles up. These were late in getting back, and returned hungry but otherwise well-satisfied. Most of the area they had found deserted, as anticipated, but they had discovered some women in hiding, which had evidently been a considerable compensation; and the sky lit up redly behind them indicated that more justice had been effected.

Duty done, all settled down for a well-deserved night's sleep even though David Lindsay, for one, had his doubts about much of the day's doings. But then he was an awkward character, and a poet into the bargain.

In the morning, leaving Craig Douglas township ablaze behind them, they set off for the Armstrong country, back over the pass to Tushielaw and then on eastwards over the Rankle Pass and the empty hills of the great watershed, past Buccleuch itself, where they halted for the night, a small and remote place to give its name to the Scott chiefs, but one which they had long outgrown, their main seat at Branxholme being many miles on, in Teviotdale. Thence, still eastwards, by Bellendean—from which came the Scott war-cry—and the rushing Ale Water, they hastened past Alemuir Loch, haunted as all men knew by a bloodthirsty water-kelpie and not to be ventured near between dusk and dawn. On down Borthwick Water, past Roberton and Highchesters, they reached the Teviot and Branxholme the second night.

Here was a major castle, one of the greatest in the Borderland, in a key position. James was so well entertained here that he decided to stay and rest his people for a couple of days after their gruelling cross-country march. Also they were now nearing the edge of the Armstrong territories and there was the question of strategy to be resolved. Johnnie of Gilnockie would not allow himself to be crept up on, undoubtedly, and would know well of their approach. James was anxious not to repeat Angus's fiasco in this respect and wondered how to get at the elusive King of the Border without having to pursue him deep into the trackless wastes and morasses of the Debateable Land—where of course the Armstrongs would have all the advantages. There were a number of suggestions put forward, none very convincing, David Lindsay's advice being merely to make a sort of royal progress through the Armstrong country, a demonstration of strength rather than taking any punitive measures, in the hope that Gilnockie would recognise realities and come to some suitable understanding with his liege-lord. The Bastard, needless to say, saw this as spineless weakness to be rejected out of hand. But Buccleuch largely supported Lindsay, knowing the problems and asserting that they would only waste their time and strength in trying to come to grips with Johnnie Armstrong in his own country. If the King was not content to do some token burning and harrying, as before, then his suggestion was that James adopted very different tactics in place of the mailed fist, that in fact he sent a messenger ahead to Gilnockie seeking a meeting with Johnnie. The man was proud, pretentious and might well respond to such invitation from the monarch. Better than the ineffectual chasing around the Debateable Land.

Despite Hamilton's jeers, with Argyll tending to agree with Buccleuch, James acceded. He would summon the Armstrong to his presence. If he did not come, time enough then to go hunting him down.

To make the summons sound suitably enticing to this arrogant freebooter no ordinary courier should be sent, it was agreed. What better than to send one of the royal heralds—and David Lindsay, Snowdoun Herald, was the only one present. He should go on, then, with a small escort, and if possible bring the Armstrong to the King.

David, although far from eager for the encounter, reckoned that it was probably all a deal better than any more pointless burning and slaying. So, provided with a royal Lion Rampant banner and a dozen Scott men-at-arms, he set off from Branx-holme up Teviot.

Gilnockie lay southwards some twenty-three miles, in the valley of the Esk, and to reach it they had to ride up past Teviothead, over the major pass of Mosspaul and down Ewesdale beyond to its junction with Esk. The Scotts knew the way, but warned that they were unlikely to get far beyond Mosspaul without being approached by the Armstrongs.

In the event, approached was hardly the word. They had only turned the second of the many bends in the twisting drove-road below the pass itself when they were suddenly confronted by a solid phalanx of mounted mosstroopers, fully a score and bristling with arms, sitting their horses silent and completely barring the way. Even as they stared, a clatter behind turned their heads, to see a similar group emerge from a ravine just passed, to block off any retreat. No words were spoken.

David, shrugging, told his standard-bearer to unfurl the royal banner. He raised his voice. "Who are you who dare to block the way of the King's lieges?" he demanded. "I am David Lindsay of The Mount, Snowdoun Herald, on business of His Grace King James with Armstrong of Gilnockie."

That produced some discussion amongst those in front. A man held up his hand, announced that he was Armstrong of Eweslees, and pointed out that it was customary for travellers seeking to traverse Armstrong country to gain permission before they did so.

David retorted that be this as it might, they scarcely could expect the representatives of the King's Grace to seek any subject's permission to ride through His Grace's realm? This elicited no response other than the announcement that the Armstrongs would conduct the visitor to Gilnockie.

In convoy, then, they proceeded down Ewesdale in dashing style and at a spanking pace. David noted how well-equipped and well-horsed were these people, Eweslees himself being finely dressed and turned-out, however rough his manner. There was little converse on that fifteen-mile ride.

They joined Eskdale at Langholm, a sizeable town and something of an Armstrong capital obviously. But they did not pause there, pounding on down the now broad Esk in a richly-wooded valley remarkably narrow for so major a river.

They came to Gilnockie in five more miles, one more typical

Border peel-tower, square and strong, five storeys high with parapet and wall-walk, but unusual in being provided with a stone beacon or fire-basket at its gable-top, no doubt for summoning the clan in haste. The tower itself was little larger than most of its kind, but its courtyard and outbuildings were much more extensive than usual, and the castleton nearby constituted a major township.

Their arrival appeared to be anticipated—which might indicate an excellent communication-system—and they were met at the gatehouse by an imposing individual wearing a heraldic cloak of the Armstrong colours of red-and-white bearing the mailed-arm device and carrying a white-tasselled staff of office. He was flanked by half-a-dozen acolytes wearing a sort of uniform in the same colours. This character bowed elaborately and intoning, sing-song fashion, requested to know who might honour the puissant, honourable and high-born Armstrong of Gilnockie, Holehouse, Enthorn and Thorniewhats with their presence this day?

Unprepared for such reception, David repeated what he had told Eweslees earlier. Bowing again gravely at this information, the unlikely functionary turned and paced back within the gatehouse-arch and out of sight, leaving his assistants impassively to face the visitor, who was still flanked by his large escort of mixed Scotts and Armstrongs.

David waited, and presently was astonished to hear music sounding from within the courtyard, the sweet music of lutes and fiddles, extraordinary for such a place at such a time. The impressive usher or seneschal, or whatever he might be, reappeared then with four instrumentalists playing as they walked. He announced, against the background melody, that Gilnockie would see King James's herald and representative, and to follow him within.

Dismounting, David was led off between the musicians in front and the silent six behind, an odd procession, while his Scott supporters were hustled off elsewhere.

Across the paved courtyard with the wall at its centre they came to the tower itself. And within its heraldic-lintelled doorway a man stood to welcome him, deerhounds at his knees.

David all but halted in his measured pacing which the music rather imposed, so unexpected a sight was this. Presumably in that stance it would be none other than Johnnie Armstrong himself. Yet anyone less like a notorious Border reiver and freebooter would have been hard to imagine. He saw a dashingly handsome dark man in his mid-thirties, slender, graceful even, and dressed in the height of French fashion, from long curled and ribboned hair, jewels at his ear-lobes, to gleaming gold dirk-belt and silver-buckled shoes. Standing smiling there, assured, at ease, he would have outshone anyone at court, even Davie Beaton.

"Greetings, sir," this elegant called out. "Do I understand that you are a Lindsay? I am John of Gilnockie."

"Then it is you that I have come to see. The King's Grace has sent me, the Snowdoun Herald, with a message for yourself."

"Ah, yes," the other nodded, as though messages from the monarch were everyday occurrences at Gilnockie Tower. "Then welcome to my humble house, Master Herald, for some small refreshment. You will be weary after your ride from Branxholme."

"You are well informed, sir," David observed, as he was ushered in through the six-foot-thick walling.

"I require to be, friend. I would not wish to have to counter what happened at Tushielaw, Henderland and Glen Douglas unprepared!"

That caused the visitor to swallow.

He was led past the basement vaults and up the turnpike stair to the roomy first-floor hall, where a cheerful fire burned under another great heraldic lintel and the long dais table was already set with an assortment of flagons, beakers and goblets, dishes of cold meats and fish and sweetmeats sufficient for a score. The walls of this chamber were hung with costly tapestries, the floor strewn with handsome rugs of skin and weave, and the window-seats cushioned in silk. David sought not to appear over-impressed.

The usher, who had followed them up, now began to ply the visitor with food and drink, snapping his fingers to have his aides bring different varieties of wine, French, Italian and Rhenish. The laird accepted a beaker to drink with his guest whilst standing easily by the fire. The sound of the music still drifted up softly from the courtyard.

Twice David began to deliver his message but each time he was waved to silence and courteously urged to finish his refreshment in peace. Only when the visitor expressed himself as more than satisfied did Armstrong dismiss the attendants and indicate that they could now talk in private.

"My errand is simple," David informed. "His Grace sends his greetings and requests your company. No more than that."

"Requests or summons?" That was mildly put.

"Requests. It is not a royal command."

"As well, sir—that is as well! When and where is this meeting desired? His Grace would be most welcome at this my house."

"Yes, no doubt. But my orders were to bring you to the King, and so soon as . . . convenient."

"Bring . . . ?"

"Escort, shall we say? As I was escorted here!"

"Ah. Convenient, you say? Now that is most . . . civil."

"Yes. Save that, to be sure, His Grace would not wish to have to wait overlong."

"At Branxholme?"

"That was where I left him, yes."

"Very well. We will ride tomorrow."

Was it to be as simple as that? David scarcely believed it.

Yet Gilnockie appeared to assume that all was settled. After some casual conversation he declared that, unfortunately, he had sundry matters to attend to, and that Wat—presumably the usher—would show his guest to his chamber. His men, Scotts though they were, would be well cared for. A woman would be available to ensure that he had a satisfactory night, if so desired. They would ride at sun-up.

Somewhat bemused, and dispensing with the proffered feminine company, David sought his couch. He heard much to-ing and fro-ing and clatter of hooves outside Gilnockie before he slept that night.

He was in no danger of oversleeping in the morning on account of similar and continuing coming and going beyond the courtyard. He was brought breakfast in his room, and when thereafter he was led down and out, it was to discover an extraordinary situation. A great concourse of men and horses was assembled outside; but these were not mosstroopers nor ordinary men-at-arms. All were dressed in fine clothing, not half-armour and helmets but doeskin, broadcloth, velvets, silk shirts and feather caps. Their mounts were as notable as themselves, as handsome a collection of horseflesh as David had ever seen at one time, all splendidly caparisoned. About them milled a host of attendants; but there was no mistaking the one for the other.

Johnnie Armstrong appeared, a sight to draw all eyes, dressed for riding but outdoing all in richness of apparel yet managing to avoid vulgar ostentation. He wore a fur-trimmed velvet cloak embroidered colourfully with the Armstrong arms over a cloth-of-gold doublet and breeches, and long doeskin thigh-boots which were gold-fringed and golden-spurred; his gold sword-belt was a hand-span in width and studded with rubies, and his flat velvet cap, hung with no fewer than nine gold or silver tassels, sat jauntily on his curled dark hair.

"Ah, Lindsay—a good morning to you," he greeted. "I trust that you had a fair night and are adequately rested and refreshed? We are all but ready to ride to meet King James. Here is my brother, Thomas of Mangerton, chief of all the Armstrongs."

Surprised, David looked from his host to the quietly-dressed, diffident-seeming man at his side, tall but apparently slightly lame. "I thought . . ." he began.

"I am but a second son," he was told. "Thomas is head of our house, and worthily so. He must represent Armstrong before King James. And these are our escort, suitable for the occasion. Here is Dod Armstrong of Kershopefoot. And this is Armstrong of Dinwoodie. And Armstrong of Whithaugh. Armstrong of Sorbietrees. Armstrong of Bruntshiels. Armstrong of Sikehead. Armstrong of Woolhope . . ."

The list went on and on. It dawned on David what was here being demonstrated. These were all *landed* men, lairds in their own right, all these well-dressed characters, not retainers nor tenants even. This was a *court* being used as escort, how many he was uncertain but not far off two score. Here was pride and display indeed, on a scale hardly to be rivalled in the land—but pride backed by might. If Johnnie Armstrong, or his brother, could produce all these lairdly supporters at a night's notice, what could he not raise amongst their mosstroopers and retainers? That he should have chosen to take these, apparently, before the King, rather than any host of armed men, was significant surely?

Introductions over, Gilnockie gave the signal to mount. Clearly, whatever their relationship, *he* was in command. David's own Scott escort was then brought forward, to fall in behind the gallant company of lairds, seemingly in good shape. And not only these, the musicians reappeared, in double the number, and horsed now, fiddles and lutes exchanged for flutes and horns. With these preceding them and playing more stirring tunes now, a start was made.

As far as Langholm they processed thus, in no great hurry, cheered and waved to by the country folk, a holiday parade. But thereafter, with the land beginning to rise up Ewesdale, the musicians put away their instruments and harder riding was called for. They settled down to covering ground expeditiously.

As they rested their horses at Mosspaul summit, Gilnockie asked what sort of man young King James was? He had heard that Angus sought to lead him into ill ways, and that he had a temper to go with red hair? David cautiously agreed with that, but declared that James had many virtues and would make a good monarch once he became a more experienced judge of character.

Riding on down towards Teviothead, they were not long in coming into view of a vast concourse of men and horses, the entire valley seeming to be filled as far as eye could see, all gleam and glitter in the sunlight.

"Ha—your King travels in some company, I see!" Johnnie Armstrong observed. "Does he intend an invasion of England, with all these?"

David was about to point out that James was as much Armstrong's King as his own, but thought better of it. "The Borderland is unsettled country and less than law-abiding," he contented himself with saying. "It behoves His Grace to show who rules, even here!"

That drew only a smile from the other.

As the two companies, so contrasting in numbers, neared each other, in the vicinity of Caerlanrig, it could be seen that the royal entourage heading the host drew up at a wide, grassy hollow, clearly to await the arrival of the Armstrongs. For his part, Gilnockie ordered the pace to be slowed, the instrumentalists to start up again and his impressive escort to form up as many abreast as the drove-road would allow—which proved to be nine at a time. They made four spectacular rows—so there were in fact thirty-six of the lairds. Thus, to the sound of music, they proceeded now at a walking pace.

James's company was, of course, illustrious, including many of the greatest names in Scotland. But all had been on the march for a week, were anyway dressed for campaigning not display, and were in no particular order. In consequence they presented a much less eye-catching picture despite the vast numbers behind, than did the Armstrongs.

Gilnockie, slightly in front, with his brother on one side and David Lindsay on the other, reined up about fifty paces from where James sat his horse under the royal standard, and so waited whilst the musicians finished the few more bars of their refrain. Then he whipped off his tasselled bonnet and made an elaborate bow from the saddle—as did all behind him in fair unison.

"Armstrong to greet Your Grace!" he called cheerfully. "Welcome to our country."

James was staring, as indeed were all his company. No response was immediately forthcoming.

David stepped into the breach. "Sire, here is John Armstrong of Gilnockie, his brother Thomas of Mangerton, and, and other Armstrong lairds. Come at your royal behest."

The King looked round at Argyll, Bothwell, Maxwell, Buccleuch, the Bastard and others flanking him. "Yes," he said, uncertainly. "All, all Armstrongs? These? Reivers? Outlaws?"

"Scarcely that, King," Johnnie corrected. "We have our own laws on the Border—and abide by them."

"Insolent!" That was the Bastard.

The change in Gilnockie was immediate and dramatic. "Who speaks so in Armstrong country?" he demanded, suddenly all the debonnaire flourish replaced by a narrow-eyed, menacing stare.

"I am Finnart, Hamilton of Finnart, miscreant! Watch your tongue!"

"I might have known it! Bastards are ever loud-mouthed! Does the King of Scots depend on such to speak for him?"

That spurred James. "You, sirrah—are you he who calls himself King of the Border?"

"No, Sire. Others may, but not I!"

There was a growl from all around the monarch.

"That is little better," James asserted, scowling. "I think that Sir James is right, sir—you are insolent!"

"Then you misjudge," the other said simply. "I assure you that I did not come here, and bring all these, to appear insolent. I came to greet you, in friendship."

"Friendship. You—to the King's Grace!" Argyll barked. "Here's a bold rogue, by God!"

211

David felt somehow responsible, having brought the Armstrongs here. "Sire," he interposed, "Gilnockie and his people, or his brother's people, have ridden far to welcome you to their lands. They hope that Your Grace will visit their houses. I have been kindly treated."

James still looked doubtful, in youthful indecision, but about him voices were all raised in offence and condemnation, the Bastard the loudest.

"I mislike his manner," he said.

"And I mislike the manners of your King's friends!" Armstrong declared, to Lindsay, but loud enough for most to hear.

"Of a mercy, watch how you speak!" David muttered, in an aside. "Inform him of your Armstrong lairds."

Gilnockie nodded. "King James—here is my brother, Mangerton, head of our house. And these are all gentlemen of the name—Kershopefoot, Dinwoodie, Sorbietrees, Whithaugh, Sikehead, Eweslees, Bruntshiels, Woolhope, Birkenbower, Patelaw . . ."

"Lord, enough! Enough! What is this? A, a retinue, a suite? All these!"

"The King of the Border's court of thieves, Sire!" the Bastard asserted.

"Aye—what lacks this knave that a king should have! See how he is dressed! Hear him! His prideful bearing, his, his train! This is an arrogant rascal!"

"And more in need of a hanging than even Tushielaw or Henderland!" the Bastard persisted.

"Aye, the rope for him! For them all. Murdering robbers! Where did they win all that finery? The gold? Those horses? Slain men's gear!" That was Ker of Ferniehurst, who was scarcely in a position to talk.

Gilnockie laughed. "Do I hear mice squeak, coneys roar? Save us from such terrors!"

"Have a care!" David warned.

"What are Your Grace's commands?" Argyll asked, clearly impatient with all the talk.

James drew a quick breath. "Take them," he said.

Argyll urged his mount forward to Gilnockie's side. "I arrest you in the King's name," he said.

"Arrest me? Why? Are you crazed, man?"

"I am Argyll, Lord Justice General of this realm. You are now in the King's custody."

"You must have taken leave of your wits, then, Campbell! We are not in your barbarous Hielands, here, see you. This is the West March of the Border, and *I* say who is in custody and who is not!"

"No more, thief! Your day is done."

"You say so? Myself, or all these?"

"You, and them all."

Gilnockie hooted an eloquent laugh.

It was his hitherto silent and retiring brother who spoke now. "My lord, you cannot mean this? You, a justiciar! What have we done to deserve custody?"

"You have robbed and slain and made terror on the Border these many years."

"We have hurt, and slain no Scots. Only the English, the King's enemies."

"Not as we have heard it. You lie, man!"

Gilnockie reined close. "No man says that to Armstrong!" he rasped. "You will take back that word, Campbell!"

"Fool! Hold your insolent tongue or I will have it torn out! Before you hang!"

"Hang . . . !" That word seemed suddenly to convince Johnnie Armstrong that this was all serious, no mere gesturing and play-acting. He gazed from Argyll to the King—and saw nothing in their faces to reassure. He saw something else, however. Hamilton, a man for action always, had utilised the period of this exchange with Argyll to summon and lead forward a troop of horsed men-at-arms, and with them was now riding to get round behind the Armstrongs with the obvious intention of cutting off any line of retreat.

For a moment or two it looked as though Gilnockie would choose to do just that and lead his people in fast retiral. But pride triumphed over such caution and he spurred forward almost justling Argyll's horse aside right over to the King himself.

"We are here at your invitation. Under safe conduct," he said to the monarch.

"I said nothing of safe conduct," James declared, almost defiantly.

"Your herald invited and brought us, at your behest."

"That does not imply safe conduct for a traitor!"

"Traitor . . . ?"

"Aye, traitor. Think you we do not know of your dealings with the English? You claim to assail only them. But say naught of your traffic with them, of payments you accept from them."

"Mail paid, that I leave them their cattle! Such as will pay, the wise ones!"

"Dacre himself pays you, they say."

"Dacre has many cattle, and owns lands near the borderline!"

"False—all false! You have boasted, man, that you acknowledge the authority of neither the King of England nor the King of Scots. Can you deny it?"

"Only in the Debateable Land. Where, as all men know, the writ of neither runs, only that of the sharpest sword."

"Well, we shall see who wields the sharpest sword here! You will hang, Armstrong—hang!"

"You cannot mean that, James Stewart! Would you hang one who can give you what I can give?"

"What you can give, I can *take*!"

"Not so. Can you take the rents of every fair property between here and Newcastle town? *I* can give you them!"

"I do not believe it. Nor would I accept them, if I could."

"Could *you* take any English noble, be he duke, earl or baron, that you named, out of all that land. I could bring you any, by a certain day, either quick or dead."

There were guffaws from the King's companions who had now gathered round to listen.

"I desire none such," James said, frowning.

"I can give you four-and-twenty fine horses, milk-white and matching beasts. And as much yellow gold, English gold, as four of them can carry. Could *you* take that?"

"You rave, man—rave! And I do not need your horses nor your gold."

"You and yours may need bread, King, if this harvest fails, as it is like to do. I can give you four-and-twenty good-going mills, and the grain to keep them grinding round the year."

"The harvest is not like to fail. Have done, boaster!"

"With such as Your Grace has around you here, scoundrels all I judge, you could do with an honest guard for your royal person, I vow! I can give you more trusty and leal gentlemen than even you see here, Armstrong gentlemen, as your guard.

214

Say forty, who would lay down their lives for you at my behest. How say you?"

"*I* say that with forty thieves around you, Your Grace would never pass another peaceful night!" The Bastard had returned. That produced grins.

James drew himself up in his saddle. "I believe none of all that you offer," he said. "And your forty thieves will hang with you, for company! My Lord Argyll, do your duty." He pointed. "Up there. There are sufficient trees on yonder ridge to accommodate them all, I swear!"

There was a shout of laughter at this royal sally, which James self-consciously acknowledged.

Johnnie Armstrong made a gesture partly resignation, partly defiance. "I was a fool to look for warm water beneath cold ice!" he said. "A fool to seek grace at Your Grace's graceless face! A fool to come at all, trusting your messenger. Had I known that you would take my life this day, I should have stayed away and kept the Border in despite of King Henry and you, both. For I know that Henry Tudor a blithe man would be this day, and would downweigh my best horse with his English gold to know that John Armstrong was condemned to die. Which proves who lacks in judgement, does it not? I tell you . . ."

"Enough!" Argyll interrupted. "Come, or we shall be here all day. We shall still this insolent tongue once and for all." And he signed for his men to grasp Gilnockie.

"A moment," James said. "What are these targets you wear on your cap?" And he pointed to the gold and silver tassels. "Eight, nine of them."

"I won them in the field, fighting the English—as your royal father dared but I think *you* would not! Each from a different knight's helm."

"Off with him!" the King jerked, turning away.

Armstrong shook off the hands which would have grasped him. "I need none to drag me to my death!" he said. He looked over towards his brother. "God be with you, Tom. We will be together again one day, in a better kingdom! Tell Kirsty . . ."

"He will tell none!" Argyll assured. "You are not parting from him. He hangs with you, as do they all. We shall see an end to the Armstrongs on the Border."

Surrounded now by overwhelming force, there was nothing that any of them could do. The Armstrong lairds, taking their

215

lead as ever from Gilnockie, did not struggle nor plead nor rail, but accepted their fate with quiet dignity. A general move was made up towards a slight grassy ridge whereon grew a group of twisted, wind-blown Scots pines.

David Lindsay hastened to the King's side. "Sire—this is madness! Wrong, wrong! And a sin. You cannot mean to go on with this? To hang him, them all?"

James turned his face away, unspeaking.

"Sire—hear me. This is shame. It will stain your royal name, for ever. The Armstrongs came here at your invitation. Safe conduct *is* understood and accepted in such case. Otherwise he would not have come. To slay him now is, is unthinkable!"

"He is a robber and a murderer. A traitor, and arrogant. He deserves to die."

"So is the Bastard of Arran! But you do not hang *him*!"

By the look the King gave him, David recognised that that was a mistake. He changed his approach. "Your Grace, I am your friend. Always have been, and I pray always will be. Yet you grievously injure *me*, in this. You sent me as herald to bring him to you. My name and repute is concerned. If you hang these men, *I* am diminished. Made accomplice, a deceiver."

"It was the only way to lay hands on him, Davie. He would have escaped justice for ever, at large in the Debateable Land."

"And you name this justice, Sire?"

"I do. Now, if you have no fairer words for me than this, leave me!"

Sorrowfully David reined away.

They hanged the Armstrongs on the trees of Caerlanrig, two or three to a tree, still in their saddles from which they had ruled the West Border, by the simple expedient of putting ropes around their necks and over a bough above then driving their horses from under them. The musicians went with the rest, the Bastard master-of-ceremonies. It was inevitably a haphazard business and not always expeditious, but they all died in the end. It was the Bastard's inspired suggestion that Gilnockie himself should be left to the end, so that he would have the benefit of watching his brother and all his presumptuous crew die first.

Thereafter a return was made to Branxholme, most in high good-humour but James himself silent and withdrawn. They left the forty-odd corpses swinging in the breeze.

Next day, with any further Border campaigning bound to seem

in the nature of an anticlimax, the return march to Edinburgh and Stirling was commenced. At Stirling, Lindsay made a stiff leave-taking of his monarch, who was still morose and difficult and who made no suggestion that David should stay at court. That man would be glad to be back with Janet at Lindifferon.

13

Davie Beaton looked from his host to Janet, and back. "The question is, do you, with all your gifts, abilities and experience, wish to use them, to do something of worth with them, of value to this our realm? Or do you seek to be only a simple Fife laird?"

"Can I not be both?"

"I fear not. I think that you must choose. Here you have no influence on men nor events. Even your poems reach little further—St. Andrews perhaps, no more. You should be at court, where events happen and are made to happen, where men are to be reached, where a little faith can move mountains!"

"I mislike the court as it now is."

"You mean that you mislike some of those who frequent the court? The Bastard and his ilk? You could help to counter their influence with James."

"I have tried that, and failed. I find James himself less and less to my taste, spoiled by the company he keeps."

"The more reason that you should seek to save him from them, and himself. Is it no less than your duty, man? You are his oldest true friend, cherishing him from infancy. James *needs* you, David."

"I think that he is scarce aware of it, then, since he never looks in my direction now."

"Perhaps he does, more than you think. I speak to him of you, and he sounds sufficiently interested. I gave him your *Dream*. He read it and praised it greatly. He even said that since King Henry had a Poet Laureate—he gives the man a yearly grant of wine!—*you* should be the Laureate of the Scots court."

"But does not want me at court to be so?"

"Do not be so thin of skin, friend! Think you all at court are there by express royal summons?"

"If James *needs* me, he can send for me. After all, I am still his Snowdoun Herald. And Janet is Mistress of his Wardrobe—leastways we have heard of no replacements."

"I think that I detect here injured pride?"

"Not so. But after Caerlanrig and the Armstrongs, I hold my distance from that young man unless, as my liege-lord, he summons me."

"Do you agree with this, Janet?"

"David knows best," she said simply.

"Ah, but we are all the better of occasional good advice, especially from our wives."

"*You* to say that!" Lindsay all but snorted.

"Indeed yes. My Marion advises me not a little. More than ever, indeed. Janet must have her views?"

"I have told David on occasion that he might find more, more fulfilment than just in farming The Mount of Lindifferon," she said, carefully.

"And you are right. I say that he has a part to play on a wider stage than some few hundred Fife acres." Beaton paused. "See you, David, I have a proposal for you, a tentative proposal. As ever, I am seeking to contain Henry Tudor, so far as Scotland is concerned. James himself is seemingly little interested. With England and France once again hand-in-glove since Wolsey's fall, the Emperor Charles is bound to be perturbed. Now, Scotland has an ancient treaty with the Netherlands, a treaty of mutual assistance, made a century ago when that land had not been occupied by the Empire and the Spanish. Few know of it, now. I did not my own self, but as Lord Privy Seal I learned of it. One of its clauses is that its term is of one hundred years, and could be renewed thereafter. Those hundred years are all but up. It occurs to me that a renewal might well suit the Emperor Charles, at this juncture, as warning to the ever-aggressive Henry—as it certainly would suit Scotland. A treaty in fact, if not in name, with the Empire, whilst France fails us. But, to be sure, Charles is unlikely to know of its existence. So I propose that James sends an embassage to Brussels to seek renewal of this treaty. How think you?"

"I think that it all sounds entirely like Davie Beaton!"

"That is scarcely the point. What would you say to going on such an embassage?"

"Me? Why me? I have no knowledge of statecraft, no honeyed tongue to persuade rulers—as I have proved!"

"Perhaps not. But you are to be trusted, as are not all. And you do not lack wits—in most matters. In some, mind you, I find you remarkably obtuse! But, see you, this embassage might serve *you* well, equally with the realm. It would bring you back into the royal service in worthy style, allow James to show you his kinder side again. For perhaps he has his pride also, David!"

"This talk of pride is foolishness. I think that you came here today to talk me into this of Brussels for your own ends! Admit it!"

"Scarcely for my own ends. But, yes, I would wish you to do this. I think that I have convinced James that the mission is important, and he suggests sending his latest drinking-companion, Campbell of Lundie. You may not know him, the late Argyll's cousin. You heard that Argyll had died suddenly? This Campbell I do not trust—but can scarcely say so to the King, who esteems him. David Paniter, the new royal secretary, I do trust—since I gained him the appointment!—and he may go also. But he is young yet and lacks experience. You would make the admirable third."

"I do not know . . ."

"I think that you should do it, David," Janet said. "You have been restless of late. There is insufficient here to content you for long, after the life that you have lived. Such a mission would be good for you."

"I shall think on it."

"Do that," Beaton nodded. "But do not think for too long. It is now June and the embassage should depart within a month or so, to gain good sailing weather there and back. Three men are always sent as such envoys—in the hope that one at least will be honest! Choosing three, who may counter each others' weaknesses, can be difficult. I shall endeavour to hold a place for you so long as I may."

"You are kind." That was Janet, not her husband.

"I am very kind, yes," the other agreed, wryly. "In especial, after all the ill things said by this character about Holy Church and its servants, such as my poor self, in *The Dream*! I could have had him excommunicated for less!"

"It all required to be said," Lindsay averred.

"That is debateable, shall we say. I told you, I see betterment, improvement, coming from within the Church rather than without."

Janet smiled. "Be that as it may, I fear that there is even worse to come, my lord Abbot. David has written two more poems in the months since the Borders expedition. And they are . . . stronger! They are named *An Answer to the King's Flyting* and *The Complaint of Our Sovereign Lord's Papingo.*"

"Sakes! The papingo? That old bird still squawks?" Davie Beaton it was who had brought the boy-King the parrot or papingo, from France many years before. "And *The King's Flyting*, you say? So, do I take it that James is the target this time, rather than the Church?"

"Not target. A, a reminder, merely, on some of the follies of the royal court." Lindsay shrugged. "Short things they are, of no real merit."

"But sufficient to destroy your repute at that court, man, I've little doubt! I would keep these from James and his friends for a time, if I were you."

"For whom they were written!"

"No doubt. But you self-appointed reformers sometimes require to be protected from yourselves. Does Janet not agree?"

She did not commit herself, but smiled quietly. She had a talent for quiet smiling, that woman.

When Beaton left The Mount, although his friend had not committed himself to Brussels and the embassy, it was understood that he would seriously consider the matter.

* * *

David Lindsay had to admit that his reception by his liege-lord, when two weeks later he did present himself at Stirling Castle, was friendly, even handsome. For, although James was guarded at first, less than at ease, very quickly he relaxed and became almost embarrassingly amiable—which tended to have something of the opposite effect on his visitor. However, when presently the King raised his voice to address a wider audience— they were outdoors on the grassy lip of the castle-rock above the terrace known as the Croft of Ballengeich, preparatory to indulging in James's favourite sport of hurly-hackit—Lindsay's embarrassment gave way to astonishment.

"Bring me a sword," James called out—for none, by custom, wore swords in the presence of the monarch, and they would have been no aid to the sport of hurly-hackit anyway. "My old gossip Davie Lindsay is come visiting, on his way to Brussels on our behalf. We have not seen him for long, and must mark the occasion. If Davie is going to chaffer with the Emperor Charles, it has been represented to me that he must needs go as better than but Snowdoun Herald. Our old Lyon King, Sir Thomas Clephane, long a sick man, has died, and a new Lord Lyon King-of-Arms is required. I therefore so now name and appoint Davie Lindsay of The Mount, our Laureate, to that office, as chiefest herald of this realm. Now—that sword."

One of the royal guard on duty produced a weapon, and taking it, James turned back to David. "Kneel," he ordered.

Scarcely able to grasp what was happening, that bewildered man sank on one knee, while his liege-lord tapped him on each bent shoulder with the long blade.

"I hereby dub you knight, Davie Lindsay, raising you to that most honourable estate, in the name of God the Father, the Son and the Holy Spirit. I charge you ever to serve me well and my realm likewise. And to remain a good and true knight until your life's end." That was said parrot-fashion and sing-song. "Arise, Sir David Lindsay of The Mount, Lord Lyon King-of-Arms."

To a certain amount of applause from some of those around, Davie Beaton leading, the new knight rose to his feet, bereft of words. It was not so much the knighthood which affected him, surprise as it was—after all, his father and grandfather had been knights before him; it was the appointment as Lyon. For this was no ordinary or merely decorative office, sufficiently decorative as it certainly was; for one thing, it was an appointment for life; it carried the rank and status of an ambassador; it ensured a unique relationship with the monarch, for whom Lyon could stand as personal representative, to the extent that to strike Lyon was the equivalent of striking the King himself, and as such high treason; moreover he ranked as one of the realm's justiciars, with his own court, supreme arbiter in more than heraldry, coats-of-arms, baronial status and feudal jurisdiction; also as master-of-ceremonies at the royal establishment, the position could be influential indeed.

James was clearly enjoying the sensation he had produced in Lindsay and in others, slapping his former usher and procurator

221

on the back and proclaiming that *he* was now the only man who could thus strike Da-Lin, his childhood name for his friend and guardian.

Beaton came up. "May I be first to congratulate my Lord Lyon, Sire?" he asked. "Sir David—my felicitations! May this Lyon roar to good effect in His Grace's Scotland, and furth of it!"

Shaking the proffered hand, Lindsay had little doubt as to where the initiative for this development had originated.

James announced that, in suitable celebration, his new Lord Lyon—who after all had first taught him the diversion of hurly-hackit, here on this very slope of Ballengeich—should now engage his erstwhile pupil in a race. Just the two of them. And let the best man win!

David, who had not taken part in this basic, indeed fairly childish sport for years, could scarcely refuse, although he had no desire to participate. For one thing, he knew his sovereign well enough to realise that he would want to win—indeed he was already wagering with his courtiers on the result; and that might be a little difficult to arrange without it being obvious—which would, in its turn, offend. Also, there was always a certain amount of danger to life and limb—not that that would greatly worry him but the man who might cause the *monarch* to become a casualty would be less than popular.

They went to choose their skulls. The sport was of the simplest and consisted merely of sliding downhill on a cow's skull, using the horns as handlebars as it were to steer with—hackit or hawkie being but the Scots word for an old cow, and hurly referring to the hurtling motion. In theory this was straight-forward enough, but in practice it was less so. For one thing, skulls, of cattle or other, are not the easiest objects to steer when sitting upon. For another, although the start of the steep slope was grassy, half-way down it became complicated with a series of outcropping rocks, little terraces and drops, some of them of a few feet, jaggy whin-bushes and other obstacles. All of which, approached at major speed, even on a wooden toboggan, would demand a deal of negotiating; on a cow's skull the hazards were not lessened. Yet this was James's favourite pastime, outdoors that is.

There is not a lot of room for a grown man on a skull, although those of typical shaggy Highland cattle tend to be broad, flattish and wide-horned. Selecting the flattest, the contestants dragged them to near the lip of the slope and there drew lots for the left or right course. The least hazardous was the right, and David gained it and wished that he had not.

James, who at eighteen now probably considered his opponent as an old man of not far off forty, was supremely confident.

The new Earl of Arran, the Bastard's half-brother—the old Earl and Admiral had died—gave the signal for off. To start well was important, for it was a test of agility, seated, to propel the skull forward the few feet to the edge, using the heels, and might in fact determine the outcome of the race there and then. But these two were experts, and David's muscles kept in good state by his outdoor life at Lindifferon. They reached the lip exactly level, and plunged over, to the yells of the onlookers, almost all, naturally, shouting for the King.

The descent started fairly moderately, with heels still urging the sleds on. But quickly gravity took over and the speed of the glissade increased. The grass slope was about two hundred yards long, and before they were half-way down this they were bounding and bouncing at an exhilarating rate, rather extraordinary for so clumsy-seeming mounts, the men perched awkwardly, with their feet up now, knees bent, soles of boots pushed against the horns between their hand-grips. Balancing in this position and at speed was an art in itself.

They could scarcely be described as running neck and neck, for the two courses diverged considerably, to take advantage of the best routes through the assorted obstacles further down, so far as this was possible with the rough-and-ready steering. But there was little for the wagerers to choose between them.

David himself was so concerned with watching James's progress that he all but came to grief at the second little ledge-and-drop, taking it a foot or two from the right spot and so careering over a fall of nearly four feet, to land with a jar. Only the speed of his descent and the consequent angle at which he hit the ground saved him from overturning and parting company with his hackit, not to speak of injury. Sobered, he reminded himself of priorities.

Going more heedfully if no less swiftly, and using the occasional heel to pivot slight changes of direction, he threaded his way through the hazards in fair style, considering the interval since last he had done this—too fair indeed, for traversing a brief levellish terrace of grass he had opportunity for just a glance leftwards, to see that he was slightly ahead of James. And for the remainder of the run, his course was, if anything, more free of obstacles than was the King's.

His thinking had to be as swift as his progress. No obvious slowing-up would serve, nor would any deliberate collision or upset. A diversion in the route, then? Only if it could be achieved as seemingly advisable.

There was a patch of wet ground ahead, drainage-water off the great rock, which normally, on this course, was avoided left-about. If he could approach this further to the right, so that to take the left side at the last moment would seem difficult, then right-about would look natural enough. And just a little too far to the right and he would be into an apron of scree and rubble thereafter, which ought to slow him up without actually capsizing him.

Even as he visualised this possibility he was acting on it, the bright green of the damp sump directly in front. Slewing right, he swept round it—and perceived that the scree was further over than he had recollected. Another jerk to the right was necessary, whether it looked natural or not to those watchers above, or he was going to win this race in only a few seconds time. He slewed again, leaning over.

Too late, he realised that he had overdone it, no doubt the effect of the speed, the incline and his heel combined. He was swinging much too far over—and that way lay trouble, actually a sort of quarry where stone had been excavated in years past.

David tried to pull round, back on course, but it was too late. He was heading straight for the rim of the crescent-shaped gouge in the hillside, and no amount of slewing was going to avoid it. He must either throw himself off his hackit, or go over the edge. He could not remember just how deep a drop there was—anything from a dozen to a score of feet probably. And one of the basic understandings of hurly-hackit was that only novices and weaklings deliberately ejected from their sleds, come what might.

It was all over in less time than it takes to tell. The new Lord Lyon King-of-Arms shot over the lip, out into space, still clinging to his cow's horns.

Because of the speed of his take-off, he and his skull did not drop with anything like verticality, hurtling through the air in a sort of sagging arc, to crash to earth, eventually near the mouth of the little quarry, into a pile of rubble, stones and nettles.

It was as well perhaps that those nettles were there in such profusion, for they helped to cushion the stones and debris. Even so, every bone in David's body was jarred and jolted, and the wind knocked out of him.

Too shaken to do more than lie there, gasping for breath, he was also afraid to try to move lest he discovered bones to be broken. He was quite unaware of comprehensive nettle-stings.

Presently, gingerly he stretched one arm, then the other, then his legs. Soreness but nothing worse, he assessed, thankfully. Slowly, painfully, he raised himself on all fours, gulping as he straightened one knee—something damaged there. The other one seemed to be all right. Cautiously he achieved the upright, actually using a clutch of nettle-stems to pull himself up. There and thus he stood, swaying, nerving himself to risk a step or two out from that uneven stance. Surely, seldom can the accolade of knighthood have been so oddly celebrated.

James himself was the first on the scene, part concerned, part amused, "Davie—here's a stramash! What happened? Are you hurt? How did you do it, man?"

"I . . . misjudged," David said briefly.

"You did so! Sakes—did you forget about this quarry? The times you have warned me of it!"

The other was in no mood nor state for any inquest. "I misjudged, I say." Scowling unsuitably at his sovereign, he held out a hand for aid to get him out of that rubbish-heap. James obliged with an arm, and stiffly, awkwardly, David clambered over to level grass, wincing with the pain of that knee.

"You *are* hurt," the King declared. "Your leg. And you have torn your breeches. I'd scarce have believed it of you, Davie."

"Nor I!" That was grimly said.

Leaning on the royal arm, and limping, David had to listen to an exposition on the finer points of hurly-hackit as regards this Ballengeich course, and where his one-time mentor must have gone wrong, the inference being that age would account for much and a failing memory was all but inevitable. This was mercifully cut short by the arrival of the rest of the company, come hurrying down the steep, in slithering disorder, to congratulate royalty on its splendid win and mockingly commiserate with the sorry loser.

Davie Beaton took over from James as support. "That was not

like you," he observed. "Were your new honours too much for you? Or do I sense something here more than met the eye?"

"I misjudged." That repetition was distinctly sour. "It was advisable that James should win."

"Ah! I begin to perceive light. Yes, I see. So it was policy, going a little astray? It happens to the best of us."

"Thank you!" Lindsay changed the subject. "I expect that it was you who were behind this of the Lyon's office? And knighthood?"

"Not altogether. James desired to show you some mark of favour. I think that his conscience might have been troubling him. I was concerned that you should be sufficiently senior, on this Brussels embassage, not to be outranked by the other two. Campbell, of course, is a knight and kin to Argyll. And Paniter is Abbot of Cambuskenneth and Bishop-Elect of Ross. So something of some standing was required for you. And Lyon is always knighted."

"I do not like being beholden . . ."

"Do not be so prickly, man! You were a senior herald anyway, and best man for the position. You will make a better Lyon than we have had for long. And Janet deserves to be Lady Lindsay."

Getting back up that hill with a damaged knee was no pleasant experience, and further converse was limited, to say the least, until Lindsay was safely installed on a settle in the Lord Privy Seal's comfortable quarters on the south side of the Upper Square.

There they discussed the forthcoming mission to the Low Countries, to which Lindsay now seemed committed. It was considered advisable that they should travel in a French ship, as less likely to be attacked by English vessels. One such would sail from Dumbarton in ten days' time, the west-coast route being infinitely safer from the said English than the east. This would entail landing at a French west-coast port, Brest or possibly St. Malo, not risking the narrows of the Channel, and travelling across France to the Netherlands, but this should produce few difficulties—even though it suited Francis to be friends with England meantime and therefore he was anti-Scotland, he had no animosity against the Scots themselves, indeed his personal guard was composed of Scots.

At Brussels they would probably have to deal with Margaret, Queen of Hungary, the Emperor's aunt, who was at present governing the Low Countries for her nephew. Beaton had never met her but she was reputed to be as plain as she was autocratic and nobody's fool. But, in his experience, plain women were more profitable to deal with than beauties, heedfully handled, being more appreciative of flattering references where looks were concerned, and of recognition of their strengths in other respects. Paniter would be little use at this, he guessed, and Campbell was an arrogant soldier who treated women like chattels.

Lindsay was extremely doubtful about all this, especially when he heard that Scotland had really nothing to offer in this treaty-renewal negotiation other than her geographical position as an ever-present threat in England's rear—that and her traditional trading links with the Netherlands, especially with the Flemings for whom she was the main source of wool for their great weaving and cloth trade. If this seemed to Lindsay precious little to offer, the other appeared to believe that, properly handled, it would be sufficient for present circumstances.

David's knee-cap was badly swollen but nothing appeared to be broken, and in a day or two the contusion went down and he was able to walk reasonably well again although the leg tired quickly. For the rest, his body was a mass of bruises, but these would fade, and there was nothing to prevent him sailing on the due date. But before that, he was eager to go back to Lindifferon to take farewell of Janet. Neither James nor Beaton had any objection, so long as he reached Dumbarton in time; but the King suggested that he should bring Janet back to court, on the way, to resume her duties as Wardrobe Mistress. David did not commit her to this, as it was not put as a royal command.

So, with riding no difficulty, he returned to The Mount, having a look at Luthric in the by-going, this modest barony in North Fife being always allotted to the Lord Lyon as a kind of fee for his services and expenses. He was reasonably well pleased with what he saw there, although the property had been sadly neglected under the ageing and ailing Clephane. Only some six miles from The Mount, it would be comparatively easy to manage it more effectively from Lindifferon.

Janet was delighted to hear of her husband's new status and what was, she declared, his long overdue promotion—she was not informed deeply on the hurly-hackit incident. But now that their parting was imminent, she was a little anxious about the dangers implicit in his mission overseas, storms, attacks by the

English, foreign travel generally and other unspecified hazards, all of which David of course pooh-poohed, even hinting that the sport of hurly-hackit was in fact more dangerous. She declared that she did not want to go back to Stirling on her own meantime, preferring to remain at The Mount until David returned, when they could resume court life together.

So, after a couple of days, farewells were said and the traveller set off for Dumbarton, knee almost recovered. He still could not really think of himself as Lord Lyon King-of-Arms nor even as Sir David.

14

It took him two days to ride across Scotland to the Clyde estuary, some of the time through the skirts of the Highland Line, MacGregor, Macfarlane and Colquhoun country, where timorous folk said that he should not venture without a well-armed escort, advice which he likewise pooh-poohed, and experienced no problems. He arrived at Dumbarton to find the quite large trading vessel, *La Couronne*, waiting and already laden with a cargo of Lammermuir wool brought by pack-horse from Lothian for the weavers of Rennes in Brittany. Abbot Paniter was therein installed, with two servants. Campbell had not yet appeared.

Paniter proved to be a serious man of about thirty, scion of a Montrose family, young to be a bishop-elect—but then, Montrose was within the Abbot of Arbroath's sphere of influence and friends and neighbours of Davie Beaton were well placed for promotion. David anticipated few problems with him but did not see him as exciting company.

The problems proved to arrive with Sir John Campbell of Lundie, last to appear, probably because he had least distance to travel. Indeed he came two days late, by which time their French shipmaster was in a state of much and voluble agitation. This did not worry the Campbell in the slightest; what did concern

228

him was that there did not seem to be accommodation on board for the dozen Highland clansmen, with less than which apparently he never travelled. It did not matter, evidently, where and how these kilted characters were bestowed, but sail they must. The shipmaster capitulated with ill grace, the Highlandmen bristling with arms, but he demanded more money. David foresaw continuing complications.

Campbell, a man of about Lindsay's own age, was cheerful enough in a loud way, big, florid and dominant, who over-ate, over-drank and over-reacted with a sort of jovial ferocity, hardly the conventional choice as an ambassador. David perceived why Beaton had felt that a counter-balancing presence, other than the reserved Paniter, would be advisable, and why such presence should be invested with some authority.

They sailed on the first tide.

Despite the greatly increased distance involved, they avoided the inner passage of the Irish Sea and voyaged instead around Rathlin Isle and Malin Head, to sail down the west coast of Ireland, where they could expect to escape the attentions of the English pirates, who could not be relied upon to know, or care, that King Henry was at present on friendly terms with King Francis, possible Atlantic gales being considered infinitely the lesser hazard. In fact, there were no storms, the breezes were consistently favourable and without incident they made excellent time—which was probably as well considering the state of the Campbell clansmen roosting in the hold amongst the smelly wool-bales.

Six days, and with hardly another sail sighted until they were into French coastal waters, they entered the Rance estuary and reached the Breton port of St. Malo on its rocky isle and defensive causeway to the mainland, David for one thankful indeed to step back on dry land. It was not that he was a bad sailor but he had had enough of being cooped up in constricted space with John Campbell, his loud voice and peculiar brand of humour. Admittedly they were going to be together for a long time yet, but on horseback, and on overnight stops in inns and hospices and the like, he could surely keep his distance better than in a cramped and low-ceiled cabin.

St. Malo was *La Couronne*'s home port, it transpired, and the travellers asked their skipper's advice as to where they might hire the necessary horses. It was then that they discovered this to be no problem, for the wool cargo would all be going by pack-horse-train to Rennes, fifty-odd miles on their way, and they could get mounts from the same source and indeed journey that far in convoy. This arrangement seemed convenient and would help to initiate them into French travel conditions. Beaton had obtained for them a safe conduct from his friend King Francis, so that no difficulties with the authorities were to be looked for.

There was considerable astonishment at the stableyard-compound across the causeway which linked St. Malo island with the mainland when it appeared that the seventeen Scots required only five horses, and three pannier-ponies, the Campbell henchmen being running-gillies who scorned horseflesh. When even David and Paniter objected that these footmen would be bound to hold up their rate of progress, Lundie hooted his scorn. They would be no such thing, he asserted, able to outrun any pack-horses, keep going longer and eat less fodder; used to traversing mountain country, this flat France would be bairns'-play for them.

And so indeed it proved. As the long cavalcade proceeded southwards through the Breton countryside, the Highlandmen, trotting at either side of their chieftain, had positively to slow their accustomed pace to avoid outdistancing the rest, with Campbell complaining that they would be better off on their own and make much better time. But David and Paniter declared that, as there was no desperate hurry and the sea voyage had been so expeditious, it was sensible to remain with the pack-train meantime, to be thus painlessly introduced to French ways and customs. Paniter spoke French of a sort, David less so and Campbell not at all, so some such assisted initiation was valuable.

They covered the distance to Rennes in two days, halting for the first night at Combourg in the Dol area, where the Stewarts had originated, where indeed they had been Stewards of Dol for the Norman Counts of Dol and Dinan. At the end of this twenty-five miles, the running-gillies appeared to be almost as fresh and unconcerned as they had been at the beginning, cheerful, undemanding individuals despite their fierce aspect, who spoke only the Gaelic and appeared to find foreign travel to their taste. The Breton horse-leaders, after eyeing them askance at first, seemed to get on well with them and in fact were able to communicate with them better than with the gentry, their own dialect sounding not unlike Gaelic, to David at least; the Bretons were themselves in origin a Celtic people, of course.

They found Rennes, Brittany's capital, to be quite a large, bustling town standing where the River Vilaine joined the Ille, the riversides lined with warehouses—to two of which their wool was consigned—mills manufacturing cloths and linen, breweries and the like. As became a commercial centre, there were plenty of inns for travellers, but here again the Campbell gillies proved something of a problem, not in themselves but in the local reaction to them and their peculiar ways—for these did not require nor desire normal inn accommodation but were happy to forage for their own food and to bed down anywhere that took their fancy, on the hay or straw of stables, on sail-cloth stocks, or just in the open air, wrapped in their stained tartan plaids. All of which somewhat disconcerted the innkeepers and town-guards. However, Sir John was liberal with moneys, and this smoothed the way for them fairly effectively. One unforeseen development, first seen at Rennes, was the attraction of these brawny and underclad clansmen for the street-women with which the place seemed to abound, and who obviously found their so evident magnificent physique and good-humoured attitudes much to their taste, a state of affairs which tended still further to complicate the bedding-down arrangements. Not that Lundie himself was in any way concerned; he found his own women and left his henchmen to it. The two other ambassadors were content to behave more conventionally, as became a bishop-elect and Scotland's Lord Lyon King-of-Arms.

The following day, on their own now, they did make much better time, reaching Laval, a good fifty miles, the clansmen, as promised, not holding up the horsemen in the least, whatever their nocturnal activities. Thereafter they crossed some higher ground to Le Mans, the capital of Maine, another fifty miles. David and Paniter were much impressed with this city on the Sarthe, the birthplace of England's Henry the Second and burial-place of Richard Lion-Heart's queen, Berengaria. The Campbells however found it less hospitable.

To avoid the Paris area, advisedly, they now turned almost due northwards by Alençon, Verneuil and Bernay, consistent fifty-mile days, making for Rouen, extraordinary progress David had to admit. At the Normandy capital, with its no fewer than three cathedrals, one archiepiscopal, its rampart-walls and its palaces, scene of the burning of Joan of Arc and tomb of Berengaria's Richard, David was greatly taken, even if his companions were less so, it bringing to mind so much that he had learned and all but forgotten, and stirring his poetic urge. He began to bless Davie Beaton.

Now in order to avoid the English-held Pas de Calais, they headed for Amiens and then St. Quentin, in both of which the great concentrations of woollen-mills and weaving-sheds along the many-channelled Somme gave David the notion of increased Scottish trade being possible. They were nearing the edge of France here, and indeed the day after leaving St. Quentin they came to the border fortress-town of Valenciennes on the Scheldt, with the Netherlands before them and only the county of Hainault between them and their Brussels destination.

After crossing Scheldt they were immediately into war-torn territory, with blackened ruins, abandoned farmsteads and wasted countryside on every hand, for this land had been fought over for generations between the Empire, France and the Dukes of Burgundy; indeed peace of a sort had only come as lately as the year previously, with the Treaty of Cambrai, the 'Ladies' Peace' as it was called, contrived by the two redoubtable queens, Louise of France, mother of King Francis, and Margaret of Hungary, aunt of the Emperor Charles. The travellers, proceeding across-country by Mons, the Hainault capital and Waterloo, became in consequence the more conscious of the problems and responsibility ahead—or two of them did. Suddenly their mission seemed altogether more real, more demanding.

In Brussels, as elsewhere, their escort of running-gillies drew much attention and comment, the like undoubtedly never before seen. It was a great and strange city, built on two distinct levels, the Lower Town and the Upper, with a hillside between them sufficiently steep to be mounted largely by means of steps and stairs, so contrived as to be used by horses. The Lower Town, built along the ditch-like River Senne, and carved up by canals, was the commercial quarter, extensive, thronged with folk, smelly, humid and foggy in this summer weather, with warehouses, granaries, mills, wharves, drinking-dens and the like packed together in the narrow streets and wynds in stirring, teeming confusion, with Flemish spoken, unintelligible to the visitors. The Upper Town was altogether different, airy, spacious, gardened and tree-girt, where was the royal palace and the houses of the nobility, with many fine religious buildings—even though most prominent of all was the renowned Hotel de Ville, below, with its seven storeys of arcading and its extraordinary spire no less than three hundred and sixty-four feet high. French was the language of the Upper Town. Here the visitors found a hospice attached to a Blackfriars monastery, not far from the royal palace, to take them in, although, as ever, the Highlanders were accepted by the friars with considerable doubts.

Paniter's French was good enough to gather from the monks that Queen Margaret was in residence but not the Emperor himself—although he was expected shortly from Italy. However, they also learned that, since it was for negotiations that they had come, the aunt was probably of more use to them than would be the nephew, for reasons unspecified.

Next morning David made his way to the palace, alone. It was felt that he, as a herald, ought to go, to announce their arrival and try to arrange an audience. Getting past the guards at the magnificent gates was not easy, what with his feeble French, his unspectacular Scots broadcloth and his lack of attendants—he had had no hesitation in refusing an escort of the Campbell clansmen on this occasion; but when it occurred to him to produce the safe conduct provided for them with the King of France's signature, that gained him entry.

Oddly enough thereafter there were no more difficulties, indeed it was all almost laughably simple. None of the handsomely-clad throng of nobles, prelates, courtiers and flunkeys who paraded and hurried or idled through the vast and ornate establishment did more than glance at him, his very modest attire probably suggesting that he was some sort of senior servant or messenger. He wandered about the seemingly endless succession of halls, salons, arcades and corridors more or less at will. Once or twice he asked obvious servitors where he would find the Chamberlain, Master of the Household or even a secretary, but received either blank looks, off-putting or incomprehensible directions.

At a loss, he was following a sauntering pair of exquisites along a mirror-walled corridor graced with highly-indelicate marble statuary when the couple in front suddenly drew aside into an alcove and bowed deeply. A thick-set, dumpy woman of middle years, almost as plainly dressed as was David him-self, was coming in the other direction, with two much more richly-clad younger females behind and a scarlet-robed cleric following on.

There being no convenient alcove available for him, David merely stood back, wondering whether this could be the Queen-Governor herself, undistinguished as she looked. He bowed, in case, but not deeply.

The lady looked at him and seemed about to stump past. Then she paused, eyeing him up and down frankly. "A stranger, I think?" she said, in French. She had a deepish voice.

David understood that, at least. "Yes, madam," he agreed. "Very much so. From Scotland." At least, that is what he meant.

"Ah—one of the Scots." That was in English very much better than his French. "More fully clad than the others, from what I hear!"

He blinked. News evidently travelled fast in Brussels. "Those are Highland gillies, running-gillies, clansmen, madam. In the train of one of my colleagues. I am no Highlandman."

"Indeed. We have differences in race and style in the Netherlands, also—but scarcely in states of nakedness, monsieur!"

"Men who run all day, even outrun horses, are best with little clothing," he asserted, a little stiffly.

"These run? All day? Outrun horses, you say? Surely not?"

"Not in speed, madam, but in distance. These gillies will run fifty miles and more, with scarce a pause. And little to eat in the running."

"You astonish me, monsieur. I must hear more of this. Come." That was somewhat peremptory.

"I am seeking the Chamberlain here, or other officer of this household, who may gain us an audience with the Queen of Hungary. So far I have not found one . . ."

"*I* am Margaret. You are one of the Scots come to sign a renewal of the treaty, I presume? So you will have to wait until the Emperor comes, for *his* signature must be appended, not mine. I am but his governor here. So, come. This of the runners? Is the like much done in Scotland? I have never heard of it."

"Only in the Highlands, Highness." David produced another little bow at that, and fell into step beside the lady as they moved along down the corridor. He tried to explain the clan system, the patriarchal relationship between chiefs and clansmen, the difference between Highlands and Lowlands, but found it hard to keep his mind on what he was saying, so affected was he by what *she* had said. She had sounded as though this treaty-renewal was almost a foregone conclusion, only formal signing to be required. Perhaps he had misheard, or mistaken? But it had sounded that way. What, then . . . ?

They turned off into a smallish apartment, lined with books like a library but equipped with paper-littered tables and desks, as in some office. Here this businesslike Queen paused, to pick out one paper amongst many, was handed a quill and inkhorn by one of her ladies, and signed the document promptly, without any of the flourish and curliques beloved of most lofty signatories; and handing the paper to the cleric, dismissed him with a wave.

"A pity that we cannot dispose of *your* concordat thus easily, but my nephew Charles insists on signing and sealing all treaties and the like in person. However, he should be here in a matter of days—and it will give me opportunity to see more of you and learn more of your country. Your name, monsieur?"

"Lindsay, Highness—David Lindsay."

"And you, Monsieur Lindsay, represent the chief of your mission to sign this treaty-renewal? Who is he?"

David coughed. "I suppose, Highness, that *I* am." That sounded apologetic almost. "At least, I represent King James. Since I am his Lord Lyon King-of-Arms, Sir David Lindsay of The Mount."

"You say so! All that! Then I am more pleased to welcome you here, Sir David. Modest men in high places are as rare as modest women in courts!" And she glanced over at her two ladies.

He smiled, feeling strangely at ease now with this Queen.

"I was only made Lord Lyon a few weeks past, to come on this embassage," he confessed. "I am scarce used to the position yet."

She gave a deep throaty chuckle and tapped his forearm. "Honest as well as modest!" she said. "I think that your King James chose well. Yet I understand that he is a somewhat loose young man, even for a king! And not always wise? Although perhaps it was Abbot David of, of Aberroath, is it?—the Abbot who chose you?"

"You are well informed, Highness!"

"I would not long remain Governor of the Netherlands if I was not, my friend!"

He accepted that. "Abbot Beaton is a power behind the throne, yes—and behind the Church. But King James, my liege-lord, is no cipher. And he has his virtues, many of them. His failings stem from his early debasement by the Earl of Angus, who long had him in his power, deliberately done to gain better control of him and therefore of his kingdom."

"Ah, yes, I have heard of Angus. Friend to Henry of England, is he not?"

"A friend of sorts! I would not wish that man as *my* friend!"

"Nor Henry himself, I think? Hence your treaty?"

He nodded. "Yes—England must ever be . . . contained." He hesitated. "This treaty, Highness, to be renewed. You anticipate . . . no difficulty?"

"Why should I? It is very ancient, and should serve both our causes. Does anything concern you over it?" That was quick.

"No." He took a chance. "It is but that it appears to be somewhat one-sided. You—or the Empire—gain an ever-present ally in England's rear. But we—what does Scotland gain? I do not look to see the Emperor ever invading England on Scotland's behalf! The Netherlands might have done so, once—or threatened it. But the Empire . . . ?"

"You think not? There are other ways to trouble Henry than by armed invasion, Sir David. But—you seek something more?"

"Only trade, Highness. Scotland is not a rich country, save in sheep and cattle, fish and salt and the like. On our way here, and in Brussels itself, we have seen much of woollen-spinning and cloth-making, tanneries for hides and the like. Clearly much wool is required, also skins. Perhaps salt, or salted fish likewise. We could supply it, to our profit—and probably yours."

"Then why do you not, friend, already?"

"In part, that we have not known sufficiently of the possibilities. But mainly in that our ships to carry the trade would be attacked and captured by the English pirates or by Henry's ships-of-war. They swarm everywhere in the Norse Sea and the Channel, as you will well know. Even this mission had to sail west-about round Ireland to escape them. Now, the Netherlands are namely for their shipping, as are the Empire's Hansa ports. If Netherlands vessels could come to Scottish eastern ports or, better still, have Scottish vessels sail protected by Empire ships-of-war, then much trade could result and wealth be created."

"I see. You are a man of some vision, I perceive, Sir David. Are you concerned in trade, as well as this of heraldic jurisdiction and the Laws of Arms?"

"No. But I do produce much cattle and sheep on my lands in Fife and Lothian."

"Ah. So you would have something to gain in the matter?"

"I, and a great many others, Highness."

"That is honest, likewise. I shall speak to the Emperor on this. And he may well approve—for he ever requires money and more money! *I* see the importance of trade, if he does not! Perhaps not a clause to the treaty, but a separate agreement?"

"I thank Your Highness."

"Now—you have gone to lodge with the good friars at the Dominican monastery, I am told. That will not do. You will bring your people here, to this palace. All, including your runners. I must see these. We shall have a demonstration, no? In the hunting-park. You, and the other envoys will dine with me tonight. Meantime, I have others awaiting me . . ."

David, bowing, was given a hand to kiss and, much heartened, took his leave.

So commenced what was, on the whole, a very pleasant interlude—even though it became rather more extended than anticipated, first by the delayed arrival of the Emperor and then by his imperial command. But meantime the Scots found themselves, as it were, in clover, most hospitably and flatteringly entertained and in great demand—indeed most embarrassingly so. This partly on account of David's obvious favour with the Queen and partly with the popularity of the running-gillies, who found themselves an unfailing attraction for not only the court but the Brussels establishment generally, all taking their cue from Margaret Hapsburg. After the first arranged demonstration of their normal abilities, they were constantly involved in races, short-distance against local champions and long-distance against each other and horsemen, with much wagering and excitement; also other feats of endurance, wrestling, cannon-ball throwing—at which they excelled, not unlike their own Highland stone-putting—Highland dancing to their own mouth-music, tossing tree-trunks, something never before witnessed here, and general display of muscular prowess. And surprisingly—at least to David and Paniter, who had looked on such clansmen as little better than heathen barbarians, in typical Lowland

237

prejudice—they behaved throughout almost without exception in exemplary fashion, modest, well-mannered and amicable, rather astonishing considering how completely novel an experience this was for men who had never before left their upland glens, and especially the way women, court ladies included, all but threw themselves at them. Sir John Campbell himself, although he gained a sort of reflected glory from his virile henchmen, became all but jealous, an extraordinary state of affairs. Although, of course, the gillies never actually dined in the royal presence, and Margaret was sufficiently tactful not to have them brought on like paid entertainers at the banquets, they certainly suffered no lack of evening and night activities and fed better than they ever could have believed possible.

In all this, significantly, there was no talk of treaty terms, although trade was discussed once or twice, particularly with the burgomaster and other city representatives introduced by the Queen.

So one August week was extended into two and three, and still the Emperor Charles did not appear. Nobody seemed very surprised, although his aunt was not exactly apologetic but understanding over her guests' delay. Not all of them were anxious to be off, admittedly, even though David was, being somewhat impatient by nature and concerned about harvest at The Mount and Luthrie, his new fief. He was also missing Janet. But the waiting was made pleasant indeed, with Paniter spending much time at the many religious institutions of the city and Campbell adequately catered for in all respects.

Then on the 2nd of September, the Emperor arrived with his vast entourage and conditions at Brussels underwent major change. It was not that Charles Hapsburg was unpleasant, domineering nor intentionally arrogant, merely that he was difficult to deal with, almost diffident in fact, with a nervous jerky manner which was apt to put everyone around him ill-at-ease. A man of thirty, he had been King of Spain since sixteen and Emperor since nineteen, and like many another youthful successor to a great man—his grandfather, the famous Emperor Maximilian—had not had an easy time of it. His natural reticence was no help. Peculiar looks likewise did not assist, a sharply-receding forehead and notably high hairline being countered by a thrusting pointed jawline, the famous Hapsburg chin, so that his features seemed to slant downwards at a distinct angle, an impression accentuated rather than aided by a bushy black beard. Emperors and monarchs admittedly did not have to depend on their looks for effectiveness, but Charles did almost appear to be embarrassed by his appearance, and in consequence embarrassed others. Perhaps to compensate he dressed dramatically all in black, with a white ruff and silver facings, his thin, bony legs in trunks and hose seeming notably long.

David and his colleagues were presented to this, arguably the most powerful man in Christendom, by Queen Margaret, and gained the impression that they were quite unimportant and indeed rather a nuisance. It took a little while for them to realise that this was the normal reaction. Charles did not look at any of them as he talked in a hurried, clipped voice, and seemed only anxious to be elsewhere. Yet, when he did move away, abruptly, it was only to go and behave the same way to other groups and individuals, and presently to pace over to one of the great windows of the ornate salon, to stare out, alone. David noted that the imperial fingers, hands behind back, fidgeted and twisted.

Queen Margaret appeared not in the least put out by this behaviour, and almost casually mentioned that her nephew would sign the treaty on the morrow. Astonished that no gestures at negotiation appeared to be envisaged, they were led off.

It was Abbot Paniter who, after discreet enquiries amongst his clerical acquaintances, came up with the likeliest explanation for this attitude towards treaty terms. The Emperor, it seemed, was much preoccupied with two main dangers to his power, now that he had more or less put France in its place—the threats from the Turks and from the followers of Martin Luther. The former was more than a threat, for the Turkish Sultan, Sulieman the Magnificent, had invaded the Empire territories, had captured Belgrade, driven the Knights of St. John out of Rhodes and was now preparing to attack Hungary. This challenge had to be met, and swiftly; but the second problem, that of the new doctrine of the so-called Protestants led by the monk Luther, seriously hampered Charles's military efforts, for his most useful and effective forces were led by the Germanic princes and *landknechts* and these were the very people most affected by Luther's demands for reform. Charles himself had at first been somewhat sympathetic towards Church reform, but the demands of the power-struggle with France and King Francis—who actually had proposed that *he* should be Emperor—required the Empire and Rome to be close allies. So Luther had to be denied. The Diet of Augsburg the previous year had been an attempt to find a middle course, but had not really satisfied the reformers. Now Sulieman was taking full advantage. It was against this background that a more positive alliance with Scotland was being envisaged. For Scotland, especially with Beaton believed to be firmly in the ascendancy, was solidly in the Papal camp—as evidenced by the burning of Patrick Hamilton—and Henry of England, since his demotion of Cardinal Wolsey from the chancellorship, was known to be toying with this reformist heresy for his own purposes. Briefly, then, the Emperor required allies, even as modest as Scotland.

All this set David Lindsay thinking. He recollected how Davie Beaton had indicated at Stirling that this ancient treaty would not be difficult to renew, despite changes in the Netherlands, without going into details. So this was behind it all. Beaton was as ever notably well informed.

The next day, nothing was said about treaty signing, but Queen Margaret was informed that Charles was anxious to see the Scots running-gillies in action and so there was another demonstration in the palace hunting-park. This apparently greatly impressed the Emperor—although he did not say so to the envoys—so much so that the Scots were to be included in a great tournament and display to be held the following week in Antwerp, in honour of Margaret herself. This was the first that the visitors had heard of such an event. It seemed that in appreciation of his aunt's effective rule of the hitherto troublesome Netherlands and to consolidate his position there, Charles was about to promote Margaret from Governor to Regent, and this entertainment was to celebrate the occasion. For political reasons it was to be held at Antwerp rather than Brussels. Antwerp was in fact the commercial capital of the world and full of foreigners apparently, with the representatives of almost every kingdom, principality and duchy in Christendom based there, for financial rather than political reasons, and so was the place *par excellence* to make any significant announcement. Seemingly this tournament and display was more important than merely a celebration of Margaret Hapsburg's promotion. When

David indicated that he was duly impressed—but when was the treaty to be signed, the Queen told him not to be impatient. Did he not desire trading concessions? Well, then—Antwerp was the place for that.

So their sojourn in the Netherlands was further prolonged.

The move to Antwerp was effected in great style, in an enormous and glittering procession of armoured knights, churchmen, carriages, horse-litters, banner-parties, mounted choirs and instrumentalists, with retainers by the hundred and caravans of elaborate refreshment and cheer, which, considering that the distance between the two cities was only twenty-seven miles, meant that the vanguard was almost at the one before the rearguard left the other. The Scots were positioned up at the front, with the Campbell gillies, running on either side of the Emperor and Queen, much admired.

They went down Senne, picking up additional numbers with the Cardinal-Primate, at Mechlin, where the lace was manufactured, and on to the Scheldt again, now a notably wide slow-flowing river dotted with vessels large and small. There was little sign of war damage here.

The visitors were all but overwhelmed by Antwerp itself, much the largest city they had ever seen, and seemingly the richest, making Edinburgh and Stirling appear like huddled villages below their rock-citadels. Although still fifty miles from the sea, the Scheldt was here navigable for the largest ships, and the city was a major port, berthing craft from every corner of the world. David was informed that Antwerp's trade amounted to forty million ducats each year, a sum quite outwith his conception. It made his notions about Scots exports seem all but pointless.

Oddly enough, although the city, within its great walls, seemed to be full of palatial buildings and splendid edifices, with a new Bourse or Exchange being erected, seemingly as much glass as wall, the largest building the Scots had ever set eyes upon, yet there was no royal palace here, only the old cramped castle down amongst the riverside wharves, many-towered but less than commodious. So the Emperor's huge entourage had to be disposed elsewhere, in scores of different premises. However, presumably through Margaret's influence, the Scots were amongst those lodged in the castle itself—although sundry courtiers observed that they might be more comfortable otherwise.

Their stay in Antwerp started inauspiciously, for when their identity was known they were met on all sides by long faces, head-shakings and condolences, since it was rumoured most persistently that their liege-lord James, King of Scots, was dead. Appalled, the envoys demanded authentification, details, but received neither. Queen Margaret was only moderately sympathetic, expressing doubts and advising caution, for it was strange that her own sources of information had sent no word of this. There appeared to be three differing versions of the story—that the young King had been poisoned, that he had been thrown whilst hunting and that he had been drowned whilst crossing a river. All could not be true—so the possibility was that none was.

It occurred to David that, if all nations maintained agents in this commercial capital, Scotland probably did so. He went seeking any such, and found one, Andrew Nisbet, a merchant from Dysart in Fife, with a dockside warehouse not far from the castle. Dysart was no great distance from Cupar and Lindifferon, and this grizzled veteran of foreign trade knew of The Mount and its lairds and greeted Lindsay warmly. On the subject of the tales of King James's death, he declared that he personally believed none of them. *He* had had no such word and in his position it was essential that he knew what went on. He had traced the rumours all to the English community here, which was quite large and very active in more than money matters. It was perhaps significant that the stories only began to circulate when it became known that a Scottish embassage had arrived at Brussels. David asked whether any of the versions indicated a date for this alleged disaster, and was told that one circumstantial story said that the drowning in the River Forth had happened on the Nativity of St. John the Baptist, Midsummer's Day. Since David himself had taken leave of James two weeks after that, he reckoned that he could dismiss the entire affair as one of Henry Tudor's extraordinary devices, presumably concocted with the aim of spoiling any Scots-Empire treaty negotiations. He reported to that effect to Queen Margaret.

The tournament was held two days later, on Holy Cross Day, on the extensive fair-ground of this staple-city in front of a vast crowd. Before the open-air proceedings commenced, the Emperor addressed the assembled princes, nobles and notables in a huge gilded pavilion erected for the occasion, jerkily announcing the elevation of his esteemed aunt, lately Queen of

Hungary, to be his Regent of the Netherlands, this in order that she should have fullest powers in all matters of policy and rule, on his imperial behalf, whereas hitherto, as merely Governor, her powers had been limited. This was of vital importance for next year he, Charles, intended to lead in person one of the largest armies ever assembled, against the insolent Infidel Sulieman, who was at present actually threatening Vienna. This great Christian crusade would require vast amounts of money; and the Netherlands, Antwerp in particular, was where moneys could best be raised.

The cheers which had greeted the announcement of the crusade against the Infidel notably died away at this emphasis on money.

Staring up at the coloured tented ceiling, so that his strange chin jutted almost horizontally, the Emperor went on. Measures would have to be taken to raise that money; and let none doubt that the Queen-Regent would have the power and ability to do so. All knew her vigour and resolution. A significant pause here. In especial there was this matter of the two million crowns ransom for the two captured sons of King Francis of France, agreed on at the Treaty of Cambrai last year. This had still not been paid and the money was urgently needed. He was reliably informed that the money-dealers and exchangers here in Antwerp could arrange a transfer of this amount from France's trade credits to his own with entire ease, indeed all but overnight. This should be done forthwith, or the Queen-Regent would have to take the necessary steps to enforce it.

Abruptly the Emperor was finished, and indicated a move out to the tourney-ground. Listening, David had conceived a new image of Charles Hapsburg. The tournament started with a lot of long faces amongst the rich and powerful.

As a sporting event, however, it all was a major success, with some dramatic jousting both of individuals and teams of knights, sword-fighting, javelin-throwing, feats of horsemanship, racing, wrestling, archery and other contests, with huge sums won and lost in wagering. Once again the Campbell gillies distinguished themselves, to general applause, even David himself winning a white rose from a lady's lips as prize for javelin-throwing at which he was proficient.

At the feasting afterwards, in the open for the multitudes and in the pavilion for the privileged, the Emperor withdrew early, to the relief of all, leaving his useful aunt to preside over the subsequent entertainment, which she did admirably. Later, back at the castle, she sent for David as he was about to retire for the night and, in her chamber, smilingly handed him the two copies of the Scots treaty, both already duly signed by the Emperor and counter-signed by herself as Queen-Regent of the Netherlands, these now only requiring his own and his colleagues' signatures. When he did not hide his surprise at this peculiar way of concluding a treaty between nations, he was informed that Charles always had his own way of doing things; but that in fact this was *her* way of ensuring that the terms would be well kept, by appending her signature for the Netherlands as well as his for the Empire. This was why she had waited until now, with her regency established. It also meant that she could add a rider to the effect that increased Scots trade with the said Netherlands was to be encouraged by all means, including the protection of Scots shipping by Netherlands warships, where possible.

So all was gained, all in the end successful, and this strange dumpy woman proved not only clever and effective but a good friend.

David took the treaty copies back to his room. He was inclined to wake his fellow envoys with the news; but recognised that Sir John at least would be too drunk to sign anything that night. Tomorrow would do. And then, home.

As a final gesture, Margaret Hapsburg arranged that the Scots party should sail back directly from Antwerp in a Netherlands vessel bound for Sweden but directed to call in at a Scots east-coast port first.

They did not see the Emperor privately again but parted from his aunt in warmest fashion.

15

The ambassadors' return to Scotland, mission successfully accomplished, indeed improved upon by the valuable trade concession, gained them perhaps less appreciation than they deserved. For they came back to something of a crisis, with the minds of those concerned with rule preoccupied with other than long-range foreign policy and trade. James, who proved to be very much alive and well, had, during the months they were abroad to some extent kicked over the traces. Allegedly under the influence of the Bastard of Arran, who now that his sire was dead and his half-brother the new Arran not very effective, was very much wielding the full power of Hamilton, the King had suddenly initiated a campaign against many of his over-powerful nobles—and incidentally those who rivalled Hamilton—as being a danger to his throne and kingdom. He had started with the Campbells. The late Earl had been not only too influential but too strong for James to overturn, Lord Justice General, commander of the army and Lieutenant of the Isles, known indeed as King of the Highlands. But his son, Colin, fourth Earl, was less experienced and potent, and when this young man had requested that the said Lieutenantship of the Isles be vested in himself, so that he could take due order with unruly clans, James had instead appointed his principal rival, Alexander MacDonald of Islay, one of the claimants of the Lordship of the Isles put down by the King's late father. When Argyll had protested, James took the opportunity to throw him into prison. So poor Sir John, returning home in something like triumph, found the Campbells in eclipse and his chief a captive—and retired to Lundie in some haste.

Argyll was not the only one in prison, it appeared. James had decided on a clean sweep. He would clip the wings of others whom he—or perhaps the Bastard—felt were waxed too mighty for his comfort. These included the Earls of Bothwell, Crawford, the Lindsay chief, Moray, the King's own illegitimate half-brother, Cassillis, and the Lords Maxwell and Glamis. And not only these, for James Beaton, Archbishop and Primate, was also in Blackness Castle. It seemed that his nephew Davie had protested against this new policy, as unwise, and against the Bastard's evil influence, and James in consequence had been going to imprison even him. However, the Lord Privy Seal's efficient warning system informed him in time to make good his escape; but his old uncle at St. Andrews, less agile, had been taken into custody instead, more or less as hostage for Davie's good behaviour. All this in the seven or eight weeks of the envoys' absence. If word of it had reached the Netherlands it would not have helped the embassage.

David Lindsay was welcomed back kindly enough by the monarch, who seemed however more concerned to hear about his reported death than about the details of the mission. But with the ominous atmosphere prevailing at court, plus his dislike of the Bastard, now so evidently in the ascendant, David sought almost immediate leave-of-absence—and had no difficulty in gaining it. Almost it seemed as though the Lord Lyon King-of-Arms was a less essential prop of the crown than the title implied.

So it was back to The Mount of Lindifferon, where he had a gently rapturous reception from Janet. He found all in order, the harvest in, and the upsets at court little regarded—save for the imprisonment of Archbishop Beaton which did worry Janet. This was no way to treat an old man, head of the Church, and who had been chief minister of the realm for so many years. He was failing in health and this might be the death of him. Davie Beaton should not allow it. He should yield himself up to let his uncle go free. Where *was* Davie?

Her husband did not know, but guessed that he would be somewhere sufficiently secure—and probably not very far from Marion Ogilvy at Ethie Castle in Angus, on whom he seemed to home when in difficulties. He did not think, however, that the Archbishop would be in any great danger nor discomfort. Blackness Castle, the state prison for the lofty, in West Lothian, was commonly asserted to be more comfortable than the houses of many of its inmates.

Janet declared that there were problems at Luthrie. The steward there and his people had been used to going their own way and in their own time with absentee lairds and little supervision; they resented a woman like herself coming and telling them what to do. But that harvest was much behind that of The Mount, both in yield and ingathering; and many of the much-neglected buildings, which David had ordered to be repaired, were still untouched. So it was decided that Luthrie must be visited, and promptly.

There was also considerable work piled up for David, sent by the Lyon Clerk and the other heralds, requests for grants of arms, complaints of infringements, genealogical descents to be proved, documents to be scanned. So he was kept busy, even though the King himself did not seem to need him.

After a few days, one evening at dusk a visitor arrived, almost stealthily, well mounted but plainly clad and without distinguishing marks heraldic or otherwise. He asked for a private interview with Sir David Lindsay.

He came, he revealed, from the Lord Abbot of Arbroath. His lordship would be grateful for some converse with Sir David. Unfortunately he could not come to Lindifferon in present circumstances, nor anywhere near St. Andrews, which the Hamiltons were watching like hawks, but he urged Sir David, for the realm's sake, to come to him in Angus. If Sir David would journey to Ethie Castle, south of Montrose, to visit the Lady Marion, the Lord Abbot would endeavour to arrange a meeting. It would be best if Sir David could bring the Lady Lindsay with him, and possibly call at the Paniter house, Newmanswalls, near Montrose first, so that the visit would not arouse the suspicions of Hamilton spies. They could make use of all the facilities of Holy Church on the journey.

David was intrigued by this rather extraordinary *cri de coeur* coming from the normally so assured and authoritative Davie Beaton. He could scarcely refuse.

The unnamed messenger left as discreetly as he had come.

Janet proved to be entirely willing to accompany her husband on an excursion to Angus in a golden autumn before winter closed in. She was fond of Marion Ogilvy, considered that she had been shamefully treated, and had not seen her for long. So, early in October, they set off northwards, modestly escorted by two armed attendants.

Janet was a less eager horsewoman than Kate had been, but there was no need to travel other than leisurely. Lindifferon was only some sixteen miles from Ferry-Port-on-Craig, where there was an established ferry across Tay, to Broughty on the Angus shore. In the interests of discretion, if not secrecy, after the crossing, they did not risk an overnight stop at the ferry-inn, so near to Dundee, but rode on a further few miles to the Grange of Monifeith, one of the many farms of Arbroath Abbey, where there was a travellers' hospice, where they put up under names of Davidson of Balgarvie and wife—this being a small subsidiary property of The Mount.

The next day, in a chilly grey haar off the Norse Sea which, however suitable-seeming for secrecy, offered no inducements for lingering, they covered a fair distance. They avoided Arbroath itself, with its great Abbey which might be watched in

247

case of a visit from its Abbot, turning inland up the Elliot Water at Abirlot to make for St. Vigeans, where there was a renowned ancient church and another grange of Arbroath, famed for its apiary. Candles made from beeswax were despatched all over the land, one of the many sources of abbey wealth; also renowned was the echo here, of no fewer than four syllables, from a nearby rock. Janet found the ancient church, its Pictish symbol-stones, the echo and the bee-management, of much interest. David, for his part, enjoyed these days in the saddle with his wife, her company considerably to be preferred to that of his recent travelling companions. She was observant, appreciative of what she saw, uncomplaining over difficulties and knew when to talk and when to keep silence. And at their halts she conformed suitably to the style of Mistress Davidson.

They learned at St. Vigeans that it was only some fourteen miles on to Montrose and that the Paniters' house of Newmanswalls was a bare mile north of the burgh. Not that Abbot Paniter himself would be there, only his uncle and aunt.

They proceeded northwards, crossing the Lunan Water at Balmullie and then mounting over the high ground of Rossie Muir and down to Montrose town beside its vast tidal basin. They had no difficulty in finding Newmanswalls, a small property on the north shore of the basin, loud at this season with the wild trumpeting of greylag geese and the quacking of mallard. Here they were well received by the laird and his lady, a quiet and well-doing couple, who were clearly very proud of their nephew, despite his birth, and whom they had brought up. He was, to be sure, the illegitimate son of the laird's brother, the still more famous Patrick Paniter, likewise Abbot of Cambuskenneth and royal secretary in the previous reign, one of the finest Latinists in Christendom. This little lairdship amongst the wildfowl-haunted marshes of North Angus seemed a strange place to have produced these two, although the brother and uncle appeared much more typical. Here, naturally, the Lindsays had to reveal their true identity, their hosts being obviously impressed. But since their nephew owed his swift promotion in Holy Church largely to Davie Beaton, there was surely no danger to the latter here. However, the visitors did not inform that they were going on to Ethie Castle, merely saying that, as Lyon, David had a number of matters to see to in North Angus and the Mearns, and had called, in passing, to tell them in some measure of their nephew's Netherlands venture. They allowed themselves to be persuaded to stay the night.

In the morning they set off southwards, but this time circling the great tidal area to the west, to avoid the town, and back up on to Rossie Muir. Ethie stood on a cliff-top position near the mighty foreland of Red Head, at the southern horn of the lovely Lunan Bay, some nine miles south of Montrose itself and six north of Arbroath, near enough to the latter to be convenient for Davie, but sufficiently remote to be suitably private.

The visitors came to Davie's real home—although it was in fact Marion's house, bought and chartered in her name—on a crisp afternoon of vivid autumn colours, with the sigh and scent of the sea pervading all and the cries of the seabirds which wheeled endlessly in the pale blue of the sky. Sky and sea were very evident at Ethie, set high on bare upland near the cliff-tops.

The little castle which Davie had bought for his wife when his abbatical revenues began to accumulate—half of Arbroath's income, of course, never reached him, being retained by his uncle—was a simple square tower of the previous century, within a walled courtyard, but with more ancient foundations. He had added a wing to it, for more accommodation and comfort, and now it was a pleasant red-stone pile of medium size, with a walled garden and orchard, sheltered by some wind-blown trees. Isolated on its grassy height, with no other house in sight, its vistas were tremendous, lovely this October day but a wild place of a winter's storm, undoubtedly.

Marion Ogilvy and a clutch of children met them at the little gatehouse—for any visitors could be espied a long way off, and three men with a woman were unlikely to represent danger. When she perceived the identity of the callers her fine features lit up and she came hastening, obviously delighted to see them. Four children, two boys and two girls, the eldest perhaps ten years, held back shyly.

Marion, daughter of Lord Ogilvy of Airlie, was a good-looking creature, still trim of figure and attractive despite all the child-bearing, now in her mid-thirties. If she felt in any way embarrassed over her peculiar circumstances, she gave no sign of it.

Out of much talk, presently, they learned that she saw Davie quite frequently, he often slipping into the castle of a night and out again before sun-up, but never risking any longer stay, for occasional parties of armed men arrived without warning, undoubtedly looking for the missing Abbot. These had never maltreated her, for the present Lord Ogilvy, her brother, lived only a score of miles away and was too powerful in these parts to offend; but Davie was determined not only not to be caught but to cause no trouble for herself and the children if possible, and to give no hint that he was dwelling in the vicinity.

And indeed he was hiding nearby, she revealed, no more than three miles away. These cliffs, some of the most lofty and impressive on all the east coast of Scotland, were honeycombed with caves; but the cliffs almost everywhere dropped sheer into the sea, so that most caves were either inaccessible or only to be reached by boat. One of the most notable of these was called the Gaylet or Geary Pot, less than a mile south of the fishing-village of Auchmithie. As well as being one of the largest, this cavern was unique in having a peculiar open shaft reaching up from its head right to the cliff-top level but some two hundred yards inland. This strange feature gave this cave an emergency escape-route for the nimble, valuable indeed. Davie was roosting in this Gaylet Pot—or at least, he was using it as his refuge and base, for much of the time he was roaming the countryside in disguise. She never knew when he would make an appearance.

That night there was no visit from the fugitive, and next day Marion proposed that, rather than waiting indefinitely, they should themselves pay a visit, discreetly, to the Gaylet Pot. Davie might not be there at present, but they could at least leave a message for him. This could be done without too much risk. The castle had its own tiny fishing community, perching on a terrace of the cliff-foot half-a-mile to the north, called Ethiehaven. The fishermen were all to be trusted there, and one of their boats could take them down the coast to the Gaylet Pot without arousing suspicion, for they had lobster-pots all along the shoreline which had to be tended. This was how Davie was provisioned.

So, leaving Janet to look after the children, dressed in the oldest clothing, Marion, wrapped in a shawl, led David to Ethiehaven, down a zigzag path at a break in the sheer cliff-face. The hamlet consisted of just a few low-browed cot-houses crouching under the precipices on a mere shelf a few feet above the tide and turning gable-ends to the sea—as well they might, for undoubtedly in a storm the waves would be battering against the walling. Below was a little harbour, part natural, where three fishing-cobles were moored, bobbing in the swell.

Marion had no difficulty in persuading a couple of the fisherman to take them, for these were their own tenants and devoted to the castle service. They would visit some of their lobster-pots on the way.

They rowed out in the high-prowed coble into Lunan Bay, to turn southwards round the mighty cape of Red Head. Seen from the sea, its soaring stacks and precipices of red sandstone, thronged by thousands of screaming birds, was a fearsome sight, even in this comparatively calm weather its base spouting high columns of white in the Norse Sea swell.

The fishermen had their lobster-creels marked in position by floating blown-up sheep's bladders attached by ropes. Drawn up, three of the wickerwork cages proved to have trapped the pink, clawing creatures, to the boatman's satisfaction, as they worked their way down the coast.

In about three miles they passed under the larger fishing village of Auchmithie, set higher this, on the cliff-edge. They exchanged hails with two boats out from its harbour.

David had noted the yawning mouths of caves great and small, all the way, in the tremendous barrier of rock. Soon now Marion pointed out a fissure rather than a cavity, a sort of wide crack in the precipice face, reaching right down into the tide. Towards this the oarsmen steered.

It proved to be a re-entrant in the towering rock formation, into which the coble nosed its way carefully, rising and falling quite alarmingly now on the surge of the seas against the cliff-tops. They turned into a narrow dog's-leg channel, all but enclosed and too constricted to row in, the men using the oars as both poles and fenders.

Rounding that bend, there was the cave-mouth ahead, hidden hitherto, and large, high, with the sea running right in. They halted just within the entrance, and hallooed. As result the hollow echoing produced a flurry of wildly-flapping rock-doves but no answering call.

There was a distinct shelf, perhaps three feet wide, weed-hung, a few feet above the water-level. The fishermen moored their coble against this and helped the passengers out and up, with cautions to tread warily on the slippery seaweed. They led the way along, deeper into the cavern.

The large mouth of it meant that light was good for a considerable distance. They passed a small side-cave opening off this shelf, in which were some wooden boxes, evidently stores. A little further and there was a larger aperture and into this the two men turned, most clearly knowing their way. There was just enough light to see that this was about a dozen feet deep and fitted up after a fashion, with a rough fireplace, cooking-pots, torch-holders, two mattresses of heather, blankets, spare clothing and so on. It seemed an extraordinary lodging for the mitred Lord Abbot of Arbroath and Scotland's Privy Seal.

They had come prepared for Beaton to be absent, and left a note on one of the beds to say that the Lindsays were at Ethie, as requested. But before leaving, they went deeper into the main cavern, to let David see the place's special feature. The light was fading noticeably thus far in, but rounding a major bend, perhaps seventy yards in, a new source of light was revealed, admittedly pale and faint. To say that it increased as they gingerly progressed would be to give a wrong impression; but it maintained and became more localised and presently developed into a sort of circular pool of luminosity ahead. This, when reached, proved to be water, a tidal pond reflecting the sky far above, down a great funnel or shaft in the solid rock, a wide chimney soaring well over one hundred feet. Down its wet walling, where ferns grew, a long knotted rope hung.

Marion pointed. "Davie's back-door," she said.

"He climbs that! Davie does?"

"If he must. Not otherwise, I think! In a storm, this cave cannot be left or entered from the sea. And he might be trapped by searchers in boats."

"I would not have believed him to be so agile, so strong of thew! To climb that, or to descend it."

"Davie is . . . . Davie! What he sets his mind to, he usually does."

"Even so . . ." David stared up. "This is a strange place indeed. How was it formed? Could the sea do this? Or is it some break in the rock?"

"Davie says that it would have been the sea. In a gale the waves come roaring in here, he says, frightening in their power, and laden with stones and pebbles. Perhaps there was softer rock here, harder beyond. So the force strikes upward into the soft stone, and over the ages this is formed. The folk here say

252

that on a very bad winter's storm spray comes spouting out of the top there, above the cliffs. But I have never seen that."

They returned to the boat, the visitor much impressed.

That very night Davie Beaton turned up at the castle, having apparently missed them at the Gaylet Pot by only an hour or two. He would have been hard to recognise as the handsome courtier and cleric, dressed now in stained and ragged fishermen's clothing, long hair uncombed, pointed beard untrimmed. But there was nothing of the fugitive and furtive about his manner, his cheerful assurance seemingly proof against present difficulties and discomforts. He greeted the Lindsays with a flourish.

"My apologies for not being present to receive you, my friends, either here in Marion's house or in my own present hermitage under the cliffs—suitable for a religious, is it not? I was haunting the port of Montrose, for news, and heard that you were come. So I hastened back."

"You *heard* that we were here? In Montrose?" David wondered. "How could that be? We told none, save the Paniters. And they did not know that we came on to Ethie."

"You would be surprised how word gets around! Not your names, to be sure—but a man and a woman, with two servants, obviously gentry, strangers, picking their careful way. I have my sources of information, see you. I have to have."

"The last who said that to me was Queen Margaret of Hungary, in Brussels," Lindsay remarked.

"Ah, yes, Margaret. An excellent woman, is she not? Your visit to the Netherlands was a success, I hear. The trade matter a useful addition."

"Your hearing is acute, attuned to near and far it seems. I know not how you do it."

"Siller, man, siller. With a sufficiency of moneys, news is . . . available! It is expensive, but it is worth it. And, fortunately, Holy Church, whatever else it may lack, has siller aplenty! Ears to hear can be bought, eyes to see, and tongues to whisper! You would scarce credit who and where and how!"

When Beaton had changed into more seemly clothing and much improved his appearance, he ate hungrily, meanwhile telling his children highly improbable stories of his adventures to hoots of laughter. But when the two women went to put the youngsters to bed, he changed his tune to the sufficiently serious.

"It was good of you to come, Davie—and so promptly. Good of Janet, likewise," he said. "I am grateful. There is need. I would not have called you, otherwise."

Lindsay nodded, waiting.

"The kingdom is in grievous danger. It always is, to be sure. But now more than usual, I fear. Our James is playing the fool, and could even lose his throne."

"That is scarce new."

"The present situation is. James is almost wholly in the grip of the Bastard of Arran. And the Bastard is more dangerous than any yet. More dangerous than Angus or Home or any of them. For he is able, as well as evil, clever as he is without scruple."

"Is that not itself of some advantage to the realm? I much mislike the man, but agree that he is no fool. If he controls the King, it may not be to James's moral well-being, but the kingdom should not be endangered. As well as being able and courageous, shrewd after his fashion too, Hamilton is a soldier. Could that not be something of what the realm needs? *You* have found him useful in the past!"

Beaton ignored that last. "Wait, you. James is unwed—however well-bedded! So there is no son, no close heir to his throne. Who is the nearest lawful heir? Who but the young Arran, since Albany rejects all, and remains a French citizen. Arran—a weakling, like his father, and the Bastard's half-brother. Have you considered that?"

The thought admittedly did jolt the other. The Hamiltons' ancient grandmother, the Dowager Countess of Arran, had been the Princess Mary, James the Third's sister. "You are not suggesting . . . ?"

"Would you put anything past that man? You who saw him murder Lennox, his own cousin. Who saw him at his hangings, in the Borderland? When I urged more than once that James should seek a wife, the Bastard each time said no haste, time enough for James to enjoy himself first. If the King was to die unwed, the Bastard would rule Scotland in the name of his feckless brother."

"You say that he is all but ruling it now."

"Aye, and to its cost. This policy of bringing down the leading nobles is his, rather than James's own. All the rivals of Hamilton are to be brought low. He started with Argyll but now it is Bothwell, Crawford, Cassillis, Eglinton, Argyll's good-brother,

Maxwell, Home, Sinclair, Buccleuch, even Moray. All imprisoned. Bishops too, my aged uncle included. And I was to be in with them! James is to rule without the aid of his nobles—only Hamilton."

"All this happened while I was in the Netherlands. Only Bothwell was in custody before that."

"Bothwell, yes. The Hepburn has escaped, however, and is now over the Border in England. And is like to join Angus."

"One more traitor will make little difference."

"Be not so sure. Bothwell is dangerous. He has renounced his allegiance to King James and calls on other Scots nobles to do the same, not only those presently in custody. He has joined the English Warden, the Earl of Northumberland, and urges actual invasion of Scotland, saying that all followers of the imprisoned lords, and others threatened, will flock to join the invaders. Bothwell is Lord of Teviotdale, so there is menace in this. Northumberland has written to King Henry to the effect that he looked to see more of the great Scots nobles agreeing to crown him, Henry, in the town of Edinburgh as King of Scots and in only short time! Friends of mine intercepted the courier—as they frequently do."

"Lord—the folly of it!"

"Worse than folly—real danger. For Angus has now sworn fealty to Henry. If only one or two others do likewise, then the thing could become a spate, especially in the Borders. If Buccleuch's and Home's clans, in the east, and the Maxwells and others in the west, let their resentment boil over, then think what that would mean. The Armstrongs are already seething. With Bothwell's Hepburns and the Douglases up in arms, the entire Borderland would be wide open to the invaders. Do you not see it?"

Lindsay wagged his head. "I see it, yes—but what can we do? You, a fugitive, and myself little more than a figurehead. Lyon has not real power . . ."

"You are James's oldest and truest friend, as I have told you before. He knows it, however little he may seem to heed you these days. You must *make* him listen to you. Seek to counter the Bastard's influence, somehow. Stay at court—you have every right to be there, duty indeed, as Lyon. Do not hide away at The Mount. Be always at James's elbow. The Bastard cannot always be there—he has all the great Hamilton interests and properties

255

to see to. James knows he is a rogue, even though he lets him sway him."

"You credit me with an influence I have not got!" Lindsay protested. "James may have some fondness for me, from times past. But he heeds me little and needs me less, now . . ."

"Be not so sure. He often mentioned you, when you were away. He acts headstrong, but he is insecure of himself beneath it all—and that is why he is so easily led by the Bastard. *You* could lead him, likewise, for he knows you to be honest, faithful. And there is your poetry, do not overlook that. James much admires it. He has little real interest in ruling his kingdom, but he loves poetry, women—and, to be sure, hurly-hackit! He thinks to write poetry himself. I have seen some of his verses and they are fair enough. Less than profound—but one could scarcely expect that. He would not show them to you, for he looks on you as the master, and would fear your scoffing. But encourage James to write poetry and you have something the Bastard has not got. James made you Laureate as well as Lyon, after all."

"I did not know of this, of his continuing writing. Childish verses, yes, but nothing more."

"He would like to rival his great-great grandsire, James the First, who was no mean poet. You mind *The King's Quair?* His verse—young James's, I mean—tends to be about women, as you might guess! Some of it is sufficiently . . . detailed!"

"I *can* guess! A pity . . ."

"Do not be over-hard on it, man. If it is women who inspire him to it, use that, and them. That way you may reach him."

"You would have me whoremonger, now!"

"Scarce that. But it is a fool who cannot use a man's weaknesses for a good cause! You will not change James over women now. So you might as well make use of them. And be careful how you talk of whores! Some of the loftiest in the land welcome our liege-lord and theirs to their beds. Margaret, daughter of the Lord Erskine is, I think, the favourite. But there is Euphemia, daughter to the Lord Elphinstone, and a pack of Elizabeths—Lord Carmichael's daughter; Elizabeth Shaw of Sauchie; my own kin, Elizabeth Beaton of Creich; Elizabeth Stewart of Atholl . . ."

"Sakes—all these! I thought that it was women of the common sort that he went for? So all the tales tell."

"Yes, yes—these also, to be sure. It is as the Gudeman o'

Ballengeich that he pursues such—not as the King! All but every night he sallies forth from Stirling Castle, alone, seeking his sport. A right potent prince our Scotland has, in some respects! Would that he was as hot on kingcraft! How many bastards has he sired already, only the good Lord knows!"

"And you would have me to encourage him in this, to make poetry out of it all?"

"Why not? Make some degree of good out of the ill. What you cannot alter, make the best of, I say! You might even use his fondness for women to spur him on to marriage! For marry he must, and the sooner the better. Scotland direly needs an heir, other than Arran. Even if he married Margaret Erskine . . ."

"Erskine's daughter, queen? Surely not!"

"No? Other kings have wed their nobles' daughters. Robert Second and Robert Third. James's own father would have wed Margaret Drummond had Henry Tudor not had her poisoned. Would God he had, then we would never have had Margaret Tudor to deal with! A suitable foreign princess, see you, would be better, I agree, to mortar together some useful alliance. Perhaps the Emperor or his aunt could find us one? But wed James should be . . ."

The return of Marion and Janet gave this talk a different slant, the two women being intrigued with the subject, both agreeing that the King should be allowed to marry for love rather than foreign policy, since he so regarded their sex, David surprised that they sounded less critical of James's amours than he, for one, would have expected. But Beaton cheerfully encouraged them, perhaps incautiously for that normally calculating individual. For it emboldened Janet to voice, however gently, what had been on her mind for long.

"I am a little surprised, my lord Abbot, to hear *you* championing marriage for love," she averred, flushing as she dared it. "After, after what you have done to your wife!" That came out in a rush.

If she feared any indication of offence from her host, she was relieved, for he laughed with seemingly genuine amusement, and turned to Marion.

"What have I done to you, my dear?" he asked. "Deserted you for Holy Church? Shamed you in the sight of honest men? Left you bereft? Now is your opportunity to belabour me!"

She smiled. "My complaint is only a small one—that so many

257

godly abbesses and prioresses now consider that you are fair game for their blandishments! Your abbatical visits to nunneries!" Marion looked at Janet. "My lord and master's embracing of Holy Church has its dangers! Although I must confess that I have seen more of him since he took holy orders and I became a fallen woman than ever I did before!"

That left the visitors with nothing to say, if somewhat embarrassed. Probably perceiving it, Beaton grimaced.

"The sorriest part of it all is the siller!" he declared lugubriously. "The cost to my purse. For now I must needs pay the Vatican, and sweetly, to legitimise our already legitimate children, suddenly become otherwise. As is necessary before they can inherit any of the properties their so loving sire intends to bestow on them in due course! You will admit that it is hard?"

Before they sought their beds that night, Beaton, declaring that he would not see them in the morning, urged his friend to return to court, to try to counter the Bastard's influence in all ways possible, to use his poetry to best advantage, to urge James towards marriage—and, to be sure, to work for the reinstatement of the Lord Privy Seal, for the realm's weal.

16

David Lindsay did not have to make any pride-swallowing gesture over returning to court, for on their return to Lindifferon they found a worried courier from the King awaiting them, with a command that the Lord Lyon King-of-Arms should attend his monarch forthwith on a progress into the Highlands. The messenger, one of the Lyon Clerk's men, had been at The Mount for three days and by this time was in a state of considerable agitation.

Enquiries as to why his presence should be required for a jaunt into the Highlands elicited for David the information that this was more than any jaunt, that it was in fact a large-scale, almost formal, expedition for the edification and entertainment of the papal envoy. Mystified, David asked what papal envoy and why any such should be taken to the Highlands, of all places, for edification?

The courier explained, as far as he was able. The Pope, informed of the imprisonment of the Scottish Primate, Archbishop Beaton, and sundry other clerics, had sent a Legate, one Antonio Campeggio, to discover the situation and make representations, indeed threatening dire reprisals, even excommunication. So the old Archbishop had been hurriedly released from Blackness, assurances given that there was no assault on Holy Church intended, and the Legate having expressed a desire to see something of the Scottish Highlands, which he had heard referred to as the arse-end of the world, the King had diplomatically arranged this progress. The nuncio, apparently, was also anxious to meet the Queen-Mother, in connection with her brother Henry's threats to divorce himself and England from adherence to Rome, because the Pope had refused him a divorce from his queen, Catherine of Aragon, and it was hoped that Margaret Tudor could act as mediator—after all, she should be grateful for her own divorce. So the said lady was to be invited on this Highland expedition also.

It all seemed a scarcely believable development to David Lindsay and he felt that there must be more behind it than the mere wish of the papal visitor to see the Highlands, even though it was necessary to placate him. Possibly it was all part of James's, or the Bastard's, campaign to bring down the power of the Lowland nobles by using the Highlanders to help. At any rate, there was no refusing the royal command to attend. Nor delay—for the messenger was urgent that they should be off at once, saying that the royal cavalcade would almost certainly have left Stirling by now. He had been waiting here for three days . . .

So, changing into finer clothing and donning his splendid Lyon's tabard, David took a hasty farewell of Janet, and set off again, westwards.

The courier, convinced that it was a waste of time to go to Stirling, advised that they make directly for Methven in Strathearn, where the Queen-Mother now lived in retirement with her third husband. No doubt the King would pick her up there and there would be almost certain delay. They might catch up at Methven.

Through North Fife and the south side of Tay, riding hard

now, they came by Lindores and Abernethy to the flat lands at the mouth of the Earn. Following that fine river westwards still, they could see, by the tracks and horse-droppings, that a great company had passed that way, probably only the day before. Darkness fell by the time they reached Tibbermore, but the wide drove-road was clear enough and they carried on. Before long they were heartened by a ruddy glow in the sky ahead, which they guessed would be from the cooking-fires of the royal escort encamped around Methven Castle.

This proved to be an accurate assessment, as presently they rode up the steep grassy slope above a small loch, its dark waters reflecting the glow, to the impressive terrace site where the fairly large castle reared its red masonry the more ruddily for the firelight. The tents and pavilions of scores of men-at-arms and retainers covered the area, and horses were tethered in long lines.

David had never thought to visit the home of Margaret Tudor, a woman he cordially loathed. As Lyon he had no difficulty in gaining entrance at least.

The first person of note he encountered was Hamilton of Finnart himself, who greeted him with a mocking bonhomie.

"Ha—the Laureate in person! Emerged belatedly from wrestling with the Muse, no doubt? We are all the richer, I swear! Welcome to this royal love-arbour, friend!"

"Thank you. Where do I find His Grace, Sir James?"

"Where but in his lady-mother's boudoir—whence I have just escaped!" Evidently the Bastard did not love Margaret Tudor either. "And scarcely happy therein. Come—I will escort you thither, but not within, my Lord Lyon—not within! I have had sufficient for one day!" And he took the newcomer's arm.

David would have liked to shake off that hand. But he restrained himself. He greatly disliked this man, but recognised that nothing was to be gained by deliberately antagonising one so much in favour with the King. Moreover, from their first meeting at Cadzow all those years ago, the Bastard had always shown a cynically amiable face to him, as though they shared some secret amusing view of life and men—although surely nothing could be further from the fact. Lindsay was scarcely an affable man, but found it difficult to be intentionally discourteous.

He was led upstairs to a second-floor chamber, where two

of the royal guard stood on duty at the door. Hamilton knocked and without waiting threw open the door.

"Your Grace," he called, "Sir David Lindsay of The Mount, Lord Lyon King-of-Arms and ornament of your court—when present!" His voice dropping to a whisper, he added, "God help you!" and pushing David within, shut the door behind him.

Four people sat in the overheated room, where too large a fire for the season blazed under a great heraldic overmantel— the King, his mother, her husband the weedy-looking Henry Stewart, Lord Methven, and a darkly smooth individual of indeterminate age, richly dressed in approximately clerical garb. All stared.

"Davie!" James half-rose from his seat before he remembered his royal dignity. "You have come, then!"

"You sent for me, Sire."

"Yes, I did. I require you, Davie. You are . . . overmuch away." Again the need to assert authority. "You have taken your time, man!"

"I was in the north, Sire. Won back to The Mount only today."

"Aye. As well." He turned towards the others. "My royal mother you know, and my Lord Methven. And here is His Holiness the Pope's nuncio, the Bishop Antonio Campeggio."

David made a composite bow.

Margaret Tudor turned a fleshy bare shoulder on him, her husband taking his cue from her. She was now in her early forties and looked older. Never a beautiful woman, she had grown heavy and coarse looking, and the display of her person for the occasion consequently a mistake. But her eyes were still vital, searching.

"This is the poet Your Majesty told me of, is it not?" That was the stranger, in good but heavily-accented English. He raised a beringed hand in something between a salute and a benediction. "I greet you, Sir David."

James coughed, mopping his brow with his doublet-sleeve, obviously feeling the heat. "Yes. Sir David has been my, my mentor, always. Sit you, Davie. Where were you in the north?"

"Angus, Sire. Monifeith, Montrose and elsewhere. As Lyon, I must needs travel the land on occasion."

"Yes, yes. Sir David is my King-of-Arms, my lord Bishop. And has lately been to the Netherlands, to conclude a treaty

261

between myself and the Emperor Charles." That was said with some emphasis.

"Ah, so. Your Majesty mentioned that."

David recognised discomfort in that room, in more than the heat, and on various levels. He saw why the Bastard had been glad to escape. He did his poor best for James.

"You are bound for the Highlands, Your Grace, I am told? Is this a progress, a surveillance, a strategy or a hunting?"

"Something of all. Bishop Campeggio desires to see those parts and their folk. He has heard much of their strangeness and would see for himself. We go to Atholl, where it is not too barbarous and there is excellent hunting. My lord of Atholl has promised me notable sport—boar, wolves, even wildcats, and deer beyond number. It will make a pleasing diversion before the winter sets in."

Atholl, David noted. The Lady Elizabeth Stewart, he recollected, was one of the high-born women whom Davie Beaton had named as welcoming James to their beds—a daughter of the Earl of Atholl.

Again the silence descended.

David tried once more. "What has His Excellency the Bishop heard of our Highlands which so interests him, may I ask?"

"Ah, much, much." Campeggio fluttered those eloquent hands. "The mountains, so strong, so fierce. Less high than our Alps but more terrible, they say. The lakes, the rivers, the torrents—most remarkable. The animals and fowls and fishes, of such abundance. And the people, savages, all but naked, but noble after their fashion, their coats of many colours—when they wear coats! Like Joseph's! Some do say, because of this, and their language, which is reputed to be like to that of the Galatians, that they are one of the ten lost tribes of ancient Israel. I would myself see, and report to the Holy Father."

Blinking a little at this, David looked at the King, who eyed them both askance. "I hope that Your Excellency may not be disappointed," was all that he could think of to say.

Methven whinnied a laugh. "A likely tale, I'd say!"

"Did any ask *you*?" his wife snapped, her first contribution since David's arrival.

"But Israelites? Hielantmen!"

"If His Excellency considers it possible, who are you to question it?"

James cleared his throat. "We ride for Atholl in the morn. By Glen Almond and Strathbraan to Dunkeld. Beyond that I know not. Have you ever been there, Davie?"

"No, Sire. Nor know any who have!"

"Wonderful! The more wonderful!" the envoy declared. "*Terra incognita!*"

"Aye, well," the King said doubtfully. "Atholl says that he will give us fair lodging and this notable sport. So, we must be up betimes. It is a long ride. I will seek my couch." He rose—so must they all. "You, my lord bishop have matters to discuss with my mother. I bid you a good night."

Margaret promptly sat down again. "You, Harry, leave us alone." That was brusque dismissal.

The two men followed James out, none reluctant. As they came to the stairway, the guard behind, the King turned to glower at Methven—who hurriedly bowed, seemed to recollect urgent business elsewhere, and went upstairs instead of down.

"*He* will not last much longer with that woman!" the monarch confided. "Nor any loss, mind!"

Discreetly David made no comment.

"She will have some other bed fellow in mind, I've no doubt. Think you she has an eye for the Florentine, Davie?"

Lindsay found the subject difficult, unsuitable. "I have no notion, Sire." He could scarcely any longer tell his liege-lord, now a grown man in his nineteenth year, that this was no way to speak about his mother, even such a mother. But it did occur to him that perhaps James was the less to be blamed for all his womanising, with such parentage—for his late father had been as popular with the ladies as with his people generally, and had never failed to take advantage of the fact.

Going down the stair the King lowered his voice confidentially. "See you, Davie—this nuncio has to be sent back to Rome happy. He came breathing threats and ill will. Excommunication, no less. The reduction of Scotland from metropolitan status, in the Church—that old story! Putting us under York . . ."

"*Only* threats, Sire, surely? No Pope today would ever revert to that folly. Especially with King Henry snapping his fingers at the Vatican!"

"Part *because* of that. Do you not see? Wolsey disgraced and now dead. If the Pope could offer *ecclesiastical* dominion over Scotland to England, Henry might change his attitude. Putting the Scots Church under York would much aid Henry's hopes. It is all part of a plan to keep England in allegiance to Rome. This Campeggio said that clearly I did not rate highly the metropolitan status, for I had imprisoned the Metropolitan, that old fool Beaton!"

They had reached a doorway on the first floor, and James drew David into what was apparently his own chamber, untidy as such always was, shutting out the guard. "So I had to release the old man, and other bishops. At least until the Florentine has gone."

"Sire—I believe you to be mistaken in this," David said, taking a chance. "This of the Primate. The Archbishop is *not* plotting against you. Indeed he is past any plotting . . ."

"Perhaps—but his nephew is not! Which comes to the same thing, since Davie Beaton rules the Church through the old man. I would have arrested *him* if I could have found him, I promise you!"

"James—hear me." It was not often that Lindsay called his sovereign by his Christian name, but he did it deliberately now, as reminder of past relationship and his own faithful service and reliability. "I know Davie Beaton—probably better than any other man in your realm. I know that he does not plot *against* you. He is a plotter, yes, a born plotter—but he is entirely loyal to yourself and your interests, Scotland's best interests. He is, I believe, the most able man you have in your kingdom, and should not be a hunted fugitive, just because Hamilton of Finnart does not like him!"

"Tut, Davie—it is more than that. We know that he was working against my policies."

"Only the policies he believed to be harmful to you and your realm, Sire. As many others believe. As do I, indeed. This of pulling down the nobles and the Church both, it cannot succeed. You need them, need them both. The Hamiltons will not replace them . . ."

"Och, man—quiet you! I did not bring you here to hear your views on policy. Nor Davie Beaton's! It is this Florentine—he is the problem, meantime. I want you to work on him. To convince him that I am a better ally to the Pope than is Henry. Send him away well content with Scotland."

"Me? How can *I* do this? I have no skills for this, no experience. Davie Beaton, yes—but not me."

"Man, did you not lead the successful embassage to the Netherlands? You did well there. You convinced the Emperor, and Margaret of Hungary. Speak with this man. The Vatican needs the Emperor's support. Tell Campeggio that Charles esteems an alliance with Scotland. That he has ordered his warships to protect Scots vessels against the English. That the Pope should be aiding me, not threatening me. You are the man to do it, new back from Brussels. He will heed you, who have been close to the Emperor."

"Scarce close, Sire. Charles is not an easy man to win close to . . ."

"To his aunt then, Davie—of whom you spoke so well. He relies on her, all know. Do your best, Davie. I need you in this."

Lindsay could be an opportunist when the occasion warranted. "I will try, James. But—it would help if I could tell him that you were recalling your Lord Privy Seal to your court. This Legate must know that you are presently at odds with Davie. Also that he is the real power in the Church here, behind the Archbishop. While you reject him, Rome cannot but suspect you. Bring him back and you will be much the stronger."

"Well . . ."

"Forby you *need* him, Sire! You need his wits. Your present Chancellor, the Archbishop of Glasgow, is a good man—but he is not experienced or very able at statecraft. Nor is David Paniter, your secretary. Nor, I swear, is Finnart, however able a fighter! Beaton is the man you require. Fetch him back, Sire."

"I do not know where he is."

"I do—or, leastwise, I know how to reach him! But, James, he will not come, I think, unless he is assured of his safety. Assured that Finnart will not prevail on Your Grace against him again. If I have your royal word on that, I will do all I can on this of the Italian. And all else."

James looked at the other from under lowered brows. "You seek to bargain with me, the King, Davie Lindsay?"

"Yes, Sire, for your own good. And your realm's." That was brief.

James nodded, laughing suddenly. "Och, Davie—you are the honestest man I know, I do declare! However prickly! Very well, it shall be as you say. Bring Beaton back—he will be safe

265

enough. And do your best for me with that nuncio. If my mother gets her claws in him, God knows what will be the end of it!"

"I thank Your Grace. You will not regret this, I promise you. Now, with your permission, I will retire. I have ridden far this day and am weary."

"Aye, Davie—off with you. I am relying on you, mind."

Next morning, David found it none so easy to play the part allotted to him, for the papal nuncio elected to ride beside Margaret Tudor, and even the Lord Lyon King-of-Arms could hardly attach himself to that pair unasked. They rode due northwards, over the high ground, out of Strathearn and into Glen Almond, David close enough behind the Queen-Mother to hear Campeggio rhapsodising over the prospect of the heather-clad mountains opening so splendidly directly ahead, his companion sounding supremely uninterested. It was this situation which presently gave David his opportunity, for, entering the quite dramatic jaws of the true Highland Line, at a dog's-leg bend of the upper valley, known locally as Glen Beg or the small glen, he spurred up alongside the envoy, to point.

"Excellency—your first Highlandman in his native heather!" he exclaimed. Up on a shelf of the otherwise steep hillside, amongst the outcropping rocks and boulders, was a single low-browed hovel, seeming to grow out of the broken ground, and beside it a man standing, watching the cavalcade pass below. Scattered around nearby were small shaggy black cattle. Even at that range the watcher could be seen to be wearing some reddish tartan and a flat bonnet. "You would look, inspect?"

"Yes, yes, Sir David. Assuredly."

The Italian followed his guide eagerly as David picked a way for the horses up that harsh incline, uncaring for Margaret's frowning. Cattle careered away, then stopped to stare. None followed the pair up.

The Highland herdsman stood his ground. As they drew near he could be seen to be a middle-aged man, distinctly fierce of appearance, with down-turning moustaches and an untidy forked beard, clad in a stained and ragged short kilt with a tartan plaid above slung across one shoulder, but otherwise bare of torso. On his feet were a pair of rawhide brogans. When they came up, he bowed strangely courteous and despite his villainous looks gave them a smile. He said something in the Gaelic.

"Good day to you," David greeted. "We are travelling

to Atholl. My friend, from Rome, would speak with a Highlandman."

The other spread a hand apologetically and spoke more Gaelic.

"I fear that he speaks only his own language," David said to Campeggio. "I have none of the Gaelic. You, Excellency, have no knowledge of this tongue you spoke of? The Galatians' was it?"

"Alas, no. Is he not a splendid savage?"

"I would scarce call him savage. He has his own manners, I think."

"The coloured clothings, they are different. The skirt, from the above. Different colours. Most manifest."

"Tartans, yes. There are many forms, designs, I am told. Perhaps with some meaning—I know not."

It was a little uncomfortable just to sit staring at the herdsman, without being able to communicate—at least for David, although the man himself did not appear to be in any way put out, nor the bishop indeed. Then the latter pointed.

"See—a woman! The house, let us see the house. So small, so miserable. Come."

Still more uncomfortable, David thought to suggest that this would be unmannerly on their part, but the nuncio dismounted and hurried forward towards the hovel. Two wide-eyed, all-but-naked children now shared the doorway with the woman.

Looking almost apologetically at the Highlander, David got down also. Gravely the other man inclined his head, and they followed the Legate.

The woman also wore a tartan plaid or shawl, evidently over some sort of brief bodice, and a skirt not a kilt, although shorter than the Lowland fashion, of homespun wool dyed a rich red-brown. She looked from the visitors to her man and smiled nervously. Behind her and the children, oddly, a cow stared out.

Exclaiming, Campeggio pointed and waved his hands about, in a flood of presumably Italian eloquence. Incomprehensible as that was, it was evident that he desired to enter the house, which was built of drystone masonry from the hillside up to about shoulder-height and thereafter thatched with turf, in rounded conformation without gables. Blue smoke curled up lazily from what must have been a hole in the roof, for there was no chimney.

267

The herdsman, still co-operative, signed to the woman and children, who retired inside, and waved the visitors within, as though it had been something of a palace. That left the cow still looking out interestedly—although it now became evident that there was a partition of about shoulder-height again, just within the doorway, dividing the premises into two, with the beast occupying the lower and smaller portion. Much intrigued, the bishop was gesticulating about this when he was rudely interrupted by some squawking poultry which came flapping out of the dark interior past him, to his sudden alarm.

"This will be a milk-cow for the family," David sought to explain. "I have heard of this—it is done in the rest of Scotland also—beasts and folk under the same roof. But always on the lower side, so that the, the glaur drains out. It helps to keep them warm in winter, I suppose."

Pushing past the cow, the Highlander ushered them into the upper three-quarters of the hovel, the visitors catching their breaths, indeed Campeggio starting to cough chokingly. It was partly the smell of cow and peat-reek and other things, but largely the actual smoke which seemed to serve for atmosphere instead of air.

Blinking and gasping, they peered about them. At first they could see little or nothing, for all seemed black within, save for a red glow in the centre of the floor from which came the smoke—for there were no windows in this building and any light came feebly from the hole in the roof and from the doorway, which of course was still partly blocked by the cow and which the visitors' own persons tended to obscure further.

Loud in his astonishment, Campeggio blundered about. It took some time for their eyes to adjust in some measure to the lack of light. When David's did, it was to perceive that the herdsman was holding out to him a wooden two-handled cup of flat design. Surprised, he accepted this, with thanks. The woman proved to have another, for the envoy, who at first did not recognise what it was and in fact spilled some of the contents on the earthen floor.

"Hospitality," David said, sniffing at it. "The drink of the Highlands. Not wine—whisky. Their water-of-life. Have a care, for it is a strong brew."

Their host had now filled a cup for himself from a dark leathern bottle, and raising it towards them said something no doubt complimentary. He thereupon tossed off the shallow cupful in a single gulp. David nodded, but sipped his carefully. However, the Italian, despite the warning, took a good mouthful—and promptly choked again, spluttering and gasping, as the fiery liquid burned his throat, spilling the rest in the process. Panting, he turned and hurried for the doorway, and out.

David, concerned over manners to match those of their host, finished his own drink, smacked his lips appreciatively, and handed the cup back with a bow. He could see better now, and noted the stark simplicity of the furnishings, if such they could be called, the benches and chests, the cooking-pots around the central fireplace, the boxed-in beds against the stone walling, all blackened with the prevailing peat-smoke. Feeling rather foolish, he bowed again and followed the bishop out.

That individual, still holding his wooden cup, met him with a flood of Mediterranean eloquence, much affected by his experiences. When the herdsman emerged, he thrust the cup back at him, and, delving into an inner pocket, produced a silver piece which he held out to the Highlander.

That man actually drew back a little, looking uncomfortable for the first time. But, the prelate insisting on presenting the coin, he took it, turned it over as though examining it interestedly and then, bowing in turn, handed it to David.

Lindsay cleared his throat. "Time that we rejoined His Grace, perhaps," he suggested, and gestured towards the horses.

Their leave-taking of the cottagers was all smiles and incoherence. When they were mounted, David handed the coin back to Campeggio. "Money they do not accept." He thought that was the best way of putting it. "A sort of pride. Forby, they would have little use for it, I think."

As they rode back downhill, the prelate was full of it all, the strangeness, the behaviour, the darkness of the hovel, the fierce liquor, the cow and poultry. Words, in English or Scots, failed him.

Back at the drove-road, they found that the cavalcade had moved on but that James had left a small escort to wait for them. David now had the opportunity he sought.

"You have travelled much in strange lands, Excellency?" he asked, as they rode on northwards.

"Much," the other agreed. "But in none so strange as this."

"Do not all lands have their own strangenesses? I am recently back from the Netherlands and France, and saw much that surprised me."

"Ah, so. France I have visited. The Netherlands, no."

"I went on King James's behalf. To conclude a treaty with the Emperor Charles, and the Regent, Margaret of Hungary. Have you met the Emperor, Excellency? Or the Queen?"

"No. I have heard that he is . . . difficult? A man much troubled in the spirit, no?"

"As to that, I do not know. But he was sufficiently gracious towards us. But then, his aunt, Queen Margaret, assured us that he thought highly of King James and the Scots nation. That may have aided us."

"Ah."

"Yes. He was eager to sign the treaty. Indeed he signed it before we ever discussed all the terms. The Queen did the bargaining, or any there was. It seems that he sees Scotland as necessary, as having its importance in his struggle against the Grand Turk, the Infidel."

"So? How could that be? This far land?"

"The Emperor fears Henry of England. Henry is like any wild bull, cunning, deceitful, unpredictable—but ever ready to take advantage of weakness anywhere, for his own gain. Does the Holy See not recognise that also?"

The other did not commit himself.

"If the Emperor marshals much of the strength of Christendom against Sulieman, as he *is* doing, and marches on Austria, then the northern parts of the Empire will inevitably be weakened for a time—and Henry might well strike. France at present is scarcely friendly towards the Empire, nor towards Rome, you will agree? So King Francis cannot be relied upon to counter any English move across the Channel. But Scotland, now—Scotland can!"

"You say that Scotland will attack England if Henry attacks the Empire?"

"That is King James's policy, yes."

"I understood, Sir David, that so it was the policy towards *France*, not the Empire? As the King's father proved, did he not, at the price of his life? The ancient alliance?"

"Yes, but not only France. The treaty with the Netherlands is

270

a renewal of one ancient also, of mutual help against England. It has stood for one hundred years."

"Henry of England could be . . . bought, perhaps?"

"By offering him *spiritual* overlordship of Scotland? The Pope reducing St. Andrews from a metropolitan see and putting in under York? It would not serve, not in any way."

"You are so sure, yes?"

"Yes. Oh, Henry would accept it and gladly. But it would not change his course by a hand's-breadth. And *Scotland* would not accept it. You might force King James into the very evil from which you would restrain King Henry—breaking spiritual allegiance to Rome."

"That is *your* belief in this, Sir David. Others may believe differently, no?"

"Not mine only, Excellency. The Queen of Hungary so believes —and therefore the Emperor, whom she much advises. Also Abbot Beaton of Arbroath, Scotland's Privy Seal."

"Ah, the good Abbot David! Where is he? I had looked to see him. His Holiness sent him a message. But he is not to be discovered. I am told that he is in disfavour, no? The Archbishop, his uncle, likewise . . ."

"That is past. A misunderstanding, just. All is well again . . ."

"Yet the good Abbot, whom we all so greatly admire, is not here with your King."

"He *will* be here, Excellency. He is at present up in his own abbatical lands. But he is recalled to court. The King told me so, only last night."

"So? And he, Beaton, will again advise your King on his policies? His Holiness has much faith in the Abbot's wisdom."

"To be sure. King James also recognises the value of his advice. And is apt to act upon it."

"That is well. In Rome they will be much pleased to hear this."

They were in sight of the rear of the main party now, strung out in file as they lifted out of the glen to cross the high pass to Amulree at the mouth of Glen Quaich. David felt that he had done as much as he could for his liege-lord, and hoped that he had not perjured himself in the process.

At Amulree, amongst high moors of heather, ringed by mountains, the company swung off east by north down Strathbraan, to reach the Tay at Dunkeld, passing the striking Falls of Braan,

271

where that river fell over three hundred feet in a mile—to the applause of the papal nuncio. Dunkeld, amongst its steep wooded ridges, was the ancient seat of the Celtic mormaordom of Atholl, the holders of which were hereditary Primates of the Columban Church—hence the name, the fort of the Keledei, or Friends of God. It was still a possession of the Earls of Atholl, although now they had their main seat at Blair, some twenty miles to the north. The Earl John Stewart had sent a large party of his clansmen to meet them here; but it was decided that a halt should be made for the night, for the Queen-Mother's and her ladies' sake, if not the nuncio's. There was a Romish abbey and cathedral here, successor of the Celtic one, and in it the travellers could put up in comfort. It was not stressed that, until a few days previously, the absent bishop thereof had been one of Archbishop Beaton's fellow-prisoners in Blackness Castle.

James was glad to hear David's report of his session with Campeggio, and agreed that in the circumstances it would be politic to send for Davie Beaton, if possible to join them forthwith at Blair-in-Atholl, a royal messenger to ride at once. Lindsay felt, however, that Beaton might well be wary of such summons, fearing a trap, and declared that it would be best if he himself were to go, to reassure his friend. He calculated that it would be about fifty miles to Ethie, certainly over some difficult country, and finding Beaton at the other end might take time. For how long did His Grace intend to remain in Atholl? Three days? Four? He hoped that they could return by that time.

So, instead of settling down for the night in the comfort of the Abbey, David, with two of the royal guard as escort, set off eastwards there and then—for it was only late afternoon and he could get in many miles before darkness. They rode hard, now, up out of Strathtay, over more high forested ground and into a long and very strange wooded valley containing a remarkable succession of lochs. Oddly enough, considering that their ultimate destination was the Angus river called Lunan, bringing them to Lunan Bay, this present twisting high-set glen was the valley of another Lunan Water, mile upon mile of it threading the hills of East Atholl and the Stormounth and enfolding the series of lochs into which the river kept widening— Craiglush, Lowes, Butterstone, Clunie, Drumellie, Rae, Fingask and Stormounth, this last in the mouth of the great vale of

Strathmore, into Angus. The horsemen did not get all that way that evening, but reached an upland grange of the Abbey of Coupar-Angus, on the shore of Loch Drumellie, where they passed the night.

Down Strathmore next day they passed Coupar Abbey itself and on to the town of Forfar, capital of Angus, where they swung off eastwards again to follow the second Lunan Water, by Restenneth and Rescobie and Guthrie, towards the sea. By mid-afternoon they had covered another thirty miles, to Ethie.

That Marion Ogilvy was surprised to see Lindsay back so soon went without saying, but she made him entirely welcome, even though she had mixed feelings about this summons for Davie back to court—for however much *he* might desire it, undoubtedly she would see a deal less of him than she had been doing lately. He had indeed been at Ethie Castle the previous night and she expected him back that evening.

Weary with hard riding, David was in fact in his bed when, late that night a knock at his door announced the Lord Privy Seal, clad, as before, like a fisherman. Davie at least had no doubts about the situation, once he had Lindsay's assurance that no trickery would be involved. The Bastard might prove dangerous, admittedly—but then he was always that; so long as James himself remained trustworthy, Davie thought that he could cope with Hamilton. He was grateful to his friend for achieving this recall. He had heard about the Papal Legate's visit and had been wondering how to contrive some secret meeting.

In the morning, then, two of Scotland's great officers of state left that cliff-top hold and a resigned woman and children, Beaton now transformed, in fine clothing, hair and beard trimmed, a glittering figure. They proposed to reach Blair-in-Atholl by nightfall, if their escort could keep up with them.

Tired indeed, and mounts all but foundered, in the event they came to the wide strath of the Garry, in which lay Blair, not by darkening but soon after—and for the last miles the sky was lit up for them adequately enough by such a blaze of fire ahead as to make the illumination at Methven a few nights previously appear as no more than candlelight. As they rode near enough to look down into the valley, it was to see that this was not caused merely by cooking-fires but came from hundreds of flaming pitch-pine torches set in long rows along the level lands where the River Tilt met the Garry. Never had they seen the like, as though a city had sprung up there in a Highland strath.

Down on the low ground the impression was less of a city than of the camp of a great army, but one where feasting, sport and jollity were the order of the day, or night, not warfare. Hundreds, probably thousands, of Highlanders swarmed everywhere, in the light of the torches and fires, singing and dancing to the music of fiddles and pipes, playing games of muscular prowess, dragging vast quantities of timber for the fires, eating and drinking. No tents were here however; presumably the clansmen despised such, sleeping in their plaids whatever the weather.

Further on they did come to a tented encampment, but this was obviously that of the royal company. Yet, riding through it, the newcomers saw no sign of the King nor his close entourage and important companions. They were looking, of course, for Blair Castle itself as destination, and were presently surprised to discover, amongst all the flaring torchlight, two castles, some little way apart, one huge, one only moderate in size, both blazing with lights. The sound of more music emanated from the larger. To this they headed.

Their surprise grew to astonishment when, drawing close, they perceived that the greater building was in fact not a castle at all; or, at least, it was a sham castle constructed wholly of timber, and green timber at that, still with the foliage attached, Scots pine and birch and rowan, in an amazing flourish. Yet it had great round towers at each end and a pair of typical drum-towers in the centre, flanking the doorway, which was guarded by the usual gatehouse and drawbridge, even its portcullis being constructed of new birchwood. The windows were glass-filled, some of colourful stained glass, and above all a row of flags flapped on poles, lit up by their own torches, mainly Stewart banners naturally but topped by a huge Lion Rampant standard.

The two Davids stared at all this in wonder, even Beaton at a loss for words.

Over the drawbridge and inside, they found themselves walking on a floor of clipped grass, the turfs fitted together closely but patterned with designs and strewn with flowers and sweet-smelling bog-myrtle. This vestibule, arched with greenery, led into a vast hall, where Highland dancing was in progress before the feasting company, with a score of kilted fiddlers playing in lively unison, a scene of extraordinary vigour, spirit and colour.

The newcomers made their way towards the dais-table, where sat the Queen-Mother, the papal nuncio, a middle-aged man in full Highland costume, John Stewart, Earl of Atholl, and sundry others. The King was not there, but a quick survey revealed him to be dancing with a dark, bold-eyed and notably low-gowned young woman, both with considerable vivacity. With his red-haired good looks, they made a striking couple. The Bastard of Arran could be seen similarly engaged nearby.

Since they must pay their respects first to the monarch, the visitors waited apart, although Bishop Campeggio waved to them. When that dance ended, James, who had evidently noticed them, came over, still holding the lady close, her prominent and delectable bosom heaving tumultuously with her exertions.

"Ha, Davie Lindsay—you have found our errant Privy Seal, I see, and brought him back to the fold!" he exclaimed. "Welcome, my lord Abbot!"

"Thank you, Sire. I was never far from Your Grace in spirit," Beaton returned, bowing. "Only I fear my so craven spirit shrank from lodgings in Blackness Castle! So . . . draughty!"

"H'rr'mm." James cleared his throat. "You know Libby Stewart?"

"I have the honour, Sire. Lady Elizabeth—your servant."

They moved up to the dais, where Atholl, who knew them both of course, offered them greeting and refreshment after their long riding. Margaret Tudor ignored them but the Legate was all but effusive in his reception of Beaton, making room for him to sit beside him, where they conversed volubly in Italian, in which Davie appeared to be fluent. Lindsay went and found a more lowly seat.

There, presently, the Bastard came to him, in passing. "So you brought our clever friend back from wherever he has been hiding," he commented. "Clever clerks are very well, in their place—but must not be allowed to get above themselves! I am sure that you will agree."

"Where do you consider that place to be, Sir James?" David asked. "After all, a long line of clerks, clever or otherwise, have governed this realm, as chancellors for the King. As at this present."

"Ah, but this Dunbar is not *too* clever, God be praised! Which makes all the difference. Your friend should note it."

"Is this some sort of a warning, Hamilton?"

"Warning? No, no—just my humble advice. Why should I warn Davie Beaton?"

"That I wondered!"

"He and our Italian visitor appear to be mighty close."

"Perhaps we may all have reason to be thankful for that!"

"You think so? I wonder."

"His Grace does not. Hence, surely, all this!" And he gestured at all their extraordinary surroundings.

"Ah, this play-acting and mummery? This is done for various reasons, not all to impress our papal friend. Admittedly, Atholl was stung when he heard that the Italian had described the Highlands as the arse-end of Christendom, and would show him otherwise. But there is more to it than that. James is concerned to use the clan chiefs to reduce the power of the Lowland lords who plague his peace. These despise the Highlanders. This display is to let them see that there is more in the Highlands than mere hordes of savage caterans. Few Lowland earls could contrive this spectacle and flourish. Save, perhaps, my brother Arran!"

"I see. But why should *Atholl* go to such expense? This must be costing him dear, indeed."

Finnart nodded towards where James sat with the young woman. "There is your answer, man. Atholl would have our James *wed* his daughter Libby, as well as bed her! This is all to aid in his project to be the King's good-sire! It will not serve, of course—but he hopes that it may!"

"You sound very sure."

"Why, yes," the other said easily, and moved on.

David sought a bed soon thereafter, finding a room allotted to him in the true Blair Castle nearby. He left Beaton still in deep converse with the nuncio. James had disappeared. So had the Lady Elizabeth Stewart.

Next day was devoted to hunting. Not the horsed chase, as practised in the south, nor yet individual stalking of beasts, but a very different kind of venery known as a deer-drive—although more than deer were apt to be involved. This was more like warfare than sport, with the hunters setting elaborate ambushes and hiding behind elaborate grass-grown ramparts specially designed for the purpose. A complicated pattern of these deer-dykes was established up on the rising ground of the hillsides a mile or two from the castle, laid out geometrically in long lines and re-entrants, so that driven deer were funnelled into strategically-placed gaps, behind which the hunters were hidden with their bows and arrows and javelins. From before sun-up great numbers of men had been out in the surrounding mountains, not exactly rounding up the herds but causing them to drift uneasily in the desired direction. This was an expert business, much more finesse being required of the deer-movers than of the killers themselves, for although the hills were full of vast herds, thousands Atholl assured, they could so easily break away in alarm and disappear into the endless mountain wilderness. To get them to move gently towards the deer-dykes area and then, at the last moment to drive them in through the gaps to the waiting hunters, was an art, the more difficult in that it had to be done in carefully-timed stages so that most of the animals did not go hurtling through in one mad stampede but in spaced-out batches, to allow maximum slaughter. If it was scarcely a sporting proposition, such as stalking or even the chase, it was certainly a most effective way of amassing large amounts of venison.

With many hunters to be accommodated, more than one of the dyke complexes were manned, and David Lindsay was sent to a different one, higher up the hillside than that appointed for the King and his principal guests. Nevertheless he had more than sufficient activity, indeed grew sickened by the killing long before the day was over. The deer came drifting across the mountainsides in their hundreds, but spread out, singly and in groups, urged on by men and dogs who now allowed themselves to be seen. But when the creatures reached the barriers of the dykes, they had to turn up or down them, and so began to bunch. By the time that they reached one of the carefully sited gaps they were packed in dense racing columns, jostling and stumbling in panic, utterly unlike their usual graceful bounding gait. Thus they streamed past the waiting marksmen, who shot their arrows and threw their javelins into the red-brown mass, and could scarcely fail to hit, so solid a target did they present, the only problem being the restringing of arrows and replacing of javelins sufficiently fast. Needless to say most beasts were not killed outright in this battue, and had to be despatched later.

277

The heaps of the slain mounted as fresh herds were driven in. Roe, blue hares, even foxes also got caught up in the stampede, providing more difficult marks.

When David had had more than enough, he moved over to join the beaters and, in fact, found their demanding activity more to his taste.

When all was over, the triumphant young monarch declared that they had slain a grand total of six hundred harts and hinds, apart from lesser creatures. Had that ever been surpassed?

That evening Atholl had a new wonder for his guests, fountains contrived in the turf spouting different wines, muscatel, hippocras and alicant—this in addition to the previous provision of claret, malmsey and whisky available to wash down the banquet of moorfowl, capercailzie, blackcock, swan, heron, even peacock, which supplemented the venison, beef, lamb and salmon.

For their final day's entertainment, they were taken hunting in different style, down amongst the flooded water-meadows and marshy scrub and woodlands of the strath floor and lower slopes, this done on horseback, more like Lowland sport. This dissimilarity was in the quarry, for although there were deer here also, heavy woodland beasts with great spreading antlers, there were also wolves, wild boar, badgers, even wildcats. The bag, needless to say, was infinitely smaller but the challenge much greater. The Bastard distinguished himself by notching up the highest score.

The royal party left Blair the following morning—and even then the Earl of Atholl had something spectacular to show them. For as they formed up to mount, taking their farewells, he ordered his gillies to light more torches and go into that great greenwood palace and set all on fire, furnishings, bedding, hangings, unconsumed provisions and wines, everything, the structure itself included. When, all but appalled, the nuncio demanded why, why, Atholl told him that it was so that quarters which had sheltered the King's Grace, his lady mother and the Papal Legate should never be profaned by less illustrious lodgers. Besides, it was an old Highland custom to burn temporary overnight accommodation behind them when the clans moved on. He said this with a grin—and not all his hearers perceived the allusion to that other Highland custom of feuding, and destroying their neighbours' property after a raid.

So the visitors rode away southwards from Blair-in-Atholl, for Methven and Stirling again, leaving behind them a great brown pillar of smoke rising high above the mountains, from their late luxurious lodging. Atholl and his daughter accompanied them, the Earl to turn back at the limits of his own territory beyond Dunkeld, the Lady Elizabeth to remain with the King. On Lindsay's suggestion they were escorted also by a large company of running-gillies, and Antonio Campeggio was just as impressed by these as had been the Emperor Charles and the Netherlanders.

Davie Beaton confided in his friend, as they rode, that Atholl had admitted having spent the almost unbelievable sum of three thousands of pounds on this three-day royal entertainment.

17

The months that followed, the winter of 1531 and the spring of 1532, although superficially an unusually quiet and uneventful period in the troubled reign of the fifth James Stewart, were in fact anything but, just below the surface, at least for those in the know, especially those at court. For an intense struggle, a battle indeed, was going on, for the will and guidance, if not the mind and soul, of the said James, a war none the less sustained, unrelenting, for being undeclared. The protagonists were Sir James Hamilton of Finnart on the one hand and the two Davids, Beaton and Lindsay, on the other. It would be difficult to say who gained most success in this tug-of-war; certainly neither could claim to win, for James, although weak in certain aspects of his character, was anything but in others, and went his own way most of the time. But, on balance, probably the Davids achieved most. Undoubtedly the Bastard lost some ground previously held—and fought the harder and more unscrupulously in consequence. And Hamilton was a fighter, whatever else.

Beaton and Lindsay held certain advantages, to be sure. The former, as Lord Privy Seal, was in a position to influence much in the sphere of government, especially with a lack-lustre although honest Chancellor; and as effective ruler of Holy Church with its great power and revenues, his uncle becoming ever more of a cipher. And Lindsay, for his part, had the effect of years of boyhood guidance on James, a reliance on him as mentor and friend never entirely outgrown. Moreover, strangely, his poetic abilities had quite a major impact on the young monarch. James had always admired David's writings, indeed envied them, for he himself sought to emulate David and compose verse. The court diversion known as flyting gave scope for this. The King's father had been a great flyter, and young James revelled in it. Flytings were exchanges of abuse in rhyme, humorous and usually ribald, often quite provocative, and James's own were the most outspoken and derogatory, as they could afford to be—although he by no means resented quite blatant attacks on himself, unthinkable on any other occasion. Most of these efforts were in fairly crude doggerel, to be sure; but David Lindsay's were apt to be of notable quality and effectiveness, and the King's own frequently far from feeble. In the long winter evenings, as the winds off the Highland mountains howled round Stirling Castle's lofty walls, flyting was a popular entertainment in torch- and firelight and over brimming beakers of wine and ale—when James was not otherwise engaged.

The King did not often single out Lindsay as the target for his wit, but on one occasion he did launch a fleering volley at his Lyon's unlionlike attitudes towards drinking, gaming, tourney-fighting and even hurly-hackit, accusing him of being a dullard in sport and a laggard in love. David did not reply in more than a few words there and then, but took the opportunity to turn the occasion to good use by composing quite a major poem as response, which in due course he read out at another flyting and then presented the written offering to his liege-lord. Simply entitling it *An Answer to the King's Flyting* he was forthright in his criticism of James's immoralities and extravagances. And he stressed the need for settling down, a satisfactory and virtuous marriage, in the interests of the succession to the throne, a vital matter for the realm's peace and weal. The younger man took this very well, all things considered. It probably had more effect on him than other more normal advice and counsel.

David also composed, at this time, another piece, *The Complaint of Bagsche*. Bagsche was the King's old hound and the poem took the form of its discussion with the current favourite dog Bawtie as to the follies of the court, a satire on the behaviour of courtiers, and incidentally the monarch himself. This earned him few friends, although it much tickled the King.

David's attempts to influence his sovereign's life-style were not confined to the poetic. For instance, on an occasion when Janet, as Wardrobe Mistress, informed him that a new master tailor was to be appointed, Lindsay, before all the King's entourage, personally applied for the position. To the monarch's astonished reaction that surely *he* knew nothing about tailoring, and laughingly doubting whether he could shape or sew, David retorted that, as he had served his liege-lord long, he looked to be rewarded as others were. That he could neither shape nor sew was of no matter, for had not His Grace given even bishoprics and benefices to many standing there amongst them who could neither teach nor preach, and other offices to those with no qualifications? Why not to himself as master tailor? James was amused, if others were less so.

The Bastard of Arran sought to counter all this by encouraging the King in ever wilder extravagances of behaviour and expenditure, catering assiduously to James's weaknesses, predilections and indiscretions, and surrounding him with as raffish a crew of courtiers, male and female, as was to be found anywhere in Christendom, Beaton asserted. Davie asserted too that Hamilton did this not only to maintain his influence over the younger man but in the hope that one or other of the many and repeated excesses might result in the death of James, since his own half-brother would then be eligible for the throne. This was no far-fetched improbability, for the King took enormous risks, in the hunting field, in sports and jousting at hurly-hackit, and especially in his night-time exploits as Gudeman of Ballengeich. Night after night he used to ride out, alone, from Stirling or Falkland, Dunfermline, Linlithgow or Edinburgh, seeking his most favoured sport, the company and attentions of strange women, seeking them in the streets of towns, in alehouses and brothels, in lonely farmsteads and cottages equally with castles and towers, insatiable. The dangers were self-evident, to his person, his health and his pocket, from angry husbands and fathers, robbers and disease. The Earl of Angus's early indoctrinations were producing a bountiful harvest. How many bastards the royal adventurer produced likewise was anybody's guess. As excuse for these nocturnal excursions James claimed that he was concerned to discover at first hand and anonymously how his subjects lived and fared, for their better governance.

These risks were well exemplified by the occasion when, riding out alone after a Privy Council meeting at Holyrood Abbey, in Edinburgh, James found his satisfaction at a low alehouse at Cramond Brig, some six miles from the city, near where the River Almond reached the Firth of Forth. Afterwards, starting off on his return to Edinburgh, he was set upon by a band of ruffians, who no doubt thought the young man a pigeon worth plucking, was dragged from his horse and belaboured with cudgels. Although able to give a fairly good account of himself, he was hopelessly outnumbered and might well have ended his reign there and then had not a stalwart countryman named Jock Howieson heard the rumpus and come to his aid. Together they fought the robbers to a standstill, then to flight. Howieson took the battered monarch to his mill-cottage, bathed and bound up his cuts and bruises and provided rough refreshment. The grateful James, ever open-handed to a fault, revealed his identity and promised his rescuer the freehold of the lands on which the assault had taken place, on condition that the new laird and his descendants should always offer the King and his successors a basin of water and a napkin, and some small hospitality, if they passed that way—a custom which was in fact to be kept up for centuries to come.

But some incidents, however romantic-sounding, were a grievous worry to the King's responsible advisers and made them redouble their efforts to bring James to a greater sense of his duties and position. Marriage, in especial, was considered ever more advisable, not only to keep him home of a night and provide an heir to the throne but to help fill the royal coffers, emptied by the years of mismanagement, hungry nobles and general extravagance. So a royal bride with a rich dowry was called for—this effectively ruling out almost all James's acknowledged Scots mistresses, such as the Elizabeths Erskine, Stewart and Beaton.

This was very much Davie Beaton's problem, for the King himself was less than interested. Davie knew all the royal houses of Christendom and approximately their state of wealth and the advantages or otherwise of their alliance with Scotland. There

282

was no lack of possibilities. By the treaty of Rouen, of course, the daughter of King Francis of France had been named as possible bride for James at some future date; but the Princess Madeleine was very delicate and probably not a practical proposition. However, Francis found three alternative names, all rich and notably high-born Frenchwomen—Marie de Bourbon, daughter of the Duc de Vendôme; Marie de Guise, daughter of the Duc de Guise; and Isabeau D'Albret, daughter of the King of Navarre. Not to be outdone, the Emperor Charles put forward his niece Mary of Hungary, like his Aunt Margaret now widowed; but she was considerably older than James, although she had proved her fertility at least. Then the King of Spain suggested Princess Mary of Portugal, while the deposed King Christian of Denmark offered either of his daughters Christina or Dorothea, plus the only firm cash commitment, ten thousand gold crowns—this in return for the promise of Scots aid to recover his crown from the usurping Frederick. There was still another possibility, the wealthiest of all, the Florentine Catherine de Medici, daughter of the Duke of Urbino, ward of Pope Clement and niece of the Duke of Albany, Scotland's recent Regent. All this galaxy of riches and influence, if not necessarily pulchritude, Davie Beaton debated, weighed up and prepared to juggle with. He would have gone prospecting Europe in person, however unenthusiastic his liege-lord, but recognised that it would be dangerous to leave Scotland for any such prolonged tour at this juncture. He prevailed on James to send Sir Thomas Erskine of Haltoun as roving ambassador when David Lindsay declined the task.

Nobody in Scotland, save perhaps Margaret Tudor, so much as considered Henry of England's daughter Mary as bride for the King of Scots, although that objectionable monarch was more or less demanding it as the price of an end to his attacks on the northern kingdom.

All this marital odyssey had unexpected results and odd repercussions. The reformation agitation in Holy Church was boiling up on the Continent and the princes of Christendom becoming involved on one side or the other. Scotland, from being a small and comparatively unimportant realm on the outskirts of Europe became quite suddenly of some moment as an ally, particularly on the pro-Romish side, especially with Henry Tudor ever more at odds with the Vatican, not so much

283

on religious grounds as at the refusal of the Pope to grant him a divorce from his Queen Catherine of Aragon. The Pope, now, instead of excommunicating James, authorised, indeed commanded the Church of Scotland to pay his treasury large sums of money, for so long as he remained faithful to Rome, the sum of ten thousand pounds annually plus one tenth of the revenues of all benefices for three years—a generosity which even Davie Beaton, and certainly his uncle, considered to be excessive. The Emperor sent James the much-prized Order of the Golden Fleece, never before awarded to a King of Scots. And not to be outdone, Francis of France conferred on him the Order of St. Michael.

All this, of course, much gratified James Stewart, especially the financial relief—for he had been reduced actually to borrowing three thousand merks from the Earl of Huntly. But Beaton, rather ruefully in this instance, finding himself or the Church, which he seemed to look upon as more or less the same thing, the victim of his own cleverness, sought to rescue something from the Pope's devious generosity with other folk's money by instituting a much needed reform in the sphere of government, a project which he and a clerical friend, Alexander Mylne, Abbot of Cambuskenneth, had long discussed—this before James might squander all the ecclesiastical windfall in riotous living. The project was the setting up of a permanent court of justice, other than the judgements of parliament, the *ad hoc* courts of the Lord Justice General, the lordly sheriffdoms and the barons' powers of pit-and-gallows, all, as it were, amateur and casual. Abbot Alexander had studied in Pavia and had been greatly impressed by the standards of justice meted out by a court established there with permanent members qualified in law and paid annual salaries to make informed and equitable judgements. None could deny that such was overdue in Scotland and this seemed an ideal opportunity. So the two churchmen devised a scheme and prevailed on James and his Privy Council, in the first flush of enthusiasm over the unexpected largesse, to endorse it. A college of justice would be established, to be called the Court of Session, in that it would sit permanently as distinct from casually, with fifteen members. And to ensure that Holy Church had major control over this, and clerics gained a suitable proportion of the cash involved—since it was Church money that paid for it—it was stipulated that seven of the members should always be churchmen, plus a clerical president—the first president to be Alexander Mylne himself. This excellent development, to become so much part of Scotland's scene, was an unforeseen bonus to come out of the King's tentative marriage enquiries.

Strangely enough, and sadly as far as David Lindsay was concerned, and the King himself to a lesser extent, one of the first cases to come before the new Lords of Session referred to another Abbot, none other than David's old friend and colleague, James's assistant tutor, Abbot John Inglis of Culross. When the monarch outgrew tutoring, Inglis had reverted to his abbatical duties in Fife and Fothriff, but he and David had kept in touch. Unfortunately he had become involved in a dispute over certain lands held by his Abbey in which Sir John Blackadder of Tulliallan claimed interest. The Abbot granted a tack or lease of these lands to the Lord Erskine, and the fiery Blackadder was sufficiently incensed actually to waylay Inglis at the Loanhead of Rosyth in Fothriff, and slay him—not so unusual an event perhaps in baronial circles, but notable in that the victim was an abbot. A warrant for the arrest of the Baron of Tulliallan was duly made out but the matter became complicated by the accused fleeing to take refuge in the sanctuary at Torphichen, in West Lothian. This ancient Girth, or traditional place of sanctuary for fugitives and wrong-doers, was an area around the Preceptory of the Knights Hospitaller of St. John of Jerusalem, marked out by girth-crosses, part of an ages-old privilege of that chivalric order, by this time little used. Nevertheless, John Blackadder claimed sanctuary there, to the embarrassment of the St. John knights and everybody else. A churchman murdered, Holy Church declared that this ancient privilege was outdated and void, and an armed party sent to Torphichen to bring the murderer to Edinburgh and justice. There however, Blackadder and his friends appealed to the King and Privy Council that he had been forcibly removed from an established sanctuary, which had never been reduced from that status. So the matter came before the new Lords of Session for decision. Cautiously at this stage, they compromised, in an awkward situation. They sent Blackadder back to Torphichen meantime under security of five thousand merks put up by his friends that he would not abscond. Then they settled down judiciously to try the double issue, first the inviolacy or otherwise of the sanctuary and secondly the murder itself—which last was more or less admitted. In due course their lordships found that the sanctuary was in fact a provision of Holy Church in the past and therefore could not be used to protect an offender against the said Church; and secondly that Blackadder was guilty of the murder of Abbot John of Culross and should be beheaded in the Grassmarket of Edinburgh in consequence.

It made a strange baptism for the new administration of justice, and a strange postscript to the life of John Inglis, who had always been a quiet and inoffensive individual. King James and his court went to witness the beheading, as indicating royal support. Sir James Hamilton absented himself, however.

An interesting by-product of this case was the unearthing of the fact that certain churchmen appeared to have been in the habit of making personal gain out of such sanctuaries, in providing criminals with protection, for reward. This discovery resulted in an act of parliament putting an end to all such miscarriages of justice.

18

All this domestic advancement and preoccupation could not last, of course, not with Henry of England's marriage offer being spurned and his burning ambition to be overlord of Scotland unabated. When he heard of Sir Thomas Erskine's bride-prospecting mission to France and the Empire, and the competition in offering James orders of chivalry, he made his own typical gesture towards his troublesome nephew—invasion. He sent the Earl of Northumberland across Tweed from Berwick, with a large army, with instructions to lay waste the lands of the Merse and Lothian, and to assist in the matter he sent also the Earl of Angus and Sir George Douglas, with the renegade Earl of Bothwell, to raise their people on the English behalf.

So it was back to normal in Scotland, after the so unaccustomed interlude, with trumpets sounding to arms again.

Unfortunately James's, or rather the Bastard's, policy of

reducing the power of the great Lowland nobles, however seemingly effective in some respects, especially in promoting Hamilton hegemony, told against the realm's needs in such sudden crisis as this. The lords' levies just failed to respond in any numbers to the call-to-arms; and producing any large host of clansmen from the Highlands and Islands took much time. So mustering to repel the invaders was slow indeed on the Burgh Muir of Edinburgh, the traditional rallying-place for warlike endeavour, and it was basically a Hamilton force of only a few thousand which presently was despatched southwards in the first instance to counter Northumberland, Angus and Bothwell, while James himself remained at Edinburgh to try to raise a large host to bring on as soon as might be. But by the same token, as well as the shortage of lords' men-at-arms, Scotland in these circumstances was notably short of commanders of any experience. The Bastard himself was probably the most able soldier available, for, whatever his failings, he was a bold and effective leader of men. Although his half-brother the new Earl of Arran in theory headed the Hamilton advance force, the Bastard was in fact in command. David Lindsay went along too, partly because of his experience of Border warfare with the late de la Bastie, partly at Davie Beaton's urging, to keep an eye on the Bastard himself, whom Beaton felt was not to be trusted in any crisis. Lindsay went with less than martial fervour in the circumstances.

Nevertheless, once they were on their way, through the western Lammermuirs by Soutra and down Lauderdale, his spirits picked up somewhat, for there was always something invigorating, enheartening, about riding at the head of a great column of cavalry. Moreover, the Bastard, in his element, could be good company when he wanted to, and he seemed to prefer David's company to that of his half-brother, whom he obviously despised.

Reaching Tweed at Leaderfoot, near Melrose, they turned eastwards, to start climbing. And almost at once, above the hills which flanked the great plain of the Merse, they saw the vast billowing clouds of smoke which soared like thunderheads to stain all the sky ahead blue-black and murky brown. To account for all that, the whole land must be ablaze. Hamilton spirits sobered. The smoke-pall extended considerably and ominously northwards.

The Bastard, perceiving sundry bands of Home moss-troopers also heading eastwards, from Cowdenknowes and Drygrange and Redpath and Brothersdene, decided to make for Home Castle, where these would be headed, in the first instance. The present Lord Home was a comparatively inoffensive character, unlike his predecessor and so many of his lairds, and had shown himself to be anxious to remain on good terms with his monarch, lest he too ended up with his head on a spike on Edinburgh's Tolbooth. Yet it looked as though he were summoning his supporters. It could be only to try to protect his lands from the invaders, of course; but in the past the Homes had all too often sided *with* the invaders, for their own gain. It would be as well to investigate.

In the early evening, topping the Smailholm ridge before the dip of the Eden valley, with all the Merse of Berwickshire then spreading before them, they drew rein almost in shock, even the tough Hamiltons appalled. It was at a credible representation of Hell that they stared, endless miles of fire and smoke as far as eye could see, the flames shooting high, but far above these the clouds streaked and glowing with scarlet and crimson. Against this terrible backcloth the walls and towers of Home Castle, on its isolated hill five miles ahead, stood out in silhouette black, stark.

Grimly they rode on.

At Home, presently, they found its agitated lord in a state of indecision, torn between his own fears and the advice of his militant supporters. Clearly his inclination was to be elsewhere and to leave his strong castle well-garrisoned enough to withstand any possible attack by the invaders, even though it looked as though these were going to leave Home alone, at least meantime, since the tide of fire and ravishment seemed to have come no nearer than a couple of miles eastwards. But some of his lairds were urging a more active programme than that, assault on the invaders; and the newcomers suspected, even though they were not so informed, others advised *joining* the English as the surest way of protecting their properties. Lord Home, in fact, appeared quite to welcome the arrival of the Hamilton force, both as added protection and as more or less taking the decision out of his hands.

All that night bands and groups of Home and other Merse residents kept arriving at the castle, as reinforcements, as refugees from the violence and as typical fishers on troubled waters prepared to pick up any advantage to themselves in a fluid and chaotic situation. It was a strong party of these last, turning up in the small hours with a considerable haul of booty taken from English raiders who had previously taken it from unspecified victims, who also brought with them a couple of Northumbrian prisoners whom they conceived to be sufficiently prosperous as to be worth ransoming, in true Border fashion. And these prisoners had been prevailed upon to talk, to the effect that this great incursion was in fact a raid rather than any major invasion, specifically ordered by the King Henry, with limited aims, these the spoiling and devastation, not the occupation, of the land, no attempt to be made on this occasion on Edinburgh, Stirling or other centres of population. The destruction of Dunglass Castle, south of Dunbar, was indeed given as the main objective—this because it was being used as the headquarters base of the Scots Chief Warden of the Marches and so had a special significance as well as being stocked with much gear, arms, ammunition, coin, horseflesh and the like, worth abstracting.

This information shed a different light on the situation, both for the Bastard's people and for Home's. For Dunglass was a Home property, their furthest north and second strongest hold, even though presently held by the crown. Although they were little concerned as to what happened to its present garrison, they had no wish to see the place destroyed. It was near Angus's great fortress of Tantallon and they suspected that this might well be another reason for making it the prime target, for the Douglases would rejoice to see it demolished, a rival strength so near. So the Homes felt impelled to do something about Dunglass.

The Bastard, and David also, saw the need to prevent the Scots Warden's base from being brought low. But still more important was the knowledge gained that this was all only a punitive raid, a short-term gesture with limited purposes. It meant that Northumberland and his host would be turning back for home before long, quite possibly before King James and his main army could be brought to bear on the situation. This, in turn, must affect any strategy of their own. Dunglass was fully twenty-five miles north of Home Castle, into Lothian, not in the Merse at all, and probably more or less the limit of the English thrust—since to go much further would be to near Edinburgh and involve major confrontation.

So next morning, with no assault on Home Castle having developed during an all but sleepless night, the Bastard announced his plans. Couriers would be sent to King James to inform him of the position and urge that he should bring on with all speed such troops as he had managed to assemble, by the shortest route to Dunglass area, that is by Haddington and the Vale of Tyne to Dunbar; whilst he and the Homes made simultaneous but separate approaches to the same area, threatening the invaders from the south-west whereas the King would come from the north-west. Between these three forces, even though they might still not equal the enemy strength, it was to be hoped that they might trap and confound Northumberland and his traitorous allies.

This seemed a sound programme in the circumstances, to all concerned, and preparations were made to move. But before the two forces separated, Hamilton informed David Lindsay that he wanted him to remain with the Homes, ostensibly to act as a sort of liaison-officer but more particularly because he did not trust them. With the Lord Lyon King-of-Arms' presence, the notoriously truculent Home lairds would be less apt to controvert the authority of their indecisive lord. David scarcely relished this employment but could hardly refuse.

It was agreed that the Hamiltons should take the more northerly approach by the Whitadder Water, into the southern skirts of the Lammermuirs, there to turn eastwards and descend on the Dunglass area of the coast by Oldhamstocks, this giving them useful hilly cover right up to the last mile or two. The Homes would advance by the twin river, the Blackadder, to cross the high ground of the Drakemire vicinity to the upper Eye Water and so threaten the English from the Colbrandspath and Pease Dean area, from the south. The conformation of the land thereabouts, with the hills coming down close to the sea, meant that inevitably the invaders would be strung out in elongated files and at their most vulnerable. David was grimly amused that it seemed that he was bound for action with the Homes at the very place where he and Antoine de la Bastie had ambushed the previous Lord Home and his people, many of them here present, all those years before.

As he rode with the Home leadership, at the head of almost

one thousand fierce mosstroopers, as wild a force as he had ever accompanied, David was interested to note that they were in fact, all the way north-eastwards, skirting just to the west of the devastated area, still smoking from yesterday's burning. The invaders appeared to have laid waste a swathe of country between five and eight miles wide, from the coast inland, proceeding northwards; but this wholesale destruction clearly had a fairly well-defined limit westwards. And it did not take him long to perceive that this limit more or less coincided with the boundaries of the major Home lands of Polwarth, Edrom, Blackadder, Wedderburn and the rest, all of whose lairds were riding here with him and their unenthusiastic lord. Obviously, then, the Homes were being deliberately spared from assault by Northumberland—and were aware of it. Why? Presumably so that the invaders' left flank would, in turn, be spared from attack. Which made David consider how genuine was this present sally, how much a mere gesture to keep the Bastard content, with no real hostilities intended? That shrewd individual had probably good reasons for his suspicions of these doubtful allies, and for leaving David himself with them as a sort of watchdog. It was all fairly typical of Borders attitudes and policies, he supposed, where national interests were quite normally subordinate to local and clan allegiances. He gathered that something of the same point-of-view was apt to prevail on the English side of the line also.

He began to doubt whether, in fact, he would see any fighting. He did not rate his chances highly of being able to persuade these Homes to war, however warlike they seemed.

They reached the Blackadder in the Kimmerghame vicinity, when a new development in the situation became apparent. This was that a mounted host, presumably enemy since the Bastard's force had ridden many miles to the west, had recently ridden this way, as evidenced by tracks and horse-droppings and hastily-abandoned farmsteads and cottages. Yet the land here was not burned nor ravaged, whereas all to the east the smoke-clouds continued to rise. Evidently therefore the invading army had divided, for some reason, and part taken this Blackadder valley. This evidently much interested the Home leadership, although none of them actually discussed the matter with David Lindsay.

A few miles further on, in the Bonkyl area, they obtained the answer to any questioning. North of Blanerne, a Lumsden place, the ground sank away to a great sump of marshland, where the Fosterland, Lintlaw and Draden Burns emptied themselves. This was the extensive swamp known as the Billiemire, covering four or five square miles. On a sort of island of firm ground in the midst, protected as by an enormous moat, rose the fortalice of Billie Castle, a remote Douglas hold belonging to Angus. David had heard of the place—indeed it was somewhere near here, in similar marshland, that his friend de la Bastie had been slain by the Homes, fifteen years before.

It was not at the Douglas castle that his present companions drew rein, to stare. At the far side of the mire, to the east, a great cavalry host could be seen to be drawn up, stationary, in ordered ranks. Even at that range, the keen-sighted could discern the prevailing colours of the many banners to be the blue-and-gold of Percy of Northumberland and the blue-and-white of Douglas.

The Homes sat their mounts, considering.

David Lindsay's mind was busy, likewise. This, of course, changed all. There could be no surprise in any force seeking to attack the Dunglass invaders from this direction. Clearly Angus, who knew the country hereabouts almost as well as any Home, had foreseen the danger and blocked off this approach, still ten or more miles from Dunglass, Colbrandspath and Pease Dean. To reach there now the Homes would have to fight and vanquish this host. Whether any similar force would be confronting the Bastard, further north, there was no knowing. But here was challenge indeed. For the enemy, first on the scene, had chosen their position with care and were strongly placed, protected in front and on one flank by all but impassable mire. Any assault on them would be difficult and costly. But, by the same token, theirs was a *defensive* position, difficult to attack from. The inference was obvious. The enemy were warning-off rather than seeking a fight. Undoubtedly they knew with whom they were dealing.

David looked at his companions. "What now?" he asked. He looked past the Lord Home to old Wedderburn, the senior of the Home lairds, and the fiercest, he who had cut off de la Bastie's head to hang at his saddle-bow and be carried to Duns Cross. Any decision made here would be apt to be his rather than his chief's.

"We wait," Wedderburn said briefly.

"Wait? For what?"

"For so long as is required, man!"

"That would be wise, yes," the Lord Home agreed relievedly.

"Wise, my lord? Is wisdom the part we are here to play, today? Are we not here rather to teach the English that it is not wise to invade and savage Scotland?"

"And how would you do that, herald?" Wedderburn demanded grimly. He pointed. "These are in a strong position. They could scarcely be stronger placed. To assail them, on this ground, we would be but throwing our lives away."

"If you assailed them from here, yes. But no need for that. Outflank them. Force them to move. You have miles of land to use. Circle to the south and east," David waved his arm right-abouts, "amongst those banks and ridges. Get behind them, between them and the Eye valley. Aye, and between them and Dunglass and their main army. Then they would *have* to move, or be trapped against this mire."

"You are bold, sir, for a pursuivant! Bold with other men's lives!" Home of Broomhouse, Wedderburn's brother said. "Why should good men die when by sitting here we can gain all that is required?"

"That from a Home! On Home ground!"

"See you, Lindsay," Wedderburn jerked. "We know what we are at, if you do not. We are here to support the Bastard Hamilton, and so King Jamie, are we not? By waiting here, we do just that. We keep that large company yonder of no use to their main host just as surely as if we fought them. More surely. For if we fought and lost, they could rejoin Northumberland, if so be he is at Dunglass. With us here, they dare not. We hold them. Hamilton should thank us!"

There were growls of approval, and some grins, from around them.

David shrugged. "This will be a tale to tell!" he observed. "How Home supports his friends and liege and fights his enemies!"

The growls changed from approval to a kind of menace, but not directed towards the foe.

So they waited. And the enemy waited, an extraordinary situation, there around the Billiemire, as the sun crept round the smoke-filled sky, hour after hour. Both sides dismounted but

293

neither moved any distance from their horses. For such fierce-seeming, heavily-armed folk the improbability of it all was striking.

David Lindsay debated with himself whether he should leave the Homes to their inaction and ride northwards alone, seeking the Hamilton force, to acquaint them with the position—if he could find them. But he decided against this. If he did leave them, these Homes, so reluctant to challenge the enemy, might quite possibly just turn round and ride home, leaving the force opposite free to rejoin and reinforce their main body, to add to the Bastard's and the King's difficulties. Besides, by the time he found the Hamiltons it might well be too late to affect the issue. In a state of impatience and disillusion, he whiled away what seemed to be an endless day.

At long last it was the enemy who made the move, as the sun was casting long shadows amongst the Lammermuir dips and hollows. Stir and mounting across the marshland heralded an orderly forming up into troops and cohorts and then, massed banners at the head, in long column-of-route they left that place. And surprisingly, at least to David Lindsay, they set off *south*-eastwards, not north-eastwards, very distinctly so, and continued in that direction for so long as they remained in sight.

This must mean, surely, that their task here was accomplished and that they no longer needed to protect Northumberland's rear and flank. And the direction taken implied that the Dunglass area was no longer of importance. So presumably Northumberland had now turned back and was heading south again, for England. And would likely be moving fairly fast, for the area he must traverse was devastated and not for lingering in. In other words, whatever had happened in the Dunglass vicinity and on the skirts of Lothian, the great raid was probably over.

This conclusion obviously had been reached by the Homes also, for they too began to pack up and mount, to turn their beasts' heads southwards whence they had come, not to follow the others, their task likewise accomplished evidently.

With no desire to remain in their company any longer, and certainly not to return to Home Castle, David announced that he would leave them, to rejoin the Bastard's force—which would no doubt be strongly harrying the English retiral, if such it was. None took him up on that, and their parting could hardly have been in less mutual esteem.

David knew the territory hereabouts only well enough to reckon that if he followed the Whitadder upwards, west by north, he ought to be on the trail of the Hamilton host—and he could see the long depression of the Whitadder valley, in the Edrom and Blanerne area, from this present position. He rode, thither, alone.

Once by the riverside road he had no difficulty, for nearly four thousand horsemen leave a trail easy to find and follow.

Up into the southern skirts of the Lammermuirs he cantered, glad enough for the action after the long hours of waiting. Quickly the character of the land changed, with the green hills drawing in closer, and now he rode in ever-deepening evening shadows. After about a dozen miles, at Nether Monynut, the tracks he was following turned from the side-valley of the Monynut Water eastwards, to commence the quite major climb over the high ridges of the Monynut Edge. It grew somewhat lighter as he mounted out of the valleys, despite the onset of the dusk, partly because there were fewer shadows up here but also in that the sky ahead was again lit up by flame, eastwards; although to the south, where before it had been so, the evil glow had now died down.

When he began dropping again into the east-facing valleys, with the glare before him outlining the remaining Eweside ridge blackly stark, it was to indicate to him that this new fire must be coming from the Dunglass area itself. When he rode into the valley-floor village of Oldhamstocks, it would have been dark but for the ruddy sky. No doors opened to him from silent church and huddled cot-houses.

He could not see the tracks of thousands of horses now, but did not need to. Surmounting the last ridge, he looked down on the narrow coastal plain, ablaze. The fires did not extend far to the north, towards Dunbar, but southwards they made a more or less continuous line of angry red until the thrust of the hill-mass hid them, where Cove, Colbrandspath, Aikieside, Aldcambus and Redheugh had been set alight. But the largest conflagration was directly below, only a mile away, obviously Dunglass Castle itself, with its castleton and fisher-haven. The smell of burning was strong on the night air.

Descending towards it all, David found the lesser fires of the Hamilton force's camp to the north-west of the burning area, which the prevailing wind kept clear of the smoke. He found the

Bastard enjoying a meal of new-slaughtered beef, of which there was no lack, dead beasts lying everywhere—and not only beasts. Hungry, he was glad to eat as he informed of the Home situation and learned in turn what had transpired here.

Finnart showed little surprise at David's account of the day's doings, indicating that he had expected little else of the Homes, especially when his scouts to southwards had reported no signs of the looked-for parallel thrust towards the enemy, from the Eye valley. But it was all another cord to hang those Homes with in due course, he asserted, grinning. For himself, he had waited, up at Oldhamstocks, not only for the Homes but for King James, who had likewise failed to appear. With his force of less than four thousand quite inadequate to attack Northumberland's main host down here sacking Dunglass, all he could do was to show groups of his people to the enemy in various strengths and positions, in the hope of appearing stronger than he was and so making the English uneasy. He believed that he had been successful in this. Northumberland had in fact not lingered long at Dunglass, nor ventured further north, but presently, after setting all afire, turned back whence he had come. The Bastard seemed quite satisfied with this, even though he had not so much as struck a blow. Now they awaited the King.

David Lindsay sought sleep that night, to the crackle of flames and the wailing of women and children, feeling less than glorious.

In the early morning a courier from James arrived, to announce that the King was on his way down the Vale of Tyne with another four thousand men and hoped to be in the Dunglass area before midday. Hamilton appeared to be quite content to wait for him; but when David protested that they ought to be hot-foot after Northumberland and Angus, harassing their rear if they could do no more, the other shrugged and asked what good that would do? Lindsay's answer that it would at least demonstrate *some* spirit amongst the Scots drew a mocking smile but the permission to take a party of Hamiltons, say five hundred, and do that, if he was so keen on profitless gestures.

David took him at his word—although he found that he had Hamilton of Barncluith as co-commander of this detachment and had little doubt as to whose lead would be followed.

So they set off southwards after the retiring invaders. As the

Bastard said, it was more of a gesture than anything else, for there was really little that they could hope to do. It was a grim business from the start, through devastated country all the way. There was scarcely a house unburned, large or small, castle or hovel, churches, barns, mills, cow-byres likewise, anything which would blaze, growing crops trampled, stock and poultry slaughtered, wells stuffed with bodies, animal and human. It was these last which especially sickened, bodies everywhere, in the villages and farmsteads, in the fields and pastures, in ditches and burns, hanging from trees, the women usually stripped naked, children frequently likewise. As for the survivors, only glimpses could be caught, for such would flee and hide from any armed horsemen soever for long to come. David's party could do nothing about all this, even if they had had time, so comprehensive was the scale of it. They could only press on after the perpetrators.

But these were not readily to be caught up with. They had had a long start and, having savaged the land on the way north, there was little for them to do or to detain them on their return. Also they would expect some retaliation and, sated with slaughter and laden with booty no doubt, they would not be apt to linger

It was not until they reached the lower lands of the Merse, where these began to slope down to the Tweed valley itself, that they made any contact with the enemy. There, in the vicinity of Mordington and Halidon, they came on fresh tracks and many cattle-droppings, which indicated that a fairly large herd had recently been driven this way, branching off a little westwards from the main retiral line—and nobody else was likely to be driving cattle at present but the invaders. So they hurried on, following this more hopeful course, until, surmounting a west-reaching shoulder of Halidon Hill, they saw before them, a bare mile off, a mass of men and beasts moving slowly southwards. How many was hard to assess at that range, but certainly nothing like their own numbers. Thankful for some action at last, the Hamiltons spurred in pursuit.

Their approach was quickly spotted by the cattle-drovers of course, and these no doubt perceiving themselves to be much outnumbered, made no bones about fleeing there and then, abandoning their stolen herd. This was scarcely surprising but what was unanticipated was the direction of their flight, for they rode off almost due westwards, whereas the Scots would have expected them to head either due east for Berwick or south for one of the nearer fords of Tweed, to reach their main army or at least English territory, at the soonest; whereas westwards, hereabouts, would bring them to a difficult U-bend of the lower Whitadder, with steep banks and deep pools, unsuitable for fording. They could well be trapped if they continued in that direction.

Once the group in front drew away from the cattle it could be seen that there would not be more than four score of them. And they rode fast, faster than the pursuers were able to do, indeed, for a smaller company always outpaces a larger; moreover the Hamiltons had been riding at a good pace for over twenty miles by this time, their horses far from fresh. Still, so long as these English continued on that course they would have them, cornered against that difficult stretch of the Whitadder.

This area off the main track of the invading host had been only partially burned. Past the blackened farm-toun of Laigh Cocklaw the two groups pounded in turn, half-a-mile apart. And still the fleeing enemy maintained their lead and their direction. It was no more than a mile now to the Whitadder.

David Lindsay was conjecturing as he spurred. These people looked as though they knew where they were going. Could it be, in fact, that it was *themselves* who were heading for a trap? Being led to what perhaps was a major force of the invaders, in the Whitadder vicinity? It seemed an unlikely spot for such, but there must be some accounting for this odd line of flight. He was about to communicate his apprehensions to Barncluith, at his side, when another thought struck him, occasioned by what his eyes now told him. For into view ahead had just appeared the topmost tower of Edrington Castle, a strong Lauder hold, strategically placed at the very apex of the river's U-bend, on a rocky bluff. Could it be there that their quarry was headed?

He shouted this suggestion to Barncluith, who shrugged.

Soon it was evident that it was indeed towards this castle that the party in front were making—a strange destination, unless it was being held by the English—although so far David had seen no tower or stronghold taken over and occupied, but all burned or made untenable.

Trees and the lie of the land presently hid temporarily both enemy and castle; but when they came into sight again, a mere quarter-of-a-mile off, the situation was resolved. The fleeing party were in fact riding in through the gatehouse arch of the fortalice on its thrusting rock, which was far from burned, indeed with a Douglas banner flying at its tower-head. Even as the Scots approached, the massive doors below the gatehouse clanged shut, the portcullis dropped into position and the draw-bridge rose.

Cursing, denied their quarry at the last moment, the Hamiltons reined up.

"Douglas!" Barncluith snarled. "Douglas there! This Edrington is a Lauder hold."

"Or was," David amended. "I know the Lauders. They hold lands near my Garleton. Indeed they own the Craig of Bass. They do not love the Douglas. So—why this?"

None could answer that.

Frustrated, they drew back out of bow-shot after a warning arrow or two came from the castle battlements, along with shouts and fist-shakings. What to do? Clearly they could by no means take this strong fortalice without cannon, and large cannon at that. David and Barncluith made a circuit and survey of the place, as close as they dared go, and saw no weaknesses. The perimeter wall was fully twenty feet high and clearly well-guarded—the garrison would now be reinforced by some eighty men, moreover. The river itself protected the place on three sides, with a wide moat cutting off the rest. And its people were unlikely to be starved out, for down at the riverside, at its only levellish access but within the curtain-walling, were actually two meal-mills, side by side, using a lade from the Whitadder for power, a highly unusual feature; so presumably there would be grain stored there.

Balked, they returned to their people. There seemed to be nothing that they could usefully achieve there. Many of the Hamiltons seemed more interested in taking over the abandoned herd of cattle than in anything else, Barncluith far from reproving them. It was decided in the end that David and a small escort should return to meet the King and the Bastard and inform them of the situation, while the rest of the force moved on discreetly down to Tweed, to discover the position of Northumberland's main army and whether or not they had yet crossed back into England. No doubt the cattle would go with them.

So, in the late afternoon, David rode north-eastwards again, over Halidon Hill and on through the devastation towards Eyemouth and Coldinghame. At Aytoun he found the royal force, now of some seven or eight thousand, settling for the night in an area blessedly saved from the general ravishment—Aytoun, significantly, being a Home lairdship and had interestingly been spared.

James greeted David warmly and seemed less distressed by all the desolation and suffering than might have been expected. He was angered, however, to hear of the Douglas take-over of Edrington Castle—anything relating to Angus could be calculated to upset him—declaring that this must be put right forthwith. They would move on towards Berwick in the morning, and then deal with the Douglases.

No doubt Northumberland and Angus were well warned of the royal approach in force, and presumably had no desire at this stage to engage in battle, for all were safely within the walled burgh of Berwick, or across Tweed into England well before the arrival of the Scots army. This, for its part, was not equipped with cannon and siege-engines to attempt the conquest of that great fortress town. So, after contenting themselves with making a large demonstration outside the massive walls and bastions of Berwick and its castle, and along the north bank of Tweed nearby, James and the royal host turned and headed westwards, upriver, for its junction with the Whitadder and thereafter northwards to Edrington Castle.

Not that there was in fact anything more that they could do here than at Berwick, for although it was not to be compared with that important citadel, nevertheless it was a very strong place, both as to site and defensive features, and not to be taken without heavy artillery, battering-rams and the like, none of which were available. But James shook his fist at the hold and its defenders and vowed that he would be back, to drive the insolent Douglases from Scottish soil, once and for all. David Lindsay was interested in this rather myopic attitude, for of course the mighty Tantallon Castle, Angus's main seat, was still firmly in that Earl's hands as were other Red Douglas strongholds, with no major campaign mounted against them.

Thereafter, less than triumphantly, the army returned to

Edinburgh. Lindsay was no fire-eater, but he felt the entire affair to have been distinctly feeble—even though his liege-lord and Hamilton of Finnart betrayed no such sentiments.

*　　*　　*

Back at Stirling, however, the Lord Lyon King-of Arms and the Lord Privy Seal, if not others, decided that some more assertive follow-up gesture and protest was required, to convince Henry and the English that such savage invasion and devastation was not to be tamely accepted and should not be repeated. Beaton's nimble wits came up with a two-part offensive, mainly diplomatic and negotiable but also with a cutting-edge, since Henry Tudor was a man more likely to be brought to the one by means of the other. He argued thus:

Henry was much preoccupied at present with his domestic affairs and policies and his ongoing battle with Rome over the denied divorce. Also he was short of money—not as James was but on a vaster scale altogether, his continual foreign wars being enormously costly and his extravagance proverbial. All knew that he was going to break with Rome, not just quarrel with Pope Clement but actually detach England from Holy Church. The English parliament had been debating this for years without coming to a conclusion. But matters were coming to a head. Henry was seeing a great deal of a certain young woman. He had many mistresses of course but this one, Anne Boleyn, was a grand-daughter of the Duke of Norfolk, Earl Marshal of England, and not to be treated in any casual fashion, even by Henry, without provoking dire trouble with the Howards, the most powerful family in his realm. Moreover, she was, Davie's spies assured him, a woman of character and spirit and was insisting on marriage before conceding her favours. Yet recently she had been considerably more free and open in her behaviour with the King—which implied that divorce was near. And since Holy Church was adamant in denying that Henry should put away his Queen Catherine of Aragon, it followed that the break with Rome must be at hand. Archbishop Cranmer of Canterbury was prepared to declare the Church in England independent, with Henry its head, not the Pope, and thereafter to grant him divorce—but the break would first have to be declared by parliament. Thomas Cromwell, who had succeeded Wolsey as Chancellor, was saying that he could be sure of a favourable majority, and the defeat of the Church party, by the spring. Therefore all would probably come to a head then—the break with the Vatican, the setting up of a new Church of England, Henry grabbing the old Church's wealth and lands, divorce declared and marriage with this Anne Boleyn.

In these circumstances even Henry Tudor was unlikely to desire any large-scale military adventures for the next few months, here or on the continent—which must be Scotland's opportunity. No doubt this raid of Northumberland's had been planned to ensure that Scotland lay low for a while. So Scotland should *not* lie low, but rather strike whilst the iron was hot. Then by the said vital spring, vital for Henry, Scotland should be in a position to wring major concessions and a substantial peace treaty out of the Tudor.

All this David Lindsay accepted, for Beaton was always well informed. But what could they do? Scotland was in no state to mount a major invasion of England. James, in deliberately reducing the power of his nobles, had also offended almost all but the Hamiltons—and they were the source of his armed power. It was not only the Douglases and Homes and Hepburns and the like who were resentful. Few of the great lords would willingly lift a hand to aid James to muster a great army.

Beaton admitted it. They could only use the tools that were to hand, therefore. But skilfully used, these might suffice. Not for any major invasion, which anyway would only unite and rouse the English. It must be to strike against carefully selected targets. They did have two tools to hand, two sources of manpower which James had not offended—the Hamiltons themselves and the Highland chiefs. A retaliatory raid on the North of England forthwith, for revenge and plunder, was just the sort of thing that the Bastard of Arran would love to lead—indeed he was already proposing it. If to that was added something much more telling, on another front, Henry could be worried. Where were the English most vulnerable? Where but in Ireland, where their occupying forces were constantly being harassed by uprisings of the Irish petty kings and native chiefs. The Western Highland clans looked on raids on Ireland as almost part of their yearly calendar. It would not be difficult, surely, to persuade say Alexander of Islay, who should be Lord of the Isles, to take a large-scale Highland host across the Irish Sea the short distance to Ulster, there to assail the English garrisons and encourage the

Irish to further rising. The Irish were strong for Holy Church and Henry's feud with Rome anathema to them. Rebellion there could spread like a heather-fire. Nothing would be more apt to worry Henry at this juncture and bring him to talk peace with the Scots.

Lindsay could not deny the validity of this reasoning—if the Highland chiefs would agree.

They would agree, Beaton asserted confidently—especially if they were promised freedom to claw back lands the Campbells of Argyll had stolen from them!

And James? Would he agree?

The other grinned.

19

David Lindsay had scarcely expected to be back at Berwick-on-Tweed so soon, especially to be admitted at its so jealously-guarded gates and to pass through its narrow streets unmolested down to the riverside and across the lengthy wooden bridge which spanned Tweed, scene of so much clash and bloodshed down the centuries, and on to English soil beyond. He had never set foot in England hitherto, and felt a strange excitement to be doing so, however similar the scenery to that which he had just left north of Tweed. Admittedly no smiles or other welcome greeted them—but then nothing of the sort had been evident as they had passed through the Merse either, that land making only slow recovery from its dire experiences of the previous autumn.

He was heading further south still, for Newcastle-on-Tyne, and under a safe-conduct letter signed by Henry of England himself, riding at the head of a well-turned-out and splendidly mounted company of about five score, under the royal Lion Rampant banner of Scotland with, at his side, Master William Stewart, the new Bishop of Aberdeen, and Sir Adam Otterburn of Reidhall, Provost of Edinburgh, as fellow commissioners.

They were on the second stage of Davie Beaton's two-part programme to tie the bloody hands of Henry Tudor, the diplomatic and negotiatory stage. That the situation had reached thus far was witness to the success of the earlier gestures. The Bastard's raid on Northumberland and Cumberland in the late autumn had been sufficiently savage and punitory to please even that ruthless individual, with Finnart boasting more towns, villages and houses destroyed, more folk hanged and more cattle, horses and sheep herded back over the border than even the thousands claimed by the English on *their* raid—however few of these found their way to the original owners. And the Highland expedition to Ireland had been even more successful—and still was, for Alexander of Islay and his fellow chieftains of the Clan Donald federation were still over there, still causing maximum havoc and stirring up the Irish to rise against the occupying English garrisons. It was, almost certainly, to get this stopped and the MacDonalds out of Ireland, that the present treaty negotiations had been hurriedly set in train at Henry's urging as early in 1533 as this March–April. That monarch was indeed having a busy spring.

Beaton undoubtedly would have enjoyed being on this Newcastle mission in person, to seek to complete the success of his planning; but a still more urgent priority had dictated that he should be elsewhere. He had gone to France to complete with King Francis final arrangements for the marriage of King James. The two monarchs had now agreed in principle that the bride should be a French princess, but there remained doubt as to which.

King Francis was still offering his kinswomen Marie de Bourbon, Marie de Guise or Isabeau d'Albret of Navarre. Sir Thomas Erskine had already been to France on this quest, but had come back bemused and confused, unable to give his liegelord any firm guidance on so delicate a matter. Not that James, less than enthusiastic for marriage at all, was in any hurry as to choice, indeed would have used the situation to postpone the entire notion of matrimony. But Beaton had been persistent. The succession must be ensured, if possible; the realm's wellbeing demanded it. A French match was much the best. So these three French ladies must be more carefully surveyed, much more thoroughly than Sir Thomas Erskine had done, and the best choice selected. Beaton was on friendly terms with King

Francis, and also the Duke of Albany, who could be helpful. It would all have to be done with much care and tact; for she who was selected had to be presentable, suitable to be queen in Scotland and above all, fertile, capable of bearing the required heir to the throne. It remained unstated that she must be reasonably attractive, physically, to James. Beaton considered himself to be apt for the task as any.

So, before departing for France, he had advised James to appoint this trio as commissioners for the English treaty bargaining, Lindsay, Bishop Stewart and Provost Otterburn, and schooled them fairly closely as to their role.

William Stewart, who had been Provost of Lincluden Collegiate establishment, and now appointed not only Bishop of Aberdeen but Treasurer of the Realm, was one of Beaton's own protégés, typical of the men he was seeking to manoeuvre into positions of power in Church and state, youngish, hard-headed, cool, shrewd, more politician than pastor. When old Bishop Dunbar of Aberdeen, uncle of the present Chancellor, had died, there had been murmurings at the appointment of this quite junior cleric, of no especially illustrious background, to one of the most senior bishoprics in the land—done in the name of the Primate, Archbishop of St. Andrews, of course—but like so many of Davie's contrivances it had gone through. Lindsay did not particularly like the man but recognised that he might well be a useful ally in any debate or argument. Sir Adam Otterburn was a very different character, bluff, hearty and jovial in manner, but alleged to be cunning, of middle years, and with keen grey eyes. He made good company—although Beaton had warned David not to trust him in all things. Lindsay was a little uncertain as to who, if any, was leader of this trio; but as Lord Lyon, one of the great officers of state and the King's personal representative, he almost certainly ranked first, however powerful the Bishop-Treasurer.

This was their third day on the road and they were due at Alnwick that night. Alnwick Castle was the principal seat of the Earl of Northumberland, now English Chief Warden of the Marches, the same who had led last autumn's invasion of Scotland. It would be as strange as riding unchallenged through Berwick to sleep under the walls of the Percy's castle.

In the event they slept *within* the Percy's walls, for on the outskirts of Alnwick, at dusk, they were met by the Earl himself, who announced stiffly that such distinguished visitors must on no account put up in any mere hospice or hostelry but should accept the hospitality of his poor house—this from the man who had laid waste half of Berwickshire. He was a tall, thin, foxy-faced individual, unimpressive as to appearance.

The same could not be said of his castle, at least, an enormous establishment, almost a town of itself behind its extensive perimeter-walls, nothing like any Scots castle the travellers had ever seen, scarcely a fortalice or stronghold at all, more of a palace, even more palatial than royal Linlithgow. The visitors eyed its proud magnitude rather askance. No doubt this reception was part of a sort of conditioning for the Scots, preparatory to the negotiations, an impression reinforced on them when Northumberland informed that it had been expressly ordered by King Henry himself. Presumably thereafter the Earl felt that he had done as much as could be expected of him, in meeting and quartering these wretched Scots, for after ushering them through his august portals and handing them over to his chamberlain, they saw no more of him. They were all, however, excellently housed and fed.

In the morning they rode on southwards, their company, formerly seeming quite imposing, now looking a mere undistinguished handful, hemmed in front and rear by what amounted almost to an army of Northumbrians, the huge concourse led by the Percy and a glittering entourage of lords, knights, squires and clerics. The Scots, in fact, rather gave the appearance of captives of a conquering host—which was no doubt intended.

By Coquetmouth and Morpeth they came at length to the shallow valley of the Northumbrian Tyne, so very different from the East Lothian river of that name, and the large walled town and port of Newcastle, a place they found comparable with Berwick in situation and size although less strongly defended and further from the sea. Here, in the late afternoon, the visitors underwent another change in conditions, being conducted to distinctly poor and cramped quarters in a monastic establishment of the Grey Friars and then left abruptly by Northumberland and their resplendent escort, without instructions or further guidance, as it were to kick their heels. In bare and basic premises, very different from Alnwick Castle, after eating plain fare, they passed the night.

And therein they spent the next day also, seemingly ignored if not forgotten, expecting all the time to be led and introduced to their opposite numbers, Henry's commissioners. But nothing of the sort transpired and enquiries from the sub-prior in charge of their lodging produced no information as to who these persons were, where they were to be found or even whether they had yet reached Newcastle—although the negotiations were timed to start that day. All they elicited from the sub-prior was that it was inadvisable for the visitors to venture out into the streets in case they were attacked by the citizens, who had no love for the Scots.

Another night passed and a second day and still they were left cooped up like prisoners and uninformed. By late afternoon, impatient and angry, Davie demanded that he should be escorted forthwith to wherever the Earl of Northumberland was lodged, to protest at the delay and the treatment of the King of Scots' representatives and to discover the situation. The sub-prior declared that he had no authority to do this nor to allow any of the Scots to be endangered in the town; but that he would send one of his monks to his lordship of Northumberland to enquire as to their disposal.

This quest, if it were indeed put in hand, produced no evident results.

It was in mid-evening that a clattering and shouting outside the monastic gates heralded some development. An officer, dressed in the English royal livery adorned with Tudor Roses, marched in on them as they sat at their frugal meal and announced in ringing tones that His Excellency Master Thomas Cromwell, Principal Secretary of State to His Majesty, summoned the representatives of Scotland to his presence.

Staring, at the newcomer and at each other, the three Scots found words slow in coming. The Bishop pursed thin lips and Otterburn hooted. David spoke.

"Summons, sirrah? Did I hear you aright? Your Master Cromwell *summons* us to his presence? The ambassadors of the King of Scots!"

The officer nodded. "Those were my instructions, yes."

"Then, sir, I must bid you return whence you come and say that King James's envoys greet Master Cromwell and will be glad to meet him in due course. At a convenient time and on suitable invitation."

The other frowned. "I was to bring you forthwith," he said. "Then your are now better informed."

"Off with you, laddie," Sir Adam advised, grinning. "While we finish this, this monkish banquet!"

"You, you refuse to accompany me? To His Excellency?"

"We do."

For moments the officer glared. Then abruptly he turned on his heel and stamped out.

The sub-prior wrung his hands.

The trio at the table were almost equally offended by the ill manners of this summons as they were impressed by the fact that it apparently came from Thomas Cromwell himself. That Henry should have sent his redoubtable chief adviser and evil genius to the negotiating table, the most powerful man in England now next to the King, was a thought to consider. That he was starting out in this fashion was likewise thought-provoking.

They debated what their further reaction should be. If a revised and acceptable invitation arrived, should they accept, at this hour? Or should they declare that they would confer next day? Bishop Stewart pointed out that if they further piqued Cromwell, he might well keep them waiting here for long enough. Having made their gesture, it would probably be wiser to go meet him now.

They had not long to wait—which seemed to indicate that the English commissioners were installed somewhere nearby. The officer reappeared, but now he had with him a cleric, who announced that he was Master Felix St. Fort, a secretary to His Excellency the Chief Secretary and Vicar-General—this last a new title for the Scots. His Excellency hoped that the King of Scots' envoys had enjoyed their repast and invited them to take wine with him in the castle, preparatory to their discussions on the morrow—this said in measured, almost fruity tones.

David conceded that, since the night was yet young, they would be pleased to come.

They were less than pleased, however, when outside the monastery they were lined up by the officer within tight files of the guard of torch-bearing men-at-arms, and marched at a brisk pace through the streets—this allegedly to protect them from the fury of the mob, which remained in fact unseen.

It was not far to the strange castle which gave the town its name, new only in that it was not the first on the site, and strange in that its walls rose directly from the town streets, not surmounting any rock or knoll, four-square and very tall, seven storeys of it, and in the darkness looming enormously hostile, like some great prison into which the captives were on their way to be incarcerated.

This impression was enhanced by the clanging iron doors and portcullis, the shouted challenges of the guards and the armed men who lined the steep mural stairway so that there was scarcely room for the visitors to climb up. However, at the third floor, past more scowling sentries, they were ushered into a large and well-lit chamber, where a great fire of coals supplemented the many flickering candles, the walls hung with colourful arras and the stone floor strewn with skins. Here a number of men lounged at ease around a long table littered with flagons, beakers and wine-cups.

"The Scotch envoys, my lords," their cleric guide announced.

Some of the loungers rose to their feet at this introduction, but three most noticeably did not. David knew two of them, the Earl of Northumberland, and Doctor Fox who had been an English envoy to the Scots court, an elderly stooping man with a long nose and rat trap jaws, never known to smile. The third was otherwise, a thick-set, bullet-headed individual, swarthy, coarse of feature, red of face, plainly dressed compared with the other two but with a grinning air of authority. In the circumstances, this could be none other than Thomas Cromwell.

For a few moments nobody spoke, as both sides eyed each other. Then Fox cleared his throat.

"Lindsay of The Mount I know. And Sir Adam Otterburn. The other, the clerk, I know not," he said. He obviously was addressing the thick-set man, and made his statement sound anything but complimentary.

"He is Master William Stewart, my lord Bishop of Aberdeen. Sir Adam Otterburn is Provost of the city of Edinburgh and lately Lord Advocate; and I am His Grace's Lord Lyon King-of-Arms," David returned, level-voiced. "You Dr. Fox, *I* know. My lord of Northumberland all know. Others are strangers to us." That was the best that he could do at the moment.

"One of you is probably the man Cromwell, who invited us to

wine?" Otterburn added, for his part, looking round the entire company enquiringly.

There was a profound hush. Then the red-faced man slammed a hand on the table-top, but barked a laugh. "I am Cromwell," he jerked. "No lord—but at your Scots lordships' service! You sound dry, as though needing a drink. Does the good friars' hospitality fail? Come—sit." The man's voice was as thick and plebeian as his person.

They moved forward to the table, David for one the more wary over the other's reaction.

Only under such as Henry Tudor perhaps could a man in Thomas Cromwell's position have risen to his present heights. The son of a Putney blacksmith and no cleric, without the Church's educational advantages, from being a mere merchant's clerk he had been sent to the counting-house of an English factory in Amsterdam, and thence to Rome, where he had made sufficiently good use of his time amongst the churchmen to be recommended to Cardinal Wolsey on his return home. That ambitious and able prelate and Chancellor, recognising a like spirit, had in due course made Cromwell his confidential secretary. So the younger man learned statecraft and the like in the toughest school, was privy to secrets which could raise or damn even the great and powerful, and inevitably came to act as go-between with his master and King Henry—who also came to recognise his abilities. He was inserted into parliament, where he was very useful on occasion. And on Wolsey's fall he defended him, in parliament, to great effect. But not sufficiently to save the Cardinal from Henry's wrath and spleen over failure to gain him his divorce. However the King did not want to lose both useful servants at the same time and took Cromwell into his own employ. Now he was not only chief Secretary of State but a sort of lay inspector of all Church institutions, properties and privileges, with the odd style of Vicar-General, assessing the wealth and personages in bishoprics, abbeys, monasteries and lands, a position of enormous influence in present circumstances. None was now more useful and close to his monarch than Thomas Cromwell, the blacksmith's son.

"You have been delayed in reaching Newcastle, sir?" David asked, pouring himself wine. "We had looked for you . . . earlier."

"Scarcely delayed, no. My lord of Northumberland took us

310

hunting. Dr. Fox is a great huntsman, although you might not think it to look at him! Myself, I find my distractions otherwhere!" That was said with a fleeting glance at the other two English commissioners.

David recognised the challenge implicit in those seemingly casual comments. This man was entirely sure of himself, despised both the aristocratic earl and the academic diplomat and their attitudes, showed who was in command here, and indicated that he had no hesitation in keeping the Scots waiting if so he pleased.

The quiet Bishop Stewart it was who answered. "We were grateful for the opportunity to rest and refresh ourselves, after the long journey." That lie was calmly declared.

Cromwell looked at the speaker assessingly.

"We hope that your hunting was sufficiently successful to outweigh your reluctance, Mr. Secretary?" Otterburn added, not to be outdone. "Putting you in good fettle for our discussions."

"That fettle you will discover in due course!" the other snapped back. Then he shrugged burly shoulders. "Not that great discussion will be required, I think. For the issues are straightforward, are they not? We both desire peace and an end to profitless bickering, no?"

"The peace, yes. It is the price to be paid for that peace which will require the fettle in discussion," David said.

"So-o-o! You Scots have come to haggle? To chaffer? Merchants, eh? Despite your so-lordly styles. I remind you, *I* was bred a merchant's clerk and know the trade—even if others do not!" Again the glance at Northumberland and Fox.

David perceived that there would be tough bargaining ahead of them. But he also thought that he perceived perhaps a chink in the English armour. There was no love lost between King Henry's commissioners, and this might be exploited. Also Cromwell was emphasising his humble origins overmuch, which could represent an aspect of weakness.

"Trade requires buyer and seller both," Otterburn observed. "*We* have much to sell. If you have the wherewithal to pay!"

"We are not here in a marketplace, sirrah!" Fox declared frostily. "*We* are here representing the King's Majesty, to conduct business of state. In, in dignity. However you deal with such matters in Scotland!"

Cromwell smiled broadly. "What have you to sell that England needs to buy?" he asked. "We have heard that Scotland is scarcely rich!"

"Yet you are here to bargain. The Secretary of State himself!" David rejoined.

"We have much that you need," Otterburn went on. "Your king desires peace on his northern borders, while he battles with Rome. He desires peace in Ireland—at which King James might assist. He desires recognition of a divorce from his queen, and his remarriage, from a monarch loyal to the Vatican. He wishes our liege-lord to wed his daughter, the Princess Mary, and an end to talk of a French match. England requires Scots wool, and could buy it instead of stealing it! England is . . ."

Bishop Stewart cleared his throat. "We are here, by invitation, to drink wine, are we not?" he suggested warningly. "Rather than to debate terms at this present. Tomorrow will serve for that."

David agreed with that. The hearty Otterburn might be forcing the pace somewhat. A more methodical approach than this was called for. "No doubt we shall rehearse all such matters with clearer heads in the morning," he declared. "Unless our English friends are going hunting again!"

Cromwell hooted. "Well said! The morrow it is. But, on your couches this night, before sleep, consider this. King Henry *requires* none of these things, however desirable they may be or may not be. Whereas his nephew King James, does require peace. His lords are in revolt—not only Angus and Bothwell and Cassillis, others also. Some are imprisoned—Eglinton, Sinclair, even Moray, we hear. Others sulk in their castles. I note that none such are here with you today! So James cannot raise an army of any size. Nor can he dare war, for fear of who may rise behind him. His treasury is empty, so that he had to get the Pope in Rome to command Beaton to give him the Church's gold, to pay his debts. He *requires* to sell his wool! He needs a wife with a large dowry; any the French can offer could be outdone by King Henry. And Highland barbarians, tasting their power, love not Lowland Scotland, and could slaughter and slay in more than Ireland, if sufficiently . . . induced! Think of these things my friends, ere you sleep."

That was plain talking indeed from a plain man, and all too true. The Scots recognised it, as they sipped their wine, even though Otterburn snorted and waved a dismissive hand.

The lists then were marked out for the morrow.

Fairly soon thereafter the visitors took their leave. The Earl of Northumberland had not said a word throughout.

Next forenoon, back in the same chamber of the castle, in a very different atmosphere and mood, they all sat down to business, formal, stiff, wary—although that last hardly seemed to apply to Thomas Cromwell. From the start he made the running, taking the line that, despite the fact that Henry it was who had called for this conference and possible treaty, England as it were held all the cards. They were here because his English Majesty, at last to be freed from the bonds of an unfruitful and deplorable marriage and to rewed, also about to take over the headship of the Church in England, with all its shamefully-gained power and wealth, desired to mark his felicity and satisfaction by a gesture of goodwill and affection towards his nephew of Scotland, and put an end to disagreements between the greater nation and the lesser.

He, King Henry, therefore proposed not any mere truce but a full and enduring treaty of peace between England and Scotland, to endure indeed for the lifetime of whichever monarch should first die—if not in fact for longer. This treaty of peace, goodwill, mutual trade and general harmony, conditional only on the most generous of terms.

Silent the Scots waited.

Firstly, the savage Highland forces to be withdrawn from Ireland forthwith, and undertaking given that they would not return. Secondly, that the Lady Mary Tudor should be wed to the Scots king at an early date, a substantial dowry to be negotiated. Thirdly, that King James should pronounce his recognition of the divorce from Queen Catherine and the marriage to the Lady Anne, and should inform the other princes of Christendom of that recognition and acclaim. Fourthly, that King James and his advisers should now consider a like rejection of the insolent shackles of Rome and declare the independence of the Church in Scotland. And lastly, that the thieves and robbers of the Scots Border Marches, especially the West March Armstrongs, should be restrained from raiding into England and due punishment and reparation made for their ravages.

Perhaps it was strange that it was this last, the least significant and far-reaching in fact, which should have the effect of

313

raising the Scots' temperatures almost to boiling point; but after Northumberland's so recent savageries in Scotland, such a stipulation seemed almost beyond belief. Otterburn half-rose out of his chair in angry protest, fists clenched. David drew a long quivering breath, but spoke before Sir Adam could find words.

"We . . . we can only believe that these terms which you have put forward are scarcely to be taken seriously," he said, seeking to keep his voice under control, "judging by that last! The folly of it! This lord," and he pointed to Northumberland, "this lord himself led an invasion into our land only a few months ago, which outdid, by a score of times and more such damage as the Armstrongs and their like may have wrought in their reivings— which, as you know well, have been part of the Borders way of living, on both sides, for centuries. If this is an example of how you seek to bargain, then we may as well leave this table here and now!"

"Aye—I say more!" Otterburn burst out. "It is bad enough to have to sit at a table with that murderer of women and bairns, there smirking! He who has boasted that he left no single tower, farmstead, house or cot unburned, or a tree without its ill fruit of hanging bodies. Without having to listen to claims for damage and punishment for a few cattle-stealing Borderers! I say that we should halt this talking here, and return to Scotland."

The Bishop raised an episcopal-ringed hand. "Unsuitable and reprehensible as that item was, I would point out that there were other references more important and no less obnoxious," he said levelly. "This of seeking Scotland's rejection of the authority of Holy Church, for instance. Not to be so much as considered."

"Ha—there speaks one who *must* so speak!" Cromwell observed, dismissively. "Lest he lose his mitre and wealth! As for the other, my lord of Northumberland's excursion into Scotland was no reiving raid but a duly authorised strategy by the chief Warden of the Marches, in retaliation for numberless Scots assaults on our territories, at the behest of His Majesty's Privy Council—an entirely different matter." He shrugged. "It is partly to end the need for further such gestures that His Majesty has called this conference."

David drew another breath. "This, sir, I would point out, is *not* a conference called by the King of England, but a possible negotiation between the representatives of the King of England and the King of Scots, with a view to proclaiming a treaty of peace. There is a notable difference."

"Call it what you may, Sir David. It comes to the same in the end."

"I think not, sir—since the end is either a treaty, or none. And on the style of your present submissions, it is like to be none!"

"Then we are but wasting our time," Fox declared. "We are not here to split hairs over nice wording and empy phrases."

"You will pay heed to our Doctor!" Cromwell added, but mockingly. "If you do not like our words and phrases, my friends, let us hear yours."

David glanced at Stewart. Was there any point in going further with these people? They seemed as inflexible as they were arrogant. Yet Cromwell was no fool, as his whole career proved. He had presumably been sent to negotiate, as had they themselves. This attitude could be only a preliminary bargaining stance designed to upset them and so impair their judgement.

The Bishop nodded as though he read David's mind. "We have our own terms," he agreed.

David had notes but scarcely required to consult them. In view of the English attitude, he enunciated the Scots headings more baldly than he might have done. All raids on Scotland were to cease, and reparations be made for damage done in the late invasion. Harassment of Scots shipping and traders was to cease forthwith. The Earls of Angus and Bothwell were to be returned to the justice of the King of Scots, as others of the King's enemies who had fled his realm. The long-trumpeted assertions of the Archbishops of York to spiritual hegemony over the Scottish Church were to be disclaimed—not difficult if the Church in England was no longer under Rome. The terms Lord Paramount of Scotland and Lord Protector of Scotland, used by English kings for centuries, were to be discontinued, Scotland having been an entirely independent kingdom always. All pensions paid by King Henry to subjects of King James were to cease, and no further interference in the affairs of the Scottish realm be permitted. The castle of Edrington in the East Merse, presently unlawfully occupied by Douglas and English invaders, along with the premises known as the Caw Mills, were

315

to be returned to the Lauder owners forthwith. These, the requirements of the King of Scots.

For a little there was silence around that table, save for the scraping of the quills of clerks sitting at another table and taking notes. Then, without consulting his colleagues, Cromwell spread his stubby-fingered hands.

"We have heard you with more patience than you heard me!" he said. "Your claims, to be sure, lack all reality and are no basis for any negotiation. But they will be duly considered, as you will consider ours. Who knows, some might be possible to grant." He smiled, as though that was only a pious hope. "Now—as to concessions. We have exchanged demands. What is there that each side might possibly concede, if such concession aided a settlement? I say only possibly. You will agree that some such indication would be useful to our further and private considerations, and save time?"

David nodded.

"Very well. Here are some that King Henry might be prevailed upon to accede to—*might*, I say. Further military incursions to cease, so long as this applied to both realms. Certain payments to be made to the Scots Treasury, as a gesture of goodwill not in any reparations for my lord of Northumberland's expedition—for anything such would be but cancelled by our similar demands from the Armstrongs. The Archbishop of York's claims might be foregone, in present circumstances. Also certain styles and titles modified. Shipping might be protected on the high seas, but only on condition that Scottish pirates such as the man Wood and the brothers Barton were restrained from attacking English ships. These might be considered."

The Scots exchanged glances. These were, on the whole, better than they had anticipated. Which in itself was suspicious, perhaps?

"Come—what have you to say to that? And what may *you* concede?" Cromwell challenged.

The Bishop it was who answered. "We stated our moderate requirements, sir. So we do not reduce these by seeming concessions. We can but assure you that Scotland will not be unhelpful in attaining a settlement by refusing to yield on a minor matter here or there."

"Your are grudging, Sir Priest. As, for instance?"

316

"His Grace could possibly request the return from Ireland of MacDonald of Islay and his people . . ."

"Request! King Henry does not *request* his lords, he commands! Is this the best that you can offer?"

David added a suggestion, something Stewart could scarcely say, as a prelate loyal to Rome. "King James might agree to recognise King Henry's divorce and remarriage," he said. James had indeed already more or less assumed this, since there was nothing which he could do to change matters—nor did the matter greatly concern him.

"And so inform other princes?" That was quick.

"It may be that could follow." Clearly this issue assumed an importance to the English, or at least to Henry, unlooked for by the Scots.

"Very well. If that is the best that you can say, we shall adjourn and consider. Tomorrow we shall meet again." Abruptly, the man stood, pushed the chair, and strode to the door and out.

Otterburn gobbled in astonishment and offence, and David all but protested, at this extraordinary way of conducting negotiations; but since such protest could only be made to Fox and Northumberland, he forbore. Bowing stiffly to the Englishmen, he led the way out.

Nevertheless, back at the Grey Friars, the Scots, on consideration, were far from depressed, however much they deplored their opposite numbers' behaviour. It seemed, indeed, as though much that they had expected to have to fight for was going to be granted. And the English demands, however arrogantly put, were on the whole less difficult than they might have been. Admittedly nothing had been said or conceded about Angus and Bothwell, nor Edrington Castle, two matters on which James was adamant. And, of course, the suggestion that Scotland should also break with Rome was not to be considered for a moment. But their other requirements, the cessation of raiding and of attacks on shipping, the end of the ridiculous York claims over the Scots Church, the English kings' pretentious titles, and the resumption of trade, appeared to be conceded—with some unspecified financial payment offered into the bargain. That left only the question of the Princess Mary's marriage not touched upon—which to be sure was not to be contemplated, with reports of the lady being plain in the extreme, a

317

matter important to James, and a French match more or less decided on.

The Scots commissioners sought their couches in a better frame of mind.

The next day's session, although no more satisfactory as regards procedure, with Cromwell acting as though he were in command of a class of students, and ignorant ones at that, confirmed the Scots' conclusions of the night before. King Henry must want this peace treaty quite urgently.

It came down then to the four outstanding issues—the marriage; the Angus and Bothwell repatriation; the yielding up of Edrington Castle; and the secession of the Scots Church from Rome. On these Cromwell would not budge, nor would the Scots.

The sitting was fairly brief. This time, before Cromwell could repeat yesterday's tactics, David proposed adjournment for further consideration. Grimly the others could not but accede.

Not that there was really anything for them to consider. On these four items the Scots could by no means give way. James and Davie Beaton, apart from others, would never concede any of them.

The next day they were informed by their sub-prior that the English commissioners would not be available for discussion. Whether it was more hunting, or just teaching the Scots a lesson, was not vouchsafed.

The day after they were still left to their own devices—which, within the confines of that small monastery, were limited to say the least. When in late afternoon, it was apparent that no call was forthcoming, David sent a message to the castle declaring that if a session was not held the next morning, preferably here in the Grey Friars' monastery, he and his colleagues would return to Scotland for conference with King James and his advisers.

That provided the expected summons, but once again to the castle. And there, with no apologies nor explanations for delay, Cromwell, after making it clear that there was no weakening in the English position, announced that he was a very busy man with many responsibilities and must return to London forthwith. Their conference should resume in one month's time—when it was to be hoped that the Scots would have come to their senses. He thereupon made one of his purposeful exits, an expert at having the last word.

His two so-silent colleagues hurried off after him, as the clerks, who had scarcely begun their note-taking, stared, at a loss.

So it was dismissed and back to Stirling for the Scots.

*   *   *

As it transpired, and as David had recognised, there was really nothing for them to debate with James and his Privy Council, as distinct from their reporting. Although most were gratified at the progress made, there was to be no weakening on their position as to the issues remaining. James was inflexible about Angus. Bothwell's treachery might be overlooked if need be, if not forgotten. But the Red Douglas was different. All James's life he had suffered at the hands of Angus; now he would have his revenge. He saw Edrington Castle's surrender in the same light, for the Douglases were holding it in the English interest. As for the proposal of an English marriage, this was still further negatived by the arrival of a messenger from Davie Beaton in France, informing that King Francis was now urging marriage with his kinswoman, Marie de Bourbon, daughter of the Duke of Vendôme. The Lady Marie was not uncomely, of a good form and a fertile family and should make a suitable match for King James. Beaton had sent a portrait by his courier, the artist painting an attractive picture of a plump-featured, well-built, smiling young woman with prominent breasts. James, although still less than enthusiastic, decided that he might do much worse in the circumstances. He sent the messenger back with a gift of jewellery for the lady and a provisional suggestion to wed. As to any break with Rome, none, even those like David Lindsay most critical of the corruption within Holy Church, considered for a moment taking any parallel action with the English. After all, it was not so much the reform of corruption which was motivating Henry but anger and spleen over the divorce, ambition to rule all himself and greed for the Church's great wealth.

So David and his fellow commissioners received no new instructions for their further negotiations, no major conciliatory gestures, save in some small matters already more or less conceded—not from Scots sources that is. But from England, during this month's interval, came a pointed and fairly typical Tudor gesture of persuasion—a lightning and particularly bloody raid on Teviotdale by a force under Sir Robert Fenwick, one of Northumberland's lieutenants. The fury this aroused at Stirling had a contrary effect from what was presumably intended. That this raid coincided with Henry's marriage ceremony to Anne Boleyn did nothing to commend the latter to the Scots; and James considered countermanding the tentative agreement that he would recognise the divorce and remarriage of his uncle and inform other rulers that he had done so. But since a peace treaty was as needful as ever for Scotland, it was decided that this rejection should not be emphasised but might be kept in reserve as a possible bargaining counter.

As an aid to the commissioners it was proposed that they should take with them, on their return to Newcastle, Monsieur de Bevois, the French ambassador, an able and friendly individual. His presence might exert a beneficial influence on Cromwell, who would be concerned not to offend King Francis, especially over the marriage proposals. A couple of days before they were due to ride, however, news arrived from England which rather made such persuasion redundant. King Henry, presumably as part of his triumph over poor Queen Catherine, or perhaps as some sort of flourish towards his new bride—who was known to be far gone with child by him—made a declaration that his former marriage having been no true marriage, it followed therefore that his daughter by that marriage, Mary, was in fact illegitimate and should on all occasions be recognised as such. This extraordinary statement, which could only confirm the impression that Henry was in some respects mad, could scarcely be expected to make any easier Cromwell's remit to try to marry the unfortunate young woman to the King of Scots.

The month's interval, therefore, far from improved the situation.

The Scots deliberately delayed their return to Newcastle for two days beyond the stipulated date, in retaliation for their own treatment earlier. Even so, their English counterparts did not put in an appearance for still a further couple of days, so the gesture fell notably flat.

There were no apologies from Cromwell and Dr. Fox—the Earl of Northumberland appeared to have been dispensed with, no doubt so that he would not have to answer difficult questions about Fenwick's recent raid. He was no loss to either side, for he had hardly uttered a word previously. Cromwell, who greeted de Bevois a deal more affably than he did the Scots, appeared to be

320

in a brisk and businesslike frame of mind, adopting from the start the attitude that all was more or less settled and that all that was now required was to agree a few outstanding details and sign the treaty. The Scots intimation that this was not quite the situation was made therefore to seem the more querulous and unhelpful.

For his part, David first made strong and vehement protest about the raid on Teviotdale since they had last met—to be countered by the almost casual assertion that this was just one more of the reivings and forays of these Borderers, something which might be expected from the Armstrongs, for instance, almost at any time. Stung, David opted for bluntness thereafter. Without any diplomatic preamble, which obviously would be wasted on this man, he stated that the Scots position was unchanged. What had been tentatively agreed previously was accepted by King James. But the four outstanding items remained, on which they were instructed not to compromise—King James would not marry the Lady Mary, the more definitely in that she was now disgraced and lowered in status from a princess; the Scots Church would not break with Rome; Edrington Castle and the Caw Mills must be evacuated forthwith; and the Earl of Angus must be returned to Scotland to answer for his misdeeds—although an exception might be made of the Earl of Bothwell, a lesser offender, who could return under pardon so long as he promised to refrain from all futher acts inimical to his liege-lord.

Cromwell's reaction was less fierce than might have been expected. He pooh-poohed these assertions, still seeming to treat them as bargaining points rather than final stances, and proceeded to whittle away at them, even when the Scots reiterated their finality. However, when de Bevois sought permission to speak, and announced that the King of France had agreed that his kinswoman Marie de Bourbon should marry the King of Scots, and that their betrothal would be officially announced shortly, it left even Thomas Cromwell without the wherewithal for riposte. And when the Frenchman added that His Most Christian Majesty most strongly advised King James not to consider any possible disloyalty to the Pope and Holy Church, the English position was still further prejudiced. In essence there remained therefore only the two Douglas matter of Angus and Edrington Castle.

It was, on the face of it, strange that the English should

consider these points as of major importance; yet on them Cromwell refused to budge. They were in fact comparatively minor matters in the affairs of both nations, and yet here they were seeming to produce the final stumbling-block. When neither side would yield, Cromwell declared another adjournment. Whether it was the presence of the Frenchman or no, he was less cavalier in his manner than heretofore.

Back in the monastery the Scots debated long. It seemed absurd to hold up this so desirable peace treaty for the sake of Angus and one small castle. Yet they were there in the name of King James, and these were the issues on which James was most determined. He was the monarch, and they just could not go back and tell him that on these they had capitulated. On the other hand, to return without the treaty, after all the rest had been gained, would be folly. In the end, they came to the conclusion that the only gesture they might risk making was to concede that Angus need not be forcibly returned to Scotland, if he elected to remain in England as an English subject—since it was apparently Henry's contention that he would not and could not deliver up one of his subjects, as Angus had become, to a foreign power. This concession made on condition that Edrington was yielded up. And of course, if Angus did return at any time to his native land, he would have to stand trial. This was the best that they could do, and they hoped that not only Cromwell but James would accept it.

It proved, in fact, sufficient, when at the next sitting Cromwell presumably saw it as a face-saver and conceded the surrender of Edrington and the Caw Mills, with the proviso that the Douglas and English occupiers thereof should be granted safe conduct into England.

So, suddenly, after so long and grievous a struggle, the thing was done. Only, lest he seem to have yielded too much, Cromwell insisted that he—and presumably the Scots also—were only competent to sign the peace treaty as it were tentatively. They would therefore commit the two nations to it for one year only, by their own signatures, although they recommended jointly that it should apply for the period of the two monarchs' reigns, to be ended on the demise of whichever died first; although it was hoped that it would then be renegotiated; it was unsuitable to commit a new monarch on either side. The clerks would draw up these terms.

322

Two days later, then, with minimal ceremony, the commissioners signed the two copies of this momentous treaty of peace between the realms—peace but scarcely love, for they parted thereafter in no more friendly fashion than they had started, their farewells less than cordial.

For his part, as they rode northwards from Newcastle, David Lindsay wondered how worth it all their efforts had been, and whether indeed the treaty would hold. Henry Tudor was namely as a breaker of truces; would a full treaty be sacrosanct? Only, he imagined, whilst it suited Henry's convenience.

Back at Stirling, James was not happy about the Angus concession, but reluctantly agreed to endorse it, along with the other terms. He was cheered by the news which arrived not long afterwards that the new Queen of England had been delivered of the child on which so much depended. But it was a girl, not the son Henry longed for, and he was reported to be beside himself with disappointment and anger, the poor mother almost as unpopular as had been her predecessor. The baby was to be called Elizabeth.

James was elated.

20

The court at Stirling was in a stir. Four arrivals ensured that. Davie Beaton was the first to come, back from France, full of news. Pope Clement the Seventh was dead, and had been succeeded by a very tough character, Alessandro Farnese, to be called Paul the Third, who was taking a much stronger line with the reformers and heretics who were plaguing Holy Church, and demanding vigorous action against English Henry from all the rulers of Christendom. Also he informed that the Duke of Albany had died lacking male offspring—this left the Bastard's half-brother, the Earl of Arran, undoubted heir to the Scots throne until James produced a lawful child, a situation which made the royal marriage even more urgent. On this subject, Beaton rather ruefully confessed very confidentially to David Lindsay that Marie de Bourbon was in fact considerably less good-looking and attractive than implied by the portrait he had sent; but she was a pleasant-enough female and King Francis was very anxious for the marriage to take place, and quickly.

The next arrivals, only a day or two later, were from England, surprisingly from Henry himself, the Lord William Howard, brother of the Duke of Norfolk, and Master William Barlow, Bishop-Elect of St. Asaphs. These revealed that Henry, despite the peace treaty agreements, had not changed. Howard, who was a son of that 'auld crooked carle' Surrey, the victor of Flodden-field, and so scarcely likely to be popular in Scotland, brought James as gift from his uncle the Order of the Garter, to celebrate the said treaty. But at the same time he pressed anew for the marriage of the Lady Mary to James, officially illegitimate or not, promising an almost unlimited dowry. And Barlow came to further urge a break with Rome, bringing with him details of the vast wealth Henry was garnering in taking over the bishoprics, churches, abbeys and monasteries in England, a magnificent windfall which James might duplicate in Scotland. It seemed as though all the bargaining and negotiations at Newcastle could be ignored, as far as Henry Tudor was concerned.

Then the fourth arrival, while the Englishmen were still at Stirling, was none other than the Papal Legate, Bishop Antonio Campeggio, back again, sent by the new Pope Paul, his remit this time to counter the English machinations, to encourage James not only to remain loyal to Holy Church but to make this evident to all by taking stern and vigorous action against the heretics and so-called reformers who were injuring Christendom in Scotland as elsewhere; and as earnest of papal favour and support to confer on the King of Scots the title of Defender of the Faith.

This explosive mixture of visitors set the court by the ears and the situation was not helped by James himself paying the while very public attentions to his currently favourite mistress, Margaret Erskine, daughter of Stirling Castle's hereditary keeper —and so conveniently on the spot—who had just had the felicity of presenting the King with a fine son, over which infant the father positively drooled. Undoubtedly he had already produced numerous bastards, but this was the first one he not only publicly acknowledged but was permitting him to be named James Stewart and promising continuing favours. Indeed the proud mother was indicating, if only privately to her friends, that it was only right that the boy should be so called, since she and his sire had gone through a secret marriage of the handfast variety.

In the circumstances, those whose task it was to steer the ship of state were not a little bemused. Even Davie Beaton was less calmly confident than usual. As well as Lord Privy Seal he was now also a bishop, albeit a French one, for King Francis seemed to have made him Bishop of Mirepoix and the new Pope had confirmed it.

Davie had come back, inevitably, to many problems which had arisen during his absence abroad, in Church as well as state, most of which he could cope with readily enough. But the matter of heresy, or at least active support for the reforming doctrines of Martin Luther, Melancthon and others on the Continent, was serious, especially in view of Campeggio's mission, the new hard line in the Vatican and the English separation from Rome which had its sympathisers in Scotland. Whilst Davie was in France, owing to the feebleness of his uncle and the *laissez-faire* attitude of the Chancellor, Archbishop Dunbar, the lead in Church affairs had been taken over by Bishop Hay of Ross, a vehement individual, who had ordered the arrest of certain determined dissenters. Most of these, deliberately given due warning to save trouble, had discreetly left the country, these including the brother and sister of the Abbot of Fearn, Patrick Hamilton, who had been burned at the stake some years before, the Canon Alexander Aless of St. Andrews, and a university divine there named MacBeth or MacBee, who was known in the city as Maccabeus. But two named 'reformers' had not taken the hint and continued their public denunciations of Church error and corruption, one David Straiton, a brother of the Laird of Laurleston, in the Mearns, the other Master Norman Gourlay, a parish priest. These now languished in prison at St. Andrews, for the Abbot of Arbroath, Bishop of Mirepoix and Lord Privy Seal to deal with.

Beaton, taking the entire situation into consideration, came up with a fairly typical gesture. He decided that Campeggio and the Pope could be satisfied, James committed firmly to the Romish cause, attention diverted from the Erskine folly, Henry

Tudor's representatives shown once and for all that their cause was hopeless, likewise due warning given to other heretics, all by staging an elaborate trial of the two dissenting culprits, with the King himself sitting in judgement along with the appointed ecclesiastics. This high court of the Church should be held not privately at St. Andrews but publicly at Holyrood Abbey in Edinburgh, and this whilst the various awkward visitors were still with them. He convinced James that this would solve many of his current problems.

When David Lindsay was told of the project he was much against it. Not only did he largely sympathise with the reformers but he felt that such trial and its results might well be counter-productive. There had been considerable unrest throughout the kingdom after Patrick Hamilton's burning. This trial would be almost certain to find the prisoners guilty, and in that case the prescribed penalty for heresy, shameful as he for one considered it, was the stake. If this were carried out there would be more trouble, and the movement for reform could well be encouraged by making martyrs of the pair. Also it would be dragging King James into controversy and endangering his popularity with not a few of his subjects.

Beaton countered that by declaring that every effort would be made to induce the prisoners to recant. They were neither of them figures of importance, and could probably be persuaded both to save their lives and gain themselves preferment in due course by taking the sensible line. Even if not, once the visitors were gone, sentence could probably be commuted to banishment.

The two so different friends agreed to differ, as so often.

It took a few days to arrange this piece of stagecraft to Beaton's satisfaction and to move the principal actors therein, along with most of the court and the audience for whom it was to be played, from Stirling to Edinburgh. James himself seemed to see it all in the nature of an entertainment and diversion, although Davie deplored this, since it would give the wrong impression to the visitors. But it was in something like a holiday spirit that the royal cavalcade proceeded by way of Linlithgow to Edinburgh, to take over the Abbey of the Holy Rood for the occasion. The King, with so many boyhood memories of the place, was much exercised. He insisted that David Lindsay and himself should make their quarters in the same chamber which had been theirs all those years before. The Bastard, for one, was incensed that he should be excluded—for he frequently nowadays shared the royal bedchamber.

Beaton had got Lindsay's Janet busy beforehand, for as the King's Wardrobe Mistress she was responsible for the royal tailoring, and it was decided that James should be clad wholly in scarlet, the traditional colour for judgement, for the occasion. So, a striking figure in rich red, to match his long red hair, rubies from Elie in Fife reflecting the sun from bonnet and breast, and wearing all the newly acquired orders of the Garter, the Golden Fleece and St. Michael, the King led the procession to the great abbey-church from the monastic quarters, where he was greeted by the Abbot of Holyrood and conducted to a throne in mid-chancel, all the rest filing in to fill the nave, although David, as Lord Lyon, followed the monarch, to stand behind the throne, as so often he had done in a different capacity. The commissioners of the ecclesiastical court were already there, at the other side of the chancel, bishops, abbots and priors. The Primate should have presided, but old James Beaton was far too heavy and lethargic to travel from St. Andrews, and Bishop Hay of Ross acted Commissary in his stead. Davie Beaton remained discreetly out of evidence. The Abbot of Holyrood, bowing to James, moved over to join the judges.

David Lindsay, however loth he was to be present, still had his official duties to perform. Once all were inside, he rapped three times on a reading-desk with his baton of office, ordered the doors to be closed and declared that they were here in the name and presence of His Grace James, High King of Scots, descendant of a hundred kings, at a consistory of the highest ecclesiastical court in the land, called by the Primate of All Scotland, to see justice done. He called upon the Lord Abbot of Holyrood to open the proceedings with prayer.

After that, Bishop Hay, a short, wiry individual whom Beaton had privately described as a mitred weasel, having requested the King's permission, declared that in the regretted absence of the Primate, the Archbishop of St. Andrews, on account of bodily indisposition, he had been appointed to head up the commissioners of Holy Church to enquire into and decide upon a matter of great concern, with His Grace's concurrence, to the realm as well as the Church. As most present would be aware,

327

there was a grievous tide of heresy flowing in various parts of Christendom, seeking under guise of reform to undermine the doctrines and integrity of Holy Church and overthrow its age-old institutions and God-given authority. This must not be allowed to happen in Scotland, however close the threat might have come. And the Bishop glanced over to where the distinguished guests sat in the south transept, Lord William Howard and William Barlow amongst them.

Under instructions from the Holy Father in Rome, the Church in Scotland had been seeking to set its house in order, in this respect as in others, reform being good and proper so long as it was ordered and undertaken with the due consent of those ordained to oversee the worship of God's people. But instigated by sources outwith this realm, for their own purposes, certain misguided persons had been seeking to persuade others publicly to rebel against divinely appointed authority and openly preaching heresy and division, even denying the very doctrines of the Catholic faith. The leaders of Holy Church had been patient, perhaps too patient, with these subverters of truth and order, and had warned them frequently. Some had taken heed, some had elected to leave the realm altogether, but some had persisted deliberately in their wrong-doing. Reluctantly the Primate and bishops had been forced to act against these determined heretics, and today two of the most inveterate offenders had been brought before this high court of the Church to make answer for their sins. With His Grace's royal permission he would call on the officers to bring them before the court.

At James's nod, the Bishop called the names of David Straiton and Master Norman Gourlay, priest.

From the chapter-house the prisoners were marched in, under guard. Straiton, young, stocky and defiant seeming, the other middle-aged, frail and bent. They were brought to stand at the chancel steps. The company sat forward, even the King.

"Norman Gourlay and David Straiton," Hay intoned, "you are here before the highest authority in Church and realm this day, in His Grace's presence, to answer charges of heresy and incitement to heresy, after due and repeated warnings and in full knowledge of the penalties prescribed for such offence. In the King's name and of his royal mercy, I give you one last opportunity to recant. Do you, either or both, repent you of your heretical statements, and urgings of others to rebel against the authority of Holy Church? If you will recant as publicly as you first proclaimed your error, and promise never again to repeat the offences, you shall go free from this place."

Hardly waiting for the Bishop to finish, Straiton spoke out strongly. "I recant nothing. I deny, in God's name, that I have ever pronounced heresy but only God's holy Word and Christ's own teaching as contained in Holy Writ."

A murmur ran round the church.

"So be it. And you, Norman Gourlay?"

The older man's voice quavered. "My lord Bishop . . . Your Grace . . . I am a sinner and one of God's weakest vessels. I have failed in much, in my ministry as in my daily life. But I cannot confess to heresy. Heresy, as I understand it, is the holding of false doctrines and the propagation of teachings contrary to the Word of God. Of such I am not guilty, nor ever would be. I but bewail, as I must as God's humble servant, the errors and malpractices which men have introduced into the observances of Holy Church. This surely is the duty of all of us, especially those ordained in holy orders. Of this I cannot recant."

David Lindsay, for one, felt like cheering, but remembered in time that he was the realm's Lord Lyon King-of-Arms.

Hay, after a glance at his fellow judges, who all displayed expressions of disapproval, offence, if not shock, gestured towards the King.

"Your Grace, you have heard these two accused, this defiance and refusal to repent, and even determination to persist in their opposition to the authority and teachings of the Church. There is, indeed, no need for any further indictment, since they have already confessed to the offences charged. But that fullest justice should be seen to be done, even to these wilful offenders, it is proposed that some examples of their offences should be put before Your Highness."

"So I would expect," James said.

"Yes, Sire. This David Straiton is brother to the Laird of Laurieston, in the Mearns, and has properties on that coast near the havens of St. Cyrus and Inverbervie. He owns fishing-cobles and smoke-houses and makes considerable moneys from the sale of fish, especially from smoking and salting. For these profits he has the duty to pay tithes to my lord Bishop of Moray, as is right and proper. But he has resolutely refused so to do. And when my lord Bishop sent his officers to collect the said lawful tithe, the man Straiton, before all at the haven, told his fishermen that they should ·throw every tenth fish that they caught back into the sea, and advised my lord's officers to go seek the Bishop's tithe where it was to be had in abundance! Such infamy . . ."

A titter ran through the company, and the King smiled broadly.

Hay frowned. "My lord King, this is a fell serious matter, not only denying the Church its due tribute on God's providence and on the labours of others, but contrary to and contesting the very right of Holy Church to its tithes and teinds. Moreover, when the Bishop's representatives upbraided him, for impiety and public denial of God's ordinances and bounty, warning him of the penalties therefor, this Straiton blasphemously there, before a large company, sank to his knees and declared in shameful mockery that Scripture said that our Saviour would deny before His Father and the holy angels anyone who denied Him before men; and he swore to God that although he was a great sinner, he would not deny Him or his truth for fear of bodily torments. We could call a score of witnesses to this wickedness and impiety. But no need, for the man has confessed and not denied it, many times since, and indeed glories in his shame."

Amidst considerable mutterings and murmurings, James cleared his throat.

"And is this heresy?" he asked. "It seems to me . . . otherwise. Play-acting and disrespect for the Bishop, perhaps. But scarcely heresy."

"With due respect, Sire, since you ask, heresy, as even the prisoner Gourlay has admitted, is the holding of false doctrines and the proclamation thereof, the propagation of teachings contrary to the Word of God. This the man Straiton has committed." And Hay turned to look at his fellow commissioners, all of whom nodded solemnly.

James shifted uncomfortably on his throne. "I must accept that assertion of Holy Church as to what is heresy and what is not," he conceded. "But since *I* would not have considered this act and behaviour of the prisoner as heresy, however foolish and disrespectful, then perhaps neither did he. So, if heresy was not intended . . ." The King's voice rather tailed away.

Bishop Hay's certainly did not. "Sire—the thing was done deliberately and of forethought, before many. Making a mock of Holy Church and its ordinances. And blasphemously calling Almighty God to aid him in his apostacy. This is heresy most vile!" Again the waspish prelate turned to his colleagues. All expressed their agreement.

James, clearly out of his depth, spread his hands. "I must bow to your decision, my lord spiritual," he said. "But in this case I suggest mercy. Also recommended in Holy Writ, is it not? Since the penalty laid down for heresy is dire, my judgement in the matter would be a warning on this occasion, on condition that the prisoner pays his tithes in future without such play-acting."

There was silence for moments, Church and state at loggerheads.

When the Bishop spoke, he sounded not a little strained. "With all respect, may I remind you, Sire, that in matters of heresy Your Grace does not have the prerogative of mercy?" he said. "Nor indeed have I!"

A single hoot, compounded of astonishment, laughter and scorn, sounded through the church. It came from Hamilton of Finnart.

James turned in his chair, features almost as red as the rest of him, to look at David Lindsay.

Almost hurriedly Hay went on. "David Straiton, you stand condemned. Norman Gourlay—do you recant?"

The whisper was barely audible. "No, my lord. God . . . giving me courage."

"So be it. You also stand condemned. For you have preached heresy from the very altar-steps of your parish church, as you will not deny."

"I have preached God's Word, as proclaimed by Christ Jesus. On that I must stand, weak as I am."

"On that you shall burn, sir! Since you set yourself up to know better than the Church which gave you any authority you have. You but add blasphemy to heresy." The Bishop turned to his coadjutors. "Does any wish to add to what has been said? Or to offer any reason why the penalty decreed by Holy Church for the vile sin of heresy should not be carried out?"

All there shook their mitred heads.

"Then it falls to me, in the name of the Primate, to pronounce sentence on both heretics. They shall be taken forthwith from this holy place to Greenside-under-Calton, outwith the Canongate burgh bounds and near to the refuge of the lepers, and there

331

their bodies shall be burned with fire. And may Almighty God have mercy on their souls thereafter. This sentence to be carried out in the presence of all true servants of Holy Church, in whatever degree. Officers—conduct the prisoners hence."

Abruptly James rose from his throne and, without a word, stamped out.

Lindsay after a moment or two followed him.

* * *

In the royal bedchamber of the monastery, a little later, Davie Beaton joined an angry monarch and Lindsay. James rounded on him at once.

"You, Beaton—*you* are responsible! You talked me into this. You contrived all. I have been made to look a fool, before all. Over-ruled by a clerk—I, the King! Brought to sit in judgement, and then ignored and controverted. In front of Henry's servants. It is not to be borne! You have failed me, man—failed me!"

"Sire—it is none so ill as that!" Davie asserted, soothingly. "Hay overstepped himself, yes, and lacked tact. But there is no great harm done. You . . ."

"I was insulted and made a laughing-stock. As good as told to hold my tongue! By that up-jumped bishop *you* appointed!"

"Scarce that, Your Grace. Hay spoke rashly, unsuitably. I have already had a word with him—and will have more! He saw his opportunity before the papal nuncio to demonstrate his own fervour and strength for Holy Church, so that the message would be carried back to Rome. Possibly he thinks to see the Primacy itself within his grasp one day! But not if *I* have aught to do with it. But you, Sire, have not suffered over it all, I swear. I have already heard men praising you, admiring your plea for mercy. You will have gained much in repute as the merciful monarch. Yet lost nothing with Campeggio and the Pope who, had the prisoners indeed been reprieved, would have been incensed against you. This way, you have the best of it. The nuncio will return to the Vatican satisfied. Henry will see that he had no hope of turning Scotland against Rome. And Your Grace will be advanced in the affection of your people. What could be a more satisfactory outcome?"

James rubbed his chin, considering.

Not so David Lindsay. "Satisfactory?" he demanded. "Not for

those two poor wretches who go to a terrible and shameful death! Have you forgot *them*, in your satisfaction? Sacrificed for your statecraft—a burnt sacrifice! For holding to what they believed . . ."

"They condemned themselves. They have only themselves to blame."

"You say that! You, who spoke to me of mercy, of reprieve, banishment at the most. Was that but lies and deceit?"

"I hoped that we could persuade them to reason. As we have tried. If not to recant, at least either to remain silent or to indicate regret, so that mercy could be shown. But they remained obdurate, knowing the penalty. They *sought* martyrdom . . ."

"Aye, martyrdom! That is what they will achieve. And your cause will suffer. Each such burning and martyrdom but further condemns the Church in the eyes of all but the clerics. I tell you, it is *Henry's* cause which may well benefit from this day!"

"Henry is concerned only with his own power and with grasping the Church's wealth. He would not care for a thousand martyrs . . . !"

James intervened. "Enough of this. The burning—must I go to this Greenside to watch? I have no wish to do so. Let your Church do its own ill work."

"I fear that you must, Sire. Not to go would look as though you disassociated yourself from the findings of the Church court, undo what good there is in it. Campeggio will be there, and the Englishmen. If *you* are not, all will say that you disagree. So all the benefit towards Rome and Henry will be nullified. These two must die, by the laws of the Church. At least let them not die in vain!"

"Lord!" Lindsay exclaimed.

"Be not so squeamish, my lord Lyon King-of-Arms!" Beaton said. "We have a realm to govern for His Grace, and cannot all afford such delicate stomachs!" He paused. "But, Sire, there is something that you could do there to, shall we say, mitigate sentence. Aye, and further demonstrate Your Grace's mercy. The Church says that heretics' bodies must burn, for the saving of their souls. But it does not say that they must be *alive* when they burn! If you were to order a quick death first, by hanging or the axe, then burning thereafter, it would be less dire, would it not?"

"Ha! Yes, that is a notion. I could do that?"

333

"To be sure. None can stop you, Sire. Certainly not Bishop Hay. And it would not do your cause any harm at Rome."

"Good! Then we will do that. See you to it, Beaton, in my name."

"There are gallows always ready at Greenside, Sire. For the hanging of malefactors outwith the burgh of the Canongate."

"Very well. Let us get the business over and done with."

"Sire, I seek Your Grace's permission not to attend you on this occasion, as Lyon," Lindsay said. "This once."

James looked from one David to the other, and nodded.

21

James Stewart paced up and down the timbers of the quayside at the port of Leith, as the last of the stores and baggage was being loaded aboard *The Fair Maid*, in a mood compounded of almost boyish excitement and impatience, tinged with annoyance that the sovereign-lord of the realm should be kept thus waiting by the laggardly efforts of common porters and shipmen who should have had all loaded and ready long before this—that, and disapprobation directed towards the man he was leaving behind, to rule, in effect, the said realm for him, even though nominally Archbishop Dunbar the Chancellor would be in charge; Davie Beaton, who stood by, expression inscrutable, David Lindsay at his side.

For Beaton was, if not in disgrace, at least in his monarch's deep disesteem. James had not really absolved him from blame over involving him in the burning of Straiton and Gourlay those months before—the resentment including all the Church's leaders, to be sure. And when the new Pope Paul had sorely failed the King of Scots shortly thereafter, the entire exercise appeared to James a sorry episode, ineffective as it was upsetting, and its instigator and moving spirit, Davie Beaton, to blame. Moreover he suspected Davie of a further offence, of secretly contriving the marriage of his favourite, Margaret

Erskine, to Sir William Douglas of Lochleven, one of the Black Douglases—this to ensure that he, the King, did not marry her, as he was every now and again threatening to do, despite the proposed French match. This secret marriage had struck James sorely, in his pride and self esteem, for he had believed that the lady loved him truly, as well as bearing his son, and he conceived that Beaton had arranged it somehow in order that nothing should interfere with the French connection. In reaction, the King had written directly to the Pope, asking him to annul this wretched union, assuming that, as Beaton had averred, the Vatican would now be well disposed towards him, after the heresy trial and such clear support of Holy Church. When the Pope had declined to do any such thing for a third party, even the esteemed King of Scots, James was the more wrathful, suspecting that here again Beaton was involved. And when, as a final blow, a Hamilton new back from France had informed the Bastard, and he the King, that the Lady Marie de Bourbon was a deal less well-favoured than the portrait Beaton had brought, in fact that she and her sister were both sore made awry, as the informant put it, his anger at his clever Lord Privy Seal reached the stage when something had to be done about it.

That something had developed into this extraordinary adventure, starting at Leith haven, the port for Edinburgh. Margaret Erskine out of the running as a wife, and the proposed French bride allegedly highly unattractive, James had decided to trust no more envoys and match-makers but to go himself, secretly, on the quest for the required wife. King Francis was offering an annual pension of no less than twenty thousand livres for the French match, to outdo Henry, so obviously to France he ought to go. But go in disguise, anonymously, to see with his own eyes what this Marie de Bourbon was like, and if, as seemed probable, she displeased, go seek another French lady more to his taste. There were allegedly plenty of highly attractive women in that fair land. This rather juvenile and romantic knight-errantry all the King's advisers, without exception, had been against; but James was not to be dissuaded. He was going, and taking only a very small company with him, in this one ship—since anything larger would reveal him as someone of importance. His Lord Privy Seal would most certainly not be going with him.

David Lindsay would, however, as would the Bastard of Arran and a few others who knew France and the Continent.

Beaton smoothed hand over mouth and neat pointed little beard. "Try to steer him, if you ever get so far, towards Marie de Guise," he advised, low-voiced. "I fear that he will have none of the Bourbon, when he sees her, in his present mood. The de Guise is not beautiful but she has her attractions, very rich, and she is an able young woman who would make a good queen. She might be good for James—and he sorely needs a good strong wife!"

"He will gang his ain gait, in this, that one!" Lindsay said. "I fear that I will be able to do little. The entire ploy is a folly . . ."

"A folly, yes. But like so many follies, we must make the best of it. I need not say to do your best for James. But watch Finnart. I would that *he* was not going. He will cause trouble if he can."

"What could he do, in this? In France . . ." Lindsay got no further with that, for heavy spots of rain began to fall and James decided to leave the quayside for the shelter of the ship. He came up to them.

"Come aboard, Davie. You, Beaton, see to all in my absence—but heedfully, see you. No clever ploys! I warn you, I shall require a close accounting when I return. They are near finished loading now. We shall sail forthwith."

"Sire, the weather is not of the best. Fishermen I spoke with say that they expect it to turn for the worse. I advise that you delay sailing . . ."

"Nonsense, man! Old wives' havers! *I* know you. You are against me sailing, at all. Be off, or you will be soaked. Come, Davie . . ."

Lindsay raised a hand to his friend, and followed his liege-lord up the gangplank on to the vessel.

The shipmaster, a burly Fifer, was also concerned about the weather, but James was already tired of delay and insisted that a start be made. At least there was no lack of wind to assist them in casting off and, sails filling, they moved out into the open water.

Beaton and the others left behind made a bolt for cover.

The steady rain which developed, the cramped and less than comfortable quarters, and the overcrowding of the small ship, made it an inauspicious start; but the King, now that he was actually on his way, was in high spirits even if nobody else was. As they heaved and tossed their way down the Firth of Forth, no wettings from rain or spray damped his enthusiasm, his interest in the handling of the ship, the setting of the sails, the views of the shores and islands of Lothian and Fife. Although the motion of the craft, in increasingly disturbed waters, together with the smells of stale bilge-water, tar and oily wool-bales from the hold, sent most of the passengers hurrying below, pale of face, not so their sovereign; he appeared to be immune to sea-sickness. Fortunately Lindsay was also a good sailor; and although the Bastard was less so, evidently, he resolutely remained on deck with his monarch.

The wind was gusting from the north-east, unusual in July, and this entailed continual tacking, much delaying their prog-ress. Not that this concerned James. He kept urging the ship-master, in his necessary beatings back and forth across the firth, to go ever closer to either shore, so that he might try to recognise the various locations and landmarks as seen from this unaccus-tomed viewpoint, exclaiming at the isle of Inchkeith, the head-land at Kinghorn where his ancestor Alexander the Third had fallen to his death, the roaring white breakers on the sand-bar of wide Aberlady Bay, and the cliffs and rocks of Elie where the rubies came from. With the mighty towering stack of the Craig of Bass off North Berwick, he was duly impressed, pointing delightedly at the basking seals and the thousands of screaming, diving gannets.

But once past the Bass, they were out of the firth and into the open Norse Sea, and the difference was very quickly apparent, as the seas grew in steepness and the wind stiffened to a steady half-gale. *The Fair Maid* rolled and pitched grievously in the cross seas as they turned due southwards, and the deck lost its attractions even for the King. Anyway, there was nothing more to see now, with night falling and the land only faintly looming on their right. Thankfully his companions led him below for a meal of sorts.

There was no great demand for food that evening, but a drinking session developed amongst those so capable and inclined. David Lindsay retired to his bunk early—but not before they had a visit from the shipmaster, who came to announce gruffly that wind and seas were still rising steadily. If it got much worse they might have to run for shelter in some haven or anchorage. Did His Grace have any views on the matter?

James, distinctly drink-taken now, told the man not to be so craven. They must be off the coast of England by now, and

337

the last place he would wish to reach was his Uncle Henry's domains. He pressed wine on the skipper to improve his courage.

Before falling asleep, David heard the King being assisted to his bed by the Bastard, who had a notably good head for liquor. Despite the strange conditions, the heaving, the creaking of timbers and the thick atmosphere, Lindsay had a fairly good night.

There was no light in that pit of a cabin when he awoke, and he had no idea as to the time. But after lying for a while, listening to the snores of his companions, he was aware of clatter and footsteps on the deck above his head. Also the motion of the ship was much less pronounced. When he smelt what he decided was cooking ham, from the nearby galley, he reckoned that it was probably morning. He rose, stretched, and made his way up the ladder to the deck.

It proved to be broad daylight, even if a dull and grey morning. Hamilton, looking enviably fresh, was standing beside a bleary-eyed shipmaster. He grinned at the newcomer.

Yawning, David looked about him. Land was visible, not much more than a mile off. It took a moment or two for its significance to register. It lay to leeward, to their *left* side, not to the right as was to be expected. Then he realised that, although there was no sun visible as yet, such lightness as the sky held was astern to them. So they were heading westwards, not southwards or eastwards, parallel to the shore. And his glance astern registered something else. Behind them, some miles, a great lump of rock rose out of the sea, and even at that range there was no mistaking its bulk and contours. It was the Craig of Bass. Bewildered, he peered landwards. Yes, there was North Berwick Law and his own Garleton Hills. They were back in the Firth of Forth, sailing for home.

Astonished, he went over to the Bastard. "What is this?" he demanded. "Why are we here? What has happened?"

"You must have slept well, man," Hamilton said. "We had to turn back. The storm grew too great for us. We could no longer hazard the King's safety. It was either this, or running for an English harbour—which James had forbidden."

"But . . . but . . . Sakes—this is beyond all! To turn back altogether. To return home. The seas are less high . . ."

"Here in the firth, yes. Out there it was otherwise. You must be a sound sleeper, my Lord Lyon!"

"But why come all the way back? We are off Aberlady Bay. Why not shelter in the south of the firth and then resume our voyage when the seas go down?"

"Because the storm has loosened some timbers, our shipmaster says. We are taking water. Some spars were broke. We must return for repairs."

"Lord! Does James know?"

"Not yet. Like you, His Grace sleeps sound! We did not think to disturb him."

"He is not going to like this."

"Better than a watery grave, man!"

"*You* may tell him, then. I prefer not!"

It was quite some time before James appeared. They were by then off Musselburgh, and with the crouching-lion outline of Arthur's Seat looming large ahead, there could be no least doubt, even at first glance, as to where they were. The King stared. His arm extended, to point at the great hill. No words came.

The Bastard produced something between a bow and a shrug. "Safe back from the storm, Sire," he greeted. "Preserved from the perils of the deep, God be praised!" he added piously

James transferred his stare from the view to the speaker. "You . . . turned . . . back!" he got out.

"To be sure. All was at stake. Your Grace's very life. The storm grew ever worse after you retired. We were in danger of sinking, timbers sprung, taking water. We could not run for an English harbour, for you had said not that. We only prayed that we could win to the calmer waters of this Forth again, in safety . . ."

"You turned back, Hamilton, without my permission! Knowing that I would not give it. You did this, against my wishes. You did it . . . because you were against this venture from the start. Would not have me to go to France. Would not have me to marry. So that, so that *Hamilton* might one day gain my throne! You, you Bastard indeed!"

"Sire—no! Hear me. We could not go on, in the storm. The seas were beyond belief. It was an English haven, or return here. You were asleep and in wine. The shipmaster was much in fear. I took the only decision possible . . ."

"You took a decision that you will regret, Hamilton! This I

will not forget." Without another word, the King swung around and went below again.

Back at Leith, James sent for David. He did not wish to see the Bastard again. Have him away and out of his sight. They would require to hire horses, to ride up to Holyrood. Send a messenger ahead to prepare all. He would speak with none. His name and fame had been brought low in the sight of all men. This was the sorriest day of his life.

Lindsay sought to comfort and reassure. A storm was beyond anyone's control, even a king's. None would think the worse of him . . .

James silenced him with a gesture and waved him out of the foul-smelling cabin.

The King would not disembark until he was assured that Finnart had gone, and the others with him. Thereafter he and David alone rode in cloaked anonymity the two miles up to the Abbey of the Holy Rood.

*   *   *

There followed a strange interlude. James, humiliated and angry, was at his sourest. He would have none of his court around him. Those at Edinburgh were sent packing back to Stirling, and none from there summoned. David Lindsay was almost his only companion, as he had been here all those years before when Angus had ruled. They went daily walks up Arthur's Seat, but these were scarcely pleasant occasions, with the King poor company indeed. He drank steadily.

Then, after five days of it, Davie Beaton turned up, unbidden, from St. Andrews, having heard the news. At first the King would not see him either; but after the two friends had had a conference, Lindsay convinced James that Beaton not only had matters of state which called for the monarch's attention, but had proposals, interesting proposals, as to the present situation and the French visit. This procured an interview.

After sympathetically listening to a diatribe against the Bastard and the shipmaster of *The Fair Maid*, Beaton, agreeing with all the King had said, suggested tactfully that the French visit should not be abandoned but amended and proceeded with forthwith. But not in any secret or clandestine fashion. Let James go openly, as King of Scots, and with a goodly squadron of ships, as befitted a royal suitor, such as would impress the

King of France, whose favour was of course essential, especially if the Lady Marie de Bourbon was to be rejected. And in view of those twenty thousand livres of pension! With a number of larger ships there would be little chance of any repetition of being turned back by storm. Also no risk of attack by English pirates.

James very quickly began to cheer up, but wondered where he could get a sufficiency of ships, and how to pay for them, in the chronically empty state of his Treasury? Davie answered to leave that to him, and to Holy Church. *He* would find and pay for the ships. There were many fine vessels trading out of Fife—from St. Andrews itself, from Dysart and Kirkcaldy, from Inverkeithing and Culross. Give him two or three weeks. And with His Grace's permission, this time he would accompany the expedition himself. And there would be no turning back!

James, much enheartened, could produce no objections.

Beaton did not actually say that he expected something in return for his generosity, but he did indicate that His Grace could usefully fill in some of the time, while the ships were being found and a suitably illustrious company assembled to accompany the King to France, by making a brief pilgrimage, which would benefit the Church and please the Pope in Rome, also further confound King Henry. A new shrine had recently been set up to Our Lady of Loretto, at Musselburgh. There had been no such place of pilgrimage in South-East Scotland since St. Margaret's Black Rood had been stolen by English Edward from Holyrood three centuries before. They had Whithorn in Galloway, St. Duthac's at Tain in Ross, and of course Iona in the Hebrides; but nothing save the small shrine of the White Kirk of Hamer, near Tantallon, where the holy well had rather fallen into desuetude. This new chapel, shrine and image at Musselburgh, founded by the hermit-monk Thomas Duthie three years before, was just what was needed for the faithful of Edinburgh, Lothian and the East Borderland. But so far few knew about it and it was therefore not attracting the desired numbers of pilgrims. If His Grace would go there, preferably on foot—it was a bare five miles from Holyrood, after all—then all the realm would hear of it and take note. Also, since it commemorated the marriage of the Virgin Mary with Joseph, as well as the Annunciation, it was a highly suitable venue for the King to offer prayers for the success of his matrimonial journey—and no more storms!

James, scarcely a religious character as he was, saw no serious reason why he could not co-operate in this, if his Lord Privy Seal thought it important. It would only take one day, after all.

Later, Lindsay taxed his friend with this pilgrimage project. Was it not all something of a nonsense? He had heard something of this hermit Duthie and his claims. Were there not grave doubts about it all?

"Of course there are, man—as there must be about anything with claims towards the miraculous. This Duthie may well be an imposter, the relics of his own devising—although perhaps not, who knows? What is important is that folk, ordinary folk, need the reassurance of such places and persons, such spiritual comfort. Their belief is what matters, not what may or may not be material. Such shrines fulfil a need amongst the faithful." He smiled slightly. "And are very profitable for Holy Church!"

"Aye—there we have it! Profitable. And it matters not that all may be pretence? Not true?"

"What *is* truth, Davie? What a man *believes* can be more potent than what may be proven fact. This of Loretto. The image and relics the man Duthie may truly have brought from Italy, or may not. But then at that Loretto itself—what of that? The tradition is that the very house in which the Virgin Mary lived in Nazareth, miraculously uplifted and brought through the air from Galilee to Ancona in Italy, was set down there three centuries ago. Do *you* believe that?"

"I think not."

"Yet many do. Sufficient, I am told, to bring one hundred thousand pilgrims there each year, giving thirty thousand crowns in offerings! Moneys which can be useful indeed for God's work."

"Or for priests' and prelates' pouches!"

Beaton shrugged. "Some of it, perhaps. But most serves its good purpose. And the Church in Scotland can do with the like." He grinned again. "If James makes a pilgrimage to this Loretto, sufficient will follow to pay for these ships I am to charter for him!"

"Sakes! So that is it!"

"Part of it. I am a practical man, you see."

So four days later a somewhat embarrassed James Stewart led his first, and probably his last, holy pilgrimage. Beaton had organised it with his usual efficiency, and all Edinburgh turned out to watch, not a few to take part. It should have been a barefoot progress, according to Vatican traditional rules, but ever since, almost exactly one hundred years before, Aeneas Piccolomini, later Pope Pius the Second, had made the pilgrimage from Dunbar to the White Kirk of Hamer in frosty weather, and suffered rheumatism in his feet for the rest of his life in consequence, he had accepted that barefoot pilgrimages were scarcely suitable for Scotland and amended the regulations for northern climes accordingly.

But walk they did, starting from Holyrood. A large choir of singing boys and instrumentalists went first, followed by a notable contingent of clergy led by David Beaton himself, for once in episcopal robes and wearing a mitre, not as Bishop of Mirepoix but as Abbot of Arbroath. Then came James, walking alone, dressed soberly, such great officers of state as were available just behind, the Earl of Erroll, High Constable and Lindsay, Lord Lyon. Then the earls, lords, barons, knights, lairds and chiefs, with the new Lords of Session. Finally the Edinburgh magistrates and guild deacons led by Sir Adam Otterburn, as Provost—who, as again Lord Advocate could have walked beside David Lindsay, but chose to lead his own grouping. A flock of citizenry trailed along behind, with children, packmen, beggars, even dogs. The royal guard was dispensed with, for this allegedly religious occasion.

In the pleasant early August sunshine, it made an agreeable enough stroll, through part of the royal hunting-park which surrounded Arthur's Seat, past St. Margaret's Loch, over a shoulder of hill to the Fishwives' Causeway and across the Figgate Whins to the coast. Less than two miles, following the sandy shore, brought them to the haven of Fisherrow, near the mouth of the River Esk. Not having horses to ford the shallows of the little estuary, they had to turn upstream to cross by the hump-backed stone bridge. Here they were met by the Provost and baillies of Musselburgh, who escorted the royal procession through their burgh, which prided itself on its ancient and honourable status as the honest toun, so called by Thomas Randolph, Earl of Moray, Bruce's nephew, regent of the infant David the Second, when it had succoured him in his and the kingdom's need. The house where the sick regent had lodged was proudly pointed out to the present monarch.

Only a little further, beyond the east end of the High Street, was the site of the new shrine, a small chapel of no real distinction, erected beside a feeder of the Pinkie Burn—to provide the necessary holy water. James was not the only one to declare himself unimpressed by the object of their pilgrimage.

They were greeted by Brother Duthie, suitably hairy but otherwise unhermitlike, a powerfully-built youngish man in the Carmelite habit, who claimed to have occupied a cave on Mount Sinai before being taken by the Infidel and held captive for years. He had eventually escaped from the Turks to Italy and gone to Ancona, where he had, he asserted, been in the famous Casa Santa, the house of the Blessed Virgin miraculously transported from Nazareth, now encased in white marble, and had actually seen the window through which the Archangel Gabriel had appeared to Mary—whose sub-angels, no doubt, arranged the said transportation.

The chapel was so small that only a very few of the visitors could get in, and Beaton murmured to Lindsay that they would have to build something better than this once the money began to flow in. Inside, amidst the incense-smoke and many flickering candles, they found an altar on which there were a number of rather gaudily-painted iconlike pictures, surrounding a small wooden statuette of the Virgin and Child, brought from Italy but which appeared to have been freshly and vividly painted for the occasion. They were assured that those privileged to touch it could be cured of sundry diseases and ills, including scrofula, cold griefs, dropsy, and it was singularly helpful in resisting witchcraft. The King duly touched, muttered a Hail Mary, and coughing in the incense-smoke, was for getting out when Beaton restrained him, and launched into a stirring petition to the Almighty for the success of the forthcoming royal journey to France in search of a fair, virtuous and fertile bride and queen, who should, they prayed, be the earthly counterpart of the heavenly one they were here to celebrate, and from whom Scotland would gain great blessing.

Outside, after depositing the all-important offerings in a capacious kist, they found the great concourse, unable to get into the chapel, settled down in holiday fashion to picnic on the banks of the burn—for enterprising hucksters and packmen had appeared, selling viands and drink as well as miniature images, pictures, beads, crosses, charms and the like. Concerned that the available moneys brought could mostly be spent in such competing fripperies instead of on the object of the exercise, the hermit-custodian proclaimed in a stentorian bellow that all should form up to file into the chapel in turn, to gain its undoubted blessings and contribute accordingly; and that meantime most there might elect to wash their feet in the burn's holy waters, duly blessed for the occasion, for which only a small charge would be made but which would banish not only weariness from walking but rheumatics, swellings, varicosity and likewise generally uplift the spirits.

James, however, had had enough, and having had the forethought to arrange for horses to come along behind them, was able to ride back to Holyrood at a brisk pace to better than any *al fresco* meal amongst the multitude.

Davie Beaton was reasonably well satisfied. A worthwhile harvest would almost certainly follow this planting of seed.

By first September, Beaton's efforts had borne fruit, and no fewer than seven fine ships were assembled at the port of Kirkcaldy in Fife—which had a more sheltered anchorage for such a squadron than had St. Andrews—one, the flag-ship, of as much as seven hundred tons. The royal procession which wound its way the forty miles from Stirling, mounted this time, consisted of no fewer than five hundred souls, an illustrious company, all clad in their best. It included four earls, Argyll, Moray, Rothes and Arran—the last taken along to keep him from mischief-making with his half-brother the Bastard, who was being most ostentatiously left behind, also, of course, he was hereditary Lord High Admiral. The Lords Maxwell, Fleming and Erskine were there, and numerous heirs and cadets of noble houses—amongst whom was a very good-looking and dashing young man named Oliver Sinclair, of the line of the St. Clair Earls of Orkney and Caithness, on whom the King's favour was increasingly being bestowed since the fall of Finnart. Davie Beaton superintended all on this occasion. There was only the one woman, Janet, Lady Lindsay of The Mount, who was considered suitable to attend on the hoped-for bride, none of the King's many mistresses being apt for the occasion.

They sailed on the evening tide, an impressive flotilla, not only the flag-ship decked with Lion Rampant standards and banners. And the sky was clear and the breeze only adequate to fill the sails—whether at Our Lady of Loretto's behest or otherwise.

22

They reached Dieppe on the 10th of September, after a pleasant, swift and uneventful voyage, admittedly dogged by English ships, but these had kept their distance, in view of the size and quality of the Scots squadron.

Their arrival at the French port created a great stir. Beaton had, of course, despatched a courier in advance to inform King Francis of their coming, and that monarch had sent what he no doubt considered to be the most suitable and illustrious deputy to welcome his royal visitor, the Duc Charles de Vendôme himself, which, in the circumstances, was something of an embarrassment to James. The Duc proved, however, to be an amiable elderly man of far from daunting character, which was something of a relief. With the Scots five hundred and the Duc's own five score, they made almost an army, to ride in leisurely fashion east by south through the Picardy plain to Aisne and St. Quentin, where it appeared that the Duc and his family were presently residing and like any and every army, they inevitably made themselves less than welcome to the ordinary folk of the countryside in passing. The provision of sufficient horses for the visitors was in itself a major undertaking, and the feeding en route likewise, with overnight accommodation a headache. All was done in the King of France's name, fortunately, and at his charges. It was almost one hundred miles to St. Quentin, and they made the two overnight stops, the first at Bethune, on the River Brette, which Beaton was concerned to show off, for this was where his ancestors had come from to Scotland in the twelfth century, the name Beaton being merely a corruption of Bethune.

The Duc Charles had brought them ill news.

The Dauphin Francis, young as he was, had died, leaving as heir to the French throne his brother Henry, a much more feeble individual with whom his father did not get on well. King Francis was prostrated with grief, at Lyons. It all made an inauspicious start to the Scots visit.

The second night they passed at Amiens, the capital of Picardy, which David Lindsay had visited on his way to Brussels six years earlier. St. Quentin also he had passed through, which they reached the next day, a large town on the Somme, with a magnificent twelfth-century church and a handsome town hall. Here the ducal palace was too small to house the great Scots retinue, presumably larger than expected, and most had to be billeted in the town—with the inevitable attendant problems of precedencies and choosing who should lodge where, a task which fell to David Lindsay, as Lyon, to arrange.

There was no lack of hospitality and entertainment, however, on the part of their host and his son, the Count Antoine; indeed a most ambitious programme of events, sports, a jousting, bear- and bull-baitings, hunting, even a carnival and circus, and of course banqueting, had been organised—which was distinctly awkward, since, within the first half-hour of arrival, the King of Scots' one preoccupation was to get away from that place as quickly as possible. For Marie de Bourbon was indeed far from physically attractive and to a man of James's all-consuming interest in women, scarcely conceivable as a wife. Without being actually deformed, she had stooped shoulders almost constitut-ing a hunched back, short legs and short neck. She was not ugly of feature but her squarish face had a masculine cast to it, very like her father's—and unfortunately an incipient moustache to go with it, which shaving could not wholly hide. Her pleasant smile, which the portrait-painter had been at pains to empha-sise, was insufficient to compensate, as far as James Stewart was concerned. And her younger sister, who might have provided an alternative choice, was very similar, but without the smile.

So the problem was how to make a fairly speedy departure without causing major offence. Beaton and Lindsay had all along recognised that some such situation might arise, and they now sought to restrain James's eagerness to be off. Their efforts were hardly aided by Marie herself, who most obviously found the good-looking and romantic prince from afar who had, she assumed, come all this way just to wed her, entirely to her taste, and made no attempt to hide the fact. In these conditions, James could not avoid her company, and not being unkind by nature, was much troubled, insisting that his closest aides should if possible never leave him alone with the lady, and in especial that Janet Lindsay should attach herself to Marie at every opportunity. At the public and outdoor events this was not difficult; but there were numerous occasions indoors, some undoubtedly contrived by Marie herself, when it was all but impossible for others to cling to the King's side. Janet found it all trying in the extreme, the more so in that she esteemed the Frenchwoman so pleasant a character.

Six days, and worse, six evenings, of this, and James was becoming desperate—an extraordinary situation for him with any woman—when unlooked for relief arrived in the shape of Henry, Duc de Guise, from Lyons. A stiffly handsome man of some thirty years, and brother of the second of the ladies suggested as possible bride for James, he came with King Francis's command to conduct the King of Scots, and all others, to him at Lyons forthwith, no explicit reason being given. However, James thankfully all but embraced the haughty de Guise, and set about preparing to depart almost too promptly for good manners. Probably their host was somewhat relieved also, since he could hardly have failed to recognise that his royal guest was hardly overwhelmed with admiration for his daughter; also the transference elsewhere of the cost of entertaining five hundred Scots could scarcely be unwelcome. What Marie herself thought, she did not vouchsafe; but probably she saw no objection to continuing her courtship amidst the splendours of Francis's court.

So a day or two later the move was initiated. From St. Quentin to Lyons involved a major journey, down through the centre of France, of almost four hundred miles, so that the royal entourage became almost an expedition, taking practically two weeks. Although James had to ride for some part of the way at Marie's side, no intimacy was called for; and since they put up en route almost entirely at abbeys and bishops' palaces, with accommodation inevitably and conveniently crowded, embarrassing proximity could be avoided. All the way they went by, and followed, great rivers, by the Oise and the Aisne to Rheims, then by the Marne to Chalon and so to reach the upper Seine at Troyes. They crossed the higher ground of Burgundy to the

Yonne and on thereafter through the Nivernais to the Saône, to the other Chalon. Finally down that river, in the Cote d'Or, to its junction with the Rhone, where stood Lyons, the second city of France. Taken leisurely, it made a pleasant and rewarding journey, although for David Lindsay it was spoiled by the continuing necessity of reconciling individuals to their overnight lodging, the Scots lords and lairds being supremely touchy about inferior accommodation.

They found Lyons to be a great and prosperous walled city, within two rows of fortifications, hilly, teeming with folk, with many great churches and public buildings. Nevertheless the dominating theme was wealth, trade and commerce, with the warehouses which lined the riverside quays seeming to represent the spirit of the place, something the visitors had not encountered hitherto, although Lindsay had seen something of the same at Brussels. King Francis, always extravagant, had recognised how much money was to be made by the manufacture of silk, and was determined to make Lyons the silk capital of the world, and so spent much time here. He had no palace, however, and made that of the Archbishop of Lyons his headquarters. Thither the Duc de Guise escorted the visitors.

Here James had a surprising reception. For they were met by the eighteen-year-old Henry, the new Dauphin, a slight, weedy and pimply young man who, when de Guise announced the King of Scots, came running forward and actually threw his arms around him, gabbling a mixture of welcome, admiration, apologies and explanations. Distinctly taken aback, James if he did not recoil scarcely responded, eyeing de Guise over the youth's head. The Duke had warned him that this Henry was not a strong character, inclined to be emotional, and all but despised by his father; but he was unprepared for such a display nevertheless.

The Dauphin, clutching James's hand and leading him onward, ignoring the Archbishop and other waiting dignitaries, launched into a breathless exposition. His father, who sadly hated him, without cause, and loved his brother, had taken to his bed in dolour and would not be comforted. He, Henry, had had done what he could. He had his brother's Italian body-squire—who undoubtedly had poisoned the Dauphin at the behest of the Emperor Charles—flayed and tortured to death; but nothing would assuage the King's grief. This God-sent arrival of His

349

Majesty of Scotland would, Heaven willing, serve to arouse his royal father and soften the pain.

They came to a door in a long corridor, flanked by resplendent guards. On this the young prince beat unceremoniously with his fists, for apparently it was locked from within. Repeated banging at length produced a hollow voice demanding to know who was there and daring to disturb a man undergoing the sufferings of the damned? To which the Dauphin shouted that he had the King of Scotland come to see His Majesty and give him comfort.

Unprepared for this role of deliverer and consoler, James was the more astonished when, after a sort of bellow from within, the door was suddenly thrown open and His Most Christian Majesty appeared in his bedgown, hair awry, beard untrimmed, tears streaming down his face, to gaze at his tall and handsome visitor and then to launch himself bodily upon him, even more comprehensively than his son had done a few minutes before, clutching him to his inadequately-clad and paunchy person and loudly thanking his Maker for His beloved goodness and great benefits in sending to him a brother-monarch to share his pain and help take the place of him whom the same Almighty had so cruelly removed.

Overwhelmed physically and otherwise by this extraordinary introduction to the de Valois father and son, James Stewart failed to respond in kind. Unprepared for such presumably Gallic demonstration, especially in one who was renowned as an inveterate fighter of battles, a notable political intriguer and the most extravagant man in Christendom, he tended to stiffen and hold off, even though his own nature was apt to be on the impulsive side. But this exaggerated mummery towards a complete stranger, although perhaps flattering, was over-much for any Scot.

Francis, however, did not appear to notice the lack of response. He drew James into the untidy bedchamber, exclaiming volubly. The Dauphin followed them in, but the others remained in the doorway, uncertain as to procedure. No more uncertain than James himself, admittedly, who glanced behind him as though for help. Fortunately perhaps, the other monarch, turning to glare at his son, perceived Davie Beaton standing amongst the others, and reacted with a further display of fervour, exclaiming his delight to see again his dear Scots David, whom the good Saviour had also sent to his aid in this pass, and beckoning him within—to James's marked relief. De Guise, Vendôme, the Archbishop, David Lindsay and one or two others, also entered now.

Thereafter, apparently recovered from his prostration, the French monarch shouted for his gentlemen-of-the-bedchamber with his clothing, these appearing from an anteroom, there before them all His Majesty was stripped of his bedgown and dressed in the elaborate finery of silken shirt and starched ruff, velvet and cloth-of-gold, padded shoulders and slashed sleeves, chains and jewellery, talking the while incessantly. He was a man of forty-two, formerly well-favoured in a dark and sallow way but now somewhat ravaged and puffy with ill-health and many indulgences, his over-large nose and heavy eyelids seeming scarcely to match his vehemence and lively facial expression. He held forth eloquently on his sorrow-turned-to-joy, his grievous loss but his new-found felicity, how he would demonstrate his welcome and his favour. They would go to Paris and forget this unhappy Lyons—and he looked balefully at his son and their unfortunate archiepiscopal host.

Thoroughly roused and revived now, Francis de Valois showed that he would prove his words. Nothing was good enough for his guests. Not only the Archbishop's palace but Lyons itself was set in a stir to provide them with princely hospitality. This king clearly did what he chose to do in no uncertain fashion, whether it entailed mourning a son or entertaining important visitors.

But not for long, here. There were restrictions even for him in playing this role, at Lyons. Paris was the place for it. Moreover, when James admitted that Marie de Bourbon was hardly his notion of a suitable wife, however admirable in birth and fortune, Francis said that he sympathised and understood, and declared that his friend must lose no time in meeting the other possibility, Marie de Guise—since tragically his own daughter Madeleine, whom with all his heart he would have had James to wed, and thus made him into a son indeed to replace the lost one, was in no state of health to marry, the apple of his eye but sadly stricken with a wasting sickness.

So, within a week, the vast train set out for the north again. This journey involved more river-following, France clearly a notable country for great and noble rivers. This time it was the Loire, which took them up through the Bourbonais and the

Orleanais, by Roanne and Digoin and Nevers, to Montargis, where they branched off due northwards to follow the Loing, as the greater river swung westwards for the distant Bay of Biscay. By Nemours they came to Fontainebleau, and the magnificent new palace which Francis had built, after two hundred and twenty miles and six days of travel. And here, strangely enough, the French king left them, with Paris only a day's journey ahead, saying that he had to ride to Rambouillet, where there was a royal chateau in which dwelt his famous and formidable sister, Marguerite, Queen of Navarre, author of the *Heptameron* and supporter of the reformers, whom James must meet. Why Francis must go for his sister in person was not explained; but de Guise hinted that a favourite mistress lived at Etampes, en route to Rambouillet. When James enquired where was the Queen of France, Eleanor of Portugal, the Emperor Charles's sister, there was a pause before de Guise indicated that the lady was not spoken of and lived in retirement. Before Francis left them, however, he sent instructions ahead for the deputies of the French parliament to be present to receive the Scots monarch at the city limits the next day, and to come dressed for the occasion in scarlet gowns—something apparently only done hitherto for the reception of a new Dauphin; of course the Dauphin Henry would be there, with James, but Francis assured his royal guest that it was in *his* honour.

The following afternoon, then, with no sign of King Francis or his sister, the great cavalcade duly arrived at the French capital, reaching the Seine at Ivry. At the outskirts the red-robed parliamentarians were waiting, with a large crowd of others in finest array, with speeches of welcome and a mounted band to lead them into the city.

Paris was undoubtedly the greatest metropolis that any of the Scots had ever seen, save perhaps Davie Beaton who had been to Rome. It was now spreading far beyond its early walls and outer fortifications, an extraordinary mixture of magnificence and squalor, of unbelievable wealth and grinding poverty, with mean stinking hovels cheek-by-jowl with palatial mansions, splendid public buildings and noble churches and monasteries set amongst crumbling ruins, wide squares and marketplaces crowded by narrow, twisting streets and lanes into which day-light scarcely penetrated.

Through all this the lengthy, brilliantly-clad company wound, de Guise's guards clearing their way with lance-butts and the flats of swords. Davie Beaton, who was very familiar with it all, pointed out the sights to the Lindsays. The mighty and lofty cathedral of Notre Dame drew all eyes with its twin towers and slender spire soaring above all else; but soon thereafter a rival edifice began to dominate the urban scene—although the word edifice might give a totally wrong impression. This was an enormous riverside citadel, of a grandeur scarcely to be taken in at first sight, curtain-walls within curtain-walls, courts within courts, with no fewer than sixteen tall, conical-roofed and parapeted towers, turrets and bastions without numbers, storeyed roofs rising row upon row, all islanded within a series of canal-like moats fed from the Seine which lapped the walls.

This apparently, The Louvre, was their destination—although there was another royal residence in the city, the Palais Royal, more modern but smaller and so less suitable for the numbers now to be entertained. The Dauphin led the company, of nearly one thousand now, in over three different drawbridges and through three outer baileys, into a vast central courtyard, where even these numbers did not appear to crowd the place—for The Louvre was itself a town within a city.

They were greeted here by a tall elegant in his mid-twenties, handsome in a saturnine way and dressed all in crimson velvet, in the height of fashion, whom the Dauphin, now seeking to assert himself apparently, introduced, although sourly, as Charles de Guise, Cardinal of Lorraine. The visitors knew this famous character to be the younger brother of the Duc de Guise, and of Marie de Guise. Next to King Francis he was the most powerful man in France despite his comparative youth, clever as he was good-looking, able as he was subtle and ambitious, effective head of the Church, and the King's all-important link with the Vatican. He and Davie Beaton, obviously well-acquainted, made a pair indeed. No doubt this was the real source of the latter's bishopric of Mirepoix.

If the Cardinal was surprised not to see his master, King Francis, with James, he gave no sign of it but welcomed the King of Scots and his entourage in a speech which could not be faulted for grace and diplomacy. It was by no means overlong, to be tedious, nevertheless James's attention strayed, taken up by a lady who waited at the forefront of the glittering throng behind the Cardinal, a tall, graceful creature, not beautiful but with an arresting appearance, dark, full-figured, with a long, swanlike neck and a glowing eye and very direct glance. Quick to notice the chief guest's interest, Charles de Guise, glancing at his brother, turned to introduce her, before any of the others, as his sister Marie, the widowed Duchess de Longueville. As she curtsied low, James hastened forward to raise her up, thereafter retaining her hand for some few moments.

Davie Beaton nudged David Lindsay, and they both looked towards Marie de Bourbon.

After the other presentations, they moved indoors and through what seemed an endless succession of splendid halls, statue-lined corridors and picture-hung galleries, unexpected in a medieval fortress, James walking between the Cardinal and his sister, the Duc de Guise and the Dauphin immediately behind. It was noteworthy how the Duc Henry, somewhat haughty and proud as he seemed hitherto, now gave place to his younger brother. Presently, leaving the major portion of their followers behind, after a wave of the Cardinal's hand towards a chamberlain, they came to a comparatively small apartment, modest in size if not in its quality and furnishings, circular in shape and obviously occupying one of the many round towers, only James's closest companions being ushered in here. It was a strange room to find there, or anywhere for that matter, giving a great impression of light and glowing brightness, for not only were there many windows but the intervening wall-space was all but filled with tall mirrors from floor to pastel-painted ceiling, reflecting the sunshine outside. Despite the warm autumn weather, large fires blazed on two white marble hearths, so that the heat struck the visitors forcibly. The plenishings and decor were all of white and gold, the floor itself white and scattered with rugs and skins. Two persons occupied this extraordinary chamber, a young woman sitting on an ornate couch, and a turbaned black slave-boy standing behind.

James was not the only one to catch his breath, and not merely on account of the heat. The girl sitting there was quite the loveliest creature that David Lindsay, for one, had ever set eyes upon. Slender, fair, great-eyed, with perfectly chiselled features, pale but with a flush to her cheeks, she was dressed simply in white silk and pearls. She gazed at James, then slowly smiled and rose.

For perhaps the first time in his adult life James Stewart was abashed. He stared, biting his lip and finding no words.

"Her Highness Madeleine, Princess of France, Sire," the Cardinal declared, bowing.

She came forward, small hand out, her whispering silk the only sound in that chamber other than the faint background crackle of the fires. James seemed rooted to the spot, so that she had to come all the way to him. She was beginning to curtsy when he came to himself, and reached out almost abruptly to stop her doing so, roughly grasping her hand, her arm, to bend over and kiss it. In that moment, Marie de Guise was as forgotten as was Marie de Bourbon, behind.

The royal pair, each so striking in appearance, continued to eye each other as though there was no other person in the room.

Cardinal Charles coughed. "I have told His Majesty of Scotland that in the absence of your royal sire that you, Princess, with His Highness the Dauphin of course, will entertain King James," he said smoothly.

"We shall do our best, Your Eminence," she acceded. "Sire, we are at your command. It is my joy to welcome you. I have heard much of you."

"And I of you, Princess. But, but nothing to prepare me for this, for your beauty and fair delight!"

After that there was no separating these two. Suddenly, completely, James Stewart was in love. Attracted as he had been to unnumbered women, he had never before been really in love, even with Margaret Erskine. Now he was so, headlong—and Madeleine appeared to be almost equally so. From that first encounter no-one else seemed to matter—and being who they were, no-one else was in a position to say them nay.

Those concerned did try at least to warn, to damp down this spontaneous combustion, pointing out that the Princess's health was precarious, that she was inevitably restricted in what she might do and the life she must live. Also of course that her father considered that she was unfit to marry. The Cardinal and Beaton were equally worried, from their different points of view, however tactful and respectful they had to be about their advice—the latter even pointing out that Madeleine was unlikely to be able to produce the necessary heir to the throne which was the object of the expedition. David Lindsay also urged caution, the poet in him declaring that the Scottish climate was scarcely one in which this lovely but frail flower would be likely to flourish. No doubt the French advisers made similar representations to the young woman. But the pair brushed all such aside. James of course could and did quote the terms of the original treaty made so long ago when, even as a boy, Madeleine had been promised to him. And the only voice which could pronounce the direct negative was that of the absent King Francis.

With that monarch still not putting in an appearance, the Cardinal did his best at least to provide distractions. He organised daily excursions and diversions, and of the sort which by their outdoor nature the Princess would be unable to attend. He took the visitors on lengthy horseback tours of the environs, visits to great houses and abbeys, even arranged a special auto-da-fé, a mass burning of fifty heretics, men and women, at Gisors, found guilty of reformist activities, himself applying the first brands to the fires. He planned a further and dramatic display of pious devotion to Vatican policy, with a mass drowning in the river for the day following—but cancelled this on indications that James was less than enthusiastic. And he urged his sister to use her very considerable abilities to provide alternative attraction for an impressionable young man. Short of actually throwing herself at James, Marie de Guise did her best, but failed to provoke more than superficial appreciation. Poor Marie de Bourbon might not have existed.

It was five days before King Francis arrived in his capital with his sister of Navarre, with no explanations as to the delay. Marguerite de Valois proved to be a handsome woman of notable strength of character, in her mid-forties. Her *Heptameron*, the book of seventy-two stories, of picturesque and uninhibited forthrightness, had made her famous, but her leanings towards the reforming heresy would have made any other woman endangered.

Whether or not Francis was upset by the association which had developed between his daughter and his royal guest, he did not show it. He may have chosen to follow de Guise's policy of trying to keep James busy, if not tired out, with strenuous activity by day and prolonged feasting and entertainment by night, or that may have been his own notion of suitable hospitality; but that was what followed at almost increased pace and endless succession, with much of which his daughter was quite unable to cope. There was hunting in the Bois de Vincennes and other royal preserves, joustings in lists set up in The Louvre's own great courtyard, full-scale tournaments elsewhere, horse-racing, archery contests, sailing regattas on the Seine, masques, balls, play-actings and nightly feastings, such as to leave even the most vigorous of the visitors all but dizzy and exhausted. But nothing quenched James Stewart's preoccupation with Madeleine de Valois, his utter determination to have her, nor her obvious joy in him; and her father, who clearly found it difficult to deny her anything, more and more came to accept the situation. Whether or not it was being in love which was responsible none could say, but the young woman showed little signs of ill health save in that she tired quickly. She attended some of the outdoor events, which apparently she had not done for long, and altogether seemed to take on a new lease of life, all remarking upon it. Francis could not but be delighted, and whatever his misgivings, gradually it became acknowledged that the royal pair were made for each other and that marriage could scarcely be forbidden. Marguerite of Navarre positively encouraged them.

September passed and October showed no let-up in the entertainment, with no word of the visit ending. Many of the Scots, Beaton and Lindsay amongst them, began to grow concerned over such prolonged absence from home and what might be happening there, with a lethargic Chancellor and ailing Primate in charge in the interim and the Bastard of Arran no doubt in resentful mood. But James showed no anxiety, wholly taken up with what was clearly the most enjoyable interlude of his life. He began to talk about the wedding-day.

By mid-November, Beaton and the others recognised that no suggestions of delay, with final decisions after the return to Scotland, were going to be effective. James was not going home without his beloved. With Francis acceding now, the matter was clinched. The actual marriage contract was signed on 26th November. They would wed here in France on the first day of the New Year.

Now all was changed, life at the court geared for preparation for the great event; and a great event it was going to be. There was so much to be done, the most elaborate arrangements made, Francis being the man he was. All was to be at his expense, his famed extravagance given free rein, his generosity almost beyond belief. Never were the tailors of Paris so busy. Everyone remotely connected with the ceremony, and many who were not, were to be dressed anew in the most splendid attire, all at the King's cost. Paris was to be transfigured for the occasion, with triumphal arches, street decorations and bunting, the thoroughfares cleaned up, beggars herded out of sight. The Louvre itself was to be turned into a palace of love and romance, with hundreds of painters, woodworkers and plasterers brought in to effect the transformation. While this was going on, Francis decreed that the court must move out, to the royal palace of Blois, near Orleans, the Princess making the hundred-mile journey wrapped in white furs in a special silver chariot with six white horses, leading a lengthy train of carriages for the other ladies. Fortunately the weather was remarkably clement for the time of year.

At Blois the tempo was maintained. James was given his wedding presents from his father-in-law to be—twelve magnificent warhorses and their full and rich accoutrements, several suits of gilded tilting armour, much jewellery and twenty thousand livres of dowry money; a thoughtful gesture this, towards one whose pockets were never overflowing and now practically empty. As well, there was the promise of two fine ships-of-war, fully manned and furnished with guns, to join the waiting Scots squadron at Dieppe.

All moved to Chambord, still another royal chateau, for Christmastide—which was by no means to be skimped on account of the wedding to follow. David Lindsay was very much interested to find the French ideas for celebrating the festive season differing in many respects from the Scots, with less emphasis on Yuletide, the new year and the sun's rebirth, and more on St. Stephen's martyrdom and singing angels on the one hand and playing curious games and not a little saturnalia on the other, echo of the pre-Christmas feast of Saturn.

Three days after Christmas they moved northwards to Fontainebleau, to be better placed to make a grand entry, or re-entry, into the transformed Paris. This was effected on the last day of 1536, to thunderous gunfire, fountains spouting wine, choirs singing at every street-junction, addresses of welcome from fir-and holly-decked arches and the scattering of largesse to the crowds.

What with all the festivity, excitement and seeing in the New Year, Scots fashion, many, including the bridegroom, never got to bed that night.

The wedding ceremony was to be at noon, in the great cathedral of Notre Dame, three different processions setting out thereof from different gateways of The Louvre. The first to leave was the clergy, and this was in itself as large as it was splendid—for, to indicate Vatican approval of the occasion, no few than seven cardinals were present, each with his own train of dignitaries; also archbishops, bishops, abbots and priors by the score. Then emerged the bridegroom's cavalcade, or rather retinue, for they did not ride but walked the bare mile to the cathedral, through the garlanded, crowded streets. This was in fact the smallest procession of the three, despite its five hundred Scots. James looked magnificent in white and gold velvet, bare-headed, his high colouring and red hair contrasting vividly, the effect only a little marred by the bruising on brow gained in a tournament at Blois. Happily the weather continued to co-operate, so that all declared that Heaven smiled on the match. The bride's array came last, the largest of all, she and her father sitting in the first of a train of white carriages drawn by white horses with tossing golden plumes and gilt harness, all behind a choir of one hundred singing boys. It was remarked upon that although Marie de Guise was well to the fore, in her own carriage, there was no sign of Marie de Bourbon who had quietly disappeared from court.

The vast church was packed with the flower of France, so that there was some considerable pushing and even altercation before all the Scots contingent could be got in. Even the chancel and transept was crowded, spacious as it was, to accommodate all the clergy, and despite being close on the heels of the bridegroom, Beaton and Lindsay had to squeeze into a corner behind sundry cardinals. Janet, for this occasion, had ridden with Marie de Guise, and did rather better. Henri D'Albret, King of Navarre, was present, with his Queen, so that there were three monarchs there—but no Queen of France. These, the bride and the celebrants, were almost the only ones who were not uncomfortably cramped as to space.

James's entry had been greeted by a great blaring of trumpets and clashing cymbals; but Madeleine's appearance, on her father's arm, was to the accompaniment of sweetest singing. She was looking at her most lovely, with a delicate and ethereal beauty to lift the heart. Dressed all in white as usual, and eschewing all fancy and elaboration, she was probably the most simply-dressed woman in the cathedral, with that very simplicity only enhancing the delight of her person. Admittedly she looked slight and frail, but it was with a willowy and not really a brittle fragility. When she came to stand beside her tall and lissome bridegroom, they made a pair to gladden the eye.

Of all the Princes of the Church present, Francis had chosen Vendôme's younger brother, the Cardinal de Bourbon, to conduct the service, no doubt as some sort of compensating gesture over the rejection of his niece. The ceremony itself was fairly brief, basic, although the musical accompaniment and priestly processional, the to-ing and fro-ing with crosses and candles, seemed to the Scots excessive, almost as though all these cardinals and prelates were more important to the occasion than were the nuptial couple. These two, however, obviously blissfully preoccupied only with each other, betrayed no impatience.

As the final benediction was pronounced, and the bells high above them began their clamorous acclaim—which was to continue for hours and be taken up by every church, monastery and religious house in Paris—James, radiant, turned his bride round proudly to face the great congregation, arm around her. Scotland had a queen again.

*   *   *

In the days and weeks which followed, as James delayed his departure, it was said that France had not known such jubilation and revelry since the days of Charlemagne. The reasons for this were hard to pin-point. French monarchs had married, their daughters had wed greater kings than James Stewart, resounding triumphs of war and diplomacy had been celebrated, yet not on this scale. It was probably Francis's especially extravagant nature, combined with his great fondness for Madeleine; and perhaps something to do with reaction from his recent prostration and mourning for his dead son. Also this closer alliance with Scotland was a gesture in the directions of both Henry of England and the Emperor Charles, a warning that France was strategically strengthening her position, likewise buttressing the Pope and Holy Church against the reformist influences in England and the Germanic states. Whatever was behind it, the scale of festivities, jubilation and revelry, hectic enough before the wedding, now attained an unprecedented pitch, attained and continued. Every day some great event was organised, every night its counterpart. Nothing appeared to overtax Francis's ingenuity, nor it seemed, his treasury—as indicated by the great chests full of gold and silver coins, kept replenished and unlocked in the corridors of his palaces, for his guests to help themselves whenever their pockets felt empty. There were mock-battles with actual armies taking part, knightly chivalry, armoured foot, squares of pikemen, ranked bowmen, cannoneers, even siege-engines to batter down temporary forts and palisades. There were sea-fights in miniature on the Seine, with fleets of small ships and barges, their gunfire, using blank shot, shaking the entire city. Pageants in every conceivable form took place almost daily, many of them with the most elaborate and ambitious refinements, for instance flying dragons spouting flame and smoke, and a complete troupe of dancing bears. Deer, rounded up from many a park and forest, were driven into the city for hunting and slaughter in the streets and wynds; and bull-baiting, cock-fighting and gladiatorial combats became part of the Paris scene.

Not that all this merry-making was confined to the capital. All France was ordered to celebrate, and the royal company and at least part of the court moved around the country attending, with great nobles and municipalities vying with each other to provide welcomes and spectacles. One of these excursions took them to Vendôme, but although her sister was in evidence, there was no sign of Marie thereof. The rumour went round that she had decided to retire from the world and enter a convent, a suggestion which did distress James Stewart somewhat.

And so the weeks passed, and many of the Scots grew more and more restive, anxious now to be gone. Beaton was kept fairly well informed, by regular couriers from David Panter and others, as to events in Scotland; and fortunately nothing of dire consequence appeared to be happening there, on the national scene at least, however many private problems might be arising. Nevertheless, few were unconcerned about this prolonged absence from home, and even their royal host's most ingenious diversions tended to pall in time. But Francis appeared loth indeed to let his daughter go; and James was probably one of the least anxious of his company to be off, the business of statecraft and rule never having much appeal to him. Also, of course, there was the excuse of Madeleine's health. On the whole this remained fairly good, although she tired very quickly and took little part in much of the excitements; but it was felt that a long voyage in winter seas would be unwise. So Francis had written to Henry Tudor seeking a safe conduct for his daughter and son-in-law through England, and Henry had made no reply, wait as they would. Despite offended pride at this discourtesy, the doting father made another approach, sending an envoy to London this time; and when this representative eventually returned, it was to announce that the King of England would not give the desired assurance of safety and non-interference for his nephew and new wife if they traversed his land, grossly insulting to all concerned as this was.

So a sea voyage it had to be.

And now it was the weather's turn to delay them. That winter had been quite remarkable for its mild geniality, at least in France; but March and April saw a change to gales and storms; and Francis would not hear of his beloved daughter venturing to sea in such conditions. The most that he would concede was that the court and guests should make the move towards the coast, so as to be ready to take advantage of any sustained improvement in the weather. Dieppe itself was scarcely a suitable place for any royal sojourn, so they would travel down Seine, in boats, to Rouen and wait there, a mere day's journey from the port.

Rouen it was, then, and here there was occasion for further festivities, for the end of April saw James's twenty-fifth birthday, a significant milestone at which, by old Scots tradition, a new dispensation began. One of the more important aspects of this was the almost automatic cancellation of all crown appointments and offices made hitherto. Most holders were re-appointed forthwith, to be sure, but not all. It was a recognised opportunity for a cleansing of the royal stables and a general reassessment. Few changes were actually promulgated there and then at Rouen, of course; but the Bastard of Arran was one of the immediate casualties, losing his positions as Gentleman of the Bedchamber, Master of the Horse and Keeper of Carrick. James, despite present euphoria, had a retentive memory. Amongst others to fall was the Lord Forbes, Justiciar of the North, and his son, the Master, suspected of plotting with the

Douglases. Needless to say, both Beaton and Lindsay retained their offices.

Eventually the winds moderated and the skies cleared, with the weather-prophets foretelling better things. So at long last the move was made to Dieppe, nine months after disembarking there.

A great host of shipping was now waiting at the port, for as well as the Scots squadron and the two wedding-gift vessels, *Salamander* and *Morsewer*, Francis had ordered a French war fleet to accompany them to Scottish waters, to ensure his daughter's safety from English attack. A tearful leave-taking followed, with Francis all but proposing to accompany them all the way to Scotland, so reluctant was he to part from Madeleine. Prolonged were the farewells, Frenchly demonstrative the endearments. Overloaded with gifts, oversated with excitements, overfed and all but overwhelmed in emotion, they sailed on the 10th of May, an impressive convoy.

As well that they were, perhaps, for the English ships picked them up within the first twelve hours and shadowed them thereafter. There were usually only two or three of these, being relieved each day, but undoubtedly, had the Scots been weaker, these could have called out a major force to try to capture James or even slay him. Without any close heir to the Scots throne, Henry would have been well placed to take over, especially with Angus his ally and his sister placed as she was.

Oddly enough, the other side of the Tudor coin was demonstrated on the fifth day out when, somewhat becalmed off Scarborough Head on the Yorkshire coast, a flotilla of small boats put out towards them, flying white flags. Suspicious but intrigued, James waited for these to approach, under the loaded guns of his escorts. They proved to be a group of Yorkshire knights and squires, who presumably had been waiting ready for the Scots convoy, come to seek King James's aid in ousting the tyrant Henry Tudor from the English throne and restoring the authority of Holy Church in England—a surprising development. Coming aboard, they were obsequious to James and loud in their complaints as to misrule and persecution, with assertions of widespread resentment, unrest in the land, faithfulness towards the Pope and Rome and admiration for the King of Scots' stand against the forces of heresy. They declared that much of England, especially the North, and all of Wales, would rise against Henry if James would provide the lead. And if France would join in, of course, victory would be assured.

This extraordinary situation intrigued James and his advisers; but in his present blissful preoccupation with Madeleine he was scarcely in a state to consider it seriously. However, he did agree to meet another and more senior delegation a little further north, off the Tees, for which it seemed this group were only forerunners; and meanwhile to ask the French admiral to chase away the English ships, which, hull-down to the south, still dogged the convoy, so that word of this meeting with the northern lords would not be reported to Henry.

In this delay in the voyage, James decided to send his Lord Lyon ahead, in a light, fast ship, to prepare a suitable reception and welcome at Leith and Holyrood for the new Queen of Scotland. Davie Beaton would have chosen to accompany him, anxious to get back to the direction of affairs in Scotland, but felt that he should remain with James during any interview with English dissenters, to try to ensure that no unwise commitment were entered into—he being very doubtful as to the wisdom of any Scots entanglement in English affairs, however tempting.

So David and Janet transferred to another vessel and set off on their own. At first they took a while to distance themselves from the others, owing to the prevailing calm, but presently the wind freshened from the south-west and, their sails filling, they began to make good speed. The Lindsays were in fact delighted to be on their own together, after nine months of crowded company.

Unfortunately the freshening wind, although timeous and in the right direction, outgrew its usefulness when it developed into an untimely early-summer storm, and the little craft, the smallest in the entire combined fleet, although seaworthy enough, reacted to the stresses in boisterous fashion, tossing and heaving and spiralling crazily in the wild waters. Janet was sick, and although David was spared that misery, he dared not eat anything substantial for two days. However, they made reasonably good progress up the Northumberland and Berwick coasts, and when they turned at last into the mouth of the Firth of Forth the land quickly began to shelter them and they went along on a more even keel.

On the fourth day after leaving the others they sailed into

Leith harbour, thankful to set foot again on their native soil. They had had sufficient foreign travel to serve them for a considerable time.

Although they would have liked to have gone straight home to The Mount of Lindifferon, they had to plunge into urgent activity. Hiring horses, they repaired to Holyrood Abbey, there to instruct the Abbot and his monks to prepare the royal apartments and in especial heat them adequately for a queen used to a warmer clime than Scotland's. David summoned Sir Adam Otterburn, in his capacity of Provost, and with him put in hand arrangements for an official welcome to the capital city. They could not attempt anything on the Paris scale, but triumphal arches, platforms and street decorations were to be erected; greenery and fir-branches hung; bonfires prepared; carriages made ready, and the folk urged to be ready to line the streets. Janet for her part informed the abbey kitcheners as to suitable cooking for the French party, and gathered a group of ladies to attend on the Queen, also filled the royal bedchamber and anterooms with such flowers as mid-May might provide. They did not know, of course, just when the royal company would arrive, which was awkward. So look-outs were sent up Arthur's Seat to keep watch, from the summit of which it was possible to see down the thirty-odd miles to the mouth of the firth. It was calculated that they probably had at least two days, although the convoy might arrive by night, hence the bonfires.

During all this activity the newcomers learned something of what had been going on in Scotland in the past nine months. The Bastard of Arran seemed to have been lying decently low in his own Hamilton country, which was a blessing. There had been some English raiding, but Scott of Buccleuch, the Black Douglases of Cavers and Drumlanrig, and other Middle March clans, had driven them off, and the Armstrongs and Johnstones, on the West March, had retaliated in kind. Margaret Tudor had been creating a new scandal, falling out with and actually leaving her third husband, and declaring that she was going to get another divorce, from the new Pope, and remarry her second spouse, Angus. Home of Wedderburn, the main firebrand of that troublesome lot, had died, and his sons, squabbling over the inheritance, tended to confine their depredations to their own Merse. And so on.

On Whitsun Eve, the 19th of May, the watchers up the hill

reported that a great fleet of ships was in sight beyond the Craig of Bass. All moved into action.

At this stage, David had concentrated on the port of Leith rather than on Edinburgh itself. Hurrying down there, he got all in train, and was ready before the first sails appeared in view from the haven. Only a small proportion of the vessels would be able to tie up at the wharves and jetties, but they had cleared as many of the harboured craft there already, as was possible, to make more room.

The King's ship, with its Lion Rampant standards, came in first, and David had a band of musicians to play it in, and a large company of notables under a gaily-flapping canopy—in case of rain—to give welcome. When the business of berthing was completed, to music, and a gangway was run out, there was a pause. Then King James appeared at its head, Madeleine at his side. And waving to the crowd he suddenly turned and impulsively scooped her up in his arms and thus burdened, strode down the gangplank on to his Scottish soil—a nice touch. Loud and long was the cheering.

For her part, when the new Queen of Scotland was set down, she swayed as though dizzy for a moment or two, then sank down on her knees before all, and in a fair attempt at Scots speech, thanked Almighty God for safely bringing her husband and herself to this their own land. Which said, she scraped at the sandy soil there with her slender fingers, to pick up two handfuls of the earth and kiss it. The crowd shouted its acclaim and James beamed on her, and all, proudly.

But David Lindsay did not, for he was shaken by the changed appearance of the young woman, however warmly she smiled and gestured. It seemed scarcely possible that there could be such alteration in three or four days. She was drawn, wan of feature, large eyes dark-ringed, thinner, slighter altogether. That storm had obviously taken its toll of Madeleine de Valois.

There was no glooming nor haste, no hustling her off to the waiting carriages, however. David would have foregone the presentation of the long line of dignitaries, but clearly both King and Queen expected to go through with this, and did so genially, James at his most amiable. Behind the notables, the ordinary folk of Leith were packed in a cheering, surging mass, and to these Madeleine smiled and waved and mouthed pleasantries. For his part, James waved forward his new favourite, Oliver

Sinclair, with a large bag of coins, into which the King dipped and threw, dipped and threw—all French silver, David noted.

At length it was over and a move was made over to the waiting carriages and horses, for the couple of miles ride up to Holyrood. David sought out Beaton, to ride beside him.

"The Princess? The Queen?" he asked, leaving the rest unsaid.

"Aye, poor lass—she took sore ill out of that storm. Not just the sea-sickness. Much worse—vomiting blood. I fear, I fear . . . She has spirit, but . . ."

"What can be done?"

"We can pray!" Bishop Davie said simply.

At Holyrood, Janet, after one look at Madeleine, to whom she had become much attached, asserted herself, as so seldom she did, and put the Queen to bed, with warming-pans and possets of curdled-milk and wine. The evening's banquet had to make do without the guest-of-honour.

A night of high fever followed, and the next day's ceremonies and celebrations were cancelled. The Queen kept her room.

Two more days of this and James at last began to show signs of worry and agitation. Madeleine herself remained quietly cheerful, but her weakness could not be denied. Physicians were sought, although James professed no faith in such—a view which seemed to be substantiated when these all made differing prognostications and prescribed different treatments.

Then the invalid rallied a little, and a limited programme of introducing her to her new subjects was put in hand, although the state entry into the capital, for which Lindsay, as Lyon, had made all the arrangements, was still postponed. But during the evening's feasting the Queen collapsed at table, amidst general consternation, and had to be carried in her husband's arms back to bed. That night she coughed more blood—which seemed to make a distinct nonsense of the blood-letting advised by the physicians.

There followed a week of prostration and consequent deep gloom, James seldom leaving his beloved's chamber. The weather by no means helped, strong cold winds and driving rain playing a mournful tattoo on the abbey windows. Deputations from all over the land, nobles, clerics, lairds, merchant and trade guilds, provosts and ordinary citizens, came with gifts, addresses of welcome and messages of goodwill. Prayers were said in the churches.

Davie Beaton, who had gone to St. Andrews on urgent business, returned and, much concerned, recommended that the Queen should be moved to the Abbey of Balmerino, in North Fife, not far from Lindifferon, renowned as the most salubrious and healthful place in the land—that is, if she was strong enough for the journey. She could go by boat—but she quailed at the thought of further sea travel. James, ready to clutch at a straw, agreed, and had a canopied horse-litter prepared. But the starting day had to be put off and put off, as Madeleine, despite her brave smiling, grew progressively weaker.

On the night of the 7th of July, six weeks after landing in her new country, Madeleine de Valois choked to death in a red flood of her own blood.

James Stewart was as a man bereft of all sense.

The bells of all Scotland tolled out thereafter, as long and loud as those of France had done so short a time before, but with a very different tempo and note.

The funeral over, and burial in the abbey-church, the distracted King went off to shut himself up in Stirling Castle, all his court dismissed.

The Lindsays rode home to The Mount of Lindifferon at long last, David thankful for only one thing—that he had not been chosen to convey the tidings to Francis de Valois. They went speaking little, he beginning to compose, in his mind, an elegy for a queen.

The Bastard of Arran may not have smiled, but the day was his.